There Ariseth Light in the Darkness

A Novel of First Century Galilee

JV Love

THERE ARISETH LIGHT IN THE DARKNESS

This book is a work of fiction. Names, characters, businesses, organizations, places, events, and incidents either are the product of the author's imagination or are used fictitiously. Any resemblance to actual persons, living or dead, events, or locales is entirely coincidental.

Information contact: www.Facebook.com/ThereArisethLight

Originally published in 2019 by One Day Press

First Edition: May 2019

10 9 8 7 6 5 4 3 2 1

For Sebastian.
May your path be less traumatic,
and your heart more easily opened.

And for my mother.
*Thank you for being an example
of patience and faith.*

Contents

Author's Note

This historical fiction novel draws from the ever-expanding, ever-evolving pool of knowledge of archaeologists and Biblical scholars. Though minor disagreements remain about precisely when certain events took place, there is general consensus about the timeframe. For example, based on the evidence at hand, most scholars agree that Jesus was likely born sometime between 7-4 BCE.

For readers interested in learning more about the setting, people, or where in the Bible a particular reference is located—including which characters and events are historical and which are fictional—please refer to the "Historical Notes" section.

Introduction

No matter a person's beliefs or religion, most everyone is familiar with Jesus and his teachings. In fact, it could be argued that no other historical figure in the history of the world is better known or has had a greater impact. And it all began in a remote Roman province on the far eastern shore of the Mediterranean Sea. So inconsequential was it to Rome that it didn't even merit its own Roman governor.

The province was no stranger to violence and it seemed that a rebellion was nearly always at hand. For that reason, authorities—both Roman and Jewish—did their best to keep a tight lid on anyone who threatened the status quo. And it seemed to them that Jesus of Nazareth's sole goal was to upset the status quo. What they failed to comprehend was that the revolution he created was never meant for Galilee and Judea alone, but the whole world. It was a revolution of inclusion. A revolution not against the tyranny of the world, but against the tyranny of hate.

Cast of Primary Characters

- ➢ **JONAH** – Jewish male
  - THOMAS – Younger brother of Jonah
  - ZEBULUN – Cousin of Jonah and Thomas
  - AMARYAH – Wife of Thomas, then Jonah
    - LUKE – Son of Amaryah
  - TIRAS – Neighbor of Jonah
    - EHUD – Son of Tiras
- ➢ **VITUS** – Roman soldier (full name: Marcus Trebellius Vitus)
  - FLAVIAN – Archrival of Vitus
  - GAIUS – General of Roman Legion X Fretensis
  - SERVANUS – Roman soldier serving under Vitus
  - PONTIUS PILATE – Roman Prefect of Judea
  - BARNABAS – Jewish male interrogated by Vitus
  - IRA – Servant of Vitus
- ➢ **AZARA** – Gentile female
  - AZIZ – Father of Azara
  - FARRUKH – Tutor of Azara
  - HADASSAH – Jewish mother whose daughters attend Azara's school
  - ESTHER – Jewish student at Azara's school
- ➢ **JESUS** – Jewish rabbi
  - PETER – Disciple of Jesus
  - ANDREW – Disciple of Jesus; brother of Peter
  - MARY (MAGDALENE) – Disciple of Jesus; Neighbor of Jonah
  - LEVI – Tax collector
  - JOHN – Disciple of Jesus

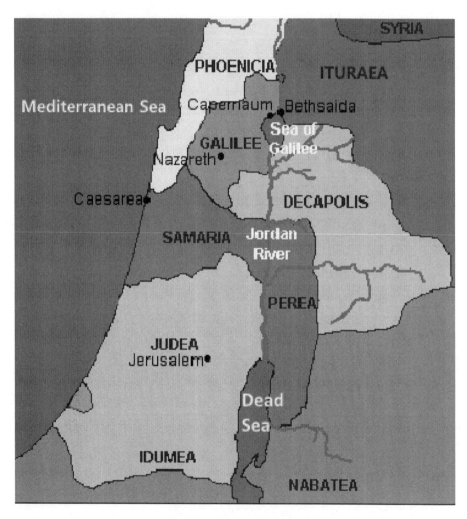

First Century Palestine

Part I

Time Period: Late in the year of 4 BCE

In the time of Jesus, Palestine was a divided land in a variety of ways. The regions of Galilee and Judea were separated not only by their geography and climate, but also by their rulers and inhabitants. While Judea was overwhelmingly Jewish and conservative, Galilee was a melting pot of Jews and Gentiles (non-Jews).

Chapter One

Jonah was rudely awakened by a smack on his cheek. He didn't bother opening his eyes. He knew it was his eight-year-old brother, Thomas, who must have once again rolled over on their straw mattress.

After gently moving his brother's arm back to his side of the bed, Jonah heard his mother's footsteps approaching. He kept perfectly still, as if he were not already awake.

She sat down on the edge of the bed, kissed him tenderly on each closed eye and softly sang in Aramaic, "Talya-Koum, Talya-Koum..." "Little boy, wake up..."

Today was Jonah's thirteenth birthday, and he had to stifle the urge to jump out of bed and shout. Pulling the blanket over his head, he pretended he wanted to sleep more. Then, as hoped, he felt the tickling. First, very lightly on his thighs, then more forcefully as his mother's hands moved up to his ribs. Jonah giggled and squirmed and pleaded with her to stop, but whenever she did, he would again act as though he were asleep until she started again.

After several minutes of the game, she mussed his hair and whispered, "Come on, birthday boy. Get started on your chores."

When she left the room, Jonah sat up in bed and softly recited the Shema prayer. He was careful not to wake his brother, who always slept in a little longer. The Shema was recited twice daily, in the morning and in the evening, and Jonah had long ago memorized it. Before getting out of bed, he kissed Thomas on the forehead and tucked the blanket in tight around him.

Once finished lacing his sandals around his feet and ankles, he went to the well to fetch water. Jonah loved their small village in Middle Galilee, home to twenty-seven families, and especially loved that his walk to the well only took a couple of minutes. The next closest village didn't have a well, and they had to walk a half mile to get water.

Jonah glimpsed the dim outline of the eastern ridge and the scrawny chickens scratching at the ground in front of the well. Though the sun wouldn't rise above the ridge for a while yet, there were already several women and children gathering water.

Of the two spigots in the wall that water poured out of, Jonah preferred the one on the right since it was cracked, slower, and shunned by most. As his jug filled, he ran his fingers along the wall. Unlike the rest of the village, the wall here was not the color of sand, because it was not made of limestone. It was built with large, gray rocks from the river and Jonah liked the smooth feel of them.

Hearing someone approach and stop behind him, Jonah looked to his left and confirmed no one was using the other spigot. That meant it must be Anna. She was madly in love with him, at least according to his brother, but was too bashful to say a word.

"Good morning, Anna," Jonah called. When there was no response, he peeked over his shoulder. Anna—dark tangled hair, pinky in her mouth—blushed and gave a shy smile.

"My brother caught a mouse yesterday," Jonah said as he lifted the now full jug of water. "Do you want to come over this afternoon to see it?"

She raised her eyes briefly to his and nodded yes. "Tell me something of my life," she said.

Jonah—a head taller than her—squatted to be on her level. He liked to play this game. Whatever he saw always came true. "What do you want to know?"

"Anything," she said with a shrug.

Jonah closed his eyes to see what came to him. He only played the game with kids, and his visions were always silly stuff, especially with Anna. The last time he'd seen her receiving a gift of a necklace made of wildflowers by her father. The time before it was that she'd soon see five baby chicks hatch.

In his mind Jonah saw the familiar cloud from which the images would appear. This time, instead of emerging slowly, an image vaulted out of the cloud. It was a horrifying picture of Anna being killed by a soldier's spear, and the shock of it caused Jonah to fall over backwards.

Anna gasped and waited for Jonah to say something. When he did not, she spun and ran away.

Wiping the dirt off his tunic, Jonah convinced himself the image had been a mistake. He'd never seen anything bad before. He thought about what his father told him time and again about his so-called visions, that it was just Jonah's imagination, nothing more.

Jonah did his best to forget about it as he carried the jug of water back to their house. Setting it down just outside the workshop, he tiptoed to the door to spy on whatever his father and uncle were working on. They were not carpenters by trade, but knew enough to do small jobs and simple repairs. Today, his father seemed to be waiting for him. He caught Jonah's prying eyes through the wide cracks in the door and signaled for him to come in. Jonah slowly pushed the door open, half hiding behind it. His uncle, who liked to sleep on the roof, was not there yet.

"Come here," his father whispered, a glint in his eye. The warm look on his father's face reassured Jonah that he was not in trouble for breaking the shovel the day before.

His father's work area was raised up a step from the ground, and as Jonah reached it, his father came out from behind the workbench and extended his hand down to Jonah. "Congratulations," he said, his deep, resonant voice breaking the silence of the early morning. "You are a man now."

Jonah shook his father's hand, happy he'd remembered his birthday.

"Tomorrow," his father continued, "we'll make it official at the temple."

Jonah focused his gaze on the blackened toenail of his father's long, bony, left foot, then gazed up at his face, noting his beard was getting more gray.

"It's a big step," his father said. "You're the one responsible for following the commandments now. No one else. And I'll expect much more from you than your brother." He folded his thick forearms in front. "Are you excited about your bar mitzvah tomorrow?"

Jonah nodded. The sun's first rays were streaming over the nearby ridge, and he regarded his father's thick chest hair sticking out from the faded yellow tunic.

With a glance at his overladen workbench, Jonah's father shook his head. "I'll see you at breakfast," he said with a sigh. "But tonight I'll teach you the proper way to shake hands like a man."

As his father returned to the workbench, Jonah pivoted and ran out the door. He brought the jug of water to his mother who was making the bread for the day. As it was still dark inside the house, Jonah had to stand in the doorway a few seconds to let his eyes adjust. As they did, he began to make out *two* shapes in the darkness. One was the familiar, delicate shape of his mother. The other was a pear-shape he'd hoped to never again see in his life.

"Jonah," his mother called, "come say hello to your cousin. He got in last night after you went to bed."

Jonah felt that old sinking feeling return, from the back of his skull right down to his tailbone. The feeling that he couldn't get away and that the more he tried— the more he *fought* it—the more firmly he ended up being stuck. He willed his legs to move forward as Zebulun's buck-toothed grin, closer to a smirk, greeted him in the dim light.

"Hey, Gladiator," said his cousin.

Gladiator. Jonah hadn't heard that nickname since the last time he saw him. Zebulun came up with it when Jonah had used his stick-sword to knock over a kid who'd pushed Thomas down a hill. Jonah flexed the muscles of his upper arms as Zebulun approached, wondering which one he would punch.

"How ya been?" Zebulun playfully slugged him on the left arm.

It hurt. It always did. Zebulun was two years older, three inches taller, and forty pounds heavier. But Jonah never let on that it hurt, even if it resulted in a bruise later.

"He's going to stay with us for a bit while his parents go to Jerusalem," his mother announced.

Jonah suppressed a scream.

"You two go help Thomas gather kindling," his mother said as she measured out grain from a large earthen-red jar.

Jonah marched out the door, the familiar nightmare replaying in his mind once again—the one where Jonah could only watch helplessly as Zebulun tortured and killed a stray dog.

His cousin pulled even with him, and pinched his arm. "Hey, Gladiator, did you—"

Jonah whirled toward him and thrust his face inches away. "Don't call me that," he snapped. He didn't want to be reminded whatsoever of the last time they were together.

"Why not?"

"Maybe I'll call *you* by a nickname too," Jonah said. "Hmm, how about Dog Killer? That's a good one."

"You still mad about that? It was just a stupid dog that wouldn't do what it was told. It deserved it."

"You had no right to kill it!"

"I had every right," Zebulun replied smugly. "The book of Genesis says so. 'Let man have dominion over the fish of the sea, and over the birds of the air, and over the cattle, and over all the earth, and over every creeping thing that creepeth upon the earth.'"

Jonah didn't know how to respond to that. When his father quoted scripture in an argument in their family, it was always the final word—unless someone could quote a scripture that countered it. When it came to memorizing the Torah, Jonah was near the bottom of his class at the synagogue, and he could think of nothing now to dispute Zebulun's quote.

"Just don't call me Gladiator anymore," Jonah demanded, poking a finger in his cousin's chest.

Zebulun grasped Jonah's hand, twisting Jonah's wrist so that he was forced around and down toward the ground to relieve the pressure. "What do you think?" said Zebulun. "A guy in our village taught me how to do this."

Jonah gritted his teeth against the pain.

"What are you boys doing?" asked Jonah's mother as she passed by with a small bowl. "I told you to go help Thomas."

Zebulun gave Jonah's arm one final sharp twist before letting go, and Jonah cried out in agony despite himself.

"We were just playing," Zebulun answered in a cheery tone. "Right, Gladiator?" He fixed his eyes on Jonah, a demented grin from ear to ear.

"That wasn't very nice," said Jonah, shaking his wrist back and forth.

"Sorry about that. I probably did it too hard for a kid."

"Stop your wrestling and get going," Jonah's mother said over her shoulder.

The two of them walked to the edge of the village, where the olive grove was, and spotted Thomas just off the road. He was in his usual talkative mood, having a conversation with one of the twigs he'd found: "Oh, hello, twig! Would you like to help me? My mother needs a fire to bake our bread, and—"

"Hey, Little Mouse," Zebulun called out to Thomas.

Jonah knew what his brother's reaction would be. Thomas hated that nickname, even if, in truth, he did look like a little mouse.

"Your mom sent us to help," added Zebulun as they drew closer. "Is that all you've got? What have you been doing out here?"

Thomas's eyes narrowed as he glared at his cousin.

Uh-oh, Jonah thought.

Thomas stretched his arm back and hurled a stick at Zebulun's head, only missing because his cousin ducked out of the way.

Zebulun howled and lunged toward Thomas. "You naughty mouse!"

Jonah jumped in front of him. "Leave him alone!" he shouted at Zebulun. "You started it."

Zebulun paused, glancing from Jonah to Thomas. Then he laughed—an abrupt cackle like a chicken. "All right, all right," he said. "We're getting off to a bad start here. I'm sorry, Little Mouse." He reached his arm over Jonah, tousled Thomas's hair, then stepped away.

Jonah straightened his brother's hair. "That temper of yours is going to get you in big trouble one day, Thomas."

"For your information," Thomas declared to Zebulun, his voice rising a notch. "This is my *second* trip. I already got enough for today. This is for tomorrow."

Zebulun surveyed the ground, then strode to a nearby bush and snapped off a branch.

"Father says to only get dead sticks, not live ones," Thomas told him.

Zebulun grinned. "This one *is* dead," he said as he snapped off another branch. "And now so is this one. Ha-ha."

"Just ignore him," Jonah suggested to his younger brother.

After they'd collected enough for the next day's fire, they returned to the house. The smell of freshly baked bread filled the air.

Jonah emptied the kindling from his basket, then quietly approached his mother by the clay oven. She was pulling out another batch of bread. "Shall we eat outside?" she asked without looking up. While Jonah thought about it, she turned to him, and he was strangely aware of how beautiful she was. He nodded yes to her question, wanting to tell her how much he loved her, but the moment had passed. She'd picked up the basket with the bread and was already heading outside. Grabbing a small jar of olive oil from the dirt floor, Jonah followed her.

Morning was Jonah's favorite time of day, because it was usually the most peaceful. He noticed that his mother and father smiled more, spoke more softly, and had more patience. News, which was nearly always bad, usually came in the evening.

These days there was no work to be done in the fields, so they got to eat breakfast early. After today's meal, Jonah's father decided he'd stay and repair the shovel Jonah had broken. He gave Jonah and Thomas their chores for the day, then made them repeat the instructions back. Thomas was to tend the flock of sheep, and Jonah was to gather figs. Both Jonah and his brother breathed a sigh of relief when Zebulun was tasked with watering the garden. Not only was it a strenuous job, hauling heavy jugs of water, but it was far away from where Jonah and Thomas would be.

Less than three hours later, Jonah had already accomplished his chore. He smiled to himself as he topped off the basket of red Sycamore figs. He'd picked them in record time, and could already see himself sneaking into his father's work area and setting the basket down in front of his workbench. His father would slowly divert his eyes from his woodworking and see the basket. Then, if Jonah was lucky, he'd see his father's ever-so-slight beam of approval, which he reserved for rare occasions like when Jonah was able to quote a scripture verbatim or, better yet, when he trumped a scripture his father said with one that was even better.

A breeze suddenly picked up, chasing away the mid-morning heat. Jonah plucked a fig from the ground, blew two ants off it, and took a bite. Closing his eyes, he chewed slowly, savoring not so much the sweetness as the sound and feel of the tiny seeds being crushed by his teeth. When he opened his eyes to take another bite, he caught sight of a solitary white cloud sailing through the sky, and became aware he was happy in this moment. He didn't recall ever noticing that before. Perhaps this ability to observe his own state of mind was another one of those things that came with age, like the hair that had started growing in his armpits and his voice randomly cracking when he spoke.

A distant clanging signified someone approaching on the nearby road. Jonah scrambled up the fig tree and peered through an opening in the leaves. Holding his breath, he scanned every inch of the dirt road for bandits or soldiers.

Jonah disliked that Gentile, King Herod, as much as the next Jew, but things certainly had gotten much worse since Herod's death earlier in the year. Without his iron-fisted rule, not a week passed by in Jonah's village when he didn't hear frightening stories about robberies or massacres or uprisings. The countryside and villages had been especially hard hit by violence.

Upon seeing a stooped man pulling an overloaded donkey, Jonah breathed a sigh of relief. It was just Old One Eye going on another trip to a nearby town to sell his oil lamps and big five-gallon clay jars. Old One Eye lived in Jonah's village and constantly scolded the children for climbing the olive trees in the orchard.

Jonah studied the patch over the man's right eye until he had passed out of sight. Then he climbed down and prepared to head home.

As he picked up his basket, he heard someone shouting in the distance. Cupping his hand to his ear, he listened intently, trying to determine the direction the voice was coming from. Uncertain, he climbed back up the tree and was surprised to see his father running down the narrow road. Jonah couldn't remember when he'd last seen his father run. And he was carrying something, the natural motion of his arm swinging it up and down, up and down. Squinting, Jonah saw it was the short, rusty sword.

"Jonah! Jonah!" his father called.

Jumping down from the tree, Jonah recalled the previous time he'd seen his father with that dull, brown sword. It was two years ago when the tax collector had come to their house. Jonah could still picture his father—bulging eyes, growling voice—swinging that old sword back and forth above his head, yelling at the tax collector to get out of his house, that he didn't have any more money.

Jonah ran toward his father, feeling just as scared now as he'd been when he last saw that sword. "Here, Father!" he shouted, waving his arms. "Over here!"

His father was breathing so hard he could barely talk. Between gasps of air, he directed Jonah to go find his brother right away.

"Why? What happened?" asked Jonah.

"Soldiers..." his father sputtered. "Soldiers all over ... raiding, killing. Get your brother and go to the secret cave. Hide there until I come get you. Zebulun is right behind me. Take him with you."

"Where are you going?" Jonah asked as his father turned away.

"They could be headed to our village. Your uncle and I will protect the house. I'll come for you by sunset," he hollered as he ran back the way he'd just come.

Jonah tied his sandals tighter while he waited impatiently for his cousin. Zebulun arrived huffing and puffing and looking as if he was about to vomit. "Come on!" Jonah yelled, then took off.

He tried to assure himself this was just another false alarm. All the stories he'd heard of bloodshed and looting had always been about a friend-of-a-friend, or a faraway village like Kefr Kennah or Shefarim. No one in Jonah's village had ever been harmed.

Jonah ran as fast as he ever had in his life. He paid no attention to the intense heat or bright glare of the sun, nor the dusty, dry air—not even to the bead of sweat slowly dripping from his temple into his right eye. As he came upon a group of spindly bushes, he slowed to a halt. The big hill loomed ahead, and he had to decide if Thomas had gone to the east of it, or the west.

Breathing heavily, legs shaking, he scoured the dry ground looking for the flock's small hoofprints. Down the road he could see Zebulun running to catch up. When Jonah found some tracks heading to the right, he motioned to his cousin where to go, then sprinted that way himself.

His mind racing even faster than his legs, Jonah tried to determine the most likely scenario. If his father was correct, that there were indeed soldiers in the area, then whose? And what did they want? Though frightening and imposing, Roman soldiers generally didn't rob and kill for no reason. Jonah had heard stories about Herod's soldiers doing horrible things, so it could be them. Or maybe it was a new invading army? Jonah's father had often told him stories of the history of the Jewish lands and of armies conquering the area, only to be replaced by a different army years or decades later. Or perhaps his father was wrong, and it was yet another group of bandits roaming the countryside....

There was another hill up ahead, and Jonah clambered up it knowing he'd have a good view and would likely spot his brother. As he neared the top, he heard voices and the panicked bleating of sheep. When he stood still and quieted his breath, he discerned the voices were all men's, but he could only pick out a few words they were saying—both because they were too far away and because they spoke with a heavy, unfamiliar accent.

After quickly surveying the landscape to ensure he hadn't been spotted, Jonah continued up the hill, turning every now and then to check on his cousin and signal to him where to go. Once on top, Jonah hid behind a thick bush. Gingerly moving branches out of the way, he spied their flock and at least a dozen soldiers he didn't recognize. They were not Roman, nor Herod's soldiers. They wore plain tan uniforms and had smooth copper helmets and shields without any sort of decoration. They were tying the sheep's legs together with rope and carrying them to a wagon with two huge wooden wheels and a jittery donkey harnessed to the front. Several sheep had already been slaughtered, senselessly bleeding out on the ground where they lay.

Zebulun, wheezing, crept up next to Jonah and studied the scene below.

"Nabataeans," he said between breaths. "My father told me all about them. He went to their capital, Petra. It's an entire city carved out of the mountains. Everybody lives in caves that are just like houses. Where's your brother?"

Jonah saw their beloved goat, Graha, lying on her side, her white fur soaked with bright red blood. He bit his lower lip to keep from crying out as he hunted frantically for Thomas. Where could he be? He wasn't among the sheep, the soldiers, the wagon, rocks, bushes.... *What if his temper got him hurt, or—*

Jonah blocked the thought immediately. "We have to *do* something," he said under his breath.

"My father says you should pray if you don't know what to do," Zebulun replied. "Let's recite the Shema and pray for God's mercy."

Jonah barely heard his words. He caught sight of Thomas's staff lying on the ground near some of the dead sheep, then held his arms tight around the pit in his stomach.

Zebulun whispered the Shema. "Hear, Israel, the Lord is our God, the Lord is One. Blessed be the Name of His glorious kingdom for ever and ever...."

Jonah's eyes darted every which way, looking for signs of his brother. One of the soldiers thrust his eight-foot-long spear into the side of a fleeing sheep, though Jonah couldn't tell from this distance whose sheep it was. Only half of the small flock was theirs. The rest belonged to other families in the village who paid Jonah's father a few coins for tending them while they grazed.

In between the soldiers' wicked laughter, Jonah heard fragments of the Shema from his cousin: "Beware, lest your heart be deceived ... And anger of the Lord will blaze against you, and he will close the heavens...."

On the verge of tears, Jonah didn't want to pray. He wanted to take action. Forcing his eyes closed, he tried to block out the voices and the laughter and the bleating and the brutality. Failing at that, he opened his eyes wide and bolted down the hill toward the soldiers. He didn't know what he was going to do, but he had to do something besides sit there and watch.

Seizing a fist-sized rock, he ran out from the bushes and into the open. "Stop it!" he screamed to the soldiers ahead of him.

They did stop. They stopped and turned to see a lone boy coming at them with a rock in his hand and tears streaming down his cheeks.

The soldier who had impaled several sheep was the closest to Jonah. He yanked his spear out of the side of the last one he'd killed. With blood still dripping off its tip, he raised the weapon, aiming it at Jonah.

"Stop it!" Jonah yelled again, holding the rock up above his shoulder. "Those are *our* sheep!" His voice cracked, prompting several of the soldiers to look at one another and laugh.

They put their weapons down and called out to the soldier with the spear, "You think you can handle him? He might be a little tougher than the sheep." They laughed heartily.

Jonah was nearly within twenty yards now. He cocked his arm back, ready to throw.

The soldier turned his head to the others, commenting, "Maybe we should put him in the wagon with the sheep. We could—"

He was unable to finish his sentence because Jonah's rock hit him squarely in the cheek, knocking him unconscious. As his limp body fell to the ground, the other soldiers hastily grabbed their weapons and charged after Jonah.

Jonah had no idea where to run to. He just ran. An arrow or two occasionally flew past him, zinging into the ground in front. He came upon a forested area and plunged into the thickest part of it, ducking underneath low-hanging branches and around thorny bushes. He ran and ran until his legs nearly gave out from under him. Then, recognizing where he was, he climbed a familiar hill to see if the soldiers had given up their quest. He discovered a few of them gathered below, peering all around. When they searched in Jonah's direction, he sunk low to the ground, finding to his dismay his right thigh was bleeding from a scrape or a thorn.

Peeking his head out from time to time, Jonah watched the soldiers congregate under the green canopy of a large tree. They sat and rested for a while, then departed. Jonah wanted to race down the hill immediately, but forced himself to wait a short eternity to be sure they were gone.

When he made his way to the flock, all was quiet. No more talking. No more laughing. No more bleating.

He counted the dead sheep on the ground and tried to figure out which ones they must have taken to the wagon. He knew all the sheep, even if they didn't have a name. As his eyes passed over their goat, Graha, he felt overcome with grief. Biting his lower lip, he willed himself not to look at the dead flock anymore. He had to find his brother. Going systematically from bush to boulder to tree, he checked everywhere in the vicinity, but to no avail. Thomas's staff still lay on the ground. *What if they took him in the wagon to sell as a slave?*

Jonah dropped to his knees with the weight of the thought. If there was one thing in life he was devoted to, it was his brother's safekeeping. How could he go on if he failed in that?

Their goat, Graha, was laboring to breathe. Jonah shuffled on his knees to her side, wishing he knew how to save her. But he didn't know anything. He was just a kid. He didn't know how to stop the soldiers. He didn't know how to find his brother. And he didn't know how to save their goat. Burying his face in her fur, he sobbed. "Graha!" he wailed. "Graha!"

He stayed like that for a long time, pouring his tears out. And when Graha took her final breath, he sat up, drained and lost, wiping his runny nose along the length of his arm. He gazed at the sky, pondering what to do next, and again saw that lone white cloud. It was drifting lazily along as though nothing had happened, as if the world was still the same as the last time he'd seen it.

But nothing was the same, and nothing ever would be the same.

Chapter Two

Long marches were the most boring part of being a Roman soldier for Marcus Trebellius Vitus, but he found ways to make them interesting. Today was the last day of his two-week Welcome Training, and also the most grueling march they'd done yet: twenty-two miles in the blazing hot sun, doing "faster step" with forty-five pounds of gear. The Welcome Training was an initiation for newcomers to Roman Legion X Fretensis and an introduction to the sweltering Syrian climate.

"No 'regular step' today!" the commander yelled. "I want 'faster step'! Anyone who doesn't finish on time is going home tomorrow!"

Vitus looked to his left at the row in front of him, spying Flavian, the taller, better-proportioned, better-looking soldier he considered his archrival. He doubted Flavian considered Vitus to be *his* archrival. After all, Vitus had yet to beat him. On every march when there were two miles left, their commander would announce, "Let's see who's the fastest today." In the beginning a handful of them would take the challenge, but after it became clear no one could come close to beating Flavian, everyone gave up, satisfying themselves with finishing the march in the time allotted.

Everyone, that is, except Vitus. He ran as hard as he could every time, but also lost every time. Flavian was plainly the strongest, fastest, and most athletic of all the new soldiers.

Knowing this would be their last march, Vitus had been quietly preparing for it for the past week. In the days they did not march, Vitus did one on his own after their day of training was over. He was careful not to let anyone, especially Flavian, see him. Instead of the standard amount of gear, he added an extra ten pounds. He knew there was only so much speed his body could give him. While he would do what he could to improve that, he concentrated his energy on his mental focus—being hyper vigilant about his breathing and heart rate, pacing, and how much discomfort and pain he could tolerate.

Out of the corner of his eye, Vitus noticed they were passing the short, fat palm tree loaded with ripe red dates and knew the two mile announcement would be coming any second.

"Two miles!" the commander shouted in his gravelly voice from behind. "Since this is the last one, whoever wins today gets a reward!"

Vitus was surprised to hear about a reward, but it gave him no extra incentive to win. His motivation was entirely to prove to himself and others that he could do it, that he could beat Flavian.

As usual, Flavian and Vitus broke formation and accelerated. Vitus contented himself with staying a steady fifteen feet behind his rival. He glanced up at the sky, hoping to see some clouds, but there weren't any. Just the scorching hot sun. Sweat dripped from his chin in a steady rhythm with each footstep. Fixing his gaze on Flavian's back, Vitus put all his attention on his breathing, trying to make it as soft and effortless as possible. He knew it took more mental effort to be the leader in a race—always wondering how far back your adversary is, if you're maybe going too fast too soon, how much reserve energy you have to handle a charge from someone behind. Vitus wanted Flavian to deal with those things for as long as possible. His own mental effort was minimal—to simply go the same pace as Flavian.

Vitus eased his breath, but kept it harmonized with his pace. He needed all his energy for his legs, so he continually scanned the rest of his body for tension he could release. When he felt his shoulders were raised, he relaxed them and told himself, "I don't need my shoulders in order to run." When he noticed his fists were clenched, he loosened them and told himself, "I don't need my fists in order to run."

He noted the grace and effortlessness of his rival's stride. Flavian's feet hardly seemed to touch the ground. Vitus felt like an oaf compared to him. To Vitus, it seemed everything came easily to Flavian. He won every contest, was popular with his cohorts, and was admired by all the young women. Vitus, with his flat nose, square face, and asymmetrical body, knew he could never be majestic like Flavian. But he could be a better soldier than him. He could be faster than him.

Flavian unexpectedly quickened his pace, but Vitus didn't allow himself any mental or emotional reaction to it. He matched his speed, staying fifteen feet behind, waiting patiently to see the small village that signaled there was only one mile left.

Not even six months ago, the Roman army recruiters had come to Vitus's village about thirty miles north of Rome. They had spoken of all the benefits of becoming a soldier: the salary of fifty dinars per year, the opportunity to own a piece of land upon retirement, the potential for promotion, but most of all the glory. They offered a chance to be a part of the greatest army in the world.

Flavian glanced over his shoulder behind himself. "Don't you ever quit, you dumb ox?" he called to Vitus. "You'll never beat me."

This race was only the latest test for Vitus in the Roman army. The first one had been when he tried to join. They'd told him he was one year too young and two inches too short, so he'd spent the next year doing whole-body stretches every day to help him grow. When that didn't work, he spent weeks on end practicing standing and walking with his heels two inches off the ground. He knew it had to be perfect, completely unnoticeable. If he wobbled while standing or bobbed up and down as he walked, they'd notice for sure.

He'd passed that test, but wasn't content merely being accepted into the Roman army. Being the youngest and smallest of his peers in his village growing up, Vitus had long made it a habit to prove himself in every way, to every person. And as he and Flavian passed the small village indicating one mile to go, Vitus set out to prove to Flavian who was faster on this day.

Pulling even with Flavian, Vitus ran side by side with him. Flavian again increased his speed, but Vitus stayed with him. Then Vitus tapped into the energy he'd been reserving and pulled ahead. His legs were on fire, but he knew his body well. He knew how much he could push himself.

With a half mile left, Vitus could hear Flavian's labored breathing and the jangling of his gear as he drew nearer. He was closing the gap between them. Vitus tried to go faster, but couldn't prevent Flavian from catching up to him. And then, a few seconds later, Flavian was out in front.

Vitus began to doubt his heart and lungs could keep up with the demand placed on them. He felt as though he might die. But unlike losing, Vitus felt no shame in dying. He commanded his body to go beyond what it told him it could do. He ran with all his might and caught Flavian. Then, with thirty yards to go, he plunged ahead, crossing the finish line a second before his rival.

The two of them collapsed to the ground. Vitus still thought he might die. He couldn't catch his breath and felt light-headed.

"I don't know how you did that," Flavian said in between gasps for air. "I beat you every time before and I didn't even have to try hard."

"I knew this was my last chance," Vitus said, still huffing.

After a moment, Flavian added, "Too bad there was no one here this time to see you win."

Puzzled by Flavian's words, Vitus said, "I don't care about that." And it was mostly true. He primarily wanted to prove things to himself, but was savvy enough to understand that to get ahead, others would have to notice. His commander, as well as those above him would have to be introduced to Vitus's qualifications.

It was many more minutes before the rest of the men crossed the finish line. Their commander, Romanus, plopped down next to Flavian to rest. He was around forty years old, Vitus guessed, with thick black eyebrows and a wrinkled, weathered face. He was missing one of his front two teeth, and told everyone a Parthian soldier had knocked it out in battle.

"What's Flavian's reward?" one of the men asked.

"First we have to find out who won," Romanus responded, prompting many of the men to laugh. When the laughter died down, the commander turned his head to Flavian. "Well?"

Before Vitus could say anything, Flavian announced, "I did, of course."

Vitus's first thought was to tell everyone that Flavian was lying, but he quickly surmised that it would end up working against him. Not only had Flavian won all the previous races, he was well liked among his comrades and even by Romanus. Vitus recognized that he, himself, would be the one labeled a liar if he tried to contradict Flavian.

"All right," said Romanus. "Now that the formalities are out of the way, here's your reward." He motioned to one of the soldiers near him, who reached into his pack and pulled out a one-liter brown jug. He handed it to Romanus, who announced, "This is the finest red wine you'll have here." He gave it to Flavian.

The commander then fixed his eyes on Vitus, but spoke to all the men. "Well, he tried at least," he said loudly. "Which is a lot more than I can say for the rest of you dirtbags!" Romanus tossed his helmet and armor in front of Vitus. "Here's your reward for coming in *second*," he said, a stern look on his face.

Vitus hid his confusion, waiting for further explanation.

"A bit dirty, eh?" Romanus said. "I want it fully cleaned by tomorrow morning." He turned to the others. "That goes for everyone," he ordered. "All your gear and armor needs to be cleaned and polished by morning. Cool off for a few minutes, then hit the baths."

Vitus was too exhausted to be angry. He watched as the rest of the men gradually left for the baths. Many of them congratulated Flavian, while others slapped Vitus on the back in sympathy. A few did both.

After a while Vitus joined them in the baths. He was in no hurry. Once finished there, he'd have to go back to the barracks, and he tried to spend as little time there as possible. The barracks housed all five thousand men of X Fretensis, and were split into eight-man rooms that were stuffy, hot, and crowded.

Vitus splashed cool water on his face, savoring every second of it after the relentless torture of the afternoon sun and the suffocating dust of their march. Then he waded into the water, took a deep breath and submerged himself. He liked to see how long he could hold his breath. After counting to seventy, he came up and shook his hair like a dog.

He loved everything about the baths: their mosaic floors, decorative statues, marble-covered walls, and columns surrounding the pool. He especially appreciated he didn't have to be in the furnace room below tending the fire. When he first arrived in Syria, the slave who did that job had suddenly died, and as a new recruit, Vitus was volunteered by his commander to do the grueling job until they found a replacement.

A soldier, conspicuous in his full uniform with scarlet red tunic among dozens of naked men, entered the bathhouse. From the other side of the pool, Vitus observed him stride over to their commander, remove his helmet, and lean his head in close to say something. After only a few seconds, he left, and their commander then climbed the six stairs leading to the changing rooms. There, he stopped and turned, calling for everyone's attention. Like the rest of them, Romanus had no clothes on, and Vitus thought it rather undignified to address the troops in this manner.

His announcement was short and to the point. "I'm sure you've all heard the rumors," he started. "Our orders are now final. We're heading to Galilee and Judea. Start your preparations this evening. Don't waste any time." Before disappearing into the changing rooms, he added almost as an afterthought, "We'll be joined by two other legions."

Vitus was thrilled to hear the Roman governor of Greater Syria was finally sending them to help restore order in the restive provinces. He soaked up every word of the discussions springing up around him. He knew very little about Galilee or Judea, except for their great distance to the south of them.

"I always wondered what would happen if King Herod died," a veteran soldier said.

"Well, now we know," a man near him answered. "Anarchy."

"I heard two thousand of Herod's troops formed their own army and are terrorizing the countryside," said yet another.

"That's nothing." A man near Vitus snorted in derision. "Did you hear about the slave who used to belong to Herod? He decided to crown himself king and burned down Herod's palace in Jericho."

"Really?"

"I'm not making it up. It's pure chaos there. I even heard about some rebel named Judas who captured an entire arsenal in Sepphoris."

"Sepphoris?"

"Yes. That's the capital of Galilee."

Vitus took a deep breath to contain his excitement. There wasn't much he could do to prove himself here in Cyrrhus, on Syria's northern border. The way to differentiate oneself in the Roman army was in battle, and he could hardly wait until they moved out.

Chapter Three

Jonah raced up the hill where Zebulun was frantically waving his arms. Despite the ominous vulture circling silently overhead, Jonah believed with all his might Thomas had finally been found and was unharmed. But once at the top, Jonah's faith drained like water from a leaky bucket. His brother, curled into the fetal position, lay motionless on the ground. Zebulun stood a few feet away scanning the area for soldiers.

Kneeling at his brother's side, Jonah placed a trembling hand on Thomas's ribs. Then he sighed in relief as his hand rose ever so slightly. His baby brother was breathing. Jonah could detect no bruises, broken bones, or blood—only a little boy with dirt all over his face from his tears turning the ground he cried on into mud.

Despite Jonah's repeated inquiries asking if he was alright, Thomas wouldn't answer. He just kept quietly weeping.

"We need to get going," Zebulun said anxiously. "They might come back."

Jonah leaned in close and squeezed Thomas's shoulder. "Can you walk?" he asked gently. "Father told us to go to the secret cave and wait for him there."

"There were so many of them. So many!" Thomas choked out in between sobs. "I was afraid."

"It's all right," Jonah said. "They're gone now."

"No!" Thomas said. "It's not all right! I ran away when they came, and then I just hid here and watched them slaughter our flock. I was a coward!"

"You were the smart one," Zebulun jeered. "Your brother was a fool. He's lucky to be alive."

Thomas wept even harder. "The whole flock is gone! Father will kill me!"

"No, he won't," Jonah said, tenderly combing his fingers through his brother's matted hair.

Zebulun craned his head to the right and cupped his hand to his ear. After holding the pose for a few seconds, he put his hand back to his forehead to block the sun. "Your father told us to go to the secret cave," he said impatiently. "Now, let's go!"

"I'm a coward!" Thomas howled.

Jonah shushed him. "Stop yelling," he begged. "There may be more of them."

"I don't care," Thomas answered. He wiped his nose on the back of his hand. "Let them come and kill us. Father will do it anyway."

Zebulun stomped over. "Stop being a baby!" he hissed. Then, leaning over Thomas and narrowing his eyes, he added, "We have to get out of here!"

"Go on without me," Thomas said. "I'm a coward."

"So what?" bellowed Zebulun. "So you were a coward! Can we go now?"

Thomas looked up at his cousin for the first time, as though verifying the words had come from his mouth. Then he sat up, the sadness on his face melting away, replaced by a blank expression. Without another word, he retrieved his small brown jug of water, hung his head low, and started toward the cave. Zebulun followed behind him, constantly searching every direction and commanding them to stop every few minutes while he cupped his hands to his ears. Jonah was at the rear, slouching forward, sighing intermittently.

Although rain clouds appeared to be forming far off in the distance, for the time being the blazing sun had the sky all to itself. The hike to the cave normally took forty minutes, but as they dragged their feet, it took them nearly an hour now.

As they climbed the last few yards of the rock face leading to their favorite hideout, they beheld a huge boulder blocking the cave's entrance. Picking thorns off his tunic, Jonah puzzled at this newest development. "Was it like this when you were here last week?" he asked his brother.

Thomas shook his head apathetically, then plopped to the ground.

Jonah studied the ridge above the cave, trying to figure out where the boulder might have come from. "How did it get here?" he asked, more to himself than to his brother or cousin.

Thomas, sitting directly in the sun despite nearby shade, gathered random pebbles into a pile. Zebulun planted his large frame in front of Jonah, blocking his view.

"God put it there," Zebulun said decisively.

Unable to tell if his cousin was serious or not, Jonah asked, "Why would He do that?"

"God punishes people if they don't follow the commandments. It makes Him angry."

The idea of God being angry was contrary to what Jonah had learned. He'd always related to God as kindly and loving. Though he didn't believe his cousin, he asked out of curiosity, "So who is He punishing? All three of us?"

"Whose flock was slaughtered?"

"That was God's punishment too?" Jonah asked incredulously.

"Of course. God is the source of all good and evil," asserted Zebulun. He then quoted the scripture to prove it. "'I form the light, and create darkness: I make peace, and create evil: I the Lord do all these things.' That's in the book of Isaiah."

Jonah, having never considered before the notion that God was the originator of both good *and* evil, made no reply. "Let's see if we can move it out of the way," he suggested.

Zebulun shook his head. "We can't move that rock."

"I think if all three of us push, we can do it," Jonah replied. "Let's—"

"No, I mean we're not *supposed to* move that rock," Zebulun interrupted. "If God put it there, then it's meant to be there."

Jonah approached the boulder, stopping a few feet away as though it might lunge at him. Using a small stick, he cleared away the numerous cobwebs around it. Then he took a deep breath, leaned in, and pushed as hard as he could.

It didn't budge.

"Told you," Zebulun said smugly. "God isn't going to let you move that rock."

Jonah left it alone and squatted under some meager shade, feeling small and helpless and wishing an adult was there.

"If Samson were here, he could move it," said Thomas. "He was the strongest man ever." After tossing some pebbles, one by one, down the trail from which they'd just come, he squinted at his cousin. "Did Samson really kill a thousand Philistines when he got mad?"

"Is it written in the scriptures?" replied Zebulun.

"Yes."

"Then there's your answer."

"But how do you kill someone with a donkey's jawbone?" Thomas protested. "It's not really long enough to be a club, and it's not sharp like a dagger—"

"I don't know how Samson slayed a thousand men with it," Zebulun said sharply, "but it doesn't matter. What matters is that we believe it's true, because God put it in the scriptures."

Thomas scratched his butt. "When I get mad," he said, "mom tells me not to take it out on others."

"Well, you're not Samson," said Zebulun. "He was holy."

Fresh with inspiration, Jonah leapt to his feet. "Who gave Samson the right to slaughter a thousand people anyway?"

"God did," his cousin answered. "God hated the Philistines. That's why you don't find a trace of them anymore."

Jonah crept on the narrow edge extending along the right-hand side of the cave, then returned a few seconds later with a thick, ten-foot long branch. "Thomas, come help me. I think I know how to move it." His voice cracked when he said the word help, prompting a snicker from his cousin.

"Who do you think you are?" said Zebulun. Then, with raised chin, he proclaimed, "From the book of Proverbs: 'Everyone who is arrogant in heart is an abomination to the Lord; be assured, he will not go unpunished.'"

Jonah grumbled under his breath. He was getting painfully reacquainted with his cousin's habit of constantly quoting scripture. He'd heard it all day long when he'd stayed with Zebulun's family last summer. They quoted scripture the way some families bickered. Instead of accusations and insults, they hurled the words of the Torah over every little thing.

Thomas peered at the heavy boulder. "Maybe Zebulun's right."

"If God really doesn't want us to move it, then He won't allow it to be moved," said Jonah. "We have to at least try."

Jonah jammed one end behind the boulder, into the cave opening, then he and Thomas grabbed hold of the other end and pushed hard. The branch bent and creaked, but finally the boulder relented, sliding over just enough for them to squeeze inside.

"Hooray!" shouted Thomas, giving his brother a hug.

Zebulun was silent, staring off into the distance as through he hadn't noticed anything.

Jonah and Thomas ducked into the cave and sat in the makeshift chairs they'd built out of the miscellaneous sticks, branches, and large stones they'd gathered over the years. Savoring the cool air, Jonah soon fell asleep. He awoke an hour later to find Thomas slumbering at his feet like a puppy.

Peeking out the entrance of the cave, Jonah spied the sun at its zenith in the sky. It was like a fiery flower in full bloom. Zebulun was sitting on the dry earth hugging his knees tight, clinging to a sliver of remaining shade.

When Thomas woke up, Jonah suggested they take turns being a lookout. There was a tall, white poplar tree on top of the ridge that provided a good view of the area around them. He volunteered to go first and spent most of his time gazing in the direction their father would come from. He also watched the clouds, especially the dark ones as they veered slowly to the east. As the time dragged on, his mood turned dreary. Where was his father? Why hadn't he come yet?

After several boring, uneventful hours, Jonah made his way down. As he neared the cave, he could overhear Zebulun and Thomas talking.

"...and then God caused the ground to open up and swallow Korah and his family," Zebulun said.

"The kids too?" asked Thomas.

"Yes, the kids too."

"But what did *they* do?"

"Nothing. They were punished because of their parents."

"That doesn't seem fair," objected Thomas.

"You really need to study the scriptures more," Zebulun advised him. "In Exodus, it talks about how God punishes the descendants of evil-doers down to the third and even *fourth* generations."

Jonah skipped the last few steps by jumping down. He landed on the ground with a thud, startling his cousin and brother. "Your turn, Zebulun."

His cousin hesitated, then snorted and began trudging up to the ridge's top.

"I'm hungry," Thomas whined. He picked up the jug and shook it back and forth to show they were out of water. "And thirsty too."

"Why don't you go down to the stream and fill it up," Jonah suggested.

Thomas perked up at the idea. "Maybe Peleg is there," he said excitedly. Peleg was the big frog that lived in the stream. Snatching the jug, Thomas hurried down off the ledge.

"Be careful of the thorns," Jonah cautioned as he observed Thomas's bare feet. Despite everything that had gone wrong that day, Jonah was at least grateful his brother was unharmed. He nearly laughed to see Thomas trotting down the trail like a horse. "And wash your face while you're there!" he called after him.

It was only a few minutes later when Thomas came sprinting back up the trail. Knowing it hadn't been long enough for him to have reached the stream and filled the jug, Jonah yelled, "What? What is it?"

"There's something there!" Thomas said with a pale face and quivering voice.

"An animal or a person?"

"I don't know," said Thomas. "Maybe a monster. I heard it, and saw it move."

"Where?"

"Near the stream."

"I'll go get Zebulun," Jonah said. "You get our spears."

When they'd go to the cave to play, they liked to sharpen sticks into spears, using them to fight off infernal armies. They were toys made of thin branches, but now they needed them for real.

Jonah led the way to the stream, moving slowly, deliberately, and looking over his shoulder now and then for Thomas to point the way toward the monster. Clutching their spears tightly, the three of them moved quiet as hunters until they were close enough to see the mysterious creature. From their distance and angle, Jonah couldn't tell what the large, brown, unmoving lump was. *Maybe a deer*, he thought. As they snuck closer, it began to take shape: legs with sandals, a tattered tunic, a partly bald head with a ring of thin, dark hair.

"He's dead," Zebulun pronounced.

Jonah kept his eye on the man to see if he moved. If he wasn't dead, he surely should have heard Zebulun's loud voice.

"It was moving earlier," Thomas whispered.

Zebulun picked up a small stone and threw it. It bounced off the man's back, and he lifted his head in response. Then he scraped at the ground with his left arm and leg. He didn't turn his head to look in their direction and his convulsions did nothing more than rake dead leaves back and forth. Jonah noted the man's right side seemed to be frozen; he only moved his left arm and leg.

"It stinks," Thomas whispered, plugging his nose with his fingers. Jonah had smelled it too, a foul mix of piss and feces with a sickly sweetness that made him nauseous.

They crept in closer. "Hello?" Jonah called cautiously.

No answer. Only more flailing arms and legs. The man's beige tunic, too small for his large frame, had holes in it, suggesting he might be a poor farmer, or perhaps a shepherd. His beard and hair were full of leaves and debris from the forest floor. Spit oozed from the left corner of his mouth and collected in his patchy beard.

"We should be careful," Zebulun advised as he scanned all around. "It might be a trap."

Jonah felt Thomas's jittery hands resting on his back. With a glance back, he said, "He might've been robbed."

"I don't see any blood or bruises," countered Zebulun.

Jonah took a few more guarded steps forward while his cousin and brother remained where they were. "Are you alright?" he asked in a louder voice.

The man spoke no words in response, just inaudible moans. After another step, Jonah was directly in the man's line of sight. His gray eyes stared straight ahead, but never directly at Jonah, always to the left or right or beyond him.

Thomas and Zebulun inched forward, rejoining Jonah. "What's wrong with him?" whispered Thomas. He stood next to Jonah, gripping his spear so tightly his knuckles were white.

"He must be hurt, or sick, or something," Jonah answered.

"He's probably possessed," offered Zebulun.

Lying on the ground next to the man, but out of his reach, was an almond-colored jug and a crude bronze dagger.

"Look! He's trying to get his dagger," exclaimed Thomas.

"I don't think so," Jonah said. "He's probably thirsty and wants his jug."

"Let's just leave him alone," Thomas said with a whimper. "Wait until Father comes."

Zebulun used his spear to hook the man's jug and get it closer to his flailing arm. "If he's a Jew, we have to help. The scriptures say so."

For the first time ever, Jonah found himself admiring his cousin and his strict adherence to the commandments.

After tremendous effort, the man was able to grab the jug with his shaky left hand and uncork it. He couldn't, however, maneuver his head so he could drink anything. His whole body was stiff as a board.

"We need to help him sit up so he can drink some water," Jonah said. He wasn't sure how to do it, though. The man was a head taller and doubtless twice Jonah's weight.

Zebulun sucked in a breath and nodded in agreement. "Let's go behind and try to lift him."

Zebulun and Jonah came close and put their arms tentatively under the man. Jonah held his breath against the stench as he lifted. When they got him a foot high, he rolled out of their arms and back to the ground.

"Thomas," Jonah called, "come help us. When we start raising him up, you get underneath his right side."

"I'm not touching him," Thomas vowed, folding his arms in front of himself.

"Don't be a chicken," Zebulun said.

That did the trick.

"I'm not scared!" Thomas yelled, then reluctantly came over.

Jonah grinned, impressed with his cousin's timely taunt.

"Ready," Zebulun said. "One, two, three...."

As Zebulun and Jonah grunted and hoisted the man up, a piece of fabric tucked inside his tunic fell out. Jonah saw it was a tallith—a prayer shawl—and thought nothing of it. All the Jewish men had one. But Zebulun gasped and abruptly let go. Unable to hold the man all by himself, Jonah's arms collapsed, and the stranger fell onto Thomas like a bag of heavy wool. With a blood-curdling scream, Thomas scrambled out from underneath.

Zebulun lurched two steps back.

"What?!" Jonah yelled at him.

"He's—" Zebulun stuttered, unable to finish his sentence.

"He's what?!" Thomas bawled, his eyes rapidly filling with tears. "Possessed?"

"No," Zebulun said. "Worse. Look at his tallith!"

Jonah stared uncomprehendingly at the piece of white cloth. "What are you talking about?"

"Look at its *fringes*."

"So they're not white," Jonah said. "Who cares?"

"Don't you know?" Zebulun said. "They're *blue*. That means he's a—"

"A *what*?" demanded Jonah.

"Samaritan," Zebulun muttered.

"A *Samaritan*?" Thomas repeated as he hid behind a nearby tree.

Jonah had never seen a Samaritan before, but his uncle, Zebulun's father, had told him all about "those half-breeds." They'd turned their backs on God long ago by intermarrying with the Assyrians, contrary to the commandments. Jews like Jonah and his brother and cousin were forbidden to have any contact with the ungodly Samaritans, lest their wickedness contaminate them.

"For Jews, the fringes of the tallith are always white," Zebulun explained. "But for Samaritans, they're blue."

Thomas tripped on a root. When he regained his footing, he fled from the scene. Jonah wasn't sure what to do. Part of him wanted to help and part of him wanted to run away like his brother.

Zebulun made the decision for him. Digging his nails into Jonah's forearm, he clasped tightly and pulled him toward the cave as the stranger made another indecipherable groan and pawed at the ground.

Chapter Four

Each footstep kicked up a little puff of dust from the road. Multiplied by fifteen thousand soldiers and hundreds of mules, it contributed to a veritable cloud that enveloped the three Roman legions. Vitus's legion, X Fretensis, was in the worst possible place—at the end of the nearly two-mile long column. Not a second went by when someone near Vitus wasn't coughing from the dust. Some even had nosebleeds. Vitus himself had a splitting headache and detested marching more than ever.

In addition to their weapons, armor, and shield, each soldier carried over his right shoulder a four-foot-long t-shaped pole with a twenty-inch crossbar. Attached to it were gear and supplies. On his pole Vitus had a woolen cloak for bad weather, a spare tunic, a waterskin, a pot for cooking, some rations, rope, and a shovel.

Though conversations had been plentiful when they'd left Cyrrhus, nobody talked now. There was just the steady rhythm of thousands of sandals on the road and thousands of gear-laden packs creaking, and thousands of pots, pans, weapons, and armor clanging. Vitus had tried to find out more about the place they were heading, but no one seemed to know much. He'd learned that Galilee was just north of Judea, and was racially mixed, with people from several different cultures living there. Judea, by contrast, was the land of the Jews and much more homogeneous.

From somewhere up the line, the order had been given to halt. Though it meant a temporary respite from the dust, it also meant it would take them that much longer to reach their destination. Vitus preferred to keep moving, miserable as it was, until they arrived at the place where they'd set up camp. It was day fifteen of their three-hundred-mile trek, and they were already marching through the hilly terrain of northern Galilee.

Vitus eyed General Gaius enviously as the general galloped past on his splendid white horse. *One day*, Vitus vowed to himself. *One day I'll be the one on that horse.*

After the troops were commanded to disassemble and rest, Vitus joined the grizzled eighteen-year veteran, Silas, under the shade of a nearby tree. Before he shed his one hundred pounds of armor, weapons, supplies, and gear, Vitus took a swig from his waterskin. Then he propped his pilum, a heavy javelin about six feet long, against a tree trunk, carefully unloaded everything he'd been carrying, removed his armor, and grudgingly took a seat on the hard ground. After another drink of his lamentably warm water, he unlaced his sandals and examined the blisters that had formed from the leather constantly rubbing against his feet.

"Pluto's ass!" Silas cussed. "This is worse than the march to Cantabria fifteen years ago."

"How much further?" asked Vitus.

"Today? Not much," Silas said as he massaged his calf muscles. "Won't be long before dusk. Maybe another two hours before we set up camp."

Vitus wondered if he'd have any luck convincing his commander to send him and a few others on an advance scouting mission before sunset. Vitus had attempted similar requests in the past two weeks, but Romanus had been none too pleased for the ideas. After Vitus's last suggestion, he'd received orders to dig holes for latrines instead.

The campaign had been incredibly boring so far. They hadn't encountered any threats or enemies, though they'd certainly seen evidence of pillaging and past skirmishes. At least half of the villages they came across had been razed to the ground. If a structure had been made of stone, it had been toppled. If it had been made of wood, it had been burned. In each afflicted village, they recorded its name and tried to ascertain who had destroyed it. Sometimes the answer was straightforward: the Nabataean army, Herod's soldiers, bandits. Other times the answer was elusive, with people giving different accounts. And for some villages, the answer was that it had been ransacked multiple times by different attackers.

After the legions resumed marching, Silas's prediction turned out to be quite accurate. Two hours into the march the order was given to stop and set up camp. While other men put up tents or constructed stables or ramparts, Vitus's role was to help dig trenches. Just as he and the others were close to finishing, a messenger dashed up and informed him he was being summoned. Vitus was to report at once to Romanus with full armor, sword, and shield.

Vitus hurried to his tent to get ready. He was thrilled at the prospect of doing something besides the tedious marching and digging that had been the whole of his life lately. As he raced to the large tent housing the camp headquarters, he spied Romanus outside it, engaged in a heated discussion with another commander. Vitus wasn't the only one who'd been summoned. There were eleven men in full armor already standing in formation. Vitus took his place next to Flavian, noting that all the men assembled had one thing in common—they were all recent additions to X Fretensis.

Romanus elbowed the portly commander next to him, and the two of them turned to address the men. "You've been called because of a grave situation," announced Romanus.

"That needs to be addressed immediately," the other commander added.

No one responded, save Flavian, who shouted, "Yes, sir!"

"Shut up!" said Romanus. "I'm not putting you in charge. Vitus, step up!"

Vitus, swelling with pride, could barely conceal a smile. He marched as straight and tall as he could to the front and stood at attention.

Romanus fixed his steely eyes on him. "You've been badgering me for a special mission," he said, "so here's your opportunity. I need you to retrieve something."

"And it's top secret," said the other commander with a slight smirk.

Vitus stuck his chin out, but otherwise hid his excitement. "What are we to get, sir?"

"We have information about a village not far from here. It's a mile and half east, and there's not much daylight left so you'll have to move quickly." Then he unrolled a map for all to see. "Follow this road and you'll come to a village called Safiel." Vitus's commander then nodded in the direction of a cluster of large, empty jugs scattered on the ground. "You'll need those," he said with a sly grin.

Vitus was confused. "For what, sir?"

"To get the water, of course!" the other commander bellowed. And with that, the two burst out laughing. Romanus guffawed and snorted like a pig as he slapped his fellow collaborator on the back.

Vitus, his face flushing red, wouldn't give them the pleasure of showing his upset. "Can't we just get it from the stream, sir?" he asked.

They always set up camp near a water source, and Vitus knew where it was because he'd already filled up his waterskin there.

"You think we're going to take a bath in that filthy water?" Romanus said in between laughs.

Swallowing his indignation, Vitus surveyed the big water jugs, noticing a dozen wooden yokes lying near them. "Very well, sir," he said as dispassionately as he could. "Do we need to get the mules? Or are they being brought here?"

"The mules?" repeated the other commander.

Stealing a glance with his partner, Romanus said, "They're right behind you!"

Vitus peered behind, quickly figuring out that he and the other men assembled were to be the pack mules.

"The mules need to rest. They've been working hard all day," Romanus added. "Unlike you good-for-nothing dirtbags! Now get going!"

Demoralizing as it was, Vitus pretended to be indifferent to the whole affair. He stepped casually to the jugs and began attaching one to each end of a yoke. Then he motioned for the others to do the same. When he observed them leaving their shields in a pile on the ground, he hollered, "We're taking those."

"But why not lighten our load a bit?" one of the soldiers asked.

"A good soldier is always prepared," Vitus replied coolly. "Tie your shield to the yoke."

The other commander was still snickering. "Good! Good," he called out. "That's a smart one you've got there," he quipped to Romanus.

"Oh yes!" Romanus howled. "You men best listen to him. He's in charge!"

Vitus and the others hoisted the yokes onto their shoulders as the two commanders continued their taunts.

"If you fail in this mission, there'll be major consequences!" Romanus yelled after them.

"Maybe decimation!" his co-conspirator added. Then the two of them fell into another fit of raucous laughter.

* * *

Vitus and his men trudged along the dirt road that curved to the top of a small hill. In front of them, the honey-colored sun was setting behind the still-smoldering village that was their destination. When the visibly tired soldier next to Vitus let out a long, dispirited sigh, Vitus attempted to console him. "Don't worry," he said. "I'm sure the well is still intact."

"It's not that," the man replied. "This just ain't what I thought it would be."

"What?"

"Being in the Roman army."

Vitus thought back to the end of his basic training, when he was notified he'd be going to Syria. He was so excited he couldn't sleep for most of the night, and when he did sleep, he dreamed of battling Parthians, Rome's enemy near the Syrian border. They were a formidable foe, and one could gain much honor by defeating them. But instead of glorious battles in an exotic land, he was in Galilee—some backward, remote province—fetching water like a slave.

"Try to keep your head up," Vitus reassured him. "All the old-timers say marching is the worst part."

A gust of wind whistled through the valley and rustled the shriveled leaves of the nearby grove of olive trees. The breeze felt good now as it wicked sweat from Vitus's skin, but it wasn't so refreshing after the sun set. The temperature had been dropping precipitously at night, to the point that Vitus had begun using his cloak as a blanket.

Vitus took in the grisly details of the gutted village, now less than half a mile away. Smashed stone walls and charred smoking posts were all that remained. The landscape outside the village was only slightly less forbidding. Spindly bushes wrestled from the rocky terrain. Barren hills stretched in every direction.

On one of the hills, Vitus recognized Gaius's magnificent white stallion pawing at the ground. The general and three advisers were on horseback, engaged in discussion and pointing to the south. Vitus kept his gaze on the general as he walked, again dreaming of becoming like him one day. Gaius had achieved the pinnacle of a career in the military. He had power, wealth, and stature. What more could a man want out of life?

The adviser to Gaius's right suddenly slumped to the side and fell from his saddle. Then Gaius and the other two plunged their horses down the dangerously steep hill.

Vitus shook his head with bewilderment until he saw the cause: Dozens of howling warriors streaming over the hill in pursuit, their savage war cry echoing throughout the valley.

Arrows sliced through the twilight sky, just missing Gaius and his advisers. The sharp hill they were attempting to descend was glazed with broken rock, and Gaius's horse lost its footing. After falling on its side and crushing its rider's leg, they both slid ignobly down the hill. When they reached the bottom, neither of them got up.

Vitus and the eleven other new recruits stared in disbelief at the unfolding scene. Everything was happening so quickly.

"Untie your shields!" Vitus yelled to the others as he dropped his yoke and jugs to the ground.

The attackers, most in leather armor with circular bronze shields, waved their swords over their heads as they made their way down the hill toward Gaius.

With shields in hand, Vitus ordered a charge. And with their own war cry, they rushed toward the wounded general. Though they were significantly further from Gaius than their adversary, Vitus and his cohorts had the advantage of mostly flat terrain. The attacking warriors had to pick their way carefully down the hill's slippery slope.

As Vitus led the way, he sized up the enemy—their number, weapons, weaknesses.... Noting their mismatched swords, ancient spears, and complete lack of armor for some of them, he decided they couldn't be an organized army. They must be bandits.

Vitus noted too that he and his men were vastly outnumbered.

Gaius's two advisers had dismounted their horses and were slipping and sliding down the hill trying to reach their commander before the enemy did. It was a three-way race to Gaius, and the general's life depended on who won.

Catching sight of enemy archers loading their bows, Vitus alerted the men to tighten their formation and prepare for the barrage of arrows. The soldiers at the head of the formation raised their shields in front of them, and the men behind held their shields above their heads, creating a nearly impenetrable wall and roof around them.

Thwack! Thwack! Thwack! Arrows plunged into the shields as others flew by or hit the ground beside them.

Vitus made sure they maintained the intensity of their charge, not allowing anything to slow them down. Though they had helmets, shields, and metal armor to protect them, each of them had only two weapons—a shortsword and a dagger. They had no bows, spears, or javelins.

When they closed to within thirty yards of Gaius, Vitus sprinted ahead of the others, hoping to beat an attacking warrior who was nearly on top of Gaius. Despite Vitus's efforts, the warrior won out, swinging his sword like an axe at the wounded general. Gaius managed to roll to the side and dodge the blow, and before the man could strike again, Vitus was there.

After lunging out of the way of the warrior's first strike, Vitus counterattacked by thrusting his sword forward at the man's exposed belly. Vitus's sharp sword penetrated the leather armor, stabbing into the man's navel. The next warrior leapt down the hill and tried to sneak in a deadly blow, but Vitus turned just in time. After blocking the attack with his shield, he then used it as an offensive weapon, striking his attacker in the face with the shield's iron edging. Before the man could recover, the rest of Vitus's men arrived. They managed to fight off the initial surge of the warriors, but soon found themselves surrounded.

"Form a circle around the general!" Vitus roared.

The other two members of Gaius's party fought their way past the warriors and made it to the circle. They stayed in the center with Gaius, keeping watch for holes in their defenses and calling out orders. Vitus and Flavian fought side by side, fending off one after another frenzied warrior. But then, out of the corner of his eye, Vitus spied Flavian falling to the ground. In a heartbeat, another soldier took his place.

The enemy lunged again and again at them, but could not penetrate their circle. When they finally gave up and retreated, eight of their comrades lay dead or dying on the ground.

For their part, two other men besides Gaius had been injured or wounded: Flavian, who was standing and looked to be alright, and another man who was lying face down. Bright red blood dripped down the side of Flavian's dirt-covered leg and onto the laces of his sandals.

"Is it bad?" Vitus asked.

Flavian seemed embarrassed, refusing to even look at his leg. "It's nothing," he said, sounding slightly annoyed. He made no attempt to stop the bleeding or clean the dirt from his leg.

Vitus recognized the soldier who was face down. He'd been in the same Welcome Training as him. Watching the man bleed out and gasp for air, Vitus felt an unfamiliar sensation in his heart. It wasn't a physical pain, more like he wanted to cry. Recoiling against the sentiment, he pushed it away and replaced it with anger—anger with the man for failing to fight off his attacker; and anger with the enemy for killing him.

One of the enemy lay nearby, bleeding profusely from his belly. Vitus remembered him as the first man he had battled. Placing his foot on the man's neck, Vitus drove his sword into him like a stake, then watched him breathe his last breath.

Chapter Five

"And many of the cities were fortified with gates and bars and high walls," Zebulun explained, stretching his meaty arms high above his head to demonstrate.

Jonah and Thomas sat spellbound, peering at their cousin's pale figure in the moonlight. They'd never heard stories from the scriptures like *this* before.

Zebulun went on to describe how Moses and his army destroyed sixty cities, plundered livestock, and slaughtered every man, woman, and child in the region of Argob. When he finished the story, Jonah and Thomas stared at him in disbelief.

Thomas was the first to break the silence, asking, "Why would God let Moses do all those bad things?"

Zebulun raised his eyebrows, clearly taken aback by the question. "*Let* him?" he said incredulously. "God *ordered* him to do it. You two really don't know the scriptures at all. How can you hope to understand God if you don't know the scriptures?"

Jonah couldn't argue with his cousin's accusation. He thought he knew the scriptures, thought he knew God, but the more he listened to Zebulun reciting stories from and quoting the Torah, the more naive he began to feel for believing God was always happy and a good friend one could count on.

Shivering against another chilly gust, Thomas hugged his knees even closer and pulled his brother's arm around him. "How do you know so much scripture?" he asked his cousin.

With a grunt, Zebulun squatted and dropped his butt to the ground. "My father takes me to the synagogue all the time to read the scrolls. He makes me study them."

Jonah reflected on how Zebulun was one of the few kids he knew who was fully literate. The ability to read was uncommon even for adults, as most were poor farmers. Squeezing his brother tight to keep him warm, Jonah thought he smelled smoke from somewhere. Lifting his head, he sniffed at the air in different directions, but the smell was gone just as quickly as it had come.

"Where's Father?" Thomas asked in a whine. "You told me he said he'd be here by sunset."

Jonah didn't know what to say, and before he felt he had to answer, a noise—perhaps a stick breaking—crept out of the dark forest in front of them.

Thomas stiffened. "What if it's that wicked Samaritan?" he asked in alarm.

Jonah pinched him on the forearm. "Don't be silly," he said. "He couldn't even sit up on his own."

Thomas pinched him back. "Maybe it was all an act," he argued. "Maybe he's plotting how to murder us right now."

"Nothing to be scared of," Zebulun said. "God looks after the righteous."

"But what if He's too busy?" asked Thomas. "What if God is helping father watch over our house?"

"Then *I'll* protect you," Zebulun answered. "We're blood. We *have to* look out for one another. If anything ever happens to your parents, you two can come live at my house. Our family will take care of you and teach you right. You'll learn the scriptures and to fear God just like the book of Deuteronomy says to."

Jonah cringed at the notion of staying at his cousin's house again.

The three of them were then quiet, watching the bright, perfectly round moon hanging in the vast, black sky. After a while, both Zebulun and Thomas fell asleep. Before joining them, Jonah prayed the Shema and also his standard petitions for his brother's safekeeping. He had bad dreams all throughout the night: vipers, floods, and a wordless skeleton who stalked him with a bloody spear.

When he next awoke, the light of dawn was already sneaking over the horizon. By habit he lay still, pretending to be asleep, then realized he wasn't at home and his mother wouldn't be coming to tickle him. With a groan, he sat up and recited his morning prayers dispassionately, then set off to refill their water jug before his brother and cousin awoke.

At the stream, Jonah washed in the chilly water and reminded himself that nothing out of the ordinary had ever happened in his village. He envisioned it fondly, nestled like a bird's nest among the rolling hills of Galilee, encircled by an ancient stone wall, inhabited by bustling chickens, lazy dogs, and warmhearted neighbors.

On his way back to the cave, he saw the Samaritan off to the side of the trail, in the same place and same position as yesterday. Holding his breath against the stink, Jonah strained to hear if his brother or Zebulun were awake yet. Not hearing anything, he decided he'd help the poor man by pouring some water in his mouth.

As Jonah approached, he heard—then saw—big, black flies buzzing around the Samaritan. They were crawling in and around his eyes, nose, and lips. Once close enough, Jonah understood why. The man had dark dried blood covering his forehead and face. A jagged rock a few feet away, nearly obscured by dead brown leaves, also had dried blood on it. The man had been murdered.

Jonah glanced about nervously as he backtracked to the trail. Then he fled from the grisly scene as fast as he could.

His unease gradually gave way to relief when he realized how fortunate they were the murderer hadn't found them sleeping just a hundred yards further up the ridge. He contemplated whether or not to tell Thomas the news. On the one hand, it might scare him, but on the other hand, he'd probably find out anyway and it would be best coming from his older brother. As Jonah pulled himself up to the ledge, he saw both his brother and cousin already sitting up. With his dirty fingers, Thomas was cautiously wiggling a loose front baby tooth back and forth.

"I got us some water," Jonah called, handing the jug to Thomas. "You know," he added as he scooched in close to his brother, "I was thinking that I probably misheard Father. He must have said *sunrise*, not *sunset*."

It was a lie, but a necessary one. Jonah knew Thomas would be worried, and he wanted to calm his brother's anxiety before it even began.

"He'll probably be here soon," said Jonah, trying to sound upbeat.

Zebulun yawned loudly and scratched his crotch.

"I wanna go home," Thomas said, leaning his head on Jonah's shoulder.

"I know," Jonah replied. "Me too." He tried to run his fingers through Thomas's hair, but it was so matted with dirt he couldn't.

The warm rays of the sun were beginning to stream over top of the ridge and down upon them.

"I have to tell you something," Jonah blurted. "The Samaritan's dead."

Neither his brother, nor his cousin had much reaction. Jonah assumed it was because they thought he'd died naturally. Though he wasn't sure he should tell them the man had been murdered, the words tumbled out anyway. "Someone killed him."

Thomas's eyes grew large, but Zebulun still had no response.

"Soldiers?" asked Thomas.

"I doubt it," replied Jonah. "He wasn't stabbed. Someone smashed his head with a rock." Out of the corner of his eye, he caught Zebulun smirking, then he had a thought that shook him to his core. Jonah remembered how he'd woken up during the night and noticed Zebulun wasn't there. Looking his cousin up and down, he asked casually, "Where did you go last night?"

Zebulun jerked his big head sharply to the side, cracking his neck. "I had to pee," he answered with a cold stare.

Jonah liked that answer. He liked it a lot. After quickly volunteering himself to be the first lookout of the day, he grabbed one of the flimsy spears and scrambled up the ridge.

He climbed to the top in half the time it usually took, wanting to put as much distance between himself and all the not knowing as swiftly as possible. He hated not knowing what to believe about his cousin, and not knowing what to do about their situation. If all this uncertainty was what it was like to be an adult, then Jonah wanted no part of it. He'd stay a boy forever—cherishing his mother as his one true love, protecting his baby brother, believing God was his best friend....

Gazing upon the dreary, green valley spread out below him, Jonah tried to block out all thoughts. Good ones. Bad ones. Happy ones. Sad ones. He didn't want any of them in his head. He just wanted to go home.

Several disappointing hours later, Jonah started back down to trade places with Zebulun. Holding his arms tight to his stomach, he couldn't remember ever being so hungry.

As he neared the cave, he once again overheard his cousin and brother talking.

"So why can't we cut a leg off one of the sheep they killed yesterday?" Thomas asked. "We could roast it over a fire. My dad showed me how to do it so that—"

"For one thing," Zebulun interrupted. "It's the Sabbath, so you can't butcher an animal or start a fire. And, besides, you can't eat that meat. It's not kosher. Gentiles killed the sheep."

"But I'm *really* hungry," Thomas whined.

Jonah jumped the last few feet down to the ledge again, and just as he was wondering how Thomas thought they could manage to cut a leg off a sheep, he saw Zebulun holding the Samaritan's bronze dagger. "Where did you get that?" he asked.

Of course he knew the answer, but he wanted to hear it from his cousin's lips.

"From that dead dog, obviously," Zebulun replied indifferently.

Jonah had heard adults refer to Samaritans as dogs, but never someone near his own age. He wasn't sure what to think and began to run through all the Jewish religious laws he could think of, trying to figure out if there was one about taking things from dead people. You weren't supposed to own property that belonged to someone else. You weren't supposed to touch a dead person. The book of Leviticus commanded one not to steal personal property, but was it personal property if the owner was dead? Jonah didn't know.

Zebulun secured the dagger in the belt of his tunic and stood up. "He wasn't using it anyway," he said with a grin.

As his cousin lumbered up to the lookout spot, Jonah slipped into the cave and lay on the ground. He tried not to contemplate the possibility his cousin had murdered an ill man, or how the sun was already high in the sky and their father hadn't come yet. He couldn't bear to think about his parents or his village or the Samaritan, because when he started to, a blackness would begin to creep over him, a morbid hopelessness that threatened to swallow his being whole.

Chapter Six

Vitus cursed his sweltering tent as he departed for a juniper tree just outside of camp. The relentless sun bore down on him as he traversed the encampment's methodical pathways. When he reached the scraggly tree, he sat under its meager shade with his legs sprawled in front and his shield in between at eye level. Desperate for something to occupy his time, he was inspecting his shield's dents and scratches to determine if they were worth repairing. The rectangular shield was about four feet tall and two and a half feet wide. Slightly curved, it was made of laminated birch wood, and painted scarlet red with the symbol of X Fretensis, the bull, on the bottom. He'd already fixed the major damage it incurred from the battle to protect General Gaius.

That was three days ago, and the three Roman legions hadn't moved since. There was no official explanation for the delay, only incessant rumors that they'd be on the move again soon.

As Vitus ran his fingers over one of the deeper scratches, he heard Silas yelling for him. "Hey, Hero! I've been looking for you. Gaius wants to see you."

Silas had started jokingly referring to him as "Hero" since Vitus led the charge that rescued the legions' venerable commander. Vitus didn't object.

Jumping to his feet, Vitus hurried back to the tent with Silas. "Me?" he asked nervously. "What does he want?" Vitus had never been summoned by such a high-ranking officer before.

Silas gave a one-armed shrug. "Blazes," he cussed as he flopped onto his bed. "It's like Pluto's pit in here."

Unsure what to wear, Vitus decided on full uniform, including his armor and helmet. Though he rushed at once to Gaius's tent, he was forced to wait many minutes before being escorted in.

Vitus found the general sitting on a bench, dressed in a simple saffron-colored tunic. His wounded leg was stretched out straight in front of him. Setting haphazardly on the edge of a crowded table near him was a silver platter filled with fresh fruit. Gaius glanced up from the map he was studying, then waved irritably at the fruit flies.

"You called for me, sir?" Vitus said, not sure what else to say.

Gaius stared absently at Vitus with his iron-gray eyes. After wrinkling his forehead and scratching the white stubble on his chin, he said abruptly, "Ah, yes." He nudged the platter of fruit forward an inch. "Please, help yourself."

Vitus picked out the biggest of the four red apples, then scrutinized Gaius's badly bruised leg, wondering if he'd be crippled for life.

"A nice shade of purple, don't you think?" commented Gaius. "It looks much worse than it is. They say it's not broken. I can already put some weight on it."

Vitus pitied him his old age. Healing probably took a long time past fifty.

"What about Flavian, the other fellow who injured his leg?" Gaius asked.

Vitus was surprised the general knew Flavian's name. "He's in the hospital."

"Yes, I know. How's he doing?"

Vitus searched for an answer. He'd been avoiding Flavian, because whenever he went anywhere near the hospital he felt that same sickening weakness he'd felt watching his fellow soldier dying on the battlefield. His knees felt shaky just passing by the hospital and smelling those disgusting smells. He couldn't imagine going *in* it.

"I haven't seen him yet today," Vitus answered, feeling pleased with his sufficiently vague response. He recalled with sadness what Silas had told him yesterday morning about Flavian's condition: the surly and combative answers to any questions, muscle spasms in his face and back, the struggle to swallow food or drink, and increasingly, the difficulty speaking.

"Well, give him my best when you do," Gaius said solemnly. "He comes from a good family. I've known his father for many years."

"Will do, sir."

There was a prolonged pause in their conversation as Gaius's deep-set eyes drifted back to the map spread out before him.

"We're moving out tomorrow, and I have many things to attend to," announced the general. "I just wanted to call you in to commend you for your bravery and skill. It's men like you that make the Tenth Legion the best there is."

Vitus, elated with the praise, kept his reaction stoic. "Thank you, sir," he said.

Gaius looked him up and down. "You look quite young," he said. "How long have you been in the Roman army?"

"Six months, sir," Vitus answered.

Gaius arched his thin, ashen eyebrows. "Basic training alone takes four months," he commented.

"Yes, sir," Vitus confirmed, raising his chin an inch higher.

General Gaius laughed, then called him by his full name. "Marcus Trebellius Vitus, you keep it up and you'll be a centurion one day!"

Vitus allowed himself a smile at the possibility. Centurions were held in high regard. They wore helmets with bright red plumes and carried short vinewood staffs as a symbol of rank. In addition to the prestige, centurions earned nearly twenty times the salary of a normal soldier.

"Here," Gaius said, holding out a half-gallon sized tan jug. "Take this wine. And have some more fruit too."

"Thank you, sir," Vitus said as he cradled the jug in one arm and used his other to help himself to an orange, some figs, and another apple.

Vitus's commander, Romanus, popped his head through the tent opening. Upon seeing the general was busy with someone, he began to apologize, "Sorry sir, I'll come back later."

"Come in. Come in," Gaius called to him. "I was just congratulating one of your men."

Romanus lowered his eyes at Vitus, then feigned a smile to Gaius.

"He saved my life," Gaius announced.

"Yes, sir," Romanus answered. "That's what I heard." He stood with one foot in the tent and one outside, his leathery face staring at the ground.

"Is he treating you well?" Gaius asked Vitus. He motioned with his head toward Vitus's commander.

Vitus thought of all the unfavorable answers he could give, decided against them all, and replied simply, "Yes, sir."

"Good to hear," said Gaius. "We need to take care of up-and-coming young men like yourself. Right, Romanus?"

"Yes, sir," Vitus's commander answered flatly.

Vitus nearly laughed, but managed to turn it into a cough. Once Gaius dismissed him and he was clear of the tent, Vitus grinned from ear to ear.

As he headed back to share his good news with Silas, he couldn't decide which treat he was looking forward to more, the fruit or the wine. He hadn't had either of them since they'd left Syria.

A sickly scent alerted him he was passing by the hospital. In such high spirits, he decided to venture inside and relay Gaius's message to Flavian.

Slipping through the opening of the large, brown tent, he contemplated what else he should say to Flavian. He wanted to chastise him for not cleaning his leg and having the doctor look at it right away, but after glimpsing Flavian's frightful condition, he thought better of it. Vitus's archrival was surely in agony. His back was arched upward off the bed with all his weight falling on his shoulders. His neck and facial muscles were grotesquely tensed, as if he was straining with all his might against something.

Vitus stumbled backward at a waft of stench, but quickly recovered, dragging himself over to the bed. He refused to look at Flavian's deformed body, once so perfect, or his face, no longer beautiful. He focused instead on the round table near him covered with miniature bottles and pouches of herbs. "Hello," he said feebly. "Just wanted to see how you were doing."

Flavian didn't answer, didn't move. Vitus wasn't sure that he *could* move.

Shifting uneasily from one leg to the other, Vitus felt exceedingly uncomfortable, guilty even, for being there with his perfect health, jug of wine, and fresh fruit. He cracked his knuckles absent-mindedly. "Just saw General Gaius," he said, peeking over his shoulder at the exit. "He sends you his best."

A handful of flies circled around Flavian's body, landing wherever they wanted. Not knowing what else to do, Vitus raised the jug so Flavian could see it. "I got the wine this time," he announced with a forced laugh.

He was hoping for some sort of recognition that Flavian understood, maybe even a hint of remorse over his cheating in their race. More than anything though, Vitus wanted an acknowledgment of their rivalry, that for all intents and purposes they were cast from the same mold. But as he forced himself to look at Flavian's face, he saw no hint of respect or regret. To the contrary, Flavian had his top lip pulled back so that his upper teeth were bared in a mocking grin.

Vitus clenched his jaw and felt his ears burning. He couldn't believe that, even in his pathetic condition, Flavian still thought he was superior. Vitus uncorked the jug of wine and took several reckless gulps.

"Mmm, that's got to be some of the best wine I've ever had," he said, using the back of his arm to wipe his chin. "You want some?"

After waiting a few seconds for a response he knew would never come, Vitus chugged some more of the wine, adding, "I thought not."

Having fulfilled his obligation to Gaius, he turned abruptly and fled toward the exit. "Hope you get better soon," he called, not meaning a word of it.

Once outside the hospital, he found his whole body quivering. He drifted through the orderly rows and columns of the camp, diverting his eyes away from anyone he encountered. Eventually, he found himself at the nearby creek, pacing along its edge. Then he sat with his feet in the shallow water, cheerlessly eating all the fruit.

Several hours later back at the tent, he came across Silas crouched on the ground, his head in his hands. He told Vitus the news of how he'd just been to the hospital and watched Flavian take his last breath.

"It's a horrible way to go," Silas said with watery eyes. "A good friend of mine died the same way—whole body stiff as a board and that same damn sneer."

Silas's words thundered in Vitus's head. He realized that Flavian's bizarre grin had not been on purpose, but rather a result of the disease which had ravaged his body. Snatching the jug of wine from beneath his bunk, he bolted from the tent. Returning to the same juniper tree he'd been sitting under earlier, he leaned against its trunk, took a long drink of wine, and hung his head in shame.

He recalled with a bitter taste in his mouth how just three days ago, Flavian had been as healthy as an ox. And only a few weeks ago the two of them had been racing at a pace few could match. In just a matter of hours, Vitus's fate had taken a decidedly upward turn, while Flavian's had plunged in the opposite direction.

Vitus could hardly believe life could be so fickle and precarious. He'd either forged his way forward, or been extremely lucky. Either way, he wasn't happy. He couldn't get it out of his head how he'd callously taunted Flavian on his deathbed with the wine.

Tipping the jug to his lips once more, he tried reassuring himself it wasn't his fault, that he couldn't have known the grin was an effect of the disease. But even as he started to believe it, something still tore at him. He couldn't put his finger on it, but his chest ached and he was acutely aware of his shallow breaths.

He took another swig of wine. Then another. And another. And before long, the whole jug was gone, and he was drunk.

Still, he didn't feel any better. There was an emptiness inside he just couldn't numb.

Chapter Seven

Jonah squinted uneasily at the copper sun, already low in the sky on the western horizon. "Let's go home," he announced.

Thomas, who was just climbing down from being a lookout, glanced at him indifferently. Zebulun was sitting on the ground using the Samaritan's dagger to carve a new spear. He paused for a second at Jonah's words, then continued sharpening the end of the thick stick.

Jonah didn't take disobeying his father's commands lightly and had been hoping for some feedback. "If we leave now, we can be there before sunset," he added, more as a question than a statement. "We can go the back way where there'll be plenty of places to hide if we need to."

Thomas retrieved their water jug and his staff, then stared blankly at the ground. Zebulun slowly made his way to his feet and tucked the dagger in his belt.

Jonah had his feedback.

He scanned the area for things they needed to take with them, but there was nothing, just the grubby tunics on their backs. "All right," he said with a sigh. "Let's go."

They left the dismal ledge and marched single-file without a word. When they passed by their dead flock from a distance, the faint smell of rotting flesh fouled the air. Jonah caught Thomas gazing wide-eyed at the vultures picking at the carcasses. "I'm sorry," he said, putting his arm around his brother's shoulder. "I know how much you loved Graha."

"I don't love that stupid goat," Thomas objected. He pulled away from Jonah's arm and wiped his tear-filled eyes with his pinky fingers. "Crying is for babies," he declared as he went out of his way to crush a purple flower blooming next to the trail. "Besides, what good does it do?"

Jonah recalled one of their mother's favorite sayings—that crying cleanses the soul of anger and grief—but kept it to himself.

From behind, Zebulun added his opinion. "Those soldiers will get what's coming to them, Thomas. The Lord's vengeance shall be upon them."

"Good!" said Thomas.

They continued on, stopping now and then for a drink of water or to listen for the presence of soldiers or bandits. But they only saw one other person for the rest of their trip, a shepherd both Jonah and Thomas knew. He was heading the opposite direction and warned them to do the same.

Like the day before, dark clouds were again gathering in the distance and floating low over the Sea of Galilee toward them. When a solitary raindrop splashed on Jonah's nose, he quickened his pace.

"Come on! Let's hurry before it rains," he called over his shoulder. The approaching storm added another drop of anxiety to the veritable flood inside him. Jonah recalled the morning of the day before and his missed opportunity to tell his mother he loved her. When he saw her this time, he vowed to say it right away. The first words out of his mouth would be how he'd love her until the end of time.

It wasn't much longer before they spotted the familiar two-dozen olive trees that marked the beginning of their village. Jonah led the way, cutting straight through the grove despite the risk of being caught by Old One Eye. As they neared the end, he was struck by the quiet. Not that his village was normally a loud and busy place, but there was complete silence now. No dogs barking. No goats bleating. No donkeys braying. No children playing. No adults in conversation. Not even a bird chirping. Just the muffled sprinkling of occasional raindrops.

The next hint that all was not well came when they saw the largest and newest building—the synagogue. It fronted the approach to their village, and the wall nearest them was partially caved in. They could see straight through to the other side.

The thick rain clouds were directly overhead now, darkening the sky. Jonah was the last to hoist himself up to the raised foundation of the synagogue. The three of them hesitantly converged on the gaping hole in the side of the building, noting the numerous black smoke stains arcing up its beige walls. Coughing against the pungent soot, Jonah stuck his head through the jagged opening and peered in.

Several of the magnificent columns that held up the second floor were broken in half. Rubble was strewn everywhere. A muted, ghastly light shined down through a foot-long crack in the roof. Besides Zebulun's heavy breathing behind him, the only sound Jonah heard was the pitter patter of raindrops striking the crushed altar table.

One by one, they squeezed through the hole and into the synagogue, ashes and debris crunching underfoot. They moved through the eerie space quickly, wordlessly, and exited through the charred front doors where they got their first glimpse of the rest of the village.

It looked much the same as the synagogue: smashed walls, half-burnt, and without a trace of life.

They staggered down the stairs of the synagogue and onto the main road of the village. The acrid smell of still-smoldering houses mixed with the nauseating scent of rotting carcasses. Ahead of them, they saw the lifeless, outstretched paws of a dog partially buried by a collapsed house.

Lightning struck in the distance and lit up everything in an intense white light for a split second. Thunder, grumbling and low, reverberated through the sky.

They saw Old One Eye's house, destroyed like the others. Old One Eye himself was sitting on a flattened wall in front, his head in his hands, mumbling softly, "Why? Why?" His donkey, weighed down with hefty, brown sacks, stood nearby, swatting at flies with its tail.

The further into the village they went, the worse the grisly smell got. Zebulun covered his nose and mouth with part of his tunic. Thomas pinched his nose. They spied a dead donkey lying in an alley, still attached to its cart.

Jonah remembered how Zebulun had said God was angry, and that He punished those who didn't follow the commandments. Jonah began to wonder if perhaps his cousin had been correct. God *did* seem to be angry. His wrath was unmistakable—in plain sight no matter which way one looked. From behind him, Zebulun was quoting scripture again, "'The heathen are sunk down in the pit that they made: in the net which they hid is their own foot taken. The Lord has revealed Himself; He has executed justice, striking down the wicked by the work of their hands.'"

Near the village well, Jonah saw a small, dark figure sprawled on the ground. Recognizing Anna's tiny, broken body, he felt his breath go out of him. His vision of the day before had not been a mistake. It had come true the same as all the previous ones.

To prevent Thomas from seeing Anna's body, Jonah diverted his attention to a dead rooster on the opposite side of the road. He felt sick, light-headed, and was afraid he might vomit. Inside of him were such intense feelings that they scared him. He was furious with God for allowing this to happen. On top of that, he felt remorse for having such a thought. And then fear—fear that God knew his thoughts and would seek further retribution.

It was then Jonah knew for sure Zebulun was right, that he'd been right all along. God *was* angry.

Very angry.

And for the first time in his life, Jonah was no longer in love with God. He was afraid of God.

As they passed by the pottery-maker speechlessly staring out at them through the window of his unbroken house, Jonah held out hope that their home too would be intact. With a sense of pride, he pictured his father confronting the soldiers who'd came, boldly proclaiming to them they could not enter his house.

But through the already dim, rapidly fading light, Jonah could see at the end of the road that he was wrong about their home being spared. It had been smashed and burned just like the others.

He seized his brother's clammy, trembling hand in his and squeezed tightly. As they moved closer and saw the utter devastation of their home, Jonah could scarcely breathe. The front door was gone. The walls were caved in. The interior was blackened and burnt. Forcing an inhale, he called out to his parents. "Father... Mother... We're home."

The three of them stood still, awaiting a response. When there wasn't one, Jonah hoped his father simply wasn't there at the moment. Perhaps he was at someone else's house, helping them with repairs.

"Father?" he called louder. "Mother? Uncle Isaac?"

The sporadic raindrops started to increase, coming down harder and faster. Jonah stepped over the rubble of their former doorway. Thomas yanked his hand away, refusing to go any further. Zebulun pointed toward the floor of the next room where two legs stuck out.

Jonah couldn't tell at first whose legs they were, but when he moved in closer, he recognized the blackened toenail on the long, bony foot. "Father?"

Jonah rounded the corner, trying to convince himself his father was merely resting, because that was the only thing that made any sense to him. For Jonah's whole life, his father had been invincible. He didn't get sick. He worked from dusk to dawn, never getting tired. He was stronger than any other man in the village, even those half his age.

Jonah knelt on the cool, wet ground. It was dark inside the house, and he couldn't see much more than the outline of his father's body. "Father?" he called again softly. He placed his hand on his father's knee to shake him, then immediately recoiled as he felt the cold, lifeless flesh.

"He's dead!" Jonah said with a whimper. Even as the words came out of his mouth, Jonah could scarcely believe them.

Thomas ran up next to Jonah, shrieking like a wounded animal. "Get up, Father! Get up!" he cried.

Jonah tried to wrap his arms around his brother to calm him, but Thomas pushed him away and kicked at his father's legs. "Father, no!" he yelled. "How could you?"

Zebulun came and tore Thomas away, shaking him forcefully. "What are you doing?" he exclaimed. "It's against the scriptures to touch a dead body!"

Thunder rumbled once more, but it was no longer distant. It sounded as though it was in the same room.

Jonah gasped for air, feeling as if he was being buried alive. He wanted to beg God for mercy—mercy for two sinful boys with no father. But he knew no such mercy would be forthcoming. God showed mercy only to those who obeyed His commandments.

He looked down the hallway, wanting to run to his bedroom, his safe space whenever he was really mad or upset. He longed to crawl into his bed, close his eyes, then wake up and find this had all been a bad dream. But he could already see their bedroom was gone. Demolished.

Thomas squirmed out of Zebulun's grip and took off down the hallway toward it anyway. Halfway there, he tripped and fell over another corpse. Jonah rushed to his brother's side, picking him up and carrying him outside.

Knowing he couldn't handle it right now, Jonah blocked out the image of his mother's half-naked, lifeless body. But he saw that Thomas could not do the same. His brother's face contorted into something less than human. He looked like a ghost. Or a demon.

Jonah shuddered at what he recognized: something had encased his brother's heart and declared itself his new master.

It was hate, and it had found a new host.

Part II

Time Period: 13 CE (Eighteen years after Part I)

The chaos that ensued after Herod the Great's death in 4 BCE was ultimately subdued by the influx of Roman troops, but it never completely disappeared. Herod the Great's son, Antipas, ruled over the region of Galilee and inherited his father's penchant for building extravagant cities. He rebuilt and expanded Sepphoris, and in 13 CE he started building a new city, Tiberius—naming it after the Roman emperor. Herod Antipas also inherited his father's habit of provoking and vexing his Jewish subjects. The city of Tiberius was a prime example. Antipas had the city built on the site of a Jewish cemetery, a clear transgression of Jewish law.

In 6 CE, Herod Archelaus, Antipas's older brother, was banished to Vienna by the Roman emperor for his inept rule. After that, Rome ruled over the region of Judea directly in the form of prefects. The Jewish populations of Galilee and Judea abhorred both Herod Antipas and the Roman prefects. At the heart of the discord was their undying belief they should be accountable to no king save the one true God. They found being subject to Roman laws and having to pay Roman taxes reprehensible.

What held the Jewish people together through all the hardships and turmoil was the covenant. It was the formal agreement made between God and the Jewish people, first carried out between Yahweh and Abraham. In the covenant, God agrees to lead the Jews, to provide them a land called Israel, and to make it a great nation. In return for God taking special care of the Jewish people, they must agree to follow laws set forth by God and live their lives in a manner that honored Him as the one, true, all-powerful deity.

The covenant was not distant or far-removed. All Jewish men were circumcised as both a symbol and reminder of the promise that had been made. The pact between God and His chosen people was something to be honored personally each day—every man, woman, and child agreeing to enter into a relationship with God. This relationship, much like a marriage, was considered holy and to be honored for better, for worse, in sickness and in health, and forsaking all other gods and false idols. Even when all hope was lost, the Jewish people could take comfort that God had promised in the covenant to never abandon them.

Chapter Eight

Azara, half asleep, only managed to dismount from the ill-tempered camel with her father's help. It was night, the city dark and cold. Pulling her robes tight around herself, she wished for a moment she wasn't a young woman of twenty-three, but instead still a little girl her father could carry in his arms. He held her close as they trudged to a large, pale tent below the low-hanging crescent moon.

It had taken them four weeks to travel from Galilee to the oasis city of Herat in the east. They'd traveled as part of a caravan through lonely deserts and frigid mountains, all the while on the lookout for robbers, swindlers, and petty thieves. Her father carried considerable money, and also goods to trade at the distant cities they'd soon be reaching.

A strong breeze picked up sand and stung Azara's ankles with it. Behind her, she heard the camels bleating and grunting. From the tent in front of her came the merry sounds of music, laughter, and conversation.

Peeling back a tent flap, Azara's father nudged her inside. Azara peeked out from her headscarf at the dozen or so men sitting or reclining on large, colorful pillows around knee-high tables. Scantily clad women prowled amongst them. Two musicians—one playing a flute, one beating a small drum—sat cross-legged at the front.

The tables were teeming with wooden mugs and plates of half-eaten food. Azara couldn't make out the food in the dim light, but her nose informed her it was some kind of roasted meat.

All eyes fell on Azara and her father as they made their way to the last remaining table at the far end of the tent. Holding her head high, Azara returned their stares. After perching herself on a red pillow, she waited impatiently for her father to take his place next to her, then whispered, "Why must we come to these places? They're detestable."

"I know. I know," he said sheepishly, "but it's the only place to get a meal at this hour."

"Then let us fast."

He held his protruding belly with his plump hands and made a long face. "My stomach has already been complaining for many hours now. We'll just eat and then go to our inn. Pay no attention to the others."

The proprietor, a slender man with a short, well-groomed beard and a striped blue and white tunic, approached and took her father's order. He then returned a few minutes later with four pieces of round, flat bread and wooden skewers of grilled meat and vegetables. Azara couldn't tell what the meat was and just hoped it wasn't camel. She couldn't bear the thought of eating a creature that had just carried her on its back for so long.

As the warmth inside the tent grew oppressive, Azara loosened her headscarf and removed her outer robe. She picked at the food, feeling more tired than hungry. And though she did her best to pay no attention to the others, she found the favor was not returned. One man in particular stared blatantly at her. Judging by his dark skin and loosely wound turban, she knew him to be from Arabia. The three women at his table—most likely his harem— were each distinct in skin color and proportions.

Their beauty and elegant robes stirred memories of Azara's miserable, failed marriage. She'd most despised her husband expecting her to be like a work of art, something to be seen and admired, but not heard. He hadn't shared her love of philosophy and ideas, hadn't been interested in answering her contemplative musings, and hadn't been inclined to let her leave the house. Even now, though, Azara didn't hate him. He hadn't been a horrible person, just impotent and boring.

With every change of the wind, the candles flickered and the roof of the tent seemed to breathe. Azara felt as if they were all in the belly of some giant, evil beast.

The proprietor approached their table with a well-practiced smile and addressed Azara's father. "The gentleman over there," he said, motioning in the direction of the man who'd been staring at Azara, "has requested me to inquire about your companion. He—"

Azara's father arched his eyebrows. "My daughter?" he interrupted.

"Ah, she's your daughter." The man laced his fidgeting fingers together and made a quick bow. "Very well. Thank you."

Azara eyed the proprietor warily as he made his way back to the man, exchanged some words, then exited the tent. She studied the women at the man's table. The bosomy one with large golden earrings and black skin, she guessed to be from Africa; the young one with pale skin and hair down to her hips was probably from Persia; and the third one with the exquisite robes and shimmering green headscarf was likely from Arabia.

The proprietor nimbly wove his way around the people, pillows, and tables, and placed two mugs of red wine in front of Aziz and Azara. "These are courtesy of the same gentleman," he announced. "He sends his regards."

Azara and her father looked from the proprietor to the man who had sent them the wine. From the other side of the tent, the dark Arabian held his mug high, nodding to them.

Azara's father nodded politely in return.

Azara pressed close, asking, "Do you know him?"

"No," Aziz answered, "but I know *of* him."

"Why did he buy us this wine?"

Her father frowned. "I don't know, but I think we're about to find out."

Azara glanced over her shoulder and saw the man making his way toward them. He was younger than her father, short and stocky, with a slim black beard that hung to the middle of his chest. His splendid, red silk robe covered his feet, and Azara half-hoped he'd trip on it and not reach their table.

Standing over them and smelling faintly of frankincense, he said in broken Greek, "Your daughter very beautiful."

Azara cringed and gripped her father's arm.

"No, she's not," her father replied, shaking his head. "It's just dark in here."

By her father's response, Azara knew what this was about. Azara's husband had died six months prior, and since they had no children and he had no living relatives, she was once again available for marriage. Her strong preference, though, was to remain a free woman.

The musicians suddenly picked up their pace, sending flute music and drumbeats swirling through the air like moths around a flame.

The Arabian grinned, showing his crooked, yellow teeth, then raised his voice over the music. "How much you want for her?"

"You don't want her," said Aziz. "She's a widow and doesn't obey very well."

The man laughed as he snapped his fingers over his shoulder, all the while keeping his gaze on Azara. The man's equally dark-skinned assistant rushed forward, handing over a small purse adorned with red rubies. The Arabian reached into it and pulled out a fistful of gold coins.

Azara's father didn't even look at them. "You flatter me," he replied. "But my daughter is not for sale."

"I take good care of her," the man said. "Maybe you want camels? I give you ten camels for her."

"Ten?" Her father's eyes widened.

Azara didn't know as much about money or trading as her father did, but she knew that ten camels was an exorbitant amount. She fixed her eyes on her plate, holding her breath.

"No. My daughter is not for sale," her father said firmly.

The man stuck his thick lips out in a pout and began twirling the narrow tip of his beard with a gold-ringed finger.

Azara's father whispered to her in Aramaic, "Come. We have to go now." After placing a few coins on the table, he stood and offered his hand to her.

"But Father, we've done nothing wrong," Azara protested. "And you haven't finished your meal."

"Please," he insisted, grasping her arm and pulling her up to her feet.

"I speak with you again tomorrow," the Arabian called as Azara and her father departed.

Once out of the tent, her father kept his clasp on her elbow. "It is not wise to displease that man," he said in a low voice. "He's accustomed to getting what he wants."

Azara understood all too well. It was not the first time someone had tried to buy her.

* * *

Waking before her father, Azara tiptoed to the broad balcony of their second-floor room. Except for her father's snoring and the occasional chirps of some clandestine cricket, the inn was quiet. In the unbroken darkness, she couldn't tell if it was the middle of the night or close to morning. She only knew her restless mind wouldn't let her sleep anymore. Questions were a constant in her life. Answers less so.

Stretching her arms over her head in a cool breeze, she tried to remember what city they were in. After traveling for weeks on end, she found it difficult to tell days and cities apart. Was it Tuesday or Thursday? Were they in Balkh or Bukhara?

She gazed up at the stars, wondering if what the rabbis in Galilee said was true, that God had placed each star there and knew each one by name. She loved the idea of it, of God being so orderly and nurturing in making his creation, but she wasn't convinced that God existed. She'd seen little evidence of an omniscient, omnipotent deity ruling over humankind. The world she saw was biased, violent, and chaotic. If a deity did rule over the land, she was certain it was the equivalent of an adolescent male: impulsive, reckless, and self-centered.

In time the eastern horizon began to glow orange, announcing the sun's imminent arrival. As the light expanded, Azara could see a fortress atop a nearby hill. As its thick, tan walls, towers, and ramparts came into view, she recognized it as the citadel built by Alexander the Great—or as he was known in these parts, Alexander the Butcher. Her tutor had given her a tour of the fortress a decade ago, telling her fascinating stories about how Alexander had conquered the area three hundred fifty years earlier.

A smile crept over her face as she realized the citadel meant they were in Herat. Her father had promised she would see her old tutor, Farrukh, here. As a youth, she had spent hours listening to Farrukh talk about religion and philosophy—her two favorite subjects. Although not a Jew herself, she was most familiar with Judaism on account of living in Galilee. She also knew a great deal about the Zoroastrian religion, since Farrukh was a practicing member of the faith. In comparison, she still regarded herself as a novice in Hinduism and Buddhism. Those were the two religions she'd been studying when her marriage abruptly ended her tutelage.

Having reached Herat also meant they'd soon be coming to her favorite city, Samarkand, with its enormous market and captivating temples. Samarkand, her father had told her, was where her ancestors had come from long ago.

She startled at a hand coming to rest on her shoulder.

"Good morning, my precious," her father's voice whispered a few inches from her ear.

She turned and eyed his chubby, smiling face. "Good morning, Father."

He took a long, deep inhale. "Don't you just love the air here? Thank God for a new day!"

"You say that *every* morning," said Azara, "no matter where we are."

"You know me too well," he said with a good-natured chuckle. After a quick kiss on the back of Azara's hand, he blurted, "About last night—"

She cut him off. "Let's not speak of it," she said, crossing her arms in front of herself. She hated being reminded about her situation. It was not only uncommon to be unmarried at her age, society deemed it unacceptable.

He gave a drawn-out sigh. "As you wish," he said, returning to his bedroom.

In the uneasy silence that followed, Azara heard him sigh five more times. She knew her father only did that when something was really bothering him, so she followed him back to his room. "All right, Father" she said with hands on hips. "What's wrong?"

He was seated on the edge of the unmade bed, staring blankly ahead. "Nothing," he replied.

Azara knew she didn't have to say anything. A dubious glance would suffice.

"I was lying awake half the night thinking," he relented.

"That's *my* job," she jested.

He didn't laugh. "About your marriage to Bahram."

Now it was her turn to sigh. She deplored recalling the seven precious years of her life wasted with that man. She'd done her best to push away the memory of that fateful day when she was wed to him—a man she barely knew, a man cold and strict and three times her age.

"I thought we agreed not to talk about it until our trip was over," she said. "Until we were back in Galilee...."

"Yes, I know," he replied. "It's just that I'd known Bahram for a long time, known him to be a good man. It breaks my heart to know how unhappy you were and how badly things turned out."

Azara saw in her mind once more the soldiers and authorities arriving at the house a week after her husband's death. They had come not to offer condolences, but to confiscate all of his property. Unknown to her, he had been delinquent in paying his taxes for many years. They'd seized everything: the house, land, furniture, even Azara's pet doves. That her husband had no male relatives had been her sole hope and benefit of the marriage. It was rare for a widow to be in the position of inheriting her husband's estate, as it usually passed to the man's sons or brothers.

"What's done is done," she said, wanting an early end to the conversation.

He fixed his glistening eyes on her. "My fear is that I bungled this one so badly you'll never want to marry again."

She folded her petite arms again and looked away from him. "Your fear is not unfounded."

Azara was relieved to be free of matrimony, free of tedious village life, free to speak her mind once more.

"But don't you want to have children?" he asked. "Do you remember growing up, when we lived in that little village, Nazareth, with your uncle for a while? Our neighbors, Joseph and Mary, had that adorable toddler—what was his name?"

"Jesus?"

"Yes, that's it. He was so joyful, I remember."

Azara thought fondly of Jesus, particularly the adventure they'd had rescuing Old Man Omri's dog, Motuk, from Baruch and his gang of bullies. Calculating that Jesus would be about twenty years old now, Azara doubted she'd recognize him.

"Wouldn't you like to have a delightful child like him?" her father asked.

Azara shook her head. Though she had borne the brunt of her village's blame for being childless, she alone knew it was no fault of her own. Despite society's scorn, she still had no desire to be a mother. "I don't want to have children, Father."

"Why not, my precious?"

She started to say it was because she could very well die doing so, like her mother had, but resolved instead to tell him the real reason. "Because there's too much suffering in the world," she answered. "It's selfish to bring a new being into that."

"But they'll come anyway," he appealed. "Whether through you, or someone who is less of a light."

Azara didn't like that argument, because it opened the possibility that she herself might have chosen to come. Why would she voluntarily submit herself to the sorrow and torment of this world?

She sat next to him on the bed, curling in close and resting her head on his chest. "I'd rather stay with you, Father," she said. "Don't push me away again."

He laughed quietly and kissed her on the back of the head. "I only want you to be happy, my sunshine."

She pulled back so she could see him. He wasn't the tallest or the most handsome man, but he always had a smile on his lips. "Happiness is a luxury of the well-to-do," she declared.

"So you're happy?"

"Unfortunately, yes," she said. "Certainly compared to all the sick, the elderly, and the poor...."

He chuckled and playfully pinched her cheek. "It's nice to have you with me on these journeys again."

"Stop that." She lightly slapped his hand. "I'm not a little girl anymore."

"Yes," he said with another sigh. "You're definitely not a little girl anymore."

Even though the sun's warm rays were finally shining into their room, the air was still quite brisk. Azara shivered and rubbed her arms against the cold. "When will we be in Samarkand?"

Her father retrieved a cloak from the back of a nearby chair and adjusted it around his shoulders. "Soon. I hope to leave here this afternoon."

"Already? I thought you had business to attend to here."

"Yes, but I'll do it all this morning."

As Azara watched him smooth out his thin, graying hair, she wondered how many more of these strenuous journeys he'd be able to do.

He wrapped an ordinary cream-colored headscarf tight around his head and ears. "Don't want to risk running into that Arabian again...."

"Are you going to get us breakfast?"

He nodded as he headed out the door. "I'll be back shortly."

After locking the door by sliding its brass bolt to the clasp on the doorframe, Azara scanned the large room. She considered lying down on her father's wool mattress, or perhaps reclining in one of the antique chairs. But the sunlight now bathing the balcony called to her, and she decided to lie there and soak up the warmth while she waited for her father's return.

She closed her eyes and reminisced about Galilee and the Jewish and Gentile girlfriends she grew up with, thinking how she could have easily ended up like them—a mother three times over before turning twenty, poor, illiterate, with no hope of improving her situation.

She felt a wave of gratitude for her father wash over her. His knack for commerce had freed her from a life of poverty; his love of knowledge had freed her from a life of ignorance; and his big heart had freed her from a life of spite.

The temperature, outpacing the sun's ascent, was rising rapidly. Down below she could hear the city coming to life—children giggling and playing, chickens clucking, carts creaking, donkeys braying, merchants advertising their wares. And a short while later, three crisp knocks and her father's voice calling out to her.

Eager to find out what he'd brought for breakfast, Azara hurried to unlock the door. One of the things she missed most about traveling with him to these distant places was all the exotic fruits and vegetables they encountered. She remembered how her father used to buy her a fruit called a mango. It had been her favorite, and she'd always looked forward to it.

Her father strutted into the room with a wicker basket and a mischievous smile. Though she suspected he'd bought some fruit, all she could see, and smell, were the freshly baked pieces of bread on top of the basket.

Noticing one arm behind his back, Azara leaned to the side to try to see it. "What are you hiding?"

He pivoted so she couldn't see, then set the basket down on the floor. "A surprise," he replied glibly.

"You know I don't like surprises."

"Nonsense," he said. "Close your eyes."

"Is it edible?" she asked, hoping for a mango.

He shook his head. "Close your eyes and hold out your hands."

She sat on the nearby wooden chair and did as he requested. When a flat object wrapped in cloth was placed in her palms, she opened her eyes and gazed up at her father's beaming face.

"Unwrap it," he said. "It's something I've always wanted you to have."

She unwound the thin, drab cloth, revealing a small, elegant mirror in a gilded frame.

Her father tapped his fingernail on the frame. "Gold," he announced.

Azara ran her fingers across it. "Does it cost more than ten camels?" she said as a joke.

Seeing he did not laugh, she rose and gave him a firm embrace. "You shouldn't have," she whispered in his ear. Though she hated the gift, she could not break her father's heart.

"Try it," he said.

"Why?" she objected. "I already know what I look like."

"Because I want you to see how lovely you are." He ran the back of his hand along her cheek. "You're just as pretty as your mother."

Azara thought briefly of the mother she'd never known, wondering what she'd look like now if she hadn't died at such a young age. Holding the mirror out in front of her, Azara feigned a smile for her father as she peered into it.

She didn't see her reflection though, because she looked past herself at the still-open door behind them, just in time to see her old tutor appear in the doorway.

"Farrukh," she exclaimed, setting the mirror down and running to hug him. Though she and her father always conversed in Aramaic, she switched to Greek for her tutor. "How I've missed you!"

"My dear Azara," he said fondly, returning her embrace. "How wonderful to see you again."

Azara's father came over and slapped Farrukh heartily on the back. "Right on time, as usual," he said.

"How could I possibly be late for my prize pupil? My favorite female student?" said Farrukh.

"What do you mean your favorite female student? I'm your *only* female student," she scolded playfully.

Farrukh chortled. He was an olive-skinned, old man with a white beard and a perpetual sly grin on his lips. "Yes, that's true," he said, winking at her. "I've never understood why your father wanted to waste his money educating a girl, but far be it from me to turn down a paying customer." He slowly scrutinized Azara and her father up and down. "How long has it been?"

"Seven and a half years," answered Azara.

"So it has," Farrukh said, nodding his head. "I always suspected you'd grow into a beautiful woman one day. Just didn't know if I'd live to see it."

She found, to her delight, that despite him being close to seventy years old now, he still had that lively sparkle in his eyes.

Farrukh turned to her father, standing tall and dignified and clasping his hands behind his back the same way he always did. "Aziz, how long will you be in Herat?"

"Not long," he responded. "I hope to finish my business this morning and leave this afternoon."

"You'll accompany us to Samarkand, won't you?" Azara asked intently.

"Of course," replied Farrukh.

Azara's father grabbed two pieces of the thin, oval shaped bread from the basket. "Now that you're here, I'll run along," he said. "I've got a lot to do." Before he disappeared out the door, he called out, "Don't eat any of the dates in the basket. They're a gift for someone."

Farrukh gathered the basket from near the doorway and set it on the small table by the chair. He moved rather stiffly and wasn't as tall as Azara remembered, though she questioned whether it was because she'd grown so much, or because he'd shrunk. Or maybe both.

"I have so many questions for you," she said excitedly.

"As always," he answered with a smile. "Were you able to find a tutor to help you with your writing? That was your one weakness, I remember."

"No," said Azara. "My husband didn't allow my studies to continue." She felt sad telling him that and pondered if she should also explain it could have been worse. If not for her father negotiating a two-year delay to her wedding, her education would have ended much sooner.

"Did you have breakfast already?" she asked, trying to move on.

"A little," he said, "but I could still eat some of those—"

"Good," she interrupted. "Then let me ask you about a statue I saw in a market. It was a woman with a bloody mouth, bloody eyes, and a blood-red garland around her neck. She held a noose in her hand and looked quite gruesome."

Farrukh reached into the basket and pulled out a handful of black grapes. "The statue was painted?"

"Yes."

"What color was the woman?"

"Black," Azara said. "She was very dark. I think I heard them call her Kalayra or Kali—"

"Kalaratri?"

"Yes! That was it."

Farrukh tugged two grapes off the cluster and popped them in his mouth. "Do you remember me telling you about the *Mahabharata*?"

"Of course," she answered, slightly offended. It was one of her favorites, and the two of them had spent weeks discussing it. "It's the Hindu story of the battle between the Pandavas and Kauravas."

"Indeed," he said, then spit tiny grape seeds out into his hand. "She's in that story."

Shuffling through the bread in the basket, Azara singled out the one with the most sesame seeds on it. "I don't remember you telling me about her. Which side is she on? Is she evil? A demon?"

"No, not a demon. She is a goddess who embodies death and time."

"So why is she so frightening?"

"Is death not frightening?"

"I suppose," she said, scraping sesame seeds off the bread with her index finger's long nail. "Why the noose?"

Farrukh stepped out to the balcony, held his hands over the edge, and wiped grape seeds from them. "The noose symbolizes death for those who provoke her wrath."

Azara contemplated his words as she popped sesame seeds one by one with her teeth. "And who would be foolish enough to do such a thing?"

"Ignorance," replied Farrukh.

"So she destroys ignorance?"

"Yes."

Having eaten all the sesame seeds from her bread, Azara returned it to the basket and took another one. "I remember you telling me once that the Buddha spoke about the need to destroy ignorance in oneself."

"So you did listen to me sometimes!" Farrukh said with a laugh.

Azara pursed her comely lips to refrain from a sarcastic retort.

Farrukh eased himself into a chair that creaked under his weight. "Yes, sometimes the religions teach the same thing," he said. He stretched out his legs and added, "Other times, not so much."

Azara rooted around in the basket, saw the dates, and stuffed two in her mouth. "I rather like her," she said in between chews.

"Kalaratri?" Farrukh said, arching his slim, white eyebrows. "She devours everything, leaving nothing but destruction in her wake."

Azara smirked. "Just like time and death, no?"

She was standing behind him, and he strained his stiff torso to turn in his chair to see her. "You are, without a doubt, one of the most astute students I've ever tutored." Fixing his piercing gray eyes on her, he shook his head from side to side. "It's a pity you're a female. With your perception and intellect, you could become a truly great man."

"I don't want to be a man," she said resentfully. "Men are petty, cruel, and full of spite."

"Azara, come now," Farrukh said with more than a hint of dismay. "Your father is a man."

"Well, except for my father." She snatched another date. "And I suppose you too. Although you still suffer from prejudice and chauvinism."

Farrukh laughed heartily. "How I miss tutoring you, my dear."

Azara twirled her long, dark hair around her pinky finger. "Kalaratri doesn't seem to be afraid of anything," she said. "And she isn't ashamed of being a woman. She was completely naked in the statue I saw."

Farrukh plucked another grape from its stem, then rolled it back and forth in his hand. "She is not all that well known," he said thoughtfully, "but there are several sects who worship her."

Azara dropped the date she was about to eat. "What did you say?"

"I said she is not all that well known."

"No, after that."

"I said there are several sects who worship her."

"Men *worship* her?" Azara felt a little chill run up her spine, as always happened when she was introduced to a new possibility.

"Yes," Farrukh answered. "Why? You sound as if you don't believe me."

"In Palestine, people do not worship goddesses," she said, choking back her indignation. "In Galilee and Judea, there are no goddesses—only thirteen-year-old girls who are married off by their fathers the same way they sell one of their livestock."

"What can you do?" Farrukh said with a shrug. "The world is what it is."

Azara peered out the balcony at the sand-colored fortress of Alexander the Great, reflecting on how its imposing towers wouldn't be there if he'd lived his life by that gloomy proverb. "Perhaps," she said. "But there are those who see what the world could be, and change it for the better so it's no longer what it was."

Another little tingle went up her spine at the prospect of *her* being one of those people.

Chapter Nine

Jonah peered east toward the rising sun and leaned into the strong wind gusting over the ridge. To his far left was Samaria. Straight in front of him was Judea. He squeezed past a few of his fellow bandits for a better view of the village of Arimathea below. By shielding his eyes from the sun, he was able to recognize the house he and Thomas and Zebulun used to call home. Squinting, he thought he saw three figures on the roof and imagined them to be children playing some sort of game, just like he, his brother, and cousin had a dozen or so years earlier.

From this distance the village looked mostly empty, and it reminded Jonah of their journey to get here. So many villages they'd gone through in Galilee— Rimmon, Cana, Nazareth, and others—and there was hardly a man in any of them. When he asked where they were, Jonah had received the same answer every time: working construction in Sepphoris or else the new city Herod Antipas was building, Tiberius.

Turning toward Zebulun, Jonah tried to determine his cousin's reaction upon seeing his old house. While Jonah and Thomas had lived there ever since their parents died, Zebulun had lived every day of his life there—from the day he was born until shortly after his thirtieth birthday. Zebulun was on a ledge that jutted over the side of the cliff, closer to the edge than anyone else. Thomas stood next to him, intense as always, and a little too close to the drop-off for Jonah's comfort.

Considering Thomas had a wife who was pregnant with their first child, Jonah assumed he would prioritize his safety and make better decisions. But that had yet to happen. Though Jonah still loved his brother dearly, it often seemed to him that reason had abandoned Thomas—replaced instead by an insatiable thirst for vengeance.

Too far away to advise Thomas to move in from the ledge, Jonah knew it would do no good anyway. He could plainly foresee his brother's reaction: Jonah would first be accused of being overbearing, next would come Thomas's incessant reminder that he's not a little boy who needs looking after anymore. Jonah would, of course, disagree, reminding him of the time a year ago when he was nearly killed participating in a robbery because he'd forgotten his shield. Then the two of them wouldn't speak to one another for a few hours.

Closing his eyes briefly, Jonah first reminded God he was obeying every one of the commandments. Then he asked, in return, for God to protect his brother from harm. In between ensuring he was keeping up his end of the covenant, Jonah implored God several times a day to look after his brother's safety.

Zebulun climbed onto a cragged, uneven rock so that he was above Thomas, above everyone. With his unique red kerchief covering his hair and tied snug with a thin white rope, he towered over the men, eyeing each of them sharply. There was no expression on his face. There never was. It was one of his defining characteristics. One never expected such ferocity to come from those placid lips. He was the undisputed leader of the tattered group of outlaws, and had been ever since the original leader, Sadoc, was killed in one of their raids a year ago.

It was Sadoc who had accepted the three of them, plus Zebulun's elderly father, into his group of vigilantes. Jonah shuddered involuntarily as he recalled those dismal days of three years ago. After their house and land had been taken from them, they had no money and no food and were wandering aimlessly along a road when Sadoc approached them.

Sadoc was notorious in those parts, both dreaded by the rich and beloved by the peasants for his generosity and daring, and also for his refusal to bow down to anyone, be they king, high priest, or Roman. Legend had it he was the son of the famous bandit, Hezekiah, who had fought against Herod Antipas's father several decades prior. Sadoc's brother, Judas, had led a revolt after King Herod's death, capturing a large store of weapons from an arsenal in Sepphoris.

Zebulun lifted his glinting sword to the sky, his signal for the men to quiet down so he could speak. After a few seconds, all was silent, save for the blustery wind blowing past them. Jonah was amazed at the transformation of Zebulun since he'd become Sadoc's prized student. His cousin commanded respect and awe wherever he went. In their group of bandits, Zebulun was simultaneously feared and admired by all the men.

"The Corrupt," Zebulun began, using his favorite phrase to refer to rich landowners, Gentiles, Samaritans, Romans, and the Herodian dynasty, "are all over the world. But nowhere are they more poisonous than here in Judea." He paused, sticking his chin out from his pudgy face. "Three years ago, the Corrupt took my family's home. They took our land. They killed my father."

Jonah took in his words from the back of the group, reflecting on the fact that what his cousin said wasn't entirely true. Though they had indeed had their house and land taken from them, Zebulun's father had died weeks later in the caves that became their new home. Old and frail, he'd lost his footing, tumbling over the edge of a steep cliff.

"The Corrupt bend the law to suit their needs," Zebulun declared. "And they mock Yahweh's commandments openly."

Jonah glanced up now and then at the three vultures circling high overhead, wondering if they'd spotted something dying and were waiting for it to take its last breath.

Raising both his voice and sword higher, Zebulun exclaimed, "The Corrupt are an abomination in the eyes of the Lord!"

The men, bedraggled and foul-smelling from a week without a bath, nodded and voiced their agreement.

Zebulun fixed his eyes on the newest member of the group, Amram. "Like you," Zebulun announced, "our misfortune began with a drought. We had no crops that year and were forced to take a loan. We borrowed one hundred dinars, and had to repay one hundred fifty. But the Lord's anger was unquenched, and the drought continued. With no crops we couldn't repay the loan, so the Corrupt came with their shameless soldiers and took our house and our land from us."

Jonah knew what was coming next, not because he'd lived the story, but because he'd heard his cousin's version of it so many times. The tragedy was merely a setup for the call for revenge.

"But *today*!" Zebulun yelled. "*Today* we return the favor!"

All the men shouted their wholehearted agreement.

Except Jonah.

He was tired of the routine, tired of diligently following the commandments, tired of repenting for the godless life he'd led before. Eighteen years with Zebulun, the last three as bandits, had exhausted him to the breaking point.

The bandits' usual strategy was to rob Gentiles, Samaritans and rich Jews who traveled on the long, winding roads of the countryside, but Zebulun was now directing them to his old village. He'd received a tip that the rich landowner who'd taken their house and land was now living in their old home.

After thrusting his sword in the air to quiet the men once more, Zebulun led them in a short prayer. "Lord, be with us this day. Help us to be humble in all ways, to submit to Your will that we might cast out Your enemies from Judea. Guide us in putting evil away from us, and allow us to proclaim Your wrath." He then quoted from the book of Psalms, "'The Lord is a God who avenges. O God who avenges, shine forth!'"

It was a familiar prayer and a familiar refrain, all the men repeating in unison the last two words, "Shine forth!"

As Zebulun turned from side to side, scanning the surrounding area, Thomas stepped up next to him and did the same. Seeing them next to one another, Jonah saw more clearly than ever how, despite their similar temperament and views, they were complete opposites physically. While Zebulun had a short square frame with wide shoulders, a nonexistent neck and a big head, Thomas was tall, nearly six feet, and skinny with gaunt cheeks and a narrow head atop an elongated neck. While Zebulun had dull gray eyes mostly hidden under a thick brow, Thomas had their father's large, penetrating green eyes that bulged outward from his all-too-fervent face.

Not spying any soldiers, Zebulun gave the command to move out. Men parted out of the way as he made a beeline through them to the opposite end.

Jonah was surprised his cousin didn't give anyone the order to stay behind to be a lookout. Jonah had traveled this exact route many times when they used to live in Arimathea and knew it would take them nearly an hour to reach the village. During that time, they wouldn't be able to see much of anything except for the evergreen trees lining both sides of the trail. Earlier that morning they'd spotted a large contingent of Romans in the far distance. Zebulun must have been satisfied, Jonah guessed, at having seen them marching in the opposite direction as the bandits were heading.

Jonah, though, wasn't so easily reassured. He took safety seriously, and not having a lookout put them at risk. But, as usual, he kept his concerns to himself. Jonah tried not to question things, because the world didn't make sense to him. It did seem to make sense to others, however, particularly his cousin. Where Jonah saw gray, Zebulun saw black and white. And when Zebulun spoke, everything seemed clear—who was at fault, who was preventing the Jews from living freely, what actions needed to be taken....

Jonah longed for that kind of clarity. His whole life was a struggle—one in which his words and actions in the outside world rarely matched what he felt on the inside.

Wanting to be last, he let all the men go ahead of him, counting each one as they stepped down the rocky edge to the meager trail. They were all dressed in dark, tattered tunics with makeshift shields strapped to their backs, and carrying a wide array of weapons. While some had swords and others bow and arrows, some had only spears, and the newcomer, Amram, had only a large dagger.

Jonah counted forty one. Forty-one outcasts from society. Forty-one Jewish men with thick, unruly beards who followed Zebulun and the scriptures zealously. Jonah was number forty-two, and he carried a beat-up, dull sword with his mother's name etched into the handle.

Chapter Ten

Vitus massaged his tight lower back while he admired the blacksmith's intense concentration on his task. Using a stout hammer, the blacksmith was turning a bright orange piece of iron into the form of a small dagger. He was so fervently focused that Vitus was sure he hadn't even noticed the small detachment of eight Roman soldiers just across from him. While much of the rest of the village had either stopped and stared at Vitus and his men or else disappeared into their homes, the blacksmith continued his methodical work—heating out all impurities and hammering out all imperfections until the piece of iron was pure and strong and free of defects.

The tax collector, a Jew by the name of Ephraim, hollered out a window that he needed help, so Vitus ordered two of his men over to the dwelling. They were there to protect the tax collector as he made his rounds in the Judean village of Arimathea. In most parts of the province, they didn't escort tax collectors, but there had been so many problems in this area, including attacks by bandits, that they made an exception.

Their original contingent of forty men had been split in two, because an elderly shepherd had informed them he saw two dozen armed men in the nearby hills. Once finished investigating the possible border incursion, the thirty-two Roman soldiers were to rejoin Vitus and his men in Arimathea, by which time the tax collector should have finished with his collections.

Of the seven fledgling recruits with Vitus, the youngest was Servanus—so baby-faced that Vitus was sure he wasn't eighteen, which was the minimum age for joining the Roman army. Vitus had to admit though, most everyone looked much younger than he thought they were. At thirty-six, Vitus was older than the majority of people in Judea.

As the blacksmith's rhythmic pounding filled the air, Servanus relaxed against a wall, provoking a rebuke from Vitus. "No leaning," he commanded. "Never forget you represent the Roman army."

Vitus recognized it was a boring job, but it was better than the alternative. Most Roman soldiers spent the majority of their time not in fighting or defending, but in constructing walls, digging, and building roads.

Noticing the thick stubble on Servanus's chin, Vitus added, "And shave that fuzz off your face."

Servanus pushed away from the wall and straightened up. "Yes, sir," he said amicably.

Vitus liked his response. Servanus never took reprimands personally. Rather, he seemed to view them as suggestions for which he was grateful.

Abandoning all hope of kneading the pain from his back, Vitus relaxed his arms by his sides and gazed at the blacksmith's shirtless, soot-covered assistant as he pumped the bellows to make the coals of the fire glow bright. Vitus had been through so many villages doing his tedious job that he'd learned to take pleasure in simply observing. Just outside the entry to the village, he'd been captivated by a brown goat giving birth, half of the kid in and half out.

Birth fascinated him. New life. A clean slate. A fresh beginning with endless possibilities. He would have enjoyed watching the rest of the birth, but the tax collector was a portly, impatient man who would have none of it. Ephraim preferred to do his job quickly, as though drinking an unpalatable tonic, so Vitus had felt obligated to order his men to move on. Starting at the far end of the village, they accompanied Ephraim as he hastily worked his way back to the main entrance.

"Hey Grandpa," one of the men called out to Vitus, "the new guy has to carry the chickens back, right?"

Vitus laughed. He tolerated the men jokingly referring to him as Grandpa. He was, after all, nearly twice their age.

"That's right," he replied. "Hope you're feeling strong today, Servanus."

It was an inside joke. They liked to pretend there would be several chickens collected as taxes, and always told the newest member he'd have to carry them all back by himself.

"Better hope there's no roosters like last time," another soldier, Damian, said. He winked at Vitus from beneath his precise-fitting metal helmet.

Vitus contained a chuckle as he caught Servanus glancing about nervously. He felt a special bond with the youngster. Servanus reminded Vitus a lot of himself at that age—ambitious, curious, always asking questions and wanting to understand the world. Vitus often reflected that had he married and had a son, he'd want him to be someone like Servanus.

"Why chickens?" Servanus asked. "Why don't they just collect coins?"

Vitus had grown up in a rural village and understood why. Knowing Servanus came from a rich household, he smirked at his naiveté. "Because most of them are *farmers*," Vitus explained. "They don't have any coins. Or if they do, don't have enough to pay all their taxes."

The tax collector's dingy, gray donkey brayed. It was attached to a wooden cart that was mostly empty now, but would soon be overflowing with more in-kind taxes: olives, figs, wine, olive oil, wheat....

Peasants and workers had to pay a number of taxes: one percent of their annual income, plus import and export taxes, sales taxes, property taxes, emergency taxes, and crop taxes. Vitus was glad he wasn't subject to them all.

The pudgy tax collector hastened to the next house while two soldiers carried baskets of dates over to the cart. Vitus instructed Servanus to pull the donkey forward, and then they all stood around waiting once again.

Arimathea was a poor village and its main thoroughfare was made of dirt. The narrow, dusty road was littered with shriveled black dog feces and occasional white splotches where chickens had relieved themselves. Courtyard walls and houses lined the sides, and the smell of smoke and baking bread wafted on a sluggish breeze.

Though it was still early, the sun was already hot. Vitus took off his weighty helmet to wipe sweat from his hairless head. The bronze headgear weighed about three pounds, and featured special flaps on hinges to protect his cheeks. It also incorporated a neck guard, which was a plate sticking out on the back to protect against downward-swinging swords. It wasn't the most comfortable thing to wear, but at least it kept his neck and bald head from getting sunburned.

Before putting the helmet back on, Vitus paused to admire its most recent addition—bright red plumes adorning the top. The plumes were a sign of his rank as centurion.

A small pack of skittish village dogs, ribs showing, sauntered down the road toward them. Servanus unsheathed his sword and charged a few steps at the barking mutts to scare them away.

"Don't do that," Vitus advised. "It just makes them bark even more."

A virile rooster paraded out from a courtyard doorway near the dogs. Vexed by a little, brown mongrel yipping at it, the rooster gave chase, and the dog retreated, its tail between its legs.

All the men laughed.

"Those dogs are just like the bandits," Damian called. "All bark and no bite!"

"That's right," Vitus added, reaching his hand up to comb the plumes on his helmet. "And I'm the rooster!"

The bandits and outlaws in the area were known for never engaging a Roman contingent head on. They usually ran the other way.

With his eyes on Vitus's helmet, Servanus asked, "How long does it take to become a rooster?"

Vitus smiled. He'd only been made a centurion six months prior. "It took me eighteen years," he answered. That was five years longer than he'd hoped, but he'd done it, and was still so proud of himself that hardly anything could bring him down these days.

The tax collector exited a doorway groaning to carry a large, brown jug. He dropped it into Servanus's arms, who then dutifully slid it to the front of the cart.

"Be sure to leave some space for Grandpa in case he gets tired on the long march back," one of the men joked.

Everyone, including Vitus, chuckled. Vitus kept himself in good shape, and felt confident he could still probably outrun any of them.

"Hey Grandpa," Damian called out. "Tell Servanus that story about your buddy who caused all the trouble in Jerusalem."

Vitus knew which story he was referring to and was tired of telling it, but when he saw the eagerness on Servanus's face, he launched into it one more time. "So we were stationed in Jerusalem for Passover—"

"What's Passover?" interrupted Servanus.

One of the men answered before Vitus could. "Another one of their endless, stupid holidays," he said, causing a handful of snickers.

Vitus, of course, knew what Passover was. He'd learned a lot about Jewish culture and could even speak a little Aramaic.

"Is it the one where they all fast and go to the synagogue?" Servanus asked.

"Well, there are actually several holidays where they do that. You're probably thinking of Yom Kippur. Passover is when they celebrate their liberation from Egyptian slavery," Vitus explained. "Anyway, we're in Jerusalem and a hundred thousand Jews are pouring into the city heading for the Temple. We're on the roofs and lining the streets watching all the pilgrims go by. They're all so serious. No one is smiling or laughing. Hardly anyone even talking.

"We've been there for hours, bored out of our minds. My buddy, Ramio, was crazy. Loved to drink, always getting in trouble. I was on one side of the street, and he was on the other, up on a ledge so he's about six feet above the street. And along comes this important looking rabbi. He's real old, dressed in black, has a big belly and long white beard down to his waist. He's got all these people following him, worshiping the ground he walks on."

Vitus swatted at a bothersome fly buzzing around his ear, then glimpsed the half-hidden faces of children gawking down at them from the rooftops.

"I look over at Ramio, and see him squinting up the left side of his face like he always does when he's trying to pass gas. That guy had more gas than a sick mule....

"So Ramio looks down the street and sees this old rabbi coming, and—who knows what went through his mind—he turns away, bends over, lifts up his tunic so his bare ass is sticking out, then lets loose with the longest, loudest fart you ever heard."

Upon hearing this, all the men burst into hysterical laughter. Vitus laughed right along with them, even if he had told the story more times than he could count.

After the laughter died down, Servanus wiped tears from his eyes, asking, "So what happened next?"

"The old rabbi stopped dead in his tracks," Vitus said. "From the look on his face, you'd think he'd just seen a ghost. They all stopped and glared at Ramio for a second."

Catching sight of the wide-eyed, curious faces of the kids on the rooftops once more, Vitus felt suddenly gloomy. "Then they all got mad," he said dolefully.

The men were still snickering, but Vitus no longer thought the way the event ended was funny.

"They got more and more upset, demanding the prefect hand him over so they could whip him. But the prefect wouldn't do it. Instead, he sent for reinforcements, because he was afraid a riot might break out. And it eventually did when it became clear Ramio wouldn't be turned over."

Vitus stared blankly at the ground as he recalled how many pilgrims died over that one foolish incident. His feelings about it had changed dramatically over the years. When he used to tell the story, he'd stress how the pilgrims got what was coming to them. He'd tended to view the world as us-against-them, the rational against the irrational, the powerful and professional Romans against the zealous and backward Jews. But now he mostly felt sad about how it had all transpired, about the role he and the rest of the Roman army had played.

The tax collector popped his fat head out the window of the house he was in, motioning to Vitus he needed two men for something. Vitus sent Servanus and Damian, who returned a minute later, each carrying a large wicker basket filled with wheat. Following them out the door was a hysterical woman pleading and clutching at the baskets.

Vitus was able to make out enough of her Aramaic to grasp her contention that the grain was their seed for next year's harvest, and that without it they wouldn't be able to plant anything. He also understood the tax collector's response to her: "That's what you liars say every time."

Vitus stepped forward and forcibly removed the distraught woman's hands from the baskets. As she fell to the ground, weeping uncontrollably, Vitus again felt somber. His heart ached as though it was frail and might burst. Instinctively, he put his hand on the middle of his chest, but all he could feel was the impenetrable metal of his armor.

He told himself this feeling of a fragile heart was simply another one of the unfortunate side effects of getting old, much like his diminished eyesight. It was just one more frequent pain, like the one in his lower back, that he'd have to learn to ignore.

Chapter Eleven

Thomas shifted his weight from one leg to the other as he listened impassively to Zebulun's usual reminders: "No harming of women or children. Neither do we inflict suffering on any man—unless he chooses to fight. And never...."

Thomas knew them all by heart, so his attention drifted to the nearby cinnamon-brown goat licking its newborn kid. From the looks of it, he guessed the kid was less than an hour old. It reminded him of when his childhood goat, Graha, was born.

The thought of Graha used to bring a smile to his lips, but not anymore. Instead, it triggered a well-rehearsed, bittersweet hatred that rose up from his belly and tingled his tongue and fingertips. Over the years, Graha had been transformed from his "beloved childhood pet" into "another victim of the vile Jewish oppressors."

"And lastly, conduct yourselves with honor and pride for you serve Yahweh, the one true God!" Zebulun concluded.

Knowing they were about to begin moving again, Thomas searched for his tiresome older brother. At first he couldn't find Jonah anywhere, but then he finally spotted him—at the very back, as usual.

The bandits advanced on the village in a disorganized way. They refused to march in neat rows and columns precisely because that was how the Romans did it. Zebulun was at the front. Like his predecessor, he liked to be the first one the villagers saw—making a grand entrance and letting everyone know just who was coming.

As they drew near, children scurried excitedly about on the rooftops or in the alleys between the houses. Thomas swelled with pride as he heard them exclaiming to one another, "The bandits are coming! Look, it's Zebulun!"

Zebulun was known by his unique and unusual bright red head covering and his equally blazing red shield adorned with fringes on the corners. The fringes, he'd told Thomas once, were to remind him of God at all times.

Seeing Zebulun unsheathe his sword and hold it in front, Thomas did the same. Then he broke away from the larger group and joined his brother and two others who were to go around the main entrance and along the right-hand side of the village. Zebulun had ordered four others to go along the left-hand side. Their jobs were to prevent the rich landowner, or anyone else, from escaping. Though Zebulun hadn't appointed a leader of their four-man party,

Thomas assumed the role, making sure they moved quickly all the way to the far end of the village where he and his brother and Zebulun had once lived.

The village, larger than most, stretched up a gentle slope. At the top of the incline, Thomas and Jonah congregated under the shade of the wide fig tree that grew just outside their old house. From there, they had a good view of the entire right-hand side of the village.

Jonah, looking more bewildered than usual, waved to get Thomas's attention. Then he signaled he heard something from inside the village walls. Thomas cupped his ear, trying to hear over some dogs' intermittent barking. The sound was faint, but unmistakable; some men were speaking in a foreign tongue, possibly Greek, which meant they were most likely Gentiles, or maybe even Romans. Thomas signaled to Jonah for the two of them to go investigate, but Jonah instead hurried over to him, whispering, "Let's wait for Zebulun."

Thomas shook his head vigorously. He didn't want to wait. He'd learned a lot from Zebulun and felt he understood so much more than his brother. Hesitation was a symptom of doubt, and was to be avoided at all costs. Doubt was poison.

That was something his brother couldn't comprehend for some reason. There was no room for indecision, for questioning if a particular action was really the best way to accomplish something. There was no room for vacillation, and Thomas thought his brother all too frequently lost in some invisible fog of uncertainty. That innocent people may be harmed, or that they themselves might die, was unavoidable if they were to accomplish their goal of restoring justice and freedom for the Jewish people. The focus needed to be solely on the goal. Nothing else mattered.

With a scowl at Jonah, Thomas stroked his long, unruly beard and remembered Zebulun's explanation of why they were not to cut or trim it. The beard was the hair that grew down from the head to the rest of the body, representing the bridge between thought and deed, intention and action. Explicitly obeying all the commandments started in the head, and with the help of the beard, spread downward to control the impulsive, undisciplined body.

Turning his back to his brother, Thomas moved toward the wall. He knew what he had to do, and he'd go by himself if necessary.

Since it was their old house, Thomas knew every nook and cranny of it, including how to sneak into the stables. As he hoisted himself over the wall, he spied Jonah cautiously following behind. Without a sound, the two of them crept into the cow's pen. Hiding behind the large animal and peeking through the wooden fence into the courtyard, Thomas was astounded to see eight Roman soldiers with a donkey and a cart. Noticing the red plumes on the helmet of one of the soldiers, Thomas knew him to be a centurion.

After ordering his brother to stay put, Thomas climbed back to tell the other two what he'd seen. He was surprised at how few Roman soldiers there were, as they usually traveled in larger numbers in these parts. While there was a good chance the villagers had already alerted Zebulun to the presence of the Romans, to be on the safe side, Thomas ordered one of the men to go warn his cousin.

The presence of a centurion raised the stakes significantly. Thomas and the rest of the bandits had learned, painfully so, that one centurion was the equivalent of several regular Roman troops.

When Thomas made it back to the cow's pen, Jonah whispered to him that he'd seen a tax collector go into the dining room. Thomas led them out of the stables and up to the roof of the house. From there, they snuck their way through an opening that descended into their old bedroom, which adjoined the dining room.

The familiar crooked door between the two rooms was partly ajar, and they could see the fat tax collector opening a chest while the occupant of the house skulked nearby. Thomas could tell immediately from the man's shabby tunic that he was not the sordid, rich landowner living in their old house, but instead just another poor farmer like they'd been.

"Tell me," the tax collector remarked dryly as he lifted a spotless cloak from the chest. "How does a 'penniless peasant,' as you call yourself, afford a cloak of this quality?"

"It was a *gift*," the man said of the linen cloak. "Part of a dowry when my daughter was married. I could never afford that on my own."

The tax collector unfolded the cloak and rubbed the material between his fingers. Then, with a few strokes of his nicely-trimmed beard, he examined it at arm's length.

"Please. Don't take it," the man appealed. "The cloak you're wearing is of much better quality. What do you need it for?"

"I?" the tax collector replied indignantly. "This is not for myself," he said with a smirk.

Thomas bit his tongue to keep from cussing aloud at the tax collector. He knew the bastard was lying. The duties of being a tax collector went to the highest bidder, and though they did collect taxes for Rome, they also collected plenty extra for themselves.

"This goes to pay for that nice road that leads to your village," the tax collector said. "And for the aqueduct, and of course," he added, motioning with his head toward the Roman soldiers outside in the courtyard, "for your security. It's not cheap to protect these remote villages in the countryside."

The fire of hate in Thomas's belly burned white hot. Like every Jew, he hated tax collectors, but seeing the hapless tenant at the mercy of this one reminded him too much of when he and his brother and Zebulun's family were evicted. They'd been powerless to do anything about it, and had felt humiliated in front of the entire village.

"If you had paid your taxes," the tax collector commented as he stashed the cloak in his basket, "I wouldn't need to be doing this."

The tenant muttered under his breath in response.

Despite the man living in their old house, Thomas held no grudge against him or his family. They were clearly farmers—no different than Zebulun's family had been—and were no doubt renting the house and land. As soon as another drought or catastrophe came, they'd be in the same peril of losing everything.

"And what's in that room?" the tax collector asked as he headed toward the doorway to the bedroom.

Thomas quietly moved to the left of the doorway and pushed himself flat against the wall. Jonah hid behind the tall dresser at the other end of the room.

"It's my bedroom," the man said. "There's nothing there."

"Well, we'll see about that," the tax collector said and pushed the door open.

Once he passed the threshold, Thomas grabbed him from behind, pressing the edge of his sharp dagger against the man's fleshy throat. Jonah stepped out from his hiding spot and signaled to the farmer not to make a sound.

Resisting the strong urge to slice the tax collector's throat, Thomas hissed in the man's ear, "Tell them you need help." The venom coursing through his veins was nearly overwhelming, and all he could think of was how to inflict more pain on the enemies of the Jewish people.

At Thomas's words, his brother's eyes grew large with alarm.

"Tell them to send *one* man in to help you," Thomas ordered the tax collector. His plan was to lure them in, one by one, and kill them. "Do it now," he whispered, "or I'll cut your throat."

The tax collector complied, calling out as he was told. "I need one man to come help me."

Thomas heard one of the Romans—the centurion, he guessed—give an order to someone. He was surprised to then hear the response to the tax collector in broken, heavily accented Aramaic: "Servanus is coming."

Thomas waved the farmer into the room and closed the door behind him. Then he signaled to his jittery brother to trade places with him. As Jonah positioned himself behind the door, Thomas pulled the tax collector with him to the end of the room, by the dresser.

Listening intently to the soldier's footsteps drawing nearer, Thomas fixed his eyes on his brother, trying to will him to do the job properly. Sweat was rolling down Jonah's temples and into his dark, scraggly beard. His timid brown eyes were wide, eyebrows stretched up high on his forehead, nostrils flaring.

Thomas despised that his brother looked scared instead of fierce. And he detested too that Jonah surely disapproved of his plan. His older brother constantly criticized him and condemned his actions. More than anything, Thomas wanted to prove to Jonah that he didn't need protecting, didn't need correcting, didn't need anything at all from his overprotective brother.

As the soldier's footsteps approached the door, Thomas motioned for the farmer to go and open it while he moved himself and the tax collector behind the immense dresser.

The room was dimly lit, and Thomas knew the soldier's eyes would take a few seconds to adjust from the intense sunlight of the courtyard. In those few seconds would come the man's downfall.

Hidden behind the dresser, Thomas couldn't see what was happening, but he could hear the door slowly creak open and the soldier's armor jangling as he entered the room.

Seconds went by like minutes as Thomas waited for the sounds of his brother pouncing. After a short eternity of hearing nothing but the tax collector's labored breathing, he started to panic. Peeping out from behind the dresser, Thomas was horrified by what he saw.

His brother, instead of killing the soldier, was trying to take him hostage! From behind, he had his arm tight around the man's throat, but he couldn't completely subdue him. *The fool!*

The Roman soldier cried out to the others as he struggled against Jonah. Quick as lightening, Thomas slit the throat of the tax collector with his dagger, threw him to the floor, and unsheathed his sword. Rushing forward, he plunged the blade deep into the soldier's belly, then watched him slump from his brother's grasp.

The courtyard resounded with sharp, urgent orders and weapons clanging.

"Come on!" Jonah called in a panic. "Let's go!"

Ignoring him, Thomas closed the door and latched it. He didn't want to leave. He wanted to stay and fight.

"We have to get out of here!" cried Jonah as he grabbed Thomas's arm. He tried to pull him to the ladder, their only way out.

Thomas shook off Jonah's grip. "Go if you want," he said coldly. "I don't need you."

"Think of your family!" Jonah pleaded.

But Thomas had already done that. He'd thought about the world his unborn child would inherit—one dominated by the Romans, the Gentiles, the unscrupulous rich. It would be better for the child to die than live in the same cage Thomas had known all his life. Better the child's father perish fighting for freedom, than he and all his descendants live like chattel.

The door broke open from a powerful kick, and the centurion charged into the room, sword and shield in hand, teeth bared, snarling like a wolf.

Thomas lunged at him, thrusting his bloody blade at the man's torso. The centurion blocked it with his shield, then swung his sword downward so forcefully that it broke Thomas's feeble sword in half. He then grabbed Thomas and rammed him headfirst into the wall.

As Thomas crumpled to the floor, everything blurred. Then there was nothing but darkness.

Chapter Twelve

After incapacitating one of the culprits by slamming his head into the wall, Vitus glimpsed the backside of the other one scrambling up the ladder to the roof.

"After him!" he commanded his men rushing into the room.

Squatting next to Servanus to check how badly he was wounded, Vitus felt sickened by the amount of blood gushing from his belly and pooling on the floor. Though the young man's breathing was still mostly normal, Vitus knew his chances of surviving were not good. Checking on the tax collector, Vitus saw the man's throat had been slashed and assumed he would soon be dead. But upon closer inspection, Vitus saw the cut was not very deep. It had been done hastily, and if the bleeding could be stopped, he'd probably survive.

When Damian squeezed past two of his stunned cohorts crowded at the doorway, Vitus ordered him and another man to wrap the wounds of Servanus and the tax collector. Vitus then climbed the ladder to the roof where he spied the other culprit already outside the village, fleeing into the countryside. Three of Vitus's men were hunting for a way down off the roof to follow him.

"Let him go," ordered Vitus. He'd learned the hard way not to scatter his men. The last time he'd done that, two of them were killed in an ambush. "We stay together."

Returning to the bedroom below, Vitus knelt by Servanus as Damian wrapped his wound. Vitus took Servanus's quivering hand in his, feeling it grow cold and clammy already. Afraid a tear might escape his watery eyes and embarrass him in front of his men, Vitus stood abruptly, scanning the room.

"Load these three in the cart," he ordered gruffly. "Tie the bandit's hands and put a blindfold on him."

Vitus clenched his jaw to try to regain control over his emotions as his men carried the tax collector, Servanus, and the unconscious bandit away. When they'd finished, Vitus followed them out to the courtyard and peered in every direction. Gone were all the children staring down from the rooftops. Shut tight was each door and window of every house.

"Let's get back to the main entrance," said Vitus, trying to conceal his nervousness. His gut told him they weren't out of peril yet.

Vitus's men, edgy and rattled, marched tensely in two precise columns. The cart, full of jugs, baskets, and now three wounded men, rumbled behind them as Damian led the donkey by a rope. It was disconcertedly quiet. Even the blusterous dogs had vanished, growling instead at someone or something further down the road.

Hyper-alert, Vitus scoured every rooftop, every window, every door they passed. He strained to hear the tiniest of sounds over the creaking of the cart's wheels and the muffled jingling of swords and armor of his men.

Raising a fist over his head—the signal to halt—Vitus cupped his hand to his left ear. He could just make out the sound of his worst fear: the faint, yet unmistakable din of a sizable group of men marching toward them.

Surveying the buildings around him, his eyes were drawn to a half-finished wooden wheel leaning against a closed door. He remembered it from their walk in: a carpenter's workshop. There were no buildings bordering it, and behind the workshop was the ten-foot wall that encircled the village.

The men he'd heard approaching began rounding the corner of a still-distant mudbrick house. A line of armed bandits, all with lengthy, unkempt beards and dressed in dark, frayed tunics, stared back at Vitus and his men. Leading the way was a bull of a man with a red kerchief on his head and a long sword in his hand. Vitus didn't need to wait until they'd all rounded the corner. He could tell from their footsteps alone that he and his men were greatly outnumbered. That alone didn't concern him. He'd won many battles where he was outnumbered. He was more troubled by the lack of experience of his men, that they were unfamiliar with their surroundings, and that the enemy could come at them from multiple directions and angles, including the rooftops.

Bandits with bows were loading arrows and taking aim, and those with spears were lowering them next to their upraised shields.

Vitus knew he and his men didn't have time to scale the village wall. And if they retreated, they risked being cut down by arrows. There was nowhere safe to flee to anyway. He saw only one viable option.

Charging at the door of the carpenter's workshop, Vitus flung himself shoulder first into it. The lock broke easily, and the door swung in with a bang.

"Come on!" he yelled to his men. "Grab the wounded and get inside!" As they hurried through, Vitus stood outside the doorway, holding his shield up to block the incoming arrows.

Thwack! An arrow plunged into his shield, its tip piercing through and barely missing his forearm. *Clang!* Another arrow bounced off a someone's helmet.

Suddenly, one of his men cried out in agony. Vitus caught sight of Damian falling to the ground. He'd been carrying Servanus toward the workshop when an arrow struck his lower leg.

As Vitus ran to help him, the bandits yelled—a tremendous roar that echoed down the dirt road. Then they charged.

A glance over his shield told Vitus he and his men were outnumbered at least five to one, that he had about six more seconds to take shelter, and that only the tax collector was left in the cart. Pulling Damian to his feet, Vitus commanded someone to grab Servanus, who was lying next to him.

After half-dragging Damian into a corner of the workshop, Vitus turned back toward the door and saw his men barricading it. "Where's Servanus?" he yelled over the clamor.

When no one answered, he strained to see in the dimly lit room, searching frantically for the wounded soldier who was like a son to him. Unable to find him, he began pulling men away from the door, shouting, "Open it! Servanus is still out there!"

But before he could remove even one piece of the barricade, a spear came thrusting through a gap in the door, nearly impaling him. Vitus grabbed the spear and pulled it to the side until it snapped in half. Then he plunged it back through the gap, hoping to stab one of the bandits.

"It's too late for Servanus," he announced, recognizing his men already understood that. He'd needed to say it for himself so he could move on.

Spotting a window next to the door, he ordered the men to make sure the shutters were locked. "And barricade it too!"

They grabbed whatever they could find to reinforce the window and the door: three sturdy sawhorses, a heavy workbench, a partially completed dresser, broken shovels and rakes, and various beams and planks they found stacked in the back.

When they'd used everything they could, they waited with shields raised and swords drawn to see if it would withstand the repeated smashing from the outside.

With the door and shutters closed, there was very little light in the workshop, and Vitus waited impatiently for his eyes to fully adjust. They'd kicked up a great deal of dust, and it hung in the air like a heavy fog. As the shouting and pounding from the bandits began to wane and Vitus was sure the barricades would hold, he went to tend to Damian.

He was relieved to see the tip of the arrow sticking out the other side of Damian's calf muscle. Wounds where arrows were lodged in the muscle, or worse, in the bone, were the most difficult to treat, not to mention the most difficult to survive. Grasping the arrow just below the bloody tip, Vitus broke it off amidst Damian's yelp of pain. Vitus then pulled the arrow out from the other end and instructed Damian to wash the wound and wrap it tightly.

Vitus could see well enough now to clearly make out all of their surroundings and the various tools at their disposal. He knew they needed to make preparations for an eventual assault. He figured the bandits would either attempt to break down the door with some type of improvised battering ram, or maybe try to smoke them out.

As he peered past the meager streaks of sunlight streaming through the cracks in the door and window, he was pleased to spot the wounded bandit against one of the walls. Because they had him, Vitus doubted the bandits would choose to burn the building down. Seeing the man begin to wake, Vitus went over and tightened his blindfold, then tied a piece of rope around his mouth to ensure he couldn't speak.

The commotion and noise from outside had all but disappeared, leaving an eerie stillness. Vitus could hear his own breathing and footsteps as he trod near the back wall trying to ensure they'd used every piece of lumber that had been stacked there. Stubbing his toe on something hard, he squatted to the floor and discovered several long boards half-buried under dirt.

"There's some more wood here," he announced. "Help me get it out. We'll use it to reinforce the window."

The boards were thick and heavy, and after he and another man removed them, Vitus was astonished to find they'd been covering a large pit nearly five feet long and two feet wide. It appeared to be empty, save for a short ladder, which Vitus used to climb down.

Once his feet touched the bottom, the floor of the workshop came to his chin. He felt around the dark pit but found nothing, guessing it was meant as a hiding spot for valuables, or maybe even people, should the need arise.

Clambering back out, he formulated a plan. While he worked to redo their hastily built barricade of the door and window, one man would begin pounding the right wall with a hammer and chisel, another would do the same to the left wall, and the remaining four men would work together in the pit to dig a tunnel under the back wall.

In a hushed voice he gave each man their orders, then handed out hammers, chisels, small axes, and shovels. Though it gnawed at him, he tried not to think about Servanus's fate. There was nothing to be done about it.

He helped Damian limp over to the right-side wall. "How's your leg?"

"Feels as if it's on fire," Damian answered. "But that isn't going to kill me."

He'd said it as though he was sure his death was inevitable. Vitus wasn't surprised. He'd anticipated his men—all young and unseasoned—would be on the verge of panic.

"You do as you're told and I'll get you out of here," Vitus called to everyone. He kept his own doubts to himself.

After motioning over the man he assigned to work the opposite wall, Vitus whispered to him and Damian, "It's very important that you don't actually succeed in making a big hole. Your mission is twofold. First, you're making enough noise so they don't hear us digging a tunnel. Second, you're confusing our enemy into thinking our plan is to break out through the walls. So go slowly and carefully. All right?"

The men nodded their acknowledgment, and Vitus allowed himself a short rest. Sitting on the floor, he took off his helmet, inhaled deeply, and sighed. He briefly considered praying to the Roman god, Jupiter, or maybe even the god the Jews worshiped. But he couldn't do it; he didn't believe in any gods. He'd gotten himself into this mess, and it was up to him to get himself out.

"The rest of our contingent will be here soon enough," he announced to the men with as much confidence as he could muster. "We just need to hold out until then."

Even with the additional thirty-two men, the bandits would still outnumber them, but Vitus highly doubted there would be a skirmish. The enemy had learned on too many previous occasions not to take on Romans unless they had an overwhelming strategic and numeric advantage.

Vitus hoped the rest of his contingent hadn't found anything to delay them. Assuming they hadn't, he estimated it would be an hour and a half, minimum, before he and his men could expect a rescue.

Chapter Thirteen

"That's not an option!" Jonah called out, just as surprised as the others to hear his voice rising in opposition to Zebulun.

All the men turned to gape at him. Zebulun arched his eyebrows and lowered his chin.

After the Roman soldiers had barricaded themselves in the carpenter's workshop, the bandits had spent nearly half an hour trying to find the carpenter in the hope of getting some helpful information. After finally determining he was out of town, Zebulun had gathered everyone together to issue his next orders.

"They have Thomas," Jonah explained. "If we set the door on fire, the workshop will fill with smoke and he could very well die."

Zebulun started to reply, but Jonah shouted over him. "Why don't we try a prisoner swap first?"

A few men nodded in agreement. "This one is nearly dead anyway," said the man closest to the wounded Roman. Jonah glanced at the soldier he'd tried to subdue and who Thomas had stabbed with his sword. His skin was pale, his breathing heavy.

With all eyes awaiting Zebulun's answer, Jonah knew this was a pivotal moment. He didn't want it to end up like the fruitless search for the carpenter when he wished he'd spoken up. Having helped build several houses, Jonah felt he could answer any questions Zebulun might have had. Jonah could tell just from looking at the workshop that its walls were impenetrable stone, and the roof constructed of solid cypress planks covered with straw mats and sealed with clay.

"I'll do the talking," Jonah said to Zebulun. While confident a majority of the men were inclined toward his idea, he recognized its execution had to be spelled out as well. He knew Zebulun would never negotiate with the Romans himself.

When Zebulun still hesitated, Jonah added, "I can do it. I heard the centurion speaking Aramaic earlier." Though Jonah and others knew some Greek, Zebulun forbade any of them to speak "that wicked language of the Romans and Gentiles."

Again, every head turned to Zebulun. He stared blankly at Jonah for a few seconds, his dull gray eyes indecipherable, then he gave a single nod indicating his approval.

Rushing away before Zebulun could change his mind, Jonah positioned himself a few yards from the workshop door. He hoped the Romans would be able to hear him above the din of their pounding.

"Centurion, let us talk!"

No answer.

The noise continued unabated, with dogs adding their barking and howling to the mix. When the Romans had first started hammering, Jonah couldn't figure out what they were trying to accomplish. His best guess was they were building something or reinforcing their barricades. But then he'd seen mortar crumble from both the right- and left-side walls and realized they were trying to break through them. He considered it a rather vain attempt, since, even if they succeeded in making a hole big enough to break out, they'd be immediately cut down by the bandits.

Jonah called to the centurion again, and this time the noise stopped. A voice in heavily accented and broken Aramaic answered.

"What you want?"

"Let us swap prisoners," Jonah said.

"No understand," came the reply.

Knowing they could see through the gaps and cracks in the door, Jonah motioned for the Roman soldier to be brought forward. "Trade prisoners," he explained. "Give us our man."

As they dumped the injured soldier in front of the workshop, he coughed, and blood began trickling from his mouth. Jonah hoped the man wouldn't die before the exchange.

"Give us our man," Jonah repeated slowly, "and you take your man."

Zebulun, standing further back, monitored the situation in between giving orders. Two bandits had climbed up to the workshop's roof and were examining it.

"Centurion!" Jonah said after another minute. "What is your answer?"

"We think," came the response. "Give time." Then the pounding started up once more.

A glance at Zebulun's shaking head worried Jonah, but fortunately no further orders were issued. Sitting on the back of the donkey cart, Zebulun was busy counting the coins from the tax collector's purse. The tax collector himself—bloody bandage around his throat, hands tied behind his back—sat nearby watching. A bandit dashing by spat on him, the spittle hanging in the tax collector's well-groomed beard.

Villagers were coming out of their houses and gathering to witness the unfolding drama. Children's dirty, inquisitive faces again peeked down from the rooftops. Dozens of working-class Jews, men and women, young and old, crowded into the area, mingling with the bandits, asking endless questions, and shouting advice on how to deal with the situation.

Jonah stood apart from everyone, close to the workshop, reciting a short prayer beseeching God to return his brother to him unharmed. As he said amen, he came up with the idea to demonstrate some goodwill. He asked a boy from the crowd to fetch a jug of water, and when the boy returned, Jonah had two villagers help the soldier sit up while Jonah helped him drink.

Then Jonah again called to the centurion. "Give us our man! You take yours!"

The pounding paused. "Give time," came the reply. "One hour."

Zebulun scowled, exclaiming, "They're stalling for time."

"No," Jonah replied to the centurion. "Give answer now."

"We think. Need time."

Zebulun held up five fingers.

"We count to five hundred," announced Jonah. "Then you answer."

Zebulun ordered his men into positions to attack should the front door be opened. Bandits on the workshop's roof pointed spears downward over the doorway; archers on the roof opposite the building readied arrows for their bows; and bandits wielding spears and swords hid around corners, ready to charge.

Jonah countered his edginess by reminding himself God would surely see to it that all ended well. After all, Jonah had steadfastly kept up his end of the bargain—living his life as the Torah taught, right down to the most trivial of commandments like ensuring he never ate a worm in a piece of fruit. Still, he folded his arms tightly in front of himself, trying to squelch the rising queasiness as his count progressed ever higher.

After reaching five hundred, he bided his time watching a rooster and three chickens peck at the tall weeds on the side of the workshop. When Zebulun hollered the time was up, Jonah demanded the centurion's answer.

"Need time!" came the familiar, lamentable answer.

Sensing his chance slipping away, Jonah impulsively changed the deal. "Give us our man," he called out. "And we give you your man *and* the tax collector."

Jonah hadn't received permission to include the tax collector and knew he was on shaky ground. He hoped if the centurion agreed to it that he could then talk Zebulun into the exchange.

The centurion's voice rose over top of the hammering. "We think. Give time."

"No!" insisted Jonah. "You answer now!"

When there was no response, Zebulun furrowed his bushy eyebrows, spat on the ground, and ordered the tax collector tied to the workshop's door. "Tell him to hand over Thomas or the tax collector dies," he said to Jonah.

Relieved the order wasn't to burn down the door, Jonah stepped forward and summoned the centurion, but before he could say anything more, the answer already came back: "Need time! Need time!"

Zebulun commanded forth six archers, and as they arranged themselves in a crooked line, a voice of objection sprang up from a throng of bandits. "He is a tax collector, yes. But he is also a Jew! A brother!"

"He is *not* a brother," Zebulun announced loudly. "He is not even a man. He's a parasite—as worthless as a dog!"

The villagers hooted and heckled their agreement. "Yes, a dog!"

"Like too many others, he made the decision to betray his people," Zebulun continued.

Jonah retreated to the shade of a nearby building as Zebulun launched into an extended denunciation of all who don't follow the commandments.

Regarding everything from a distance, Jonah was mesmerized by Zebulun's ability to direct and control, and simultaneously fearful of where his direction might lead. Jonah couldn't help but think of when they were kids and he'd found the murdered Samaritan. He still suspected Zebulun of having done it.

After a lengthy tirade, Zebulun unsheathed his sword, clutching it over his head as he gave the order to fire. Arrows sliced through the air, plunging into the tax collector's chest, throat, and stomach. Villagers and bandits cheered as he slumped forward, the ropes bearing all the weight of his hefty body.

The Roman soldier was then tied in the tax collector's place. The lame man could barely hold his head up, and his skin was so ashen he already looked like a corpse.

Unprompted by Zebulun, Jonah shouted for the centurion's attention once more. "Give us our man and you take yours!"

There was no answer at first, and Jonah swallowed against his rising apprehension that things might not resolve well after all.

Then the pounding stopped, and the answer he'd hoped for came. "Yes."

Holding his palm to his fluttering heart, Jonah asked for confirmation. "You agree?"

"Yes," said the centurion. "We open door. Give time."

Jonah breathed a sigh of relief at Zebulun's order to stop tying the soldier to the door. Spotting a grimy, long-haired boy offering water, Jonah waved him over. As he sipped from the boy's jug, he saw a two-inch chunk of stone fall from the right-side wall of the workshop. The Roman working inside had finally succeeded in breaking through.

When an archer came over and aimed an arrow through the hole, Jonah chided him. "No! Wait until we've finished our negotiations."

Zebulun was occupied with returning the in-kind taxes to their owners. Villagers were charged with carrying back the grain, wine, dates, olives, and other containers in the tax collector's cart. In appreciation, most of the villagers offered a small portion of it back to him. Some even went into their homes and returned with additional items for Zebulun and the bandits: fresh bread, pomegranates, almonds....

Jonah paced back and forth in front of the workshop, puzzled by how long the Romans were taking. Despite the agreement, all the loud noises and pounding continued and the door remained closed.

"Open the door!" Jonah demanded.

"Yes," came the response. "We open door. Give time."

Zebulun raised a chubby fist and extended four fingers.

"We count to four hundred," said Jonah. "Open the door or no deal."

Jonah counted in a soft voice as he glimpsed three vultures circling high overhead. He wondered if they were the same ones he'd seen earlier that morning. When he reached four hundred he said another prayer pleading with God for his brother's safekeeping.

After Zebulun finished accepting donations from the villagers, he returned his attention to the workshop. He glared at the still-closed door, then at Jonah. "Time's up," he said crossly, then commanded the door be sealed from the outside and the Roman soldier tied to it once again.

"Time's up!" Jonah repeated loudly. "Open the door!"

As they strung up the Roman soldier, Jonah tore at his hair trying to understand what the miscommunication could have been, why their agreement wasn't being fulfilled.

"Give us your prisoner," Jonah said, speaking as clearly and slowly as possible. "And we give you ours. Open the door."

The centurion's silence enraged him, and Jonah, red-faced, tightened his hands into balls as two men passed by. One bore hot coals, and the other a bucket of thick, black tar.

Villagers' panicked voices cried out.

"Don't burn it! The fire may spread."

"Stop! You'll torch the whole village!"

Zebulun gave them a dismissive wave as Aaron, one of the bandits who'd been sent to patrol the left-hand side of the village, pushed his way through the crowd and hurried up to him. Aaron whispered something, to which Zebulun asked, "How long?"

Jonah couldn't hear the response over the clamor from the crowd and the workshop. But shortly thereafter Zebulun advised the villagers to gather water to douse the flames if they threatened to spread beyond the carpenter's workshop. Then he abruptly ordered the fire set.

"No!" Jonah screamed at the top of his lungs.

The firestarters hesitated, gazing first at Jonah then at Zebulun.

"You heard me!" Zebulun snarled. "Do it now!"

As they coated the door with tar and set it ablaze, Jonah dug his nails into his face until he drew blood. Snatching a jug of water from one of the villagers, he rushed toward the flaming door.

"Stop him!" Zebulun commanded.

Two men tackled Jonah, his jug crashing to the ground and splintering into a dozen pieces.

"Bring him to me," said Zebulun.

Jonah twisted and strained, but was unable to escape the hold on him. Bright orange flames licked the door, burning the Roman soldier alive.

Some of the villagers cheered. Some stared silently. A mother holding a toddler covered its eyes.

Jonah desperately wanted to put his fingers in his ears to block out the bloody screams, but then, as suddenly as they began, the screams stopped and the man's head hung limply. Jonah was both surprised and relieved at how quickly the man had died.

Zebulun spoke from behind Jonah. "I know your brother better than you," he said. "This is what he would want, to be a martyr."

His cousin's calm voice grated on him. "You lie!" Jonah snapped. "My brother would choose to *live*."

"He was a good man," said Zebulun, peering at the fire as he walked away. "If I had a hundred like him, we'd already be a free people."

As the door burned, Zebulun took time to dole out coins to every outstretched villager hand.

"When they come to question you," he announced, "tell them the tax collector had already taken your taxes when Zebulun came and killed him. Tell them Zebulun stole *everything* from the tax collector. Then they'll leave you alone."

The crowd gave him an ovation, including a hearty chant of "Long live Zebulun! Long live Zebulun!"

Jonah hated his cousin like never before. He wished he had the strength to free his arms and break Zebulun's neck. Instead he could only watch helplessly as the flames consumed the door and spread to the roof.

Zebulun handed out the last coin from the tax collector's purse, then studied the fire for a few seconds before puffing out his chest and reciting his favorite scripture: "'The Lord is a God who avenges. O God who avenges, shine forth!'"

As black smoke streamed out the shuttered window of the workshop, Jonah could hear the Romans inside coughing and choking. He nearly collapsed as all the fury within succumbed to the certainty that it was too late to save his brother. Everyone inside would be dead within a matter of minutes.

After the bandits repeated their refrain of "Shine forth," Zebulun gave the order to move out, a sense of urgency in his voice.

As they marched away, Jonah only partially blamed God for Thomas's impending death. He mostly blamed himself. It was his reluctance to slay the Roman soldier in their old bedroom earlier that had caused this calamity. If it weren't for his own weakness, for his inability to kill the part of him that was confused and doubtful, none of this would have happened.

Chapter Fourteen

When the bandits set fire to the door, Vitus had immediately begun clearing away the barricades he'd erected. If he and his men couldn't make it out of the tunnel before the smoke incapacitated them, then they'd open the door and charge out. He knew they'd be slaughtered, but he was of firm belief that if one had to die, it was best to die standing on one's feet, fighting.

Pulling barriers from the door, he'd heard the shrieks of Servanus being burned alive. In the dim light he'd searched with his fingers for adequate cracks in the door. When he found one about navel high and another two inches above it, he plunged his dagger into each, resulting in the end of Servanus's screams.

After wiping blood from the dagger, Vitus felt wobbly and was afraid he might pass out. He couldn't blame the smoke since it was all outside. For now, at least.

The room started to spin when he'd finished mouthing the words, "I'm sorry, Servanus." Then he staggered to the floor and held his hands to his face amidst a flood of emotion. It came in violent convulsions and waves of tears. Unable to stem the flow, he wept as he hadn't since he was a child.

While regaining his composure, one of the soldiers in the pit cried out in alarm that they'd encountered a rock.

Vitus crawled over to where they were digging tunnels. They'd started with just one tunnel, but Vitus had ordered them to start on a second tunnel a foot away from the first. He didn't think they'd use it. He'd only wanted to keep every man occupied, because he could sense their panic when they had nothing to do but sit there, waiting their turn to dig, pondering whether they were trapped inside their own tomb.

"What's wrong?" Vitus asked.

The men in the pit were pulling a man from the first tunnel. "There's a rock!" he screamed when he was out. "It's too big. We can't get past it. We're going to die!"

"Are you sure? Someone else go in and try," Vitus ordered.

He doubted they'd find anything different, but he needed a minute to think. He'd received training in sieges—both how to lay them and how to survive them. One of the most important things he was taught was to stay calm, even if the situation seemed hopeless. If you dwelled on all the obstacles to be overcome, you could easily fall into overwhelm and indecision. Vitus knew that in any situation, one had to focus solely on the next step, the next problem to be solved. That was all that mattered.

The second man came out, confirming what the first had said. Vitus smelled the smoke more strongly now as it started to seep into the workshop. "How close are you?" he asked the men working the other tunnel.

They were changing diggers, and after they pulled the current one out, he replied breathlessly, "I don't know. I can't tell."

As Vitus deliberated what to do with the now three idle men who'd been digging the first tunnel, he heard the fire outside crackling and hissing. "You men come with me," he ordered.

Once away from the pit, Vitus pointed at the door. "Remove the rest of the barricades," he commanded one of the men. "And you two get your armor on and get ready to hand out weapons. We may have to charge out the front if the second tunnel fails."

Vitus cussed as he wiped his stinging eyes. The top of the room was already filling with smoke. "Work on your hands and knees," he advised everyone. From his training he knew the effects of smoke inhalation firsthand: the lack of coordination, inability to think clearly, nausea, fatigue. He had a good guess of how much time they had before the effects of the smoke immobilized them. They needed every minute, every second they could get. He'd done his best to stall for time with the bandits, but there was only so much he could do. He could never have agreed to their prisoner swap, because he'd lose his sole bargaining piece. If that happened, he was sure the building would be set ablaze immediately.

"Stay low!" Vitus shouted. "The lower you are, the better the air."

Because of the heat and their intense labor, all the men had long since removed their armor and tunics, working in nothing but loincloths. Vitus snatched a tunic from the floor and doused it with what little drinking water he had left. Then he hung it over the door in the hope it would keep some smoke out and slow the fire. It seemed futile, but if it bought any extra time whatsoever, it was worth it.

He could hear the men counting in the pit. Only one man at a time could be inside a tunnel, so he would dig feverishly while another man gathered the loose dirt and threw it into a pile outside the pit. The third man would count aloud. Once he reached fifty, the three of them would rotate, the counter taking the digger's place.

At some point Vitus would have to decide whether they'd storm out the door, but he wanted to wait as long as possible before making that decision. His first preference was for them to escape through the tunnel. If the smoke got so thick they were in danger of passing out, he'd give the order to break down the door and charge.

"Take this," he directed the man to his right, handing him another tunic. "Tear it into swaths, like you would for a large bandage." To the man on his left he ordered, "Gather everyone's waterskin."

Of the six waterskins that came back, four were completely empty, and two were nearly empty.

"Wet the swaths and hand them out," commanded Vitus. As they did that, he instructed everyone to cover their mouth and nose with them. "Breathe through them," he yelled. "It will help with the smoke."

Once each man had a swath, Vitus wet the last one and tied it around the prisoner's face.

With his eyes burning and his head pounding, Vitus knew they were down to their last few minutes. "Be ready," he said to the men lying near him. "On my order, hand out the weapons and we charge out."

He crept snakelike along the floor to the tunnel where the men were rotating out the digger. "Let me go next," he called.

Climbing into the pitch-black tunnel, Vitus felt with his hands for the end of it, then started jabbing at the dirt with a chisel in one hand and a small axe in the other. It was grueling work digging with both hands simultaneously, and he feared his lungs would burst.

In the cramped, stifling tunnel, he wondered if his life, like Servanus's, was about to end. And if so, what had it all been for? To earn a little prestige? To win a few battles? He'd always imagined his death would be glorious, fighting for something he believed in with all his heart and soul. But no matter how quickly his mind raced, he couldn't find anything he believed in that deeply. He promised himself that if this was not the end of his life—if he somehow made it out of this—he would find *something* he believed in with all his heart and soul.

As he felt hands gripping his legs and yanking him out of the tunnel, Vitus gave one last stab at the never-ending dirt. "Damn you!" he screamed.

Then he saw it.

A beam of sunlight shining through a small hole.

He shouted to the men drawing him out of the tunnel, "I'm through! I'm through! Quick, finish the job!"

The next man scrambled in. Fresh air was already streaming into the workshop through the opening, making it momentarily easier to breathe, but also feeding the flames. Every single man was coughing against the thick, acrid smoke.

After Vitus saw the digger's legs disappear up the tunnel, he handed the next man a sword and sent him through. He hoped with all his might there were no bandits waiting on the other side.

"Remove your armor!" he yelled over the raging fire. The men would never be able to squeeze through the narrow tunnel while wearing it.

One by one Vitus ensured his men escaped out the tunnel. When the last one, Damian, didn't respond to his orders, Vitus backed into the tunnel legs first, then took hold of Damian's arms and dragged him out. On the outside, Vitus was relieved to see there were no bandits. As he crawled back into the tunnel, a voice called after him, "Everyone's already out! What are you doing?"

"The prisoner," Vitus answered. He didn't want him to die of smoke inhalation. That would be too easy. The bandit needed to answer more fully for his crimes.

Back inside the burning building, Vitus choked on the dense smoke. What had been clear to him only a moment ago was now fuzzy. What was he doing here? Why had he come? The intense heat burned his skin. He slumped to the bottom of the pit and tried to vomit, but nothing came out.

No longer aware of where he was or what he needed to accomplish, he knew only that he wanted to sleep. It called to him relentlessly.

When something rolled on top of him, he recognized the legs of a man. But everything was so hazy. Thoughts were like sludge, slow and amorphous. Even as the legs kicked at him, Vitus didn't know what to do. The simple act of breathing was a chore he could barely accomplish.

As he slipped further and further away, something within began to make itself known, something that *did* know what to do. It was simultaneously *not* him and yet *more* him than he ever imagined possible. He'd glimpsed this essence a few times before, but not understanding it, had always maintained a safe distance. Now, he gave in to it completely.

His hands took hold of the stranger's legs and he felt himself working his way back through the tunnel. Through it all Vitus regarded himself as a spectator, watching his body pull and squirm and strain up the tunnel.

"We can see the rest of our unit. They're coming this way," Vitus's men exclaimed as they pulled him out.

Once he caught his breath, Vitus willed himself to his feet, an act that seemed to force the essence within to recede. It was as though there were two wills at work—one that belonged to Vitus, and one that belonged to the essence.

Though still light-headed and dizzy, Vitus peered into the distance, grateful to observe thirty-two Roman soldiers marching in tight formation toward the village. Over a mile in front of them, heading away from the village, Vitus spotted the bandits.

"Cowards," he muttered under his breath.

Sneering at the disorderly way they retreated, he wished he could destroy all people like them. If he were king of the world, he'd put an end to all dishonor and cruelty. He'd build a society based on fairness, integrity, and justice. No one would be burned alive.

He glared at their prisoner lying on the ground, glad the bandit was in for a cruel death when he was crucified.

Then, without warning, the essence within returned with a roar, revealing to Vitus his hypocrisy. It crushed his chest as if someone had dropped a large wicker basket filled with wheat on him. Clutching at the sharp pain in his heart, Vitus felt full of shame.

Chapter Fifteen

From his lookout post in a poplar tree on a ridge, Jonah peeked from behind olive-green leaves at the Roman soldiers marching toward the village. He estimated their numbers at several dozen, but his vision wasn't the best and they were still a long way away.

"Are you sure they won't be able to see us here?" Aaron called from the branch below him.

"I'm sure," Jonah replied. "Besides, I can get us out of here quickly if we need to. They'd never be able to follow us. I know this area like the back of my hand."

The two of them had been assigned to monitor the fire and, more importantly, the approaching Romans. The rest of the bandits were pulling back. Jonah and Aaron were to meet up with them on the other side of the ridge in two hours.

While Aaron climbed further up the tree, Jonah gazed numbly at the soaring flames of the carpenter's workshop.

"Thirty-two," Aaron announced from a few branches above Jonah.

Jonah was impressed with Aaron's eyesight. "Are you sure?"

"I told Zebulun there were *fifty*," Aaron added with a tone of disappointment. "But I couldn't really see them all before."

"Don't worry about it," Jonah reassured him. He knew that Zebulun would have ordered them to withdraw whether there were thirty-two or fifty Roman troops approaching. Zebulun didn't like to take them on directly unless he had an overwhelming advantage.

"Ay-yay-yay!" Aaron blurted, pointing toward the fire. "Look at that!"

Jonah couldn't see anything different, just roaring flames and thick smoke. "Look at what?"

"You can't see from down there," said Aaron. "Come up here."

After clambering up, Jonah followed Aaron's pointing finger to the wall behind the burning building. He spied a group of men in loincloths there. Squinting, he was astonished to see another man crawl out of the ground and join them.

"A tunnel," exclaimed Aaron. "How on earth could they have dug that in such a short time?"

Jonah closed his eyes against a gust of wind that blew smoke at them. Once it passed he climbed over to a thicker, safer branch and counted the men. "How many do you see?" he asked Aaron.

"Five."

"Me too."

"Do you see Thomas?" Jonah asked anxiously.

"No, but look! Another one's coming out."

The man emerging from the tunnel was pulling an unresponsive and possibly dead man.

"That's not Thomas," declared Jonah, though he couldn't tell for sure.

"No. Can't be," confirmed Aaron. "He doesn't have a beard. But it looks like one of them is going back in."

Jonah held his breath in anticipation and glanced at the methodical, scarlet streak of Roman soldiers flowing toward the village.

When the half-naked man re-emerged from the tunnel, he was again pulling someone out.

"It has to be Thomas!" Jonah cried.

"His hands are tied and he has a beard," replied Aaron. "It must be him!"

Jonah smiled from ear to ear. God had not abandoned him after all. He'd heard his prayers!

"I'll follow them," said Jonah. "You go and tell Zebulun what happened, that Thomas is alive. They'll take him to Lod for sure. We can break him out of prison there, but we'll need to do it tonight. Tomorrow may be too late. Have Zebulun come with as many men as possible. I'll meet him at that cemetery, the old one on the hill two miles outside the city. Tell him to be there an hour before sunset."

"All right," answered Aaron. He descended to the bottom branch, then swung from it down to the ground. After scanning uneasily in every direction, he sprinted away.

Jonah straddled a branch and leaned against the tree's trunk as he waited for the thirty-two Roman soldiers to arrive. When they did, they united with their cohorts who had escaped through the tunnel. Then all of them joined the villagers in a human chain from the well to the carpenter's workshop. Passing buckets of water hand-to-hand, they worked to tame the blaze.

Once they'd extinguished it, they retrieved their armor from the burnt-out building and prepared to move out. As Jonah watched them load Thomas into a donkey cart, he wondered how God would free his brother from their hold. He was sure it would happen. Somehow. Some way.

He chastised himself for having lost faith earlier that day. God had been there all along.

Chapter Sixteen

Annoyed with his dry mouth and throat, Thomas pulled on the chains binding him to the wall and shouted to the guards again. "I want water!"

There was no response. There never was. Just a distant drip, drip, drip from somewhere down the dank hallway.

His skin, red and painful from the fire, bothered him even more than his thirst or pounding head. He particularly disliked the tight metal cuff on his right ankle. Wrapping his hands around the shackle, he tried once more to pry it open a notch. Failing at that he used all his strength to attempt to pull the chain free from the wall. Once. Then twice. Then three times. With each fruitless yank, his frustration and anger grew until his face was raging red and the pulsing of his blood made his headache throb unbearably.

Abandoning the struggle, he gingerly pressed the bulging bruise on his scalp from where the centurion had slammed his head into the stone wall. He was busy fantasizing about getting revenge when a loud shriek echoing down the hallway interrupted him. He pondered what the scream was in response to. Someone being tortured? A howl of desperation? Or maybe an act of defiance?

Settling on the last one, Thomas did it himself—releasing a rage-filled scream, before shouting at the guards. "I want water!" He again pulled at the cuff around his ankle, but the shackle, heavy and indifferent, bound him just the same.

"It's no use," his cellmate, Hezron, advised. "They don't know Aramaic."

Thomas glared at the feces lying on the straw near him. He hated its stench, and he hated that it had come from him. "Bring me some water," he yelled at the top of his lungs. "You devils!"

Hezron arranged some filthy straw into a pile, pulled his clean onionskin-colored tunic above his knees, and sat cross-legged. "Don't you know any Greek?"

Thomas banged the back of his head on the hard wall. Of course he knew some Greek, but damned if he was going to speak a foreigner's tongue in his own land.

"You have quite the temper," commented Hezron.

Thomas gave him a scowl, wishing he could reach far enough to slap one of the old man's wrinkled, sunken cheeks. "Did I ask what you thought?"

Hezron shrugged and turned away.

"You sound just like my brother," Thomas grumbled, more to himself than to his cellmate.

He was sure Jonah was judging him for what had happened at the village. His brother was always accusing him of being irresponsible, like the time he'd gone on a raid without a shield. What Jonah didn't understand was that Thomas had left the shield behind on purpose. His real shield had been damaged beyond repair, and the only replacement they had was a dead Roman soldier's shield. Thomas could never allow his integrity to be tainted by using an enemy's shield.

That was just one of many things his brother couldn't grasp about him. For years Thomas had tried to survive in his brother's world where everything was a varying shade of gray, but he couldn't live in a place where every word and action was relative. He needed clear lines and boundaries. There had to be an us and a them, a right and a wrong, a good and an evil.

Zebulun had mastered that, and Thomas longed to be like his cousin. Thomas's dream was to one day rise above all his flaws, frailties, and doubts. He wanted to have complete control of himself, be fearless, unwavering in his beliefs, and ruthless in pursuit of what was right.

Peering glumly at the lock and chain on his ankle and the four thick walls surrounding him, he had to concede that dream was dead. Like all his other dreams, it wasn't going to come true. There was nothing to do or say now that would make any difference in his life. All his past words and actions defined him. He couldn't change any of it. It was too late to rededicate himself or turn over a new leaf. There would be no next month or next year. Time—the most precious thing in the world, he now knew—was rapidly running out for him.

"I was in here once before," Hezron announced. "Got caught stealing grain during the drought."

"Which one?" asked Thomas.

"Fifteen years ago," Hezron answered.

"That's when they took our house from us."

"Yes, those were awful times." Hezron inhaled deeply and sighed. "Not that they're much better now...."

"They didn't execute you for stealing grain?"

"No, the judge was in a good mood that day for whatever reason. There were five of us, and no matter the crime, he gave us all the same sentence— twenty lashes. They whipped us right after the trial. The first man got it the worst, and he wasn't in the greatest health to begin with. He died the next day. The rest of us got it a bit easier. I could never move my left arm much after that, but I lived."

Thomas leaned back against the wall and tried to kick the straw with the feces further away from the two of them. "Will I get a trial?"

"Oh yes," Hezron replied. "They always want to make everything look legal. Mine should have been today."

Thomas thought of his family and how he would likely never see his wife, Amaryah, again. Nor would he be there for his child's birth. "They pardon people sometimes, don't they?"

"I've only seen that happen once," said Hezron. "I don't remember his name, but he was well-known and his family was wealthy. He'd committed a petty crime and was due to be sentenced. But it was after a Roman soldier had committed an atrocity in some village and there were terrible riots all over. They pardoned him in the hope of appeasing the angry mobs."

"What did the soldier do?"

"He set fire to several scrolls from the Torah."

Thomas hoped there had been another appalling transgression recently so he might be pardoned as a result. But then he felt like a hypocrite for harboring such a desire. That was exactly what he'd been fighting against his whole life—corruption and immorality.

"Maybe you'll get off easy," Hezron said. "What did you do?"

Thomas knew a light punishment was next to impossible. "I'm with Zebulun," he said.

"You're a bandit?" asked Hezron, his voice raising a notch.

Thomas nodded.

"I'm so sorry."

Thomas understood Hezron's apology. He knew the consequences. The Romans liked to send messages to the public about the dangers of resisting their rule. Those messages were always put on display for all to view. He'd seen it himself enough times to know that he'd be crucified near the main gate of the city. If it came to that, he hoped it would be quick, not like the most gruesome one he'd seen when a man took nearly three days to die, birds of prey picking his flesh before he'd even taken his last breath.

"Why are you in here this time?" asked Thomas.

Hezron stuck his chin out. "I told people they didn't have to pay taxes to Rome, and to stop doing it."

Thomas's impression of his cellmate changed abruptly. Hezron may be old, but he was clearly not a coward.

"I've lived longer than most," added Hezron. "I don't have much time left in this world, and I'd rather die speaking the truth than submitting to their lies."

The more Hezron spoke, the more Thomas admired him. He wished there were more Jews like him.

They talked for a long time, until the sun had sunk below the horizon and it was pitch black in the prison cell. Hezron eventually fell asleep, mid-sentence, and began to snore. Though tired, Thomas resisted the urge to rest, instead using the time to examine his life.

He saw how he'd been so caught up in getting things accomplished, on learning new skills, on lecturing others, that he'd rarely allowed himself time to reflect, to just think about what was important and what wasn't. He had all the time in the world now, but his thoughts were mostly torturous for him. What had he really accomplished? Where had his beliefs gotten him?

At the notion that his whole life had been in vain, he was overcome with grief. He felt convinced that death awaited him in the morning. There would be no rescue from Zebulun and the bandits, who most certainly believed him already dead.

All his hopes, his dreams—his very life—rested on his trial.

Chapter Seventeen

Jonah received Aaron's news glumly. In hindsight, he knew he should've expected it.

He'd waited for hours for Zebulun in the cemetery—even after the sun had sunk below the horizon and the light of dusk faded. The situation had reminded him of that terrible time eighteen years ago when he'd been waiting in the secret cave for their father to come. Like Zebulun now, Jonah's father was supposed to have arrived before sunset.

Jonah had already been to Lod to scrutinize the layout of the city, the guard posts, the prison where Thomas was held, and the spots where they might sneak over a wall if needed. But his plan to rescue his brother was destined for failure without help from his cousin and the rest of the bandits.

"Zebulun said it was too risky," Aaron explained sheepishly. "He said they'd be sending Roman troops to hunt us down, so he took everyone back to Galilee to hide out in the hills for a while."

Jonah collapsed onto a nearby tombstone and shook his head.

Aaron reached into a pocket, pulled out a piece of bread, and handed it to Jonah. Then, leaning against the stone wall of a tomb, he kicked at the dirt. "So what shall we do?"

"I don't know," Jonah answered with a sigh. "What *can* we do in this darkness? With no moon, I can barely see ten feet in front of me." As he took a big bite of the bread, he contemplated how he'd been so eager to free his brother from the workshop earlier that day. None of his efforts had borne fruit, and yet his brother had been saved from certain death nonetheless. Maybe God had had a plan all along for rescuing his brother....

Aaron retrieved another piece of bread. "Here," he said. "Have more."

Just a few moments ago, Jonah had been despairing of his hunger, and now he was unexpectedly eating. As he felt how grateful his stomach was to receive the food, the cemetery abruptly filled with pale light. It was the moon. Less than a quarter full, faint and distant, but it was there. It had just been hidden behind massive clouds.

"It was there all along," Jonah exclaimed.

"What?" asked Aaron.

"The moon," Jonah explained. "I didn't think it was there, but it was."

"I don't understand."

Jonah leapt to his feet, pointing up at the night sky. "Don't you see? It was the same earlier today. Thomas was rescued from the fire."

"Yes, I know," said Aaron. "I saw the Roman soldier pull him out, but—"

"No," Jonah corrected him, "it was *God* who rescued him. Don't you see? *God* saved my brother."

Aaron gazed up at the moon, and Jonah stretched his arm around him.

"We have so little faith," Jonah whispered in his ear. "When we left Arimathea, I blamed God for not being there looking over Thomas. But He was!" Jonah held the bread to his nose, inhaling its subtle scent. "And just before you came, I was so hungry," he added, his voice choked with emotion. "Then you brought me bread."

Squeezing the back of Aaron's neck, Jonah put his forehead to his. "It's time," he said solemnly. "It's time we surrendered to God's will."

"All right," Aaron said with furrowed eyebrows, "but—"

Placing a finger over Aaron's lips, Jonah shushed him. "There is no but," he declared. "No more. God rescued Thomas from the fire. He'll rescue him from prison as well. God promises in the covenant to never abandon us. We need to start trusting in that promise."

Aaron's face softened. "You're right," he said.

Jonah pulled him into an embrace, feeling Aaron's scruffy beard on his cheek, and also himself filled with hope.

The two of them made their beds on the hard ground under a nearby tree. Before giving in to slumber, Jonah reaffirmed to himself that Thomas would surely be freed. God knew everything, so He certainly knew that Jonah's life would mean nothing without his brother.

Chapter Eighteen

"Azara," Farrukh hollered over the clamor of the market. "Where are you?"

Hearing his cry, Azara tore herself away from the fascinating leopard-like cats in wooden cages. She waved her arms high for Farrukh to find her, then wove her way through the thick crowd back to him.

They'd arrived in Samarkand the day before and Azara had insisted they go to the market first thing in the morning. Her father had business elsewhere in the city, but promised to join her for dinner.

"I've never seen cats like those before," she said upon reaching Farrukh's side. "They're much smaller than lions. They have spots like a leopard, but their fur is thick, and black and white, instead of yellow."

"Those are snow leopards," Farrukh explained, then chided her. "You must stay close. Your father would never forgive me if anything happened to you."

Azara raised her eyebrows. "Why are you so worried?" she asked. "We've never had a problem here before."

"Have you not noticed anything different since you were last here?"

Azara glanced around. It had been nearly eight years since she'd been in Samarkand. She definitely hadn't seen the snow leopards, rhino horns, or huge tortoise shells before, but she doubted he was referring to the things for sale.

The market was crowded, noisy, and overflowing with smells. She detected the heavenly scent of myrrh wafting over top of the odors of animal dung and sweaty men. To her left she spied the incense vendor selling the myrrh. To her right were perfume vendors offering samples to prospective customers. Buyers and sellers were haggling over prices. Vendors were shouting out their wares. And in between was a cacophony of conversations in different languages.

It was just as she remembered, and she loved every bit of it. "It looks the same as ever to me," she said.

"Look closer," Farrukh suggested.

A scrawny black and white dog scavenged rotting fruit from the ground. Azara thought it odd to see only one stray mutt, but it wasn't completely out of the ordinary. Then she noticed all the people dressed in rags standing around the edges or meandering through the crowd with big eyes and outstretched hands. That was nothing new, but....

"Now that you mention it," she said. "There do seem to be more beggars than I recall."

"Yes," confirmed Farrukh. "It is more dangerous these days. You can't trust anybody. I saw a man get robbed right in front of me recently."

"Did they catch him?"

"Surprisingly, they did," Farrukh said over the din of the market. Although they were walking side by side, they had to raise their voices to be heard.

"What do they do with those they catch stealing?"

"It depends on what they stole and how they did it," said Farrukh. "If they physically assaulted someone and stole his money, then the punishment would likely be death."

"What about for stealing, say, a piece of bread?"

Farrukh said nothing, but pointed to a boy who looked to be about twelve years old. Azara saw that his right hand had only stubs for fingers. She shivered involuntarily, feeling guilty for being so fortunate. She'd never gone hungry or had to beg for anything.

"Come," Farrukh called, veering left down a different road. "The food market is just ahead."

Despite his age and rigidity, Farrukh still walked just as fast as Azara remembered. Even now she had trouble keeping up with him.

They had come to the market in search of watermelon, but that was mostly an excuse for Azara. She just wanted to peer at all the people and things for sale. She was particularly enamored with the items made of glass that came from the East. It was a wonder to behold something you could see through that, at the same time, was solid and impenetrable.

The market was comprised of roughly four separate sections, though they often intermingled. One section was for food: fresh fruits and vegetables, rice and grains, tea, spices, and meat. Another section was for wool, cotton, and silk. One could buy either bulk raw material or finished products like rugs, blankets, or robes. Her favorite section—for vendors of precious metals, stones, and wares—was a feast for the eyes. Azara liked to spend hours there looking at pottery, ceramics, terracotta, silver and gold ornaments, swords, armor, furs....

The last section was for livestock, and Azara tried to never go there, because that was where they also sold slaves. Though she encountered slaves and indentured servants on a daily basis, it had always been difficult for her to accept that one human could own another. When she'd been married and unable to leave the house, she'd felt like a slave herself.

They squeezed through the bustling, disorderly throng of mostly men, then rounded a corner and the food market came into view. Vendors lined the sides of the street, hawking an assortment of colorful fruits and vegetables. Farrukh guided her down an alley where rows of baskets, many half-empty, sat on makeshift tables. Azara recognized a few of the items: brown lentils, white rice, fresh green garbanzo beans alongside dried yellow ones, turmeric root, coriander seeds. Many others she didn't recognize and simply marveled at, curious how one would cook and eat them.

Upon exiting the alley Azara saw they were surrounded by vendors selling all sorts of melons. She pointed out one selling watermelon, and Farrukh went over and began to speak with the seller. A few seconds later he called Azara to his side. "Come, my dear," he said. "Let's see if you remember any of the Sogdian I taught you. Get us some watermelons."

Azara spoke slowly, certain she'd butchered the words terribly, but the man understood her request for two ripe watermelons nonetheless. She even managed to barter him down to a price Farrukh deemed acceptable, though she suspected the man was agreeable only because Farrukh was with her.

Farrukh cradled the round, medium-sized watermelons in his arms and led them out of the food market. "Let's get back to the inn," he called to her. "We'll work on languages today."

Azara smiled to herself. It was just like old times. Even though she knew her father was paying Farrukh simply to keep her company while he tended to business, she saw Farrukh couldn't step out of his lifelong role as tutor.

Holding her nose as they approached the smelly animal market, Azara noted all the dingy sheep, goats, cattle, and camels with equally dingy ropes wrapped tight around their necks. As they neared the end of that section, Azara saw the beginning of the slave market.

Grasping Farrukh by the elbow, she pulled herself close and complained in his ear. "You know I hate this section," she said reproachfully. "Why did you take us here?"

"My apologies," he answered. "This was the shortest path back to the inn, and I forgot how you detest it so."

Azara cast sidelong glances at the dozens of slaves standing or sitting in rows. Nearly all of them had light skin and brown or black hair. The men had beards, something forbidden of slaves in Palestine.

"Where are these slaves from?" she asked.

Farrukh replied over his shoulder without slowing down, "Eastern and Northern Europe."

Azara observed a man in turquoise robes examining a young female slave. The man's head and nearly his entire face were covered by a white scarf. He had the seller disrobe the young woman so she was completely naked. After inspecting her body, he stuck his fingers inside her mouth to check her teeth. Awaiting sale behind her were three male slaves dressed only in loincloths. One long rope had been looped around each slave's neck. A stout, dark-skinned man with a cow's horn hanging on a necklace held the end of the rope. In his other hand he bore a short black whip.

"In Galilee some Jews in extreme poverty sell themselves," said Azara. "Is that the case with these, as well?"

"Doubtful," remarked Farrukh. "They're likely spoils of war."

Two of the slaves looked up at Azara as she passed by. She was struck by their blond hair and bright blue eyes, and also their despondent gazes.

"How much do they cost?" she asked.

"Why?"

"Because I want to buy one and set her free."

Farrukh stopped and turned to her. "First," he said, "you don't have enough money. Second, what good would it do? Thousands of slaves come through here every week. What difference would it make setting just one of them free?"

"It would make a difference to *that* person, that's what," Azara said indignantly. She studied Farrukh's face, searching his perpetual sly grin and the deep creases in his forehead for signs of sympathy. Finding none, she said, "Why are you so cold-hearted?"

"I'm not indifferent to their plight," Farrukh answered and began to walk again. "I'm just being rational. Even if we did buy one and set him free, what would he do? He'd just be another beggar. Or worse yet, a thief."

"Or he could have both his dignity and faith in his fellow man restored and live an honorable life," Azara asserted.

"My child," Farrukh said and sighed. "You are such a dreamer."

"I am *not* a child," Azara protested, "though I proudly admit I'm a dreamer. This world needs more dreamers—people who are changing it for the better."

"All right, you are not a child," conceded Farrukh. Then, grinning at her, he added, "But you are a woman. You can't argue with me about that."

He winked at her, but Azara remained aloof. She was not in a playful mood.

"And tell me," he went on, "what exactly is this woman named Azara doing to change the world for the better?"

Azara wanted to lash out at him, but he'd asked it not in a condescending tone but in a way that suggested he genuinely wanted to know. The problem was she didn't know the answer. What *was* she doing to change the world for the better?

As she pondered the question, Farrukh steered them out of the market. The end was marked by a handful of vendors selling kebabs, bread, cups of tea, and fresh fruit. Squatting or leaning on the walls behind them was a row of penniless vagrants—thin men with bare chests and visible ribs, expressionless women with gaunt cheeks, barefoot children in rags.

Overcome with pity at the sight of the wretched beggars, Azara called to Farrukh, "Give me the change from the watermelons."

Farrukh looked about cautiously, then opened his purse and retrieved two coins. "What do you want to buy? Some bread?" he asked. "I'll tell you if it's a fair price or not."

Azara held out her hand impatiently.

"Let me hold them, dear," Farrukh advised. "There are thieves everywhere. I had fruit stolen from my basket once by a five-year-old."

"It's my money," she said sharply. "Give it to me."

Farrukh scrutinized the crowd again. A young woman, perhaps no more than fifteen years old, was approaching. Her robes were tattered, and one arm held a squirming, crying baby while the other was outstretched in need. Farrukh waved her away and made a loud shushing sound, as if scaring off a dog. Azara snatched the two bronze coins out of his hand and hurried after her.

"Here," said Azara as she tapped the woman on the shoulder.

The woman took the coin, but said nothing, only staring blankly in return.

Azara held her gaze, feeling peculiar, as though she was seeing herself in a reflection. The sensation lasted no more than a few seconds, but it frightened her, because she somehow felt what it was like to be a young mother with a child and no home or money. A deep sense of hopelessness and despair engulfed her until she pulled away and caught the shy eyes of a little girl peeking around a corner.

Azara squatted and motioned with her finger for the girl to come. Brushing the bangs of her unkempt hair out of the way, the girl inched forward. Her cheeks were stained purplish-black by some fruit she'd eaten, and her robes were hopelessly grimy. But she had an enchanting smile that reminded Azara of the toddler Jesus many years back.

After placing her second coin in the little girl's palm, other beggars came forward. With an exaggerated frown, Azara displayed her empty hands. Though she felt good about helping two unfortunates, she felt even worse for those she couldn't help.

Farrukh shook his head, then took her by the arm and led them toward the inn once more. "My dear," he said, "the compassion of the heart must be balanced by wisdom. What you've done will feed them for only a short while, and then what? They'll still be poor and in need."

Azara pulled her arm free. "If the world listened to you," she said bitterly, "nothing would *ever* change." She tried to pass in front of him, nearly bumping into a woman balancing a large plate of red and green apples on her head.

Though Azara was furious with Farrukh's words, she knew that what he'd said contained more than a grain of truth. Changing the world for the better was not as straightforward as she'd thought.

As they approached the entrance to their inn, Azara spotted five monks in bright orange robes standing quietly one next to the other. Their heads were shaved and they held out empty wooden bowls. Farrukh spoke to them, but Azara was behind him and couldn't hear what he'd said.

Managing to hold both watermelons in one arm, Farrukh opened the heavy wooden door of the inn for Azara.

"Are those Buddhist monks?" she asked.

He nodded as he followed her through the door.

Once back in the room, Azara found a small piece of papyrus on the table. Recognizing her father's handwriting, she scanned the first line, then handed it to Farrukh. "It's for you."

Farrukh read the note, then placed it back on the table. Dipping a five-inch-long reed into a small inkwell, he wrote on the back of the papyrus. "Your father has asked me to do a few errands for him," he said. "I'll be back in a couple hours, and then we'll resume our lessons for the day." He held out the papyrus for Azara. "Here's some Sogdian words I want you to memorize."

Feigning interest, Azara held the list in front of her face. Once she'd closed the door behind Farrukh, she slumped in a chair and gazed vacantly at the dozen words. Farrukh had written them out phonetically and had included one-word definitions in Greek. Two of the Sogdian words—*traditional* and *reverent*—were familiar to her, and she realized she'd learned them a decade prior but had since dismissed them like useless relics of the past.

Unable to study, she set the list aside and went up to the inn's roof. As she'd hoped, no one else was there so she could unwrap her scarf and enjoy the sun and breeze on her uncovered head.

The two-story inn was on a slight hill and provided Azara with a good view of Samarkand. The city spread out beneath her like a giant raven, its wings stretching far and wide, dwellings upon dwellings as far as she could see. To the east she spied the large Zoroastrian temple with its endless stream of white headscarf clad disciples going in and out. Farther up the road she spotted a Hindu shrine where devotees were doing prostrations before a statue of the male god, Shiva.

Even the religions are dominated by men, she thought. Their deities are male. Their prophets are male. Their priests are male.

Turning her face to the sun, she twirled a strand of her long, black hair around her finger and dreamed how things would be different if women ruled the world. It would surely be a kinder, more tolerant land, without the incredible disparity in wealth and justice. A place less violent, without wars and stonings and crucifixions....

Then she grinned, remembering one of Farrukh's favorite sayings whenever they discussed philosophy: "Or perhaps that's just a seductive lie." He used that phrase to demonstrate when one of them was falling into the trap of believing their thoughts and ideas without critical analysis or actual evidence. Azara had to admit she had no proof the world would be any better off with women in charge. She wondered how many well-intentioned rulers in history had tried to mold kingdoms to their ideals and failed miserably.

Going to the edge of the roof, she leaned over and watched the scene below. Carefree children dashed to and fro playing tag, and the statuesque monks stood silently with their begging bowls. Azara thought the monks noble. She admired their sacrifice. They were following the Buddha's teachings in the hope of finding truth just as he did. People passed them by without so much as a glance, let alone food or coins. She pitied them for relying on their indifferent brethren for support. Then she heard Farrukh's accusation in her head again: "*And what exactly is this woman named Azara doing to change the world for the better?*"

An idea seized her. She ran back to the room and rummaged through her belongings until she found the mirror her father had given her. After folding a cloth around it, she rushed out the door toward the market in search of the place where she'd seen several vendors selling jewelry.

The sprawling market extended down every alley and crossroad, and Azara constantly stopped, peeking tiptoe over the crowd, to ensure she didn't pass the spot. As she did so she began to notice the same two men always a short distance behind her. They didn't wear the elegant robes of rich merchants, nor the rags of beggars, and every time Azara looked their way, they turned their heads as if they hadn't been peering at her. Azara argued with herself she was being unreasonably suspicious simply because of her father's and Farrukh's earlier warnings about the dangers of the market.

When she finally found the jewelry vendors, she approached one who was not busy, unwrapped her mirror, and held it out to him. "You buy," she said in Sogdian. "How much—silver drachmas—you give?"

The man tapped the handle with a long fingernail, then parted his lips to observe his yellow teeth in the mirror. He gave it back and held up nine fingers.

Azara shook her head. He squinted at the mirror for a few seconds, then held up ten fingers.

"No, not enough," she replied, walking away. She had no idea if that was a fair price or not, but now at least she had something to compare other offers to.

On the other side of the street was a table filled with opulent jewelry. The man sold gold pins for fastening cloaks, dozens of rings with precious gems, earrings with brightly colored stones, silver bracelets, and necklaces galore. Azara headed toward the vendor, catching out of the corner of her eye the same two men ogling her from a distance. She clutched the mirror with both hands, then breathed a sigh of relief to see four Market Guards—soldiers with leather armor, long staffs, and swords around their waists—approaching from a side alley. They ambled at a leisurely pace, and Azara passed in front of them and waited in line at the jewelry vendor's table. The vendor was a jovial man who seemed to laugh at everything. Azara enjoyed haggling with him, and successfully bargained him all the way up to thirteen.

Feeling confident about how much she could get for the mirror, she moved on to a third vendor who sold exquisite perfume bottles and finely decorated cosmetic dishes and applicators. Handing him the mirror, she asked for twenty silver drachmas. He laughed contemptuously as he immediately gave the mirror back, saying he'd pay no more than fourteen.

"Make it fifteen," she countered.

He stroked the lengthy, black whiskers on his pointy chin, then, to her surprise, agreed.

Delighted with her sale, Azara calculated how many coins she'd be able to donate to each of the five monks. Though not enough to last them for years, it should nevertheless provide them with food for many months.

As the vendor retrieved the money, Azara gritted her teeth to find the two cagey men closer than ever. In addition, when she glanced their way now, they no longer turned their heads, but instead stared straight back at her. One had a scar that extended from the stained green scarf covering his head, through his right eyebrow, and into his patchy, dark beard. The other man kept his right hand underneath his shabby cloak near his chest, as if hiding something.

The Market Guards had long since passed, and after receiving her coins, Azara deposited them into a small purse and tucked it inside her robes. The safest path back to the inn, she decided, was whichever way was most crowded. But after only a few steps, she caught sight of three men who looked to be Galilean, so turned to follow them.

She saw fellow travelers from Galilee every now and then, recognizing them sometimes by their tunics and mannerisms, but more often by hearing them speak Aramaic in that familiar Galilean accent.

Her plan was to strike up a conversation with the men, then ask them to escort her back to the inn. Unfortunately, when she caught up to them, she heard a language unknown to her.

With her two dreadful followers only a few yards behind, Azara tried to quickly distance herself from them. But not only was the crowd dense in this area, the street narrowed and was rife with beggars. A filthy urchin with shoulder-length hair pulled on Azara's robes asking for a handout. Azara tried to wave her off as she'd seen Farrukh do, but it had no effect. The girl held fast, slowing down Azara even more.

When she glimpsed only one of her followers behind, Azara began to panic. Where was the other one? Desperately wanting to go faster, she grabbed a handful of coins from her purse, opting to give one to the urchin so the girl would leave her alone.

It didn't take long for Azara to realize that had been a mistake. In handing out the coin so conspicuously, she found herself surrounded by a dozen boisterous children with outstretched hands.

"No. No more," she yelled to them.

Though vexing, Azara saw the urchins had at least drawn the crowd's attention, hopefully safeguarding her from her two followers.

Amidst all the grubby, pleading faces, Azara noticed the girl she'd already given a coin to. Instead of smiling in gratitude and scurrying away, she was still there, holding out an empty hand as if she hadn't received anything yet.

Since she was no longer able to donate an equal number of coins to the monks, and because she wanted to remain in the safety of the spotlight, Azara picked out four more coins for the pitiful children.

She tried to award one to a cute five-year-old boy, but the other kids grabbed it out of her hand before she had a chance to. Azara scowled at the perpetrators, then excused their rude behavior by reminding herself how little they had and how hungry they must be. On her next attempt, she swatted away the older kids' hands and made sure the little boy got the coin meant for him. Once firmly in his grasp, however, the bigger kids pried his fingers open and stole it. Then they began tearing at Azara's hand as well.

"Stop it," she yelled. "Give him back that coin!" Whenever she became distressed, she found it impossible to speak anything other than her native Aramaic. "Behave yourselves or you won't get anything!"

The children yanked hard on Azara's hand and all her remaining coins tumbled out and scattered on the ground. The children dove after them, fighting and clawing with one another. The chaos was exasperated when nearby adult beggars joined the fray.

Azara let out a high-pitched scream, then bawled in desperation.

Vendors hurried over from their booths, berating the urchins and beggars, and swatting at them with sticks. After several tumultuous minutes, a half dozen Market Guards arrived on the scene. Using their long staffs as a threat, they forced the children and beggars into a dead-end alley. One of the guards took Azara aside, asking her a couple of questions, but she was too distraught to understand him. The only thing she could remember to say in Sogdian was, "I don't understand."

As two guards led Azara away, the rest used rope to tie the urchins and beggars one to the other.

Inside a busy building several blocks away, Azara was nudged into the office of a harried, middle-aged man in plush crimson robes. He dabbed at his perspiring forehead with a sweat-stained cloth, then asked impatiently, "Do you speak Sogdian?"

Having calmed down, she answered, "Yes, a little. Please send a man for my father." She then told him the inn they were staying at.

After dispatching a guard, the official disappeared into another room, leaving Azara alone with her thoughts about how her good intentions had backfired terribly. To her, it was further proof there was no God. If He existed, surely her efforts would have been welcomed. There wouldn't have been turmoil at the market, only thankfulness and rejoicing. Full of bitterness, she slouched on the bench and muttered under her breath how foolish people were to believe in that malicious fallacy known as "God."

As the time passed, she prepared herself for the impending scolding her father would surely give her. She rehearsed her defense with charged points that she wasn't a child, and that she had every right to do whatever she pleased with the mirror since it was a gift. If she were his son, instead of his daughter, she reflected bitterly, he wouldn't dare admonish her.

Azara was pacing back and forth when her father finally arrived. Beside herself with resentment, she crossed her arms and sneered as he approached. Before she could tell him she didn't want to hear his patronizing lecture, he rushed forward and wrapped her in a tight embrace.

"Are you alright?" he asked, his voice choked with emotion.

In his loving arms her temper drained in a heartbeat, her rigid body melting into sobs. Burying her face in his chest, she blurted, "You're not angry with me?"

"Oh, my precious, no," he replied. "Thank God you're safe."

Azara cringed briefly. There was that word again: God.

Farrukh peeked in the room and made eye contact with Azara. Then he began conversing with the official.

"Come," her father said, guiding her to a well-worn wooden bench. "Let's wait here while Farrukh clears things up."

Azara sat close to him, leaning her head on his shoulder and letting him hold her hand in his.

"Father, why are you always thanking God?"

"God is the master of all," he answered matter-of-factly. "Nothing happens except by His hand."

"All the brutality and unfairness?"

"Yes," he said. "And all the beauty and kindness too."

"But I don't understand it," she protested.

"Neither do I."

"And yet you're always thanking Him."

"Yes. God has been very good to me in this life."

"God took your wife from you."

"True."

"You're not bitter about that?"

"No. I'm thankful to God for allowing your mother to be a part of my life for as long as He did. He certainly didn't have to let her be my wife and bear my beautiful daughter."

"And what about your hip? You tell me it gets a little worse each year, and that it hurts terribly sometimes."

"I'm grateful God still allows me to walk on two good legs."

"So you're grateful for *everything*?"

He made a little laugh and said, "It's all a choice, my sunshine. You can be mad or you can be glad. God doesn't care which one you choose, but being grateful makes for a much happier life."

Skeptical it could be that simple, Azara tested him. "I went to the market and sold that mirror you gave me."

He pulled back, his eyes wide with surprise. "But why?"

Azara observed Farrukh taking leave of the official and heading toward them. "Are you alright, my dear?" he asked as he arrived.

She nodded to him, then answered her father. "I sold it so I could contribute the proceeds to the Buddhist monks outside our inn. I was giving coins to some children when they tore them from my hand and made a terrible scene."

"So that's what this is about?" her father asked in an incredulous tone. "They took all your money?"

"They told us you'd been robbed," added Farrukh.

Azara shook her head. "They were rude," she said, "but they weren't thieves." She knew if she blamed the children for what had happened that they'd be punished severely.

"My goodness," said Farrukh. "I'd better go tell the official."

Azara and her father waited quietly, watching Farrukh's animated conversation with the official and his men. Probing the bottom of her purse, Azara was pleased to find she still had four coins left.

Farrukh returned a moment later. "Aziz, I've talked him into releasing the children and beggars," he said. "But what about the coins? They've managed to confiscate eight of them."

Azara's father tugged at his beard, then turned to her. "You want them back?"

Her ire long since vanquished by her father's tenderness, Azara pictured the grievous children and was immensely saddened by their plight. "No," she answered softly.

"See to it that they're distributed equally among them," Azara's father called to Farrukh, who was already heading back to the official. "You'll probably need to exchange them for smaller coins."

"Thank you," Azara whispered in her father's ear, first in Aramaic, then in Greek, and finally in Sogdian. With a chuckle, he caressed each of her cheeks. Then he helped her up from the bench and led them through the jam-packed room to thank the official.

Once out the door and departing for the inn, Azara questioned her father a last time. "You're really not mad at me?"

Despite the midday heat, he wrapped his arm around her as they walked. "I'm indebted to God I have such a big-hearted daughter," he said, kissing her on the forehead. "You teach me more than you'll ever know."

Azara still wasn't sure if there was a God, but neither could she believe it was sheer luck or coincidence that had bestowed upon her the privilege of having such a gracious man as a father. She silently addressed a short prayer to "*Whatever it is that I don't understand but has blessed me nonetheless.*" She was brief and to the point. "*Thank you for this gift of life with a father whose love for me knows no bounds.*"

When they came to the Buddhist monks in front of their inn, Azara retrieved her four coins. As she put one in each of their bowls, they smiled and bowed appreciatively. Disheartened she didn't have a coin for the fifth monk, she averted his gaze. But as her father opened the door of the inn and waited for her, she ventured a glance, noticing the man bore the same half-smile she always saw etched into the faces of the Buddha statues at the market. That smile had always piqued her interest. It was as if the Buddha knew some secret and was profoundly joyful because of it.

Longing to know it herself, Azara asked the monk, "Why do you smile so?"

"You are asking the wrong question," came his response.

"What do you mean?"

He pointed to the side of her head. "The question you should be asking is, '*Why do* I *not smile?*'"

Azara considered the question absurd. The world was prejudiced and unjust, and she could list a thousand reasons why she didn't smile. And yet something changed in her in that moment. She wasn't interested in her thousand reasons. Instead, she was deeply curious why a man with so little— not even food to eat that day—appeared to be so happy, and yet she, who had everything in comparison, was so troubled.

Before entering the inn, she peeped back over her shoulder. The monk seemed so peaceful, as though he was in a dream and none of this was real.

Chapter Nineteen

Awakened by the sound of jangling keys and a creaking cell door, Thomas rubbed his bleary eyes. By the light of the sun's early morning rays coming through the barred window, he made out a centurion looking down at him. An instinctive urge to fight stirred in Thomas's belly, but quickly dissipated. He was simply too dehydrated, too groggy, too weak to put up any resistance.

The centurion barked orders in his vulgar language, then two guards unlocked Thomas's chains and pulled him up by the arms. Thomas shot the centurion a look of hate, but the man's face was annoyingly placid and he did not return the animosity. For some reason he had a small white flower tucked into the red plumes of his helmet. Thomas couldn't figure out if the Roman had put it there himself, or if someone had snuck it in as a joke.

They marched Thomas and Hezron down a murky, windowless hallway, then prodded them up two dozen stone steps before shoving them into a small courtyard. Three wide archways lined the far wall. In front of the middle one, on a wooden bench, sat a young, clean-shaven man with blazing orange hair. He wore an impeccable white tunic. With his head lowered to his knees, he was rubbing his temples with his fingers and slowly opening and closing his jaw.

The centurion and the guards stood at attention in front of him. Thomas gazed down at the clean patchwork of stone squares, trying to decide what he would say in his defense. He could lie and try to convince them they had the wrong man. Or he could beg for mercy. Or he could do what he truly wanted to— denounce the Gentile intruders to their face. While the first two options offered a small chance at living, the third would seal his fate outright.

After an unbearably long silence, the centurion cleared his throat emphatically, prompting the young Roman to lift his head and notice them. As the centurion began loudly announcing something, the legate frowned and squeezed his hands over his ears until the centurion stopped talking. Obeying the legate's downward pat of his hand, the centurion began again at a softer volume.

Usually when Thomas heard Greek, he blocked it out, but now he listened attentively. He couldn't make out every word, but managed to figure out the centurion was listing the charges being leveled against him and Hezron.

Sunlight seeped through the archways. A pigeon strutted by, pecking at the ground, then abruptly flew away. Thomas took a deep breath, trying to calm himself. The biggest decision of his life would soon be upon him.

Once the centurion finished, the legate made a short reply Thomas couldn't hear. Then the man rose and careened out of sight through the archways. Confused, Thomas looked to Hezron for an explanation.

Hezron made no response, but the centurion translated to them in his broken Aramaic: "Punishment is crucifixion."

Thomas couldn't fathom it. "What?" he exclaimed. "I didn't even get to speak. That wasn't a trial!"

The centurion gave an order to the guards, who then began pushing Thomas and Hezron out of the courtyard.

Thomas struggled against them. "You damn liars!" He turned his head to scowl at the centurion still standing there.

After holding his gaze for a second, the Roman said in Aramaic, "Sorry." Then he followed the legate through the archways.

Thomas didn't know what to think. So many questions swirled in his head. *Are they taking me back to the cell? Or am I going to be crucified right now? Why did the centurion say sorry? Why wasn't I allowed to speak at my trial? Am I already breathing my last breaths?*

When the guards passed by the dingy stairwell that led to the dungeon, Thomas knew the sentence was to be carried out immediately. He'd seen the Romans dole out punishment on numerous occasions and knew what came first. It was something Thomas dreaded even more than being crucified.

First, he'd be scourged.

He and Hezron were taken to another courtyard with two large tree stumps and a foul smell. A tall soldier with a puffy face received them with a listless frown. Another soldier lurked in the shadows behind him. Thomas realized they were the lictors, the men responsible for administering the scourgings. Too far away to reach them, he spat in their direction nonetheless.

While the guards held Thomas's arms, the lictors came and ripped his tunic off. A sharp elbow to the back knocked Thomas down over one of the tree stumps. Then they fastened his wrists so he couldn't get up.

Twisting his head to the side, he saw they'd done the same to Hezron. With a crude snigger, Thomas's lictor brandished his flagrum in Thomas's face. It was a short whip with a wooden handle and three leather thongs. Each thong had knotted into it small pieces of metal at two-inch intervals.

When the lictor swung the flagrum back, Thomas clenched every muscle in his back to brace himself. But the flagrum smacked the stump instead. His lictor, howling in delight, pried it out from the stump and dangled it in front of Thomas once again.

Thomas heard a whack, followed by Hezron's bloody scream.

"You devils!" Thomas swore at them. "If I—"

Thwack! An intense burning immediately blotted out everything. The torment seared through his body as if he'd been stabbed with a red-hot sword.

As the next lash struck his back, Thomas gasped for air. It was just as he feared it would be—the most agonizing affliction he'd ever experienced.

The lashes came quickly, one after the other. Thomas tried to stop wailing, as Hezron had, but couldn't help himself.

Eventually, all of Thomas's thoughts ceased, and he knew nothing but agony—complete excruciating pain that knew no end.

When his lictor finally paused, Thomas had no idea if he'd been whipped twenty times or two hundred. All he could do was try to catch his breath.

After a few more seconds without a lashing, Thomas hoped it was over. He couldn't feel his back, just a raw throbbing sensation throughout. He found he couldn't keep up with his torso's spasms and relentless violent throes, and that they began to push him out of his body.

Then the scourging began again.

Thomas screamed as he'd never screamed before, and something even more powerful than the torture erupted from within.

Rage.

He could not, would not, allow himself to be defeated by his enemy on his own land. Willing himself not to close his eyes, not to leave his body, he let the pain crash down upon him like an angry sea's waves against a rudderless dinghy. And when the scourging again paused, he cussed at his tormentor.

Feeling himself on the verge of losing consciousness, Thomas forced his eyes to stay open. "The Lord will avenge me," he cried. He'd intended to shout it, but all he could manage was a whisper.

When another lash came down, Thomas saw only blackness and couldn't breathe. He sensed death so near that he could cross the boundary in a heartbeat.

The centurion entered the courtyard, yelled a command, and then the scourging stopped. Thomas again tried to catch his breath, but no matter how quickly or deeply he inhaled, it was never enough.

He and Hezron were untied and prodded out of the courtyard toward the city's main gate. Naked and senseless, they staggered down the dusty road. Hezron veered close to any and every wall, using them to help him stay on his feet. Thomas wanted to help, but was too weak himself to offer any assistance.

A small crowd congregated near the city's main gate up ahead: merchants with donkeys and carts preparing to leave for the day, farmers with rakes and shovels going to tend their fields, day laborers awaiting work, woeful beggars with outstretched hands. When Thomas and Hezron approached, they all stopped, stared, then backed away. A boy leading a young cow by a rope hurried through the gate ahead of them.

Outside the city's walls, a soldier hollered an order and pointed to two wooden beams lying on the ground. Thomas hadn't understood a word the man said, but knew those sentenced to crucifixion had to lug their own beam. He fixed his eyes on the thick, ten-foot piece of wood, unsure he had the strength to haul it.

Hezron had collapsed and was reduced to crawling on all fours. Thomas tried to go back and help, but two soldiers blocked him from doing so. While he waited for Hezron, he sat on a beam and looked directly at the bright yellow sun floating above the eastern horizon. He'd been taught all his life to never look directly at the sun, but he did so now with impunity.

He had often cursed the sun for its overbearing heat and headache-inducing brightness, but now he appreciated its warmth, its light.

An old man from the crowd approached and offered a small wooden bowl of water. Thomas recklessly gulped it down, spilling half of it. "Thank you," he uttered, truly meaning it. Gratitude was not something he was familiar with, and its presence now eased his suffering.

When Hezron finally arrived, Thomas strained to lift the end of one of the beams. It was even heavier than it looked.

Hezron, wheezing and unable to stand, did not even attempt to lift the other beam. Instead, one of the Romans heaved it up to his shoulders and carried it for him. After only a few steps, he was stopped by another soldier. A few terse words ensued, then a villager was yanked from the crowd and directed to take on the burden.

Under the weight of his load, Thomas stumbled over his own feet and fell to the ground. The same soldier who'd assisted Hezron came to help him back to his feet, but Thomas shook off his grip and pushed him away.

"This is *my* pole, you devil," he hissed. "And this is *my* land. Not *yours*!"

Eyeing him quizzically, the soldier withdrew.

"I don't need help," added Thomas, though the truth was more that he wouldn't accept it from someone he considered his enemy.

Since staring into the sun, his vision had been partially obscured by dark splotches. In their place now were glimpses of a strange veil—a nearly invisible cloak that surrounded him. Thomas found he could see on both sides of this veil. On one side he saw his bare feet trudging on the dry dirt road, and on the other side he saw random events and experiences from his past. He viewed them not as the person who had lived them, but as an impartial observer. Here he was as a baby in his mother's arms; next, a young man learning how to fight, kill, and condemn with Zebulun. Then he was a child with Jonah, pretending to be warriors fighting off an invisible enemy.

Thomas recalled how he used to plunge himself so deeply into fantasies that his brother would have to convince him none of it had been real—that there were no monsters in the cave, no enemy soldiers attacking from the top of the ridge.

In one terrifying glimpse, Thomas suddenly understood his whole life had been like that. None of it had been real.

Coming to the base of the crucifixion mound, Thomas felt extremely weak. He was unsteady and light-headed, but for reasons he couldn't comprehend, his thinking was becoming more and more clear. The closer he came to death, the more clarity he found.

Using every last ounce of his strength, Thomas ascended the small hill. Then he dropped his beam and collapsed to the ground. He again stared into the sun, as Hezron, ashen and limp, was carried up by two villagers.

With his newfound clarity, Thomas began to come to terms with a growing understanding that he'd voluntarily chosen to travel the wrong path in his life. No one had forced him. No one was to blame. It had been his decision all along.

Still, he was filled with resentment. Where was this clarity when he'd needed it? Why had this clear reasoning been denied him in his day-to-day life?

As a soldier directed him to lie down on the beam, Thomas saw that his entire adulthood had been a lie. The only time he'd lived the truth was as a child, when he'd loved his parents, his brother, and his goat, Graha, for no reason whatsoever.

They tied his legs tight to the pole, then stretched his arms over his head, tying them as well. With his remaining breaths, Thomas gazed up at the brilliant blue sky. Seeing a lone white cloud in the distance, he was filled with an urge to live his life again, to choose correctly this time. If he had that chance, he'd choose kindness and compassion no matter the costs, no matter the pain.

Why couldn't someone have taught him about love and goodwill while he still had a life to live?

Those rabbis and high priests, he thought with disgust, *were not teachers at all*. They were gatekeepers, guardians of the current state of affairs. Their only purpose was to keep things the same as they'd always been.

The veil between the two worlds shrank further, enabling Thomas to see, for the first time, that the rabbis and high priests had never been taught the truth themselves. How could they teach about something they didn't understand? It was like asking someone who had lived their entire life in the desert to teach you about the sea.

"Thomas!" a distant voice called.

Thomas heard it, but couldn't tell which side of the veil it was coming from.

He was so very tired. He just wanted to sleep. Closing his eyes, he pondered how things surely would have been different if only there had been someone to teach him the truth.

Chapter Twenty

"T homas!" Jonah called out again.

He and Aaron were sprinting toward a mound where Roman soldiers were preparing to crucify two men. Jonah tried to assure himself this was a false alarm. It couldn't really be Thomas. God wouldn't let that happen.

Still, he ran as fast as he ever had in his life. He paid no attention to the heat or bright glare of the sun, nor the dusty, dry air—not even to the bead of sweat that slowly dripped from his temple into his right eye.

"I see five soldiers," Aaron said breathlessly from behind. "Romans, with armor and weapons."

It was Aaron, with his amazing eyesight, who had first spotted what was happening. The second he'd announced it, Jonah had begun running—despite Aaron's assertion that he couldn't tell if one of the condemned was Thomas or not.

Jonah reached the small hill completely out of breath, but forced his shaky legs to dash up it without pause.

"Wait," Aaron called from behind. "There's a centurion there too. It might be the same one from the village."

Jonah heard him, but didn't slow down in the least. Though he'd seen the centurion's face when he'd burst through the bedroom door, he was fairly certain the centurion had not seen his.

At the top of the mound, Jonah saw two bloody figures sprawled on their backs. There were no crossbeams. Their arms were high above their heads, hands tied with rope to the wooden poles. The first man, old with gray hair, already had nails through his arms and legs. The second man was skinny with a narrow head and gaunt cheeks, and Jonah bit his lower lip to keep from crying out. It was Thomas. He'd been stripped of his clothes, and his long, naked body was stretched out on the wooden beam.

"Thomas!"

"Jonah?" his brother murmured. "Is that you?"

"Yes. I'm here."

The centurion hollered an order, and not paying attention to what he'd said, Jonah feared it was directed at him and that he was about to be arrested. When none of the soldiers advanced on him, Jonah glanced at the Roman commander. After eyeing Jonah and Aaron suspiciously for several seconds, the centurion resumed his work, withdrawing a six-inch tapered nail from a leather pouch and handing it to another soldier with a severely crooked nose. For reasons Jonah couldn't discern, the centurion had a white flower tucked into the red plumes of his helmet.

Stepping too close to his brother, Jonah was shoved to the ground by one of the other soldiers. The Roman then unsheathed his sword and held it in front as a second soldier joined him.

"Stop it!" Jonah yelled at the centurion and the soldier with the crooked nose. "That's my brother!"

They did stop. They stopped and turned to see a grown man walking on his knees toward them, tears streaming down his cheeks.

"Please, stop it. Leave him alone," Jonah pleaded. As they nailed his brother's feet to the pole, Thomas shrieked in pain.

"God!" Jonah screamed. "God, help me!" Scrambling to his feet, he snatched a fist-sized rock from the ground. Holding it over his head, he lurched forward, but before he could assail his brother's tormentors, Aaron grabbed him from behind and knocked the rock out of his hand.

"Don't," Aaron implored in Jonah's ear. He motioned to the two soldiers standing guard, who were now peering warily back. "They'll kill you on the spot."

Writhing on the pole, Thomas called out to his brother, "Jonah!"

Jonah didn't hear a fully-grown adult call for him. He heard his little brother—just a boy who'd climbed too far up a tree and was scared to climb down. Jonah tried to free himself from Aaron's firm grip, but could not.

"Where is God?" Jonah bawled over and over. "Where is God?"

After the soldier nailed Thomas's wrists to the pole, the centurion slapped him on the helmet and yanked the hammer away. Jonah recognized why. The soldier had mistakenly pierced an artery, possibly both.

"Thomas, I'm sorry," Jonah cried as he wiped away tears. He wished he knew a way to save his brother. But he didn't know anything. He was just a kid himself—a kid in a man's body.

Three soldiers lifted the pole with the old man, and Aaron chastised them. "That man is already dead. Why are you putting him up?"

Seeing the man's head and body hanging listlessly, Jonah knew Aaron was right. He knew, too, that his brother wouldn't be far behind. Thomas was bleeding profusely from his back and wrists, and when he wasn't whimpering in pain, his breathing was rapid and shallow.

People going to and from the village passed by on the road next to them. Some stopped to watch. Others refused to turn their heads, walking by as quickly as they could.

When they set Thomas's pole in the ground, Jonah was finally able to look his brother in the eyes. They were no longer the penetrating green eyes he'd grown accustomed to. They were dull now and distant.

Aaron let go of Jonah's arms and held him in a tight embrace from behind.

"This is my fault," Jonah said, his voice quivering. "I let you down."

Thomas's head lifted for a second to meet his brother's gaze, but then dropped again. "Tell Amaryah," he said in a whisper Jonah could barely hear, "to name our child Luke if it's a boy."

"I will," Jonah answered.

Luke. That was their father's name. It had been so long since Jonah had thought of him.

The centurion hung a well-worn sign below Thomas's feet that read simply "Bandit." After some last instructions to the soldiers under his command, he turned and left. As he walked down the hill, a gust of wind caught the flower in his helmet and blew it off. It landed at the base of Thomas's pole in the little puddle of blood forming there.

The four Roman soldiers stood together in a circle off to the side. They talked amongst themselves, snickering and chuckling every now and then. After a while they departed for the shade of a tree a short distance away.

Jonah stared at his brother's gaunt body, ribs protruding. Thomas's breath had become extremely shallow, and Jonah could barely discern the ever-so-slight movement of his abdomen.

Unable to tolerate looking at his brother's gruesome form any longer, Jonah fixed his gaze at the bottom of the pole, noticing the white flower that had been blown there by the wind. It was mostly red now, as blood dripped onto it from above. Suddenly, Jonah recalled a premonition he'd had nearly fifteen years earlier. It had all come true—the white flower sailing through the air, the drops turning it red, and his brother being crucified.

It was after that premonition that he'd fully denied his supposed gift, deciding it was actually a curse. He'd never again searched for the cloud and its mysterious images. He didn't want to know anything about his future and the misfortune and misery awaiting him.

"Is he still breathing?" asked Jonah.

"I don't think so," Aaron answered.

Forcing himself to look at Thomas one last time, Jonah saw he was indeed dead, and that his failure to protect his younger brother was complete.

At first Jonah just stood there. It didn't seem real. Then his sense of betrayal boiled over. Not only had his lifelong appeals to God to protect the Jewish people gone unanswered, his simple, well-meaning prayer to keep his brother safe had been ignored as well.

An urge to run away tingled down his arms and legs. He resisted it at first, but then bolted down the hill.

He had no idea where to run to. He just ran. Coming upon a forested area, he plunged into the thickest part of it, ducking underneath low-hanging branches and around thorny bushes. He ran and ran until his legs nearly gave out from under him; then he buried his face in his hands and wept.

He stayed like that for a long time, pouring his tears out. At last he sat up, drained and lost, and wiped his runny nose along the length of his arm. He recalled growing up with his cousin's family how Zebulun's father never let them forget that each affliction that befell them was a result of someone disobeying the commandments. At every unfortunate event, he'd questioned Jonah and Thomas mercilessly until they'd finally confessed to some recent sin.

Jonah interrogated himself now, trying to find some transgression of the commandments he'd committed that would have resulted in his brother being crucified before his very eyes.

Then he stopped. Squeezing his hands into tight fists, he raised them to the heavens. "God!" he shouted at the top of his lungs. "I'm through with you! You broke the covenant, not me!"

He waited for a response, some kind of sign. If God wanted to punish him—maybe have the earth devour him like He'd done to Korah and his family—then Jonah was ready for it.

"You won't be hearing from me anymore," Jonah continued. "I'm sure you're glad to hear it. One less thorn in your side, yes?"

He slugged the tree in front of him relentlessly until his knuckles were bare and bloody.

"I give up on you!" he declared, his voice fading into hoarseness. "Why don't you drown the world again! Kill us all! This world you created is a failure!"

He glared at the sky, waiting for God to cause the ground to open up and swallow him into oblivion.

But there was nothing. Just a lone white cloud drifting lazily along as though nothing had happened.

Part III

Time Period: 26-27 CE (Thirteen years after Part II)

The violence in Galilee and Judea continued in fits and spurts, and there always seemed to be an incident that threatened to be the spark that would start the fire of a new Jewish uprising. At least two dozen competing Jewish factions each had their own vision of how to effect change. They rarely agreed with one another and often detested each other. Two circumstances united them, though: they were Jews, and as such celebrated the Sabbath; and they were decidedly unhappy with the current state of affairs. The opinion that the Jewish people had been, and still were, on the wrong track would elicit no argument.

Chapter Twenty-One

While she waited in line at the fruit vendor's mostly empty table, Azara scanned the market for any interesting items for sale. Though Capernaum was a small fishing and agricultural community in Galilee, it was also a port city. Perched on the northern end of the Sea of Galilee, it sometimes had rare items on display, like those she used to see a dozen or so years prior in Samarkand and other cities of the Far East when she'd traveled there with her late father.

She saw the old basket-seller, Isaiah, surrounded by his myriad baskets and weaving yet another one. She waved to him and received his precious one-tooth grin in return. Jebediah and his family, who sold sandals, were busy packing up their things, as were most of the vendors still there. Now past noon, many had already gone home for the day. To her immediate right, a middle-aged man and a much younger woman were selling honey. Azara didn't know them and studied the way they interacted with one another, trying to discern if she was his daughter or his wife.

Before she could decide, the fruit vendor called to her from behind. "Yes? Can I help you?"

Azara pointed to the remaining mound of raisins behind the leftover dried figs. The vendor shooed a bee away from his grapes, then placed two handfuls of raisins on the scale. Biting her lower lip as she calculated the price, Azara tried to determine if she had enough money. "A little more," she said.

He added one more small handful, then Azara nodded and handed him a wooden bowl to put them in.

In addition to raisins, she'd already bought some extra bread and a gorgeous bouquet of flowers the vendor told her had come straight from the Garden of Eden. It was the first day of her new school and she wanted it to be special. She anticipated some of the poor would come and planned to reward them with food. The poor rarely had enough to eat, often supplementing their meager diet with tiny sardines from the Sea of Galilee and wild figs foraged from the wilderness.

After filling Azara's bowl, the vendor took her coins for payment, then rummaged through his leather pouch and frowned. "Sorry," he said. "Need to get change." As he strode across the road, he spoke sharply to his big-eared son. The adolescent boy promptly abandoned throwing pebbles at a nearby rooster and rushed over to tend the fruit stand.

Azara returned her attention to the honey sellers to spy on their two new customers who were speaking loudly.

"...but you are quite right, Moshe," one of them announced. "The Jews here are like a fine wine that's been watered down." Though there was no festival and it wasn't the Sabbath, he wore a pristine white prayer shawl covering his head.

Azara groaned. She encountered men like them more often than she preferred—braggarts from Jerusalem who scorned all things Galilean.

The insult struck a nerve with the man filling their order, and he waved his bony fist in the air. "At least we are not under the tyranny of a Roman prefect!"

"What did he say, Shem?" Moshe asked. "Something about Galilee being ruled by that corrupt Gentile, Herod?"

"Yes, I believe so. It's terribly hard to understand them sometimes. It's that vulgar accent."

Inspecting the two more closely, Azara recognized the contrived piety on their bearded faces, as well as the exaggerated fringed borders of their garb. They were Pharisees, devoutly zealous Jews who followed a rigid set of rules and rituals in their day-to-day life.

"What say you, Shem, are there any true Jews in Galilee?"

"Not sure. Not sure," came the reply. "Certainly not in Tiberius or Sepphoris."

"Ugh. Must you mention those abominations?"

Azara held her hand between her breasts at the mention of Tiberius. She had often wished she could sell everything and move back there. Like Sepphoris, it was a magnificent city—diverse, wealthy, respectful of differences. A far cry from the largely Jewish and conservative Capernaum. Azara lived here not by choice, but circumstance. Before her father died, he'd sold his lavish home in Tiberius and bought a modest one in Capernaum, solely because of the port city's location.

The house with all its furnishings had been Azara's sole inheritance, the rest of her father's wealth having been stolen at his death.

The fruit vendor, apparently unsuccessful in his first attempt to get change, was now treading toward Isaiah through his sea of baskets. Azara gave him a look of dismay, hoping it would prompt him to hurry back. She wanted to get away from the two Pharisees from Judea as quickly as possible.

"Shem, do you suppose they have rabbis here?"

"Perhaps, though it's a pity to call them by the same name as our esteemed priests in Jerusalem."

The honey vendor's wife held out the men's change, but Moshe put a cloth over his hand before accepting it. Some Pharisees would not even allow physical contact with those not of their sect.

"Now be on your way back to Judea," the honey vendor called. "Go pay your taxes to Rome!"

The two men took their time gathering their things, then turned away as if nothing had been said to them.

"I wonder, Shem, if they even follow the Torah in these backwaters."

"I suppose they pick and choose which laws they care to follow," came the reply. "Depending on the day, of course."

Not wanting to draw their attention, Azara pulled her headscarf down tight and looked away. Her vendor finally returned and began counting out her change.

"Look here, Moshe," Azara heard from behind her. "A woman out and about without an escort. What sort of depravity is this?"

Azara spun around and scowled, her thin black eyebrows angling down and her eyes flashing. She had no children or male relatives to accompany her when she left her house. All the regulars at the market knew this.

"Thanks be to God," Shem announced emphatically, "you would never see that in Jerusalem."

"Indeed," Moshe said. "Thanks be to God, the Jews in Judea are faithful and diligent about following the commandments."

"Indeed," Azara said sarcastically. "The Jews from Judea are presumptuous and arrogant." She yanked her basket from the vendor's table.

The two men strolled slowly away, hurling one final insult in Azara's direction. "Thanks be to God," Shem announced, "the Jewish women where we live are respectful and virtuous, and know their place."

"Thanks be to God," Azara nearly screamed at their backs, "I am *not* a Jew!" In her hurry to leave, she collided with a man coming from the other direction. Her basket fell from her grasp, bread and flowers tumbling all over the ground.

She cursed bitterly in Sogdian, an old habit from her father. "I'm so sorry," she said, switching back to Aramaic.

He waved his hand dismissively as he knelt down and gathered up her purchases. Fortunately, most of her raisins only spilled from the bowl, but remained within the basket.

Seeing he was Jewish, she felt even more embarrassed by her outburst. "Please," she said, her cheeks flushing, "that's not necessary."

"Of course it is," he replied, continuing to put everything back in her basket.

Azara appreciated his help, as it was often painful for her to bend down. She was thirty-six years old and seemed to have inherited her father's problem hip.

When the young man handed back her basket, the sun suddenly broke free of a cloud and glinted off the Sea of Galilee in front of them. Shielding her eyes against the glare, Azara admired her helper. "The world needs more people like you," she said. "Thank you."

"Someone's got to make up for all the rudeness around here," he replied with a nod toward the men who had aggravated her. He held his hands up to the sky, whispered something inaudible, then shared a smile with his eyes as he departed.

Azara stood still, absorbing the feeling of gratitude flowing from the middle of her chest. In just a matter of seconds, she had experienced both the worst and best in man. It made her think of her old tutor, Farrukh, and the Zoroastrian creation story he'd told her. In it, two forces—one of light and goodness, and one of darkness and ignorance—existed independently of one another for all time. And it was only in this world, where humans abided, that these two forces existed side by side. The human realm was one where love, truth, and knowledge were forever trapped alongside hate, lies, and ignorance. A place half peaceful and half violent; half paradise and half hell.

Azara believed it her mission to strengthen the side of righteousness, to help spread truth and knowledge. But it was an upward battle and her victories few and far between. The thought of her school sent her heart racing with hope and joy, but fear was never far behind. After all, she'd never seen nor heard of a school like hers before—one for girls only.

She quickened her pace on the way home to make up for the longer-than-expected time at the market. Her house was not as tightly clustered as most in Capernaum. She even had a stone wall that separated it from the road and enclosed a narrow L-shaped courtyard with a pomegranate tree and tiny garden. A short distance before her house, at the top of the slight hill, she could see her front door if she stood on her tiptoes. She exhaled in relief at seeing no girls or their parents waiting for her.

Once inside, she arranged the flowers in a vase and set it at the front of her improvised classroom, which used to be her living room. Four knee-high tables were arranged in two rows to use as desks. They were rectangular and long, and three girls could sit at each one. The desks had not been cheap, and she'd had to take out a small loan for the carpenter to build them.

Originally, she'd planned on holding her classes at the local synagogue. That was where the boys were schooled. It was also used for communal meals, political meetings, as a court, a hostel, a place to collect and distribute charity, and, of course, as a place of worship on the Sabbath. Azara thought it the perfect place for her school, but the village elders had laughed at her audacious request, leaving her little alternative to hosting it in her home.

Spreading out several small wax tablets on the front desk, Azara felt pleased the girls would have at least one thing the boys wouldn't. The rare writing implements could be reused, and Azara planned on having the girls practice their writing and arithmetic on them.

After setting out the bowl of raisins, she scrutinized the room one last time. She had parchment for writing, scrolls of the Torah, scrolls of the alphabet, even cups and a jug of water in case anyone got thirsty. She was as ready as she'd ever be. There was nothing left to do but wait.

She began to pace, from the front door to the far wall of her classroom, twelve steps there and twelve steps back. An anxious voice in her head began yet again to question all her plans: *You have no experience in teaching. You'll probably be horrible at it. Girls have been raised with low expectations for their intellect. Some of them will likely be completely illiterate. They won't even want to learn.*

Though she tried not to be bitter about the educational disparity between girls and boys, it wasn't easy. Education for boys was compulsory, and their classes started at the age of five. They began by learning the Hebrew alphabet, then moved on to reading, writing, and some basic arithmetic. When they were ready, they would study the book of Leviticus and all the customs and laws it contained. By age ten they were studying the oral traditions of the Torah, memorizing long passages and key points.

The education of girls, on the other hand, was left entirely to the parents. Azara considered this a tragedy as it was, more often than not, neglected.

To restore her faith, she retrieved the letter from Farrukh and read it for the hundredth time.

> *My Dear Azara,*
>
> *I regret to inform you that I am not long for this world. I lie on my bed knowing I shall never rise from it. I have been blessed to walk this earth for over eighty years. And though I am no Moses— who parted the Red Sea at my age—I have no complaints. I have lived much longer than most, and am weary of seeing all whom I love pass before me.*

I received the letter you sent with your father's old acquaintance, and your anxiety about telling me your plans for a school were unfounded. Time has taught me the error of my ways. You are right to teach girls. Education is the only means by which society can be freed from the chains of ignorance. You have my blessing in your endeavor. Please accept these wax tablets as a gift for your new school.

Azara, you are a bright star. Don't let anyone dim your light. The world desperately needs it.

With love, Farrukh

Azara held the letter to her heart. It was her firm belief that the world would never know peace or harmony until an abundance of educated women came into positions of authority and power. That this would never happen in her lifetime, or in the foreseeable future, was a forgone conclusion. Her only intention was to plant the seed and hope it would take root, sprout, and one day far in the future grow into a towering, vigorous tree that provided shade and safety for all. She could help educate girls, and show them an enormous, enchanting world lay beyond their tidy, compliant village. Hopefully they would see the importance of education and pass it on to their daughters.

She replaced the letter, then arranged the flowers once more, trying to get them to face every direction. They were wildflowers, a mix of small red, white, pink, and purple flowers that she often saw when she ventured into the countryside. Next she revisited her lesson plan. For the first day, she planned on evaluating each girl's existing level of reading and writing. The older ones would have their mathematics assessed as well. She would tell a story each day and planned on starting with one about Alexander the Great and his conquests.

The boys' classes in the synagogue offered no secular subjects in the curriculum—no history, no philosophy, no study of other cultures or religions. The purpose of their schooling was strictly moral and religious indoctrination. Azara thought that short-sighted, and had told the teachers precisely that on numerous occasions. As was usually the case, her advice had not been received gratefully.

Peeking out the window again in the hope of seeing someone approaching, she sighed to behold only a scrawny hen and her week-old chicks pecking at the ground outside the door.

Knowing the girls would be tasked with chores in the morning, Azara had decided on the afternoon as an ideal starting time. She had also carefully selected this time of the year to open her school. The grain harvest of spring was over, and the only crops currently being harvested were chickpeas and grapes. Azara hoped that would allow the girls enough free time to attend school for a few hours a day, just like the boys.

She began pacing again, trying to reassure herself that everyone was simply running late. Nearly every mother she'd spoken to about her school had liked the idea. Only a few had declined outright. Some said their husbands saw no point in a girl receiving an education, while some of the Jewish mothers said their husbands were not opposed to the idea, but couldn't tolerate it being done by a Gentile.

A breeze suddenly gusted through the window of her house, carrying with it the glorious sound of children's laughter. Azara rushed to the front door and flung it open. She saw her friend with her two daughters coming around the corner of the stone wall.

"Hadassah!" Azara practically shouted.

"Helloooo..." she called out in response. Waving her arm in the air, her numerous gold and silver bracelets jangled against one another. "Sorry we're late." Her two daughters, wearing fashionable lavender-colored robes with fine embroidering, bounded up to the front door. One of them peeked inside at the classroom, while the other ventured toward the baby chicks.

"You're not late," said Azara. "I'm so happy you came!" She was doubly pleased by her friend's arrival, because Hadassah and her daughters were Jewish. Azara had been worried she might only get Gentile families to come.

"Come on, Father," Hadassah chided the old man with a cane lagging behind. He was badly hunched over and made no effort to speed up. Hadassah gave Azara a quick one-armed embrace and then glanced around. "Are we the first ones?"

Azara nodded.

"Well, I stopped by and convinced your new neighbor to bring her daughter," said Hadassah. "She should be here any minute."

"Salome? How lovely," Azara replied. "She only lives a few houses away, but I rarely see her."

"Yes, her husband works construction. You know how they are. He's rarely ever home. Plus, they're rather conservative so she can't get out much."

Azara brought out a chair for Hadassah's elderly father. He sat in it without a word and stared at the space between his feet. Then Azara and Hadassah followed the two girls, who were doing their best to get as close as possible to the baby chicks. Azara was fond of Hadassah's daughters, particularly the younger one, who asked endless questions. She watched her now as her tiny body crouched like a cat moving in on its prey.

"I thought you'd hired a tutor for your daughters," remarked Azara.

"I did," Hadassah said, "but when you told me about your school, I got rid of him. I never liked his narrow views anyway."

Azara smiled.

The two girls had managed to corner some of the baby chicks, who were peeping and hopping and searching for a way out. The younger daughter was low to the ground, holding her arms wide to prevent any escape.

"Careful not to scare them," Azara called out.

"You know," Hadassah said. "I was thinking that if we really want to get more parents to bring their daughters, we'll have to come up with more incentive than simply a free education."

Azara was surprised by her use of the word "we."

"You have to understand their situation," continued Hadassah. "If their daughters stay home, they can put them to work planting, weeding, or cultivating their pathetic little plots of land. They don't contribute much, because they're featherbrained kids, but every little bit helps, I suppose. So what if we paid them for coming to school? Then their parents would view it differently, yes?"

Azara tilted her head to one side and looked at Hadassah. "I suppose." Like the male teachers in the synagogue who made their living through their vocations as carpenters, farmers, blacksmiths, and fishermen, Azara was also teaching solely as a public service. Unlike the men, she did not expect to receive any nominal payments from the parents. Her only desire was that some girls would show up and take an interest in their education.

"Not much, you know," Hadassah added. "Just a trifling amount. You know how poor they are."

"It's a wonderful idea, but I certainly can't do it," Azara said. "My income is quite limited."

Though Azara was secure in owning the land, house, and some opulent furniture her father had imported, her monthly income was meager. It came entirely from her little shop selling herbs, minerals, perfumes, and ointments.

The younger daughter lunged toward the chicks, just managing to grasp one of them in her tiny hands.

"You misunderstand me, Azara. My *husband* will give you the money."

Unsure of how to react, Azara withheld a response until she could determine if Hadassah was serious.

"Don't get me wrong," Hadassah said, laughing. "He doesn't know he'll do it. I manage the finances of our household." She shook her arm to bring her bracelets back down to her wrist. "Of course, I may need to buy a little less perfume from your shop to make it work...."

Azara felt her eyes begin to water. She was speechless.

Hadassah put her arm around her. "My darling," she said, "if we women don't help one another out, who will?"

Azara nodded in agreement as she wiped her eyes with the back of her hand. Whichever perfume Hadassah had on, she smelled like an angel.

"We must keep this our little secret, though," added Hadassah. "Don't go around bringing unnecessary attention to the school."

The sound of additional children's voices brought the two of them back to the front door. They arrived just in time to see Salome with her daughter, followed by three Gentile girls and their parents.

"Welcome! Welcome!" Azara called to them. "You're just in time!" She went into the house to retrieve the bread she'd bought. Before she picked up the basket, she did a quick scan to make sure no one could see her. Then she twirled in place, flinging her arms above her head in celebration.

After she offered everyone bread and made sure they knew one another, Azara asked the parents to either wait in the courtyard or come back in a few hours. She was eager to begin her first class.

She led the girls into the classroom, then let them choose their seats while she stood at the front trying in vain to be calm.

"Now before we begin," Azara said, her voice nearly breaking, "does anyone have any questions?"

Hadassah's youngest daughter raised her hand, and Azara called on her.

"Why are there so many different languages in the world?"

Azara couldn't help but laugh. She had expected questions along the lines of how long the class would be or whether they would get raisins every time. She beamed as she surveyed the classroom and the six girls sitting at the brand new desks. "Good question," she said. "Let's answer it using logic—"

"What's logic?" the girl interrupted.

Azara thought fondly of Farrukh, then gave her best imitation of him. "Logic is a way of thinking. It's concerned with what is true and how we can *know* whether something is true."

Before she could finish her explanation, another two hands shot in the air. Azara couldn't stop smiling.

Chapter Twenty-Two

"Centurion," Pontius Pilate called out to Vitus, "please." He motioned to an ornate wooden chair opposite him.

Vitus studied the garish chair with its elaborately carved back and armrests, concluding it had been built more for pageantry than for comfort. Though he felt certain it would hurt his back, he decided to sit anyway. It was the first time he was meeting the newly appointed Roman Prefect of Judea and he didn't want to risk offending him. He'd heard that Pilate had rather firm convictions about many things.

Vitus, dressed in full uniform for the occasion, removed his helmet, set it on the floor next to the chair, and sat down gingerly. An unsmiling adolescent boy dutifully stepped forward and began to fill two bronze mugs with red wine. As the boy poured, Vitus stole a look at his new commanding officer. Pilate wore immaculate white robes. He had short cropped hair and a receding hairline that gave prominence to deep creases in between his eyebrows. His light skin probably burned easily in the sun, and he seemed short, but since he was seated, Vitus couldn't be sure. Pilate's thronelike chair was set atop a tiger-skin rug, the fearsome cat's jaws open, fangs bared.

The servant finished pouring the wine, then wiped away any drops on the cups or the table.

"You'll enjoy this," Pilate said in a nasal voice. "I had it brought from Rome— not that swill they drink here."

They were in an open area inside the Antonia Fortress, near the largest of its four towers. A light breeze wafted through the large archway to their right and down the long colonnade behind them. The sun was just beginning to set. Through the archway Vitus could see rose-hued clouds float by.

After Pilate lifted his mug, Vitus raised his own. "To your success in Judea," Vitus toasted, then gulped down half the wine.

Pilate waited for him to finish.

"Delicious," Vitus pronounced, lowering his mug to the table. The wine was sweet to his tongue, but he noticed it left an unusual, bitter aftertaste.

Pilate nodded, but did not smile. He took a drink himself, keeping his eyes on Vitus all the while. When he finished, he blotted the corners of his mouth with a napkin. "How was your trip?"

Vitus had anticipated that question, but still wasn't sure how to answer it. Before turning fifty later that year, he'd decided to visit his childhood village north of Rome. He'd hoped to see his old house, family, and friends, but the trip had been a disappointment. He'd been away for over three decades—far too long, he came to realize—to expect any kind of homecoming. When he'd arrived at his old village, he didn't know anyone, nor did anyone know him. Unable to find any of the family, relatives, or friends he'd left behind, he'd searched for the house he'd been born in. But time had washed that away too. It had burned to the ground, the charred remains still jutting out like the bones of a skeleton in an abandoned grave.

Glancing at Pilate, Vitus guessed he wasn't interested in a lengthy, genuine answer. "It was splendid," he replied.

"I assume you spent some time in Rome," Pilate said. "You were gone for quite a while...."

Vitus nodded. He'd been away for nearly eight months. When he left, Valerius Gratus had still been the Prefect, and now Pilate had already been in the position for many months.

"Rome has changed a lot since I was there last," said Vitus, wondering if he should share any of his observations. "My trip ended up being much longer than I'd planned. I broke my leg at the Colosseum. It took a while to heal."

Pilate arched his eyebrows. "In the Colosseum?"

"Yes, sir. I was in the stands watching the gladiators when I got pushed from behind. Fell down a number of stairs."

"Sorry to hear that," Pilate said. "The crowds can be rather rough there, I know." He sipped some more wine, then turned in his chair toward Vitus. "I'm certainly pleased to have you back," he announced. "Everyone speaks quite highly of you."

"Thank you, sir."

Although it was summer, the day had been only lukewarm. The breeze, noticeably cooling as the sun set, picked up, and Vitus pulled his cloak around his shoulders. He remembered how when he was younger, he never used to get cold. Even in the winter when Jerusalem would have a rare snowfall, the temperature hadn't bothered him.

"Is it true you're proficient in the barbarian's language?" asked Pilate.

"The language of the Jews, sir? Aramaic?"

"Yes. Is that what they call it?"

"I'm no native speaker," Vitus replied, "but, yes I can speak Aramaic." As he chugged down the other half of his wine, he heard a pigeon cooing from somewhere above them.

Pilate clinked the top of his mug with one of the several gold rings on his fingers. The servant, who'd been standing at a distance, glided over and refilled both mugs.

"I don't know what possessed you to learn it. It is they who should be learning Greek, not us learning their language and customs. These dolts," he said with a dismissive wave of his hand, "are so stubborn."

As the longest-serving centurion in all of Judea, Vitus felt it his responsibility to educate Romans who were new to the land. His advice and counsel on Jewish customs and beliefs had oftentimes been sought by the former prefect, and Vitus fell easily into that role once more. "Many of them are actually quite learned, sir," he said.

Pilate raised his mug to his lips, eying Vitus suspiciously over the rim of it as he drank.

"The boys learn to read and write in the synagogue," Vitus continued, "so—"

"Yes, but they cling to their antiquated beliefs, don't they?" Pilate interrupted. "They refuse to work on the Sabbath. They refuse to eat pork. And they do this barbaric thing to the penises of their baby boys."

Vitus took a deep breath in preparation to explain. He'd found that the three things Pilate had mentioned were the most difficult for Romans to understand.

"Circumcision is—"

"And why is there no image of their god in their temples?" Pilate again interrupted. "These people make no sense to me."

Listening to his gut instinct, Vitus kept his mouth shut. He felt rather hopeless that, while he'd come to appreciate differences, he rarely saw the same desire in others. Having lived through four Roman prefects of Judea, Vitus wondered which group Pilate would end up in—the first three, who had served for only three years each, or the last one, who had served for eleven. If the rumors he'd heard since arriving were true, Pilate was certainly off to a rocky start.

"I agree, sir," Vitus said flatly. "It's difficult to understand the depth of the Jews' allegiance to their ancient teachings."

"Anyway," Pilate said, "I'm glad you can speak their language. I suspect I'm going to require your services on a regular basis."

Vitus felt relieved to hear these words. He knew that Pilate had dismissed many of his predecessor's advisors. His goal was to come into a position of trust with the new prefect, like the high priest Caiaphas already had.

"Any assistance I can provide will be my pleasure," said Vitus.

"Excellent. I'm glad to hear that. Rome has already warned me this place is seething with radicals and heretics, and that any uprising whatsoever would be quite detrimental to my record. Not to mention my family's position." Pilate leaned toward Vitus, stretching his head close. "I will not allow *anything* to get out of hand. Do you follow?"

Vitus returned his gaze and nodded.

"In fact," Pilate continued. "I intend to stamp out the smallest of fires before they even have a chance to do any damage."

Vitus agreed. That was usually a good policy in Judea, but one did have to be careful in carrying it out. He'd seen too many times the disastrous results of offending or antagonizing the Jews.

Pilate turned to the servant, who stood like a statue behind them. "Bring us some bread," he ordered.

They sat in uncomfortable silence until the boy returned a moment later with a small basket. Pilate selected a piece of bread from it and began scraping off any blackened or burnt spots.

"Is this where you stay?" asked Pilate. "Here in the Antonia Fortress?"

"Yes, sir," Vitus answered. "I spend a lot of time traveling, though, because of my duties."

After taking a bite of his bread, Pilate spit it out and threw the rest back in the basket.

"In Caesarea," he muttered, "I've already got them trained how to make bread properly. They're still clueless here in Jerusalem."

Vitus had long since gotten used to the way they made bread and rather liked it. "What brings you to Jerusalem?" he asked.

"The usual," Pilate sneered. "Problems." Tipping his mug a little too high, wine streamed down his cheeks. He cursed under his breath and snatched the napkin from the table. "Seems all I ever do is deal with problems when I come here. And they're all on the other side of that wall."

Vitus understood what Pilate meant. The Antonia Fortress bordered the walls of the Temple.

"I'm getting rather tired of it," added Pilate. "I think I need to put my foot down, strike a bit of fear into them. Make sure these priests and Sadducees understand who's in charge."

A Roman soldier with freshly polished armor and helmet respectfully in hand entered the area through the archway. A gust of wind lifted his crimson cloak as he marched up to Pilate.

"What is it?" Pilate asked irritably.

"We've brought the man you requested."

"Did he resist arrest?"

"Not in the least, sir. We told him to come with us, and he did. What shall we do with him?"

Pilate paused, then looked sideways at Vitus. "Bring him here."

Two more soldiers, each carrying a javelin, escorted in a young man. He wore a white tunic, dusty but in good condition, had a rope for a belt around his waist, and a white kerchief covering most of his thick, black hair. He didn't appear particularly dangerous to Vitus, quite the opposite actually. He was of slight build and somewhere in his twenties. His hands were tied before him, and he began to giggle for some reason.

"What are you laughing about?" demanded Pilate.

The man inhaled deeply and stopped snickering, but his eyes retained a distant, maniacal quality. "Why have you arrested this man?" he asked.

Pilate turned to Vitus. "What did he say?"

Vitus was momentarily confused. First, by the man referring to himself in the third person. Second, by Pilate not understanding what was said, since the man had spoken in Greek—heavily accented Greek, but Greek nonetheless.

"He wants to know why he was arrested," Vitus answered.

Pilate raised his chin. "You are here to answer questions," he said, "not ask them. Tell us what you were speaking to the crowd about."

"About Master's teachings," he answered. "Preaching to them about God."

The man continued to speak in Greek, and Vitus repeated his words for Pilate.

"Which god?" asked Pilate.

"There is but one true God," the man replied. He wore a silly grin on his face, and Vitus wondered if he was drunk.

Pilate ignored the man's response and turned to Vitus. "This quaint god they worship, what do they call him?"

"Yahweh."

"He seems rather pathetic; don't you think?" Pilate said to Vitus. "If he had any power, they'd be a free people." Pilate took another sip of wine, then held his chin up even higher than before. "Who would you wager on in a fight? Mars? Or this Yahweh?"

Vitus wasn't sure whom he was speaking to. "Are you asking—"

"Speak up," Pilate commanded the man. "I asked you a question."

"Juno," the man replied, smirking.

Vitus thought him mad. Juno was the wife of Jupiter, king of the Roman gods.

Pilate seemed not to have heard his answer, or else paid it no attention. "These people confound me." He crossed both his arms and his legs and leaned forward, looking slightly effeminate. "Rome is the mightiest empire in the world thanks to its gods. Mars in particular. And what of this god they worship?" He regarded the man with a haughty stare. "You are a backwards people with no knowledge of engineering or warfare. A conquered people! Your god is nothing."

Pilate relaxed back into his chair, a sly smile on his lips.

Vitus, sadly accustomed to displays of contempt, was unimpressed. As he tilted his head back to get the last few drops of his wine, he saw the pigeon he'd heard earlier. It was roosting on a crossbeam high above them.

When there was no reply, Pilate became impatient. "Why isn't he answering?" he asked, turning to Vitus. "Did he not understand me?"

Vitus asked the man in Aramaic if he understood what Pilate had said. The man nodded his head.

"He understands, sir."

"So why doesn't he defend his god? I just said he was nothing."

Vitus began to repeat the question in Aramaic, but the man interrupted him by answering Pilate directly.

"Because He asks for silence in response to that," he said in Greek.

"Did he say his god asks him not to reply?" Pilate asked Vitus.

"Yes, sir."

Vitus was intrigued by the man's response. Pilate less so.

"And what *precisely* does this god of yours ask of you?" Pilate asked. "To slaughter a bird or a sheep for him at the Temple?"

Pilate had said it with more than a hint of condescension, and the man's demeanor changed abruptly to one of seriousness. Puckering his lips, the young man lifted his bound hands so he could point to himself. "The comprehension contained within this form is very limited and prone to error," he answered.

Vitus found his curiosity further aroused, certain it wasn't strictly due to the intoxicating effects of the wine. "Understood," he announced. "Despite that, tell us what you *do* comprehend."

"Master teaches that God desires only our growth and learning," the man said. "God loves us no matter what we say, what we do, or what we don't say, or don't do. God does not defend nor does He attack. Seek ye to emulate this."

"You see what I mean, Centurion?" Pilate said after a prolonged sigh. "I can't understand these people."

Unclear on whether Pilate meant it literally, figuratively, or both, Vitus began to repeat the man's answer in Greek.

Pilate cut him off. "Get this lunatic out of my sight," he ordered the soldiers.

The man bowed cordially, a strangely serene smile on his face, then turned and began to leave the area of his own accord. The soldiers ran a few steps to catch up with him, taking him by the arms the rest of the way.

Once they were gone, Pilate tilted toward Vitus and said in a low voice, "I'm going to keep him under arrest until I can figure out what he's all about. I'd like you to speak with him and tell me what you think."

Vitus pulled back from Pilate's foul-smelling breath before answering. "Certainly, sir. What are the charges?"

Pilate stared blankly until Vitus rephrased the question. "What was he arrested for?"

"He was preaching to others outside the Temple," replied Pilate. "Quite a large crowd had gathered. Caiaphas told me he had some rather alarming ideas, so I told my men to take him into custody."

Pilate picked up his mug, frowned at the inside of it, then set it back down. "I'd like to know what his views are; what he was preaching," he added. "But I don't speak their sordid language and I can't understand his garbled Greek, so I want you to interview him."

"Will do, sir," Vitus answered routinely. If there was one thing that had served him well in his career, it was making sure his superiors were pleased with him.

"Report back in two days," said Pilate, standing up. "Mornings are best."

Vitus carefully bent and retrieved his helmet from the floor, then stood at attention. He saw that Pilate was even shorter than he'd imagined. As the prefect walked away, the pigeon fluttered off the crossbeam above, simultaneously defecating as it flew out the archway. Vitus watched the feces fall onto the back of Pilate's head.

He waited for Pilate's reaction, but there was none.

"I'm eager to set an example," Pilate called over his shoulder before disappearing from view. "So hopefully he's a good candidate for crucifixion."

Of all the responses Vitus imagined a man might have to being shit on—from anger to grief to laughter—the one he couldn't fathom was no response at all.

His stomach complaining about the wine, Vitus departed for the latrines. Nothing from Rome sat well with him anymore.

Chapter Twenty-Three

"There is no end to this," the black beast hissed to Jonah. The fat swinelike fiend was sitting atop Jonah's chest, slowly suffocating him.

With his whole body in a state of paralysis, Jonah longed to cry, but no tears would come. He didn't try to argue with it, for he knew it was right. There didn't seem to be an end to his misery, and though he was somehow awake within his dream—completely conscious of all that was happening—he could neither wake himself nor fight the beast off. He was completely at its mercy.

"You asked for this," the beast growled, bearing all its weight down. "And you cannot escape it."

Jonah wished for someone or something to awaken him, because he couldn't do it himself. He knew Amaryah lay next to him and Luke just down the hall, but it didn't matter. Jonah was alone.

He'd been that way for a long time.

His nightly torture finally ended, the way it always did, with his heart insisting that it could not continue to beat without air. He awoke with a gasping inhale, then lay there several minutes catching his breath.

He gazed at Amaryah's shapely figure illuminated by the moonlight falling through the window. Even after thirteen years, he still couldn't think of her as his wife. She would always be Thomas's wife, just as Luke would always be Thomas's son.

Quiet as a stillborn, he crept from the bed and sneaked down the hall to retrieve his cloak against the cool morning air. Running his fingers along the wall, he decided he'd miss the house most of all—the intricate designs of its mosaic floor, the smooth, even walls, and the comfortable pine chair he sat in to tell Luke stories before bed. Jonah had done much of the work on the house himself, spending countless hours in absent-minded labor, consumed by grief over the miscarriages he and Amaryah had endured over the years.

Passing by Luke's bedroom, he peeked his head in and tried to feel sad about seeing him for the last time. But, as usual, no feelings came. He didn't seem capable of emotions anymore.

Opening the front door painstakingly slowly so it wouldn't squeak, he left the house and headed to the nearby cliff.

With each step, he felt as if he was leaving a part of himself behind: Jonah the carefree child; Jonah the orphan; Jonah the angry teenager; Jonah the bandit; Jonah the family man; Jonah the thirty-three-year-old apprentice; Jonah the respected physician; Jonah the admired elder of the community of Magdala; Jonah the failure....

After a twenty-minute walk, he pulled on the branch of a wild fig tree to help him clamber up the last few steps to his destination. The sun had only begun to shine its burdensome light over the far horizon. He'd been venturing to the cliff more and more over the past few years. At first, he'd merely liked to sit in stillness, doing nothing more than breathing and feeling the breeze on his skin. But in the last few months it had become an escape for him. He longed each day for the mental quietude he could only find sitting there at the cliff. And lately his yearning had deepened even further, to an unbearable level. Now, more than anything, he longed for the eternal quiet of death.

Though it had mostly been a long, listless descent into despair, Amaryah's latest miscarriage—her fourth—was the event that pushed him to consider taking his own life. With Luke nearly a man himself now and in no need of bedtime stories or learning how to tie his sandals, what point was there to it anymore?

Marching along his well-trodden path to the edge of the cliff, he peered down at the pointed rocks thirty feet below and contemplated how nobody had known him when he entered the world. Nobody had expected him. The world had been going about its usual routine. Fighting wars. Making money. Losing money. People falling in love, falling into prison, falling into power, falling into fathomless holes they couldn't climb out of.

All this had been happening before he arrived in the world, and his birth had no effect on any of it. Everything had continued as before, forcing Jonah to conclude his life was so insignificant that the world would continue just the same after he died too.

He'd been a fool when he was a part of the bandits, thinking he could change things in some way. All he'd done was add to the hatred and violence of the world. It had been a mistake.

My whole life has been a mistake, he thought. *All forty-four years.*

Inching closer to the edge of the cliff, he watched as a few loose stones tumbled over. When they hit the sharp rocks below, some of them bounced off while others split in two. Jonah knew which one his body would be like. It wouldn't be bouncing.

He took in the placid Sea of Galilee spread out before him, wanting its dispassionate ripples to be the last thing he ever saw.

Squeezing his eyes shut, memories of his deceased parents and brother assailed him. He nearly lost his balance, coming close to prematurely plummeting to his death. He thought that would be fitting, an accidental death to complete an accidental life.

Taking one final inhale, he bent at the knees in preparation to jump.

"Jonah?" a voice called from behind him.

He didn't want to turn back. It was Amaryah's voice.

"Jonah, what are you doing?" she asked sincerely.

Last chance, he told himself. But it was too late. He couldn't do it in front of her.

Straining to find her among the shadows, he began to suspect a ghost until he spotted a nebulous form moving toward him. She had her tan cloak wrapped tightly around her shoulders, blending in perfectly with the cliff walls. When she emerged from the darkness, the sun's amber rays settled on her face.

Jonah switched his gaze to ground, calculating the distance between them. He'd told her the previous evening that if he wasn't there when she awoke, he'd be at the synagogue praying.

She moved close and stretched her arm out, taking him by the elbow and pulling him back from the edge. Then she tried to lift his face to hers.

Jonah felt her small childlike hand against the stubble under his chin. Ever since he quit the bandits, he'd refused to grow a beard.

"Look at me," she whispered.

Jonah would not. Having been caught in a lie, he couldn't bear to look her in the eyes.

A white dove landed on the fig tree—its gentle cooing filling the silence.

Amaryah stroked the hair on Jonah's head. "You can't go on like this," she said softly.

"Like what?" he asked, keeping his eyes on the dirt below his feet.

"Going against God."

Jonah felt every inch of his face begin to burn, all his buried indignation promptly clawing its way out of the tomb he'd stuffed it into.

"Forgive me," Amaryah added quickly. "I can see my words missed the mark. I only want you to see the truth."

Jonah glowered at her. "The truth?" he said incredulously. "I'll tell you the truth. There is no justice in this world. There is no freedom. There is no fairness. Our lives mean nothing, because there is no God! That's the truth!"

He waited for her horrified reaction at the blasphemy he'd just uttered. Years ago he'd seen a young man stoned to death for exclaiming those very words denying God's existence.

Amaryah had no shock on her face, though, only water filling her eyes.

"Did you hear me?" Jonah shouted. "Did you hear what I said?"

She nodded, her expression blank, tears trickling down. "Were you expecting me to be surprised?" she asked. "It might as well be written on your forehead that you don't believe in God. You can't hide it."

Astonished she knew his deepest secret, Jonah felt his knees give from under him. Collapsing to the ground, his body began convulsing in violent sobs.

Amaryah knelt and spread her warm body over his. When his weeping began to recede, she spoke again. "It doesn't matter what you believe about God. You're still a good man, Jonah. Why can't you see that?"

While Jonah admitted most people said that about him, he alone knew the truth. He alone knew all the malicious thoughts, the faithlessness, the violence and dark secrets of his past.

Amaryah squeezed her arms around him. "I'm not going to quote any scripture about what you should or shouldn't do. I'll just tell you the way I see it," she said. "I see you clinging to your sorrow and your resentment like an old man to his cane. He can't walk without his cane, and you can't seem to live without your bitterness. You rehash all these painful memories to justify your 'specialness,' your uniquely unbearable life."

She paused and massaged his scalp with her fingertips. An intermittent wind carried the scent of the sea. On the wild fig tree behind them, another dove landed, answering the call of the first one.

"But Jonah," she said, her voice pleading, "*everybody* suffers. There is no one for whom death, sickness, and sorrow has not visited."

Jonah wasn't sure he believed her, but he let every word in nonetheless.

"This has to end," she continued. "You can't keep living as if you're already dead. In death, there is no change, no growth. All remains as it was and shall be forevermore. But you're not dead yet."

He sat up and faced her, his tear-stained face a few inches from hers. He knew, undeniably, in that moment, she truly cared about him.

"Please, Jonah, stop pretending," she implored. "Stop pretending that you're strong enough to carry all this, that you've gotten over the past. You haven't, and you never will. It's part of who you are. You carry this heavy burden on your shoulders and you think no one else sees it, that no one knows your daily struggle not to fling yourself off this cliff."

Again she knew one of his deepest secrets.

"I am no prophet and I am no priest," she said, "but I know untruth when I see it. And the way you live your life now is full of untruth, Jonah. There is a poison within you, in your heart."

Jonah focused on the Sea of Galilee and the reflecting stream of sunlight that extended in his direction from the far shore.

Amaryah took his calloused, trembling hands in hers. "Jonah, Luke has already lost one father. I don't want him to lose another. He's not a child anymore, but he still needs you to be there for him, to teach him the things he needs to succeed in life."

Jonah found himself nodding in agreement with her words.

"Get this poison out of you," she said. "Don't see any patients. Stop working. Leave if you have to. Do whatever it takes so you can be the father Luke needs you to be. I beg you, please, don't turn your back on him."

"But there's nowhere to go," Jonah protested. "I don't know what to—"

Amaryah spoke over him. "Our neighbor Tiras said he's going to Jerusalem for Sukkot in a few months. Take Luke and go with him. Make a pilgrimage to the Temple for Sukkot, and commemorate Luke's bar mitzvah."

It was a long trip to Jerusalem and one that Jonah didn't enjoy, but he agreed with her idea. At a minimum, he had to get away from this cliff. He didn't know how much longer he could resist its call.

Chapter Twenty-Four

The stench increased tenfold after the heavy door creaked open. Resisting the urge to pinch his nostrils, Vitus stepped into the dark prison cell and remained still for a moment to let his eyes adjust. In the corner he could just make out the outline of a man sitting cross-legged on the floor, his body rocking gently back and forth.

"Where's the candle?" Vitus asked the guard standing in the hallway.

"Sorry, sir. We're out."

"Damn it to Pluto!" Vitus cussed. He didn't want to come in the first place, and it was asking too much to shut himself up in a tiny cell filled with a torch's eye-watering smoke. If not for Pilate's directive to make a report the next morning, Vitus would've left. Instead, he grudgingly ventured inside. "Bring me a fresh torch," he growled. He thought about seizing the one the guard was carrying, but it was nearly at the end of its life.

Vitus hated going down into the prison; despised the reek of moldy straw, urine, and feces. His preference was to conduct interrogations in the courtyard above, but Pilate's directive forbade this prisoner from ever leaving his cell.

The guard returned with a freshly wrapped torch, and Vitus recoiled against its brightness. Holding it at arm's length, he scanned the walls of the narrow cell, searching for the holder to affix it to. The prisoner remained sitting in the corner, eyes closed, a slight smile on his lips, seemingly oblivious that anyone had entered his cell. The stone floor had hardly any straw, as if someone had started to replace it, but had abandoned the job halfway through. In the corner opposite the prisoner was a pile of shriveled, lifeless ants—their blood long ago sucked out of them by a spider.

After Vitus affixed the torch to the wall, the guard left, latching the door with a loud clink behind him.

Vitus pressed his hands into his lower back, noting with disdain how sore it was. It was the end of the day, and he wanted to finish the interrogation as quickly as possible so he could go to the baths and get a massage. All he had to do was figure out which category the prisoner belonged in: bandit, heretic, radical, or falsely accused. He only hoped it wasn't the last category, for, although rare, they proved to take the most time and effort.

Vitus first sized up the prisoner, noting with envy his thick, dark hair that hung nearly to his shoulders. A full head of hair wasn't a matter of vanity for

Vitus, but practicality. Being bald, he got cold easily when the temperature dropped, and in the summer, sweat rolled down from the top of his head into his eyes.

The prisoner's white tunic was noticeably dirtier than the day before, but what struck Vitus the most about him was his youth. His recollection was of a man much older, and before the torch was brought in, he'd gotten that same sense—that he was about to speak to an elder.

Before Vitus could address him, the man opened his eyes and blurted, "You look familiar." His voice was soft, so Vitus moved in to hear better.

"Ah, remembrance," the man said, sounding pleased. "You were with the king yesterday, yes? You had all your armor on then, though."

Vitus thought it odd to hear a Jew refer to Pilate as a king, but remembered from their first meeting that the man seemed a bit peculiar. "Yes," he replied. "I was with the prefect when they brought you in."

"Have you come to release this one? He has done nothing wrong."

At first Vitus glanced around the cell, searching for a second prisoner, then he recalled how the man referred to himself in the third person for some reason. "No," Vitus answered. "I don't have that authority. I just came to speak with you."

Upon hearing the response, the man began to moan and shake his head from side to side as he pulled on his beard. "Recognition," he pronounced solemnly. Then his demeanor changed suddenly, and with a genial grin and cheerful tone he said, "Very well then. With whom does this one have the honor of speaking?"

Vitus had never given his name when doing an interrogation and realized this was the first time he'd been asked. "My name is not important," he said.

"Nonsense. Your name defines who you are. It is *quite* important."

Vitus hadn't really meant what he'd said and felt annoyed the prisoner hadn't understood the conventions of the situation. He'd only been trying to set the stage for the interrogation. He wanted to make it clear he was there as a tool for the Roman command, to ask questions and gather information. He was not there to engage in a friendly chat.

To combat the foul odors, Vitus tried breathing through his mouth instead of his nose. It didn't help.

"State your birth name and the place of your birth," Vitus demanded in his well-practiced voice of authority.

The man opened his mouth as if to answer, but did not.

Vitus pounced. "Why do you hesitate?" he asked suspiciously.

"This one was about to say Barnabas, but then realized you asked for his *birth* name," he answered. "His mother named this one Joseph, but he now goes by the name of Barnabas, the name given him by Master."

Vitus was familiar with Jewish men getting spiritual names when they submitted to a particular teacher, so he didn't find it unusual. The man's bizarre way of not using the first person to refer to himself was far more perplexing.

"And your place of birth?"

"Barnabas was born in Salamis on the island of Cyprus."

"And do you still live there?"

"No."

"Where do you live now?"

"Here in this prison."

Vitus, in no mood for games, began to anger, but saw from Barnabas's face that he'd answered earnestly. "Where is your *home*?" he asked irritably. "What *city* do you live in?"

"This one has no home. He has been traveling with Master for many years."

"Who is your master? What is his name?"

"His name is Jesus."

"I've met over a dozen men with the name Jesus."

"Yes, it is quite a common name," replied Barnabas. He ran his fingers across his thick eyebrows, grooming out-of-place hairs. "Master comes from a small village in Galilee called Nazareth."

"And does he still live there?"

"No."

"Where is he now?"

"Barnabas does not know."

Vitus had become fairly adept at telling when people lied, and he studied Barnabas for the telltale signs: heavy breathing, a shallow voice or difficulty speaking, a sudden jerk or tilt of the head before answering, covering one's mouth with one's hand, or repeating an answer—as if trying to convince oneself that the lie is true.

Vitus detected none of these in the man before him. If anything, Barnabas seemed to have a childlike, almost guileless way about him.

"What is your relationship to this Jesus of Nazareth?" asked Vitus.

"Barnabas is a student, a disciple."

Suppressing a grimace as the pain in his back flared, Vitus continued on. "Why are you not with your teacher now?"

"Master sent me away," Barnabas answered. He began to hum and rock back and forth again.

"Why?"

"Unknown. One does not question Master."

Being a Roman soldier, Vitus understood that. To try to ease the pain in his spine, he shifted his weight from one leg to the other. "Or else you would be punished," he remarked offhand. "But I want to—"

"Oh no," Barnabas quickly interjected, "never punished. One doesn't question Master because he is never wrong. Even if what he says makes no sense, do it anyway, because he knows better."

In his mind, Vitus pictured all the generals and prefects he'd served under who thought they, too, were never wrong, and how miserably they'd failed when they found out otherwise. He pitied Barnabas for believing in his teacher so completely, certain he'd regret it one day.

"Master's only instructions to Barnabas were to go to Jerusalem and begin introducing people to the truth," the prisoner added. "Master said that he, himself, would come one day and gather those who listened."

"Gather them for what?" asked Vitus.

"He did not say."

Vitus leaned his shoulder against the damp stone wall in search of relief. He felt like a hypocrite, knowing he would reprimand any soldier he saw do the same.

"What do you think he would gather them for?"

Barnabas closed his eyes and became very still, then after a few seconds answered, "Perhaps to teach them further about truth. Barnabas can only introduce people to it. He is not Master."

Vitus admired Barnabas's humility, but felt perplexed by his candid answers. He expected a certain amount of fear and loathing from prisoners during an interrogation, and its complete absence now unnerved him.

"You said yesterday that you were speaking to the crowd at the Temple about your master's teachings," Vitus said. "Tell me more about what you were saying to them."

Barnabas smiled broadly. "Of course," he exclaimed. "So delighted you are interested in learning. The world needs more men like you."

Vitus scowled. Was this prisoner truly this naive? Did he not recognize he was being interrogated? That his words could be used to keep him in prison? Or even to put him to death?

"This one had started speaking about how people misunderstand who and what God is," Barnabas explained, "but did not get very far."

"Why?"

"Because half of them kept asking *why* God had not punished Israel's enemies yet. And the other half kept asking *when* God was going to intervene." Barnabas shook his head and laughed gaily.

Vitus clenched his jaw, cringing. It was the first time anyone had ever laughed during one of his interrogations.

He rubbed his eyes against the accumulating smoke, then regarded the dead ants in the corner. When the spider had sucked their life out, had it been brief and painful, he wondered. Or did it occur so slowly and imperceptibly they weren't even aware of what was happening until they slid numbly, irretrievably into death's awaiting arms?

"And what was your response to them?" Vitus asked.

"Barnabas answered them as Master would have," he said. "The god of hate and vengeance that you seek exists only in your head. Therefore, seek ye first the one true God, the God of love and forgiveness."

Vitus searched Barnabas's answers for clues about which category to put him in, but felt lost thus far.

"And then a man from the crowd waved his arms," Barnabas said, imitating him by flailing his arms above his head. "He shouted at Barnabas, 'What is it that God wants of us?' And this one answered him, saying that God wants him to treat his wife and children better, to stop beating them. He became very upset with Barnabas." He paused to laugh yet again. "The man cursed Barnabas and left, and when the others also asked what it is God wants of them, this one replied that God desires nothing more than we humbly seek Him, every day and every night of our lives."

Vitus thought how, not all that long ago, he would have been interested in the philosophical questions Barnabas was raising. But now, he didn't care. They were just words, meaningless ideas from yet another man who would probably be hanging lifelessly on a pole soon.

"Master says when we seek God," Barnabas continued, "our lives are not fruitless, but in accordance with God's divine plan."

Vitus repeatedly held his breath against the stink and the smoke, but found it exhausting to breathe so shallowly. He reflected on what Barnabas had said, knowing that when Jews spoke of a divine plan they meant restoration of their land and the defeat of their enemies, Rome in particular. "And what is this Jesus of Nazareth's role in your god's divine plan?"

"It is he who has come to lead us, to teach us the good news."

"The good news?"

"Yes, the good news that has been obscured for so long. The good news that all is not in vain, that God has not abandoned his people, that the light of knowledge has come to dispel the darkness. That the transformation has begun."

"The *what* has begun?" Vitus asked, not understanding the Aramaic word Barnabas had used.

Barnabas said the same word, but a little slower. When Vitus shook his head that he still didn't understand, Barnabas chose a different word: revolution.

That got Vitus's attention. He stopped slouching and stood up straight. "This revolution you speak of, is Jesus preparing for it?"

"Oh definitely," answered Barnabas. "He has been preparing his whole life for it."

Vitus hadn't expected such a straightforward affirmation. The punishment for inciting rebellion was crucifixion, and the penalty for being an accomplice was the same.

"The day will soon come when Master begins his ministry," Barnabas added enthusiastically.

Vitus barely heard him. There were several key words he always listened for in an interrogation, and he'd just caught two of them: revolution and preparation. Vitus was beginning to sense that Pilate really had stumbled upon something.

"And this revolution," Vitus said, "how will it take place?"

"Once people hear the good news and see it reflected in Master, they will throw off their old clothes for new. They will rise up, with one voice, proclaiming righteousness."

"They will rise up with swords and spears?" Vitus asked, half-hoping Barnabas would take the bait so he could be done with the interrogation.

Barnabas chuckled. "Not at all, my friend."

Vitus winced at the last word. No Jew could ever be friends with a Roman. Didn't this fool understand that Vitus was not his ally, but the one sent to judge him? To determine if he should live or die?

"There will be no weapons, no violence," Barnabas said. "Master teaches to burn the other cheek."

"*Burn* the other cheek?" Vitus repeated. He pictured a blacksmith holding a red-hot coal with his tongs and forcing it to someone's face.

"No, no. Barnabas said *turn* the other cheek. Master teaches that if someone strikes you on one cheek that you should not respond in kind, that you should then offer him the other cheek to strike as well."

Vitus imagined being struck by someone else. In his younger days, he would have returned it with a fist to their face. He'd probably do the same now, but he wasn't so sure. He was a little more dead now, a lot less passionate, and more unwilling to start something he might not be able to finish.

"You could, of course, retaliate," Barnabas added. "An eye for an eye, as it says in the book of Exodus."

Vitus considered for a second that Barnabas had just read his mind, but quickly dismissed the idea. He didn't believe in that.

It was quiet for a moment, the only sound coming from the flickering torch. Then Barnabas cleared his throat and said, "But you need to ask yourself if that response—an eye for an eye—gets you where you want to go."

Vitus rolled his shoulders, cursing under his breath at his body's stiffness. The only place he wanted to go right now was to the baths.

Barnabas fixed his eyes on him. "Centurion," he implored, "if you do not know where you want to go, then how can you take steps to get there?"

Shifting uneasily from one leg to the other, Vitus contemplated who was interrogating whom. He couldn't shake the sense that Barnabas somehow knew him and genuinely cared about him. But he dismissed the idea. Man, in his view, was inherently selfish. And Jews hated Romans.

Unable to bear Barnabas's gaze, Vitus turned away. A burning sensation flashed up his spine, and despite his stoic resolve, he groaned aloud.

"Pain," Barnabas announced, "is an invention of the mind to keep us from discovering the truth."

Inhaling slowly to regain his composure, he retorted, "You speak from experience?"

"Yes. This one was in near constant pain for many years."

Vitus had actually been more interested in whether Barnabas claimed to have discovered the truth. Afraid he'd already lost control of the interrogation, he dropped the subject. He was beginning to feel unsettled and tried to re-establish his authority. "When you spoke to the crowd about these things, did they believe you?" he asked.

Barnabas waved his hand dismissively. "This one's intention is merely to open their minds a crack in preparation for Master."

Coughing against the acrid smoke filling the room, Vitus tried to figure out what conclusion he could possibly draw from the interrogation. Turning the other cheek seemed an odd teaching for a revolutionary. Most of the subversives he'd known had done the exact opposite. They stoked people's resentment, building their outrage so they'd act out violently, perhaps even sacrifice their life for some cause.

Having no idea what to tell Pilate, Vitus sighed loudly. "I fear I shall have to return to speak with you some more."

"Why *fear*, my friend? It has been Barnabas's pleasure talking with you."

"Stop calling me friend," Vitus ordered as though Barnabas was a soldier under his command. He stepped to the opposite wall to retrieve the torch. In addition to being a long way from any kind of verdict, he felt perturbed with Barnabas's sense of camaraderie, as though they were on the same side.

"You don't believe we're friends?" asked Barnabas with a look of surprise.

Vitus lifted the torch from its holder on the wall. He felt its heat on his skin and recalled the time he and his men had been trapped in the carpenter's workshop while the bandits set it on fire. He remembered the vow he'd made if he got out of there alive: to find something he truly believed in with all his heart and soul.

It had been thirteen years since then, and he still hadn't found it. In fact, he'd quit looking.

"No," Vitus replied. "I don't believe..." He'd thought to complete the sentence with "...*we're friends*," but what actually came out was, "...in anything." The words felt strange escaping his lips. He'd felt it—this apathy, this despair—but had never actually expressed it before. He used to feel proud to be Roman, believing he was part of a great movement spreading knowledge, engineering, order, and stability. But that seemed a lifetime ago. Now, the only thing he knew for sure was that the world he lived in was a violent, prejudiced mess, and he'd contributed to it.

Barnabas interrupted Vitus's reverie. "Persevere, Centurion," he called softly. "Confusion always precedes clarity. Know that what you seek, your mind cannot show you. Listen, instead, to your heart."

Vitus heard him, but had no intention of heeding the advice of someone he was interrogating. He was tired of holding his breath and longed for the fresh air above ground.

"Question," Barnabas advised in a near whisper from behind him, "if it was your mind or your heart speaking in that burning building. Which one told you to run your sword through your friend to stop his pain?"

Vitus stumbled backwards into the door, shouting for the guard to let him out. He had no idea how Barnabas could have known about that horrible time with Servanus. He'd never told anyone.

As the guard opened the door, Vitus intentionally frowned and stuck his chin out. But his tears betrayed him.

The guard eyed him curiously. "Are you alright, sir?"

Vitus wiped his cheeks with feigned indifference. "This stench and smoke make my eyes water. I want this cell cleaned and new straw brought in."

"Yes, sir."

"And there had better be candles available next time."

Vitus took slow, measured steps toward the stairs leading out. It took every last ounce of exertion to keep from dropping to his knees and bawling like a baby.

Chapter Twenty-Five

Jonah's neighbor, Tiras, filled the cracked yellow cup with water and held it out. Accepting it with a nod, Jonah sipped the water slowly, swishing it around in his mouth and then savoring the feeling as it flowed down the insides of his dry throat. It had been another long, sweltering day and they were taking a rest at the well of a small village north of Jerusalem.

"What did you do before you became a physician?" asked Tiras.

Jonah always chose his words carefully when discussing his past. If word of his involvement with the bandits got out, he could find himself arrested by the Romans or Herod's soldiers. "Construction," he answered, which wasn't a complete lie. He had helped build a fair number of houses in his life.

He did his best to never mention the bandits for another reason: he hoped time would wipe the memories away. There was one aspect he missed though. He'd awakened each day back then knowing what his purpose was—to protect his younger brother. And he'd fallen asleep each night knowing if he'd been successful or not. When he awoke each morning now, he often lay in bed staring at the ceiling, searching for a reason not to just stay there the entire day. His reason used to be Luke, but at age thirteen now, Luke was nearly an adult himself.

Hoping to change the subject from his sordid past, Jonah passed the cup to Tiras's ten-year-old son, Ehud, and commented, "You two boys have done well today. Are you tired?"

Ehud shook his head, then gulped down the rest of the water. He was a skinny kid with a small head who rarely laughed or smiled around adults.

Jonah slumped against the short stone wall surrounding the well and inspected the blister forming on the back of his heel. It was the fourth day of their pilgrimage to Jerusalem, and he regretted not heeding Amaryah's advice about his sandals. When Jonah had bought them several months ago, Amaryah suggested he either break them in first or wear his old pair on the journey.

He regretted many things about the pilgrimage so far. It had even started out on an auspicious note. The night before they left, Jonah had been surprised by a visit from the mysterious cloud in which he'd received visions of the future as a child. Unlike long ago, when he'd had to consciously call the cloud, he'd received the vision this time whether he wanted it or not.

It hadn't been anything astonishing, just Tiras stepping awkwardly on a loose stone and twisting his ankle. But Jonah had worried that every event he'd ever seen emerge from the cloud had come true, and an injured ankle would surely imperil their journey. He'd been hyper-vigilant the first day of their pilgrimage, warning Tiras repeatedly to be careful. He'd even spotted the exact stone he'd seen in his vision and alerted Tiras to steer clear of it.

Despite everything, the incident had unfolded exactly as Jonah foresaw it.

With Tiras's gimpy ankle, they hadn't been able to walk their planned twenty miles a day, but only fifteen. And instead of reaching the Temple by today, the first day of the Sukkot festival, they wouldn't get there until the next morning.

Jonah pressed gingerly on the blister. "Where did Thomas go?" he asked.

When neither Ehud nor Tiras answered after a few seconds, he looked up at them. Ehud gazed back blankly. Tiras wrinkled his forehead and asked, "You mean *Luke*?"

"Yes. Isn't that what I said?"

"No," Ehud answered. "You said Thomas."

Hearing that name, Jonah intentionally pinched his blister until the pain from it was all he could feel. He hated how often he called Luke by his father's name. Luke didn't even look that much like Thomas. The only physical characteristics they had in common were brown hair and green eyes. And even then, Luke's hair was short and curly, and his eyes deep-set and gentle— unlike his father's. Where Thomas had resembled a mouse as a child, Luke looked more like a lamb.

Ehud pointed behind Jonah. "Here he comes."

Jonah saw Luke conversing with a stranger as they rounded the corner of a nearby house.

"He's the one on the left," Luke said as they approached.

The gaunt man with a sparse gray beard hurried over, taking quick, but tiny steps that made him bounce up and down slightly. "Kind sir," he addressed Jonah. "Your son is most helpful. He tells me you're a physician. I beg you to come help my wife. She's been lying in bed all day, moaning and telling me how much her tooth hurts."

Ehud had passed the cup back to Jonah, and Jonah purposefully took his time drinking from it so he could decide how to respond. The festival was seven days long, and the first day of it was to be observed like the Sabbath. On the Sabbath, one was not to buy, sell, or do any kind of work. Even baking and food preparation was to have been done the previous day so as not to violate the commandment.

"Ignore him," Tiras advised as he filled his son's waterskin.

"Please, sir," the man said. A gust of wind twirled the long sidecurls dangling from the top of his ears down to his shoulders.

Tiras raised his voice, admonishing the fellow Jew. "You should be ashamed of yourself. Asking pilgrims to work on the first day of Sukkot!"

"Our village is small. We have no physicians." The man shakily lowered himself to one knee in front of Jonah. "You must help."

"Which tooth is it?" asked Jonah.

"Come, I'll take you to her," the man said, sounding much relieved. With Luke's assistance, he stood up and motioned to the right. "It's just—"

"It doesn't matter," Tiras interrupted. Fixing his eyes on Jonah, he exclaimed, "We can't help them. It's bad enough that we're walking so much."

On the Sabbath one was not to walk more than one thousand cubits; otherwise it was considered work. When Jonah and Tiras realized they wouldn't reach Jerusalem on the day they'd planned, and with no rabbi to consult, they'd argued endlessly about this prohibition. The main point of contention between them was that the first day of Sukkot was to be observed *'like* the Sabbath,' though it was not technically the Sabbath. Not wanting to miss the festivities at the Temple, they'd finally decided they would walk, but Tiras insisted they fast for the day to make up for it.

Giving his son a nudge from behind, Tiras began to march away from the well, his limp more pronounced, as it always was after a rest. "Jonah, let's go," he said as though he was in charge. "We still have a lot of ground to cover."

Catching Luke's disappointed gaze, Jonah lowered his head, sighing as he pushed himself up from the wall. The man called to him as he passed by. "Please, sir. I beg of you!"

Tiras turned and berated the man from a distance, his voice dripping with scorn. "Leave us be! If your wife suffers, then it is God that must be appeased. Offer up an animal to atone for her sins!"

"But we are poor," the man explained. "We have no money to buy an animal for sacrifice."

Jonah felt an ache in his heart upon hearing that. He knew what it was like to be poor. It was only in the past decade that he'd experienced prosperity, ever since Amaryah's uncle had returned from living in Egypt and taught Jonah to be a physician. Dragging himself away, Jonah resisted the urge to look back. He hated denying a person in need, but on this journey he wanted to follow the scriptures to set a good example for Luke.

As the two boys dashed up the road chasing a butterfly, Jonah groaned to himself at the prospect of spending further time alone with Tiras. He dreaded having further conversations with his neighbor, coming to realize on this journey how little he'd really known him before.

It didn't take long before Tiras turned to Jonah, fuming. "The nerve of some of these people! Why didn't you just tell him *no* right from the start? You know you mustn't do any work today. What would God think of you?"

Jonah wanted to tell Tiras he didn't believe in God, but that was something a Jew didn't announce unless he wanted to be ostracized or stoned to death.

Thankfully, Luke and Ehud came scampering back before Jonah felt he had to answer.

"Father, could you settle an argument for us?" Ehud asked. "When God killed all the babies in Egypt, he killed the babies of animals too, right?"

"That's true," Tiras said. "God struck down all the firstborn in Egypt, including the Pharaoh's own son, and all the firstborn of the livestock as well."

"See?" Ehud said to Luke. "Told you so."

The two boys again ran up ahead, stopping at a lone olive tree outside the village to pick olives from the ground and throw them at each other.

"Ehud's a smart boy," Jonah commented, hoping to find at least one subject that wouldn't end up being confrontational.

"Yes," agreed Tiras. "His teacher at the synagogue says he's at the top of his class. I'm hoping to keep up his education, maybe get him accepted for instruction by a prominent teacher."

Jonah scoffed at Tiras's plan, but kept it to himself. It was a rare thing for a boy's education to continue past adolescence.

"He's already close to being able to quote more scripture than I can," Tiras said. "When he grows up, he could be a venerable rabbi. Maybe teach those pompous Jews from Jerusalem a thing or two."

"Maybe," Jonah said, "but you never know. I remember how, as kids, my cousin could quote more scripture than anyone I knew. And he turned out to be an arrogant, iron-handed tyrant."

"Who's your cousin?"

Jonah wished he'd kept his mouth shut. "You wouldn't know him. He's long since dead," he lied. The truth was he heard about Zebulun from time to time—his latest exploits, the attempts to capture him.

When they reached the olive tree, Tiras stepped under its shade. "Wait a minute," he said as he knelt and began untying the leather straps that wound around his ankle. "Got a rock in my sandal that won't come out."

Even though Jonah had just drunk at the well, he was in the habit of drinking from his waterskin whenever they stopped. Lifting it from his shoulder, he realized it was nearly empty. "Oh, shit," he said, immediately covering his mouth, hoping Tiras hadn't heard his expletive. "I forgot to fill my waterskin. You and the boys continue on. I'll go back to the well, then catch up with you."

"Have Luke do it," Tiras suggested. "He's young. He can run."

"No, I've been trying to teach him responsibility and accountability," Jonah called over his shoulder. "What kind of an example would that set?"

When he reached the well, he was surprised to see the same man waiting there, only now he was accompanied by his wife and son. The man tousled the boy's hair, exclaiming, "You were right!" He then took his tiny steps, bouncing up and down toward Jonah. "I knew you'd be back," he said. "Thanks be to God."

"What do you mean?" asked Jonah.

"To be honest," the man said, "*I* didn't know. It was my son." He squeezed Jonah's arm by the elbow and led him forward.

The boy, about Luke's height, was helping his mother up from her seat on the small wall surrounding the well. Without him holding her, Jonah was afraid she might collapse. She stood barefoot and stooped over, with her hand on her bony right cheek, her face contorted in pain.

"Our son has a gift from God, some way of knowing things," the man continued. "I don't understand it. He said you'd be back."

A deluge of memories rushed forth for Jonah. He remembered how he used to make predictions for other kids when he was about the same age. And he recalled, with great sadness, how he'd believed in God wholeheartedly back then. He'd trusted God was on his side and that He had Jonah's best interests in mind.

Without Tiras or the boys around, Jonah decided to give whatever aid he could. He hastily rummaged through his bag for some gum of the terebinth tree. Then he briefly inspected the tooth, wriggling it to make sure it wasn't loose, and handed the medicine to her.

"You'll be fine," he said. "Take this. It will help."

He actually had no idea what the cause was or whether or not she'd be fine. That happened often in his profession, but Amaryah's uncle had taught him that quite often simply telling people they'd be alright was enough for healing to occur. Jonah had found this advice to be invaluable. The only people it didn't seem to work for were those who clung tightly to the belief that God had inflicted the pain as punishment. For them, Jonah would give a frown and leave feeling defeated.

"Thank you," the woman said, her face softening. "May God bless you."

"It's nothing," Jonah replied, waving her off.

The man tried shoving some bread in Jonah's hands as payment, but Jonah pushed it away. Then the three of them left, the husband and son each holding one of the woman's arms.

Jonah was refilling his waterskin at the well when he caught Luke spying at him over the top of a partially built wall across the road. He motioned him over, asking, "You saw everything?"

Luke nodded. "Tiras didn't want us to get separated," he said meekly as he approached. "He showed me where they'd be waiting and sent me back for you."

"Listen," Jonah said. "I'm not a good Jew. I don't follow the commandments very well. I don't say the prayers every day. I know I don't set a good example for you." As they departed down the road, he searched Luke's face, wondering if it was even necessary to say that.

Luke stared down at the ground. "Sometimes I skip my evening prayers when I'm tired," he confessed.

Jonah watched the little clouds of dust that briefly formed after each of their footsteps. It had been dry for a long time, and the winter rains wouldn't begin for at least a few more weeks.

With a sidelong glance, Luke added, "In the synagogue, I heard the rabbi telling us many times that the scriptures *command* you to help people if you are able. Why was it a sin for you to help that woman?"

"It's confusing, I know," Jonah replied. "You *are* supposed to help—unless there's some commandment saying you cannot."

Before Jonah could elaborate, Luke asked in a curious tone, "Did my father obey God's word?"

Jonah sighed, recalling how fervent Thomas had been when they were with the bandits. "Your father tried harder than anyone I knew to obey the commandments," he answered.

"Then God loved him," Luke said decisively.

Jonah nodded, though he was unsure what exactly Luke meant. "Yes, I suppose so."

"The teacher in the synagogue tells us God loves people who do their best to obey all the commandments," Luke added.

With a heavy heart, Jonah understood the implications of what Luke had said. Since both of them had admitted to falling short in their effort to follow the scriptures, Luke believed that God did not love them.

"I wish he weren't my father," Luke blurted unexpectedly.

Jonah stopped mid-stride, pulling on Luke's arm to halt him as well. "Why do you say that?"

"Because then I wouldn't have to avenge his death."

"What makes you think you have to do that?"

Though Luke had been told his father had been killed, Jonah and Amaryah had kept the details of Thomas's death a secret. On Luke's insistence, they had promised to tell him once he was a man. Jonah frowned to himself as he realized he'd have to fulfill that promise when they returned home to Magdala.

"Ehud says I'm a coward if I don't avenge his death. He says my ancestors won't be able to rest unless I do."

Jonah glared up at the sky in exasperation. "Are you taking advice from ten-year-olds?" he said, regretting the words as soon as they'd left his lips. He sped up, and when they neared Tiras and his son, he shouted, "Ehud, what is this nonsense about you telling Luke he has to avenge his father's death?"

Ehud had been squatting like a chicken over its eggs. He stood up and stretched his scrawny arms out wide. "I was only telling him what it says in the book of Exodus," he explained. "'Life for life, eye for eye, tooth for tooth, hand for hand....'"

Jonah blamed Zebulun and his malicious scripture-quoting for ruining Thomas's life. He wasn't about to let the same happen to Luke, but he knew the sole way to win an argument was to cite more extensive, or more applicable scripture than your opponent. The Torah was the ultimate authority on all things.

After grinding his teeth in contemplation for a few seconds, Jonah initiated the debate as they walked. "Does God not set the example for us to follow?"

Ehud looked to his father. The sun, still as fierce as at midday, was low in the sky, nearly blinding them from straight on.

"Yes, of course," Tiras said.

"And do the scriptures not say 'The Lord is gracious and compassionate, slow to anger and rich in love'?"

"They do," Ehud affirmed. "That's in the book of Psalms."

Though determined, Jonah felt nervous. He tended not to engage in scriptural debates, because even though he knew a lot more scripture than when he was a kid, he still usually lost. The teachings of the Torah simply didn't match his beliefs.

Ehud again gazed expectantly at his father, who patted him on the head, then said, "There can be no doubt that God is gracious and compassionate." He let the words hang in the air before continuing. "But is He not also vengeful? Did He not destroy the cities of Sodom and Gomorrah? All the firstborn in Egypt? All the people of Jericho? All the Amorites? If we are to follow God's example, then it seems very clear that we are to avenge injustices done to us—not just personally, but as a people as well."

Jonah searched his memory for something that would counter that, but the only story that came to him was the one about God commanding the earth to swallow up Korah and his family.

"But God is merciful too," Luke said, trying to squeeze between Jonah and Ehud. "Did He not lead our people out of Egypt and to the Promised Land? Did He not end the plague that sickened so many under King David?"

Jonah was pleased with Luke's decision to participate, even more so because he was taking his side.

"God is indeed merciful, " Tiras affirmed. "But sins must be atoned for, justice served. As it says in the second book of Chronicles, 'Fear the Lord and judge with integrity, for the Lord our God does not tolerate perverted justice.'"

Jonah felt Luke's eyes on him, but try as he might, he couldn't think of any passages that opposed Tiras's words.

"A leopard!" Ehud suddenly shouted, pointing up at the ridge ahead of them. "It was on that ledge over there."

Jonah studied the dull yellowish rocks ahead of them, but saw nothing out of the ordinary. His eyesight wasn't the best, and the landscape seemed perfectly suited to a leopard. He was relieved by the interruption and hoped nobody noticed his red ears. He could feel them burning with embarrassment at the brevity of the debate.

"It was probably an ibex," said Tiras. "Or maybe a deer."

"No," Ehud insisted. "I saw its face, and it had a long tail!"

Jonah felt grateful for it, whatever it was. Its appearance brought a merciful ending to his vain attempt to win an unwinnable argument.

He despaired that he was destined to have lost the debate. He believed the future—like Moses' Ten Commandments—was written in stone, and there was nothing you could do to change it. All the calamities and sorrow and good fortune in one's life were predetermined. You might think you're doing something different that will change your future, but in fact you're just doing exactly what had already been planned. His earlier experience with Tiras hurting his ankle only strengthened his conviction on the matter.

The boys—certain the leopard must have been hunting something up ahead—sprinted away, leaving Jonah alone with Tiras once more.

"So, do you know who killed Luke's father?" Tiras asked.

Jonah grimaced at his neighbor's knack for asking the exact questions he didn't want to answer. Of course he knew who killed his brother—not his name—but he'd never forget that centurion's face. It haunted his dreams. If he told Tiras that Thomas had been crucified by the Romans, that would open up a whole series of unwanted questions. Everyone knew that crucifixion was mainly reserved for those who had committed high crimes or gotten on the wrong side of the Roman authorities.

"No," Jonah said, then sped ahead to discourage any further conversation.

They walked in silence for the next mile, Jonah passing the time noting his surroundings. Everything was a varying shade of beige, from the sun-bleached, rocky slopes to the sandy hills that towered all around. There was very little green to be found anywhere—just tiny pockets of half-dead cedar trees and grass lucky enough to be in the shade. He wondered how people managed to make a living in such an infertile place. It was certainly a sorry contrast to the fruitful landscape of Galilee, with its orchards and fields of wheat and barley.

The boys raced back before long, shouting, "We saw it again! The leopard!"

"You *both* saw it?" asked Tiras.

They nodded excitedly and pointed to where they'd spotted it.

Jonah surveyed the area they indicated, but still saw nothing except the same old monotonous ridges they'd seen for most of their journey that day.

"Is it stalking us?" Luke asked.

"No, they're afraid of humans," Jonah said, although he didn't entirely believe his own answer. "What did it do when you saw it?"

"It ran that way," Luke said, pointing in the direction they were walking.

Instead of a leopard, Jonah spotted a potential campsite. "Then why don't we sleep here?" he said. "It's getting late anyway."

The sun turned orange as it began to dip below the distant mountaintops.

"Yes, it will be twilight soon," Tiras said. "You boys go pee and then meet us over there." He pointed at the same spot Jonah thought was promising.

Luke and Ehud disappeared behind a handful of withered cedars nearby while Jonah and Tiras made their way up a small slope to a relatively level area carved out of the side of a ridge.

Jonah was kicking stones out of the area he'd chosen for his bed when he heard the boys returning, and then Tiras's shrill voice.

"What in God's name are you doing?"

"Gathering sticks for a fire to keep the leopard away," Luke answered.

"Fools!" Tiras shouted, knocking the sticks from Ehud's arms. "You can't do that. Today is to be observed like the Sabbath!"

Ehud, on the verge of tears, whimpered, "I told him we weren't allowed—that Moses sentenced a man to death for gathering sticks on the Sabbath."

"You didn't tell me they *killed him*," Luke protested.

Tiras slapped his son across the face. "But you did it anyway, didn't you?"

"Tiras, stop!" Jonah said. "They're just kids."

"Yes, and who do you think pays the price for their sins?" Tiras shot back. He curled his lips in so his crooked teeth showed.

It was taught that up until a boy's bar mitzvah, the father suffered the consequences of the child's ignorance, for not obeying any commandments. Once a boy turned thirteen, he was responsible for his own spiritual progression.

Jonah took the sticks from Luke's arms and tossed them a short distance away. "Why don't you let me look after them getting ready for bed," he said to Tiras.

Tiras picked up a stick he'd knocked from Ehud's arms and growled like an enraged dog as he whipped it sidearm toward the road. Then he stomped away.

* * *

When Jonah finally stretched out on the hard, unforgiving ground, Luke and Ehud were already fast asleep. They'd been sleeping so deeply every night that nothing woke them, not even Tiras's loud snoring.

Feeling the tiredness wash over him, Jonah yawned and beheld the black sky of a moonless night above. Seeing millions of stars usually made him feel small and insignificant in a comforting way—his problems so minuscule in the grand order of things. But tonight he felt anything but comforted. Hateful thoughts about the day flew through his mind like half-starved bats: scorn for his new sandals that had given him blisters; anger with Tiras for not letting them eat and for being such a grievous companion; and resentment against Ehud for telling Luke he had to avenge his father's death.

But the most hateful thought of all he reserved for himself. He hated that he kept failing. He'd failed to protect Thomas. Failed to raise Luke to be a dutiful, devout Jew. Failed to be happy when he had so much. Failed that very day in winning the scriptural argument with Tiras.

This trip was supposed to heal the poison in his heart, but Jonah felt the opposite was happening. The poison was spreading, claiming more and more territory within him. Instead of feeling less confused and wretched like he and Amaryah had hoped, Jonah identified more than ever with Moses after the Exodus from Egypt—a desperate nomad in exile, wandering aimlessly.

Moses had led Jonah's ancestors through the wilderness for forty years, enduring God's punishment for refusing to wrest control of the Promised Land from the people currently occupying it, the Canaanites. In the end, Moses himself died before ever setting foot on the "land of milk and honey." But he'd at least glimpsed it. He'd at least known that all had not been in vain—the struggle out of Egypt, the four decades in the desert, all the death, hunger, and disease God had inflicted on them for their faithlessness.

Jonah had no such hope for his own life, that any of it would prove to be worth the pain and suffering. He felt like his namesake who'd lived eight hundred years prior: both of them having been swallowed by a great beast of the sea and stuck in its belly, with no hope of escape.

When Tiras ceased his snoring, all was still, and Jonah closed his eyes to sleep. He longed for the cliff back home, for the quietude of death. It was the only thing he knew of that held any hope of relieving him of his misery.

But death did not call. The cloud that gave him visions of the future did. It showed him two images. The first was of the black beast, gripping Luke's throat in its mouth and dragging his lifeless body away. The second was of himself lying nearby, witnessing the tragedy unfold. Though very much alive, he was completely immobile, like a corpse.

Jonah halted the disturbing vision by forcing his eyes open. Tiras injuring his ankle was one thing, but Luke's welfare was another. He felt angry with himself and remembered Amaryah's words about death ceasing all change, all growth.

There were many things he didn't know for certain, but in that moment he knew without a doubt he didn't want to die as he was—full of resentment, full of regret. He may have lived his life always holding back, afraid to take risks, but he couldn't allow himself to die that way. He made a silent vow to escape from the belly of the beast, to stop living his life like an apology.

The words stirred a strange sensation in his navel, and a shiver spiraled up his back. Convincing himself it was merely a result of the temperature having dropped significantly since the sun set, he pulled his cloak tight and turned on his side.

That's when he saw them.

There, no more than fifteen feet away, were two big, glowing green eyes. No face. No body. Just eyes floating in the darkness.

It was the black beast. It had come for Luke already.

Jonah could not move, could not speak, could barely even breathe, but the energy in his navel was growing quickly, like a fire expanding tenfold because it encountered a rush of air.

The wind picked up, whistling through the landscape's innumerable ravines and crevasses, sounding like a demonic howl of triumph.

The gleaming green eyes moved quickly, and when they were within a few inches of Luke's throat, Jonah saw the outline of a leopard's head and body take shape. He sprang to his feet and charged toward Luke—the raw, primal force in his belly exploding up his spine. The leopard snarled and lunged at him. Jonah wrapped his arms around it, and together they crashed to the ground. The big cat clawed at him furiously, tearing at his torso with its hind legs. But its claws couldn't penetrate Jonah's thick leather cloak. Using all of his strength, Jonah squeezed the leopard tight and sunk his teeth into its side until he felt warm blood coat his chin.

Then, almost as soon as the fight began, it was over. The leopard managed to free itself of Jonah's grasp and, defeated, withdrew into the shadows from whence it had come.

Tiras sat up and rubbed his eyes. "What was that?"

"It was nothing," Jonah told him as he sat on the ground and searched through his pack. Both Luke and Ehud were still soundly asleep.

"I thought I heard something," Tiras persisted. "What are you doing?"

"I said it was nothing," Jonah repeated.

But he knew that it wasn't nothing. *Something* had happened.

After cleaning the bloody scratches on his arm, he applied some olive oil and balm of Gilead to them. Then he lay down and picked fur from his teeth. As the intense energy continued to pulsate through his body, he could think of only one thing. It was the first time a vision from the cloud hadn't come true.

Perhaps the future wasn't written in stone. But just to be on the safe side, he stayed up the rest of the night watching over Luke.

The stars above were so bright and thickly clustered that they looked like a river in the sky.

Chapter Twenty-Six

Vitus knocked forcefully on the side of the sentry's helmet. "You may be new, but that doesn't entitle you to do something foolish. Never confront or try to arrest anyone if you're by yourself. Maintain your space and report the incident at the end of your duty. Did I not already speak to you about this?"

"Yes, sir. Won't happen again, sir."

Vitus wasn't surprised at the confrontation between the soldier and the Jewish man. It was the second day of the Sukkot festival, and tensions were running high. The city was overflowing not only with pilgrims, but also rumors. And the biggest rumor of all was that the prefect was planning to raid the treasury of the Temple to pay for the incomplete aqueduct project.

Even with all the sentries, like this one, posted throughout the city as a reminder for the Jews of who was in charge, Vitus knew from experience how careful they still had to be. He'd seen firsthand the effect that a large crowd had on people. With their strength in numbers, they became more brave, more insolent. Passover was usually the worst, but any of the three festivals could cause trouble. Vitus always stressed to the prefects the importance of bringing in more troops during these times. Even though that advice had been heeded, he estimated that with all the pilgrims streaming into the city from north, south, east, and west, Jews probably outnumbered Romans a hundred to one now— maybe more.

The soldier walked sharply back to his post and stood at attention as Vitus scanned the crowd.

"They're trying to provoke you into doing something stupid," Vitus called over his shoulder as he departed. "Don't oblige them."

Descending the stairs, he had a bad feeling about the day. Yesterday had been relatively calm, as the first day of the festivals usually were. Today, he was sure, would be a different story. His biggest concern was the Jewish zealots, who liked to hide in the colossal crowds. Their main goal was to aggravate the Romans into a heavy-handed response they could use to their advantage. Vitus had learned that the boiling point of Jewish indignation was never far away, so even something minor might set them off.

Though Vitus had been avoiding him, he was glad the prefect was back in the city after a hiatus of several months. Just after Pilate had instructed Vitus to interrogate Barnabas, he'd abruptly left Jerusalem to deal with some urgent matter in the capital, Caesarea. Vitus had been sidestepping him because, even with all the extra time, he still hadn't reached any conclusions about Barnabas. While most prisoners took only a few visits for him to reach a decision, he'd visited Barnabas at least a dozen times, but still didn't know what to say about the strange young man and his peculiar beliefs.

He knew what verdict Pilate wanted him to reach. The prefect had made it abundantly clear before he'd left that he was in search of someone to make an example of, and that Barnabas was an ideal candidate. Vitus understood all too well that if he cooperated, he could expect things to go easily with his commanding officer. But if he failed to comply, his life would become much more burdensome.

Eager to get out of the sun, Vitus hurried to the Antonia Fortress and climbed the stairs two to a time. There were nearly as many stairs here as to the esplanade of the Temple, except the fortress's wide staircase was mostly empty. Near the top he paused in the shade to drink from a fountain, watching as the "Samarian unit" marched by. They were a cohort of Roman soldiers who were not from Rome, but who had instead joined from the neighboring region of Samaria. As Samaritans, Jerusalem and the Temple held no reverence for them. The Jews didn't allow them to make sacrifices there, and the Samaritans had built their own temple on Mount Gerizim. Besides having slightly darker skin than those from Rome, the soldiers of the Samarian unit were also smaller. Vitus was taller than all of them.

Pilate's unmistakable nasal voice suddenly rang out. "I said I wanted the area cleared!"

"My apologies, sir," came the response. "They're arriving now. It'll just be a moment."

Curious about what was happening, Vitus climbed the remaining steps and peeked around a large column. He saw two archers marching side by side toward Pilate. One of them loaded an arrow in his bow, aimed nearly straight up at the archway, and fired.

A second later a dove with a bloody arrow in its neck fell to the ground.

Vitus thought it ludicrous and would have laughed if not for the fact that the dove looked to have been an extraordinary specimen—brilliant white without a single blemish.

Hoping the prefect was sufficiently occupied, Vitus tried to sneak by without being noticed. Exiting the colonnade, he veered right and cut across the sun-drenched courtyard.

Pilate caught him anyway. "Centurion," he called out. "I'm still waiting for your report on that provocateur."

"Sorry, sir. I've been caught up with other things," Vitus shouted back. "I'm heading there now."

"Come find me afterward," Pilate said. "I want an update when you're done."

Though dismayed at Pilate's words, Vitus kept his expression stoic. His conversations with Barnabas sometimes wandered off topic into philosophical and even metaphysical questions, but today he wouldn't be able to allow that. He'd have to stay focused.

At the entrance to the stairs leading to the prison below ground, Vitus recognized the paunchy guard leaning against the wall scratching his groin. It was Stone. Vitus didn't remember the soldier's actual name. He thought of him as Stone, because he seemed about as refined and as intelligent as one.

When Stone saw Vitus, he dragged himself a few steps over to a small basket, then started down the stairs with it.

"Did you get everything?" Vitus asked as he followed behind.

"Yep," Stone answered, then spat in front of himself.

"That's 'Yes, sir.' Not 'Yep,'" Vitus said crossly. He regretted their policy of assigning the least competent soldiers as prison guards.

With each step down, the light decreased and the stench increased. Even though Barnabas's cell had been cleaned and didn't smell as bad, the rest of the cells more than made up for it. Vitus could hear conversations between the prisoners. They talked to one another from across or down the hall, speaking softly and slowly because of the echo.

Stone, carrying a nearly lifeless torch that provided the only light, castigated them. "Shut up, you prigs!" he yelled, his words reverberating off the rock walls.

When they passed by the door of one who had been speaking, Stone pounded on it and said, "You want a beating? I told you before: No talking."

At Barnabas's cell, Stone handed the torch to Vitus, then jangled his numerous metal keys, muttering under his breath as he struggled to find the correct one.

While he waited, Vitus retrieved the candle he'd brought. He didn't trust the guards to provide them and brought his own each time. He contemplated his forthcoming recommendation to Pilate and the no-win situation he felt himself in: a verdict of guilty would wrack his conscience with guilt, while an innocent verdict would wreck his career.

Vitus's candle sputtered and refused to burn, but he persisted until it complied and provided a dim flame. Stone, having finally managed to find the right key, turned away from the door and kicked it open like a donkey. It banged loudly when it hit the wall. Through the cell's foglike darkness, Vitus spied Barnabas sitting in his usual position in the corner. Unfortunately, the scant light of the candle didn't allow him to see Barnabas's facial expression. Vitus used that to judge how to begin. A foolish grin and wide eyes meant flippant and mostly useless responses. A slight smile and calm eyes meant dependable, rational answers. But Vitus had learned that Barnabas could switch from one to the other quickly and without warning.

After closing the door and setting the candle down, Vitus considered that if—instead of joining the Roman army—he'd married and had a family, his eldest son would be about Barnabas's age now.

"Greetings, Centurion," Barnabas called to him. "Will this one get to learn your name this time?"

Vitus couldn't understand why it was so important for Barnabas to know his name. He took his helmet off and set it on the fresh straw. Then, instead of his routine refusal, he said, "I'll make a deal with you. I'll tell you my name if you promise to do something for me."

"My friend," came the response, "if you desire something of Barnabas, you need only ask."

Even after several months of coming to Barnabas's cell to speak with him, Vitus still cringed every time Barnabas called him that. "Why do you keep calling me *friend*?" he protested. "You are a Jew. I am a Roman. You are a prisoner. I am your jailer. You are—"

Barnabas interrupted him with his own list. "Barnabas has a beard. You do not. Barnabas is still young, and you have already led a long life. Barnabas's penis is circumcised. Yours is not." He started to laugh, his snickers sounding like a cackling hen, then he abruptly stopped. "What does any of that have to do with friendship?"

Vitus stubbornly conceded the point. It was true he'd had friends throughout his life who were very different from him.

He twisted in a gentle stretch from side-to-side, noting with great apprehension his back didn't hurt in the least. It had been two days now that it hadn't bothered him, and whenever that had happened before, the pain returned with such a vengeance he could hardly get out of bed.

"A friend," Barnabas continued, "is someone you respect, listen to, and wish the best life has to offer. You are indeed a friend in my eyes. Is Barnabas not in yours?"

Vitus clenched his jaw tight. It was an impossible question. He fixed his eyes on the hint of blue in the mostly yellow flame of the candle, then said, "My full name is Marcus Trebellius Vitus, but you may call me Vitus."

"A majestic name," exclaimed Barnabas.

As Vitus's eyes slowly adjusted to the dark, he thought he could see Barnabas smiling. "My father told me it means *lively*," he added.

"Brilliant! Brilliant!" Barnabas said gaily. "You are, indeed, full of life. Full of questions, thirsty for both adventures and answers." He briefly looked upward, proclaiming, "Creator, you never cease to amaze this one."

Vitus had never thought of that before, that his name *did* fit him. He wanted to ask Barnabas again why he referred to himself in the third person, hoping he might understand the answer this time. But he quashed that urge before it escaped his lips. Reminding himself to keep a professional distance, he straightened up, frowning intentionally as he decided which question to begin the interrogation with.

"You brought something today," Barnabas said, gesturing to the basket on the floor near the door.

Vitus had forgotten about it. He picked it up and set it in front of Barnabas. "I brought some bread and olives."

"A present in prison!" Barnabas chuckled. "How kind of you. Barnabas is accustomed to eating one meal a day, but the others here are not. They say they are quite hungry during the day."

"There are a few figs too," Vitus said. He'd convinced himself earlier that bringing in food didn't violate anything, that it was simply a ploy to get a prisoner to cooperate, but he wasn't so sure anymore. Now it seemed inappropriate, and he wondered if he'd crossed a line.

"Hmm, this isn't very much," Barnabas said as he rummaged through the basket. "There are ten of us down here."

Vitus furrowed his eyebrows. "You misunderstand me," he said. "I brought this just for you, not everyone."

"But why? Barnabas is no different than any of them."

The candle suddenly popped and hissed, then resumed its quiet flickering. A faint moan echoed down the hall.

Vitus smirked as he scanned Barnabas's face to check if he was being coy. Seeing that he wasn't, Vitus said, "You're not like the others at all. When I speak with them, they're deceitful and disrespectful. Some of them, I'm quite sure, would attack me if they weren't in chains. The criminal in the cell next to you is here because he tried to kill one of my men. He told me it was a moral obligation of Jews to kill Romans."

"Barnabas *is* like the others," he insisted. "If this one had lived *his* life, fed his heart nothing but hate, then this one, too, would have done the same thing."

"I don't believe that for a second," Vitus replied sharply. "I've seen no inkling of hostility in you."

"This one is no different than him or you," Barnabas reiterated. "Vitus, you must understand this."

The sincerity with which Barnabas had called him by his birth name made Vitus want to sit at his feet like a schoolboy.

"It is the same as if Barnabas had lived *your* life up to this point in time," he continued. "Then this one, too, would be filled with confusion, despairing as to life's meaning."

Vitus didn't try to hide from the truth of what Barnabas had said. With anyone else he would have taken the words as an insult and been incensed. But Barnabas had said the words matter-of-factly, without a hint of judgment.

Remembering Pilate's command to provide an update, Vitus reluctantly moved on. He had to finalize something. It was always so much easier when the prisoner was hostile, and clearly—or even just *mostly*—guilty.

"If you were released today, what would you do?" Vitus asked.

"This one would continue to do as Master instructed," said Barnabas as he tore the bread into pieces. "Await his arrival and preach the good news that the pain and suffering of this world is only temporary, that it is not meant as a punishment, but as a catalyst to spur one in making a choice. And—"

"What choice?" Vitus interrupted. "The choice of whether to pay taxes? The choice of whether or not to rise up in rebellion?"

Barnabas giggled. "Vitus, *the choice* is between inclusion and exclusion, between seeing others as oneself and seeing others as separate. That's what each of us has to decide—whether to serve others or serve one's self. Whether to listen to the heart or ignore it. This is the most important thing Master came to teach."

Vitus didn't want to get sidetracked, so he logged Barnabas's words to contemplate later. "If you are released from prison and stand outside the Temple preaching once more, Pilate will have you arrested again," he said. "Only he won't call on me. He'll simply have you executed."

"Rabbis are constantly teaching outside the Temple. They are not arrested. Why this one?"

"Because the high priests do not consider *their* teachings heretical," Vitus answered. He chastised himself at first for sharing that information, but then decided he didn't care. "They are the ones who reported you to the prefect."

Barnabas peered over Vitus's shoulder, grooming his beard with his fingers. "Master warned Barnabas about them...."

"What I want you to promise to do for me," Vitus said slowly, "is to leave Jerusalem if you are released. Go to some other city far away from here."

"No. No. Impossible," Barnabas said. "That would be disobeying Master's instructions."

Vitus felt his sunburned skin flush even hotter. Here he was, going out of his way to help this ill-fated man, and he wouldn't cooperate. "I told you my name," Vitus reminded him. "We made a deal."

"But Barnabas already made a deal. It was with Master. This one agreed to surrender to him two things: who Barnabas thought he was, and what Barnabas thought he knew about the world. In exchange, Master gave Barnabas new eyes and new ears. Please," he implored, "ask of Barnabas something else."

"Damn it!" Vitus yelled, pounding his fist on the wall. "You're going to get yourself killed with these absurd ideas of yours."

"Oh, yes," confirmed Barnabas, "Master has already made that clear."

Vitus bent toward him. "He told you that you'd die as a result of following his instructions?" he asked in disbelief.

Barnabas nodded. "Perhaps not today or tomorrow, but in the future, yes."

Vitus had often wondered over the past few days if Barnabas might be mad. Now, he was almost certain of it. "Then why would you do as he says? Is not your life the most precious thing you have?"

"Vitus," Barnabas answered. "We will die anyway. Why not die doing something you believe in with all your heart and soul?"

His words, charged and impudent, caught Vitus flat-footed. He scrutinized Barnabas's expression to see if this was yet another example of him knowing things he couldn't possibly know—that Vitus had made a vow using those exact words on that awful day in the village of Arimathea, when he was sure he was going to die in the fire.

Vitus still hadn't found anything he believed in with all his heart and soul, and recalled how on his first visit to Barnabas's cell, he'd said he didn't believe "in anything." But that wasn't true, he now knew. He *did* believe in something. He'd just been denying it, because it seemed foolish—impossible even—to believe in something so magnanimous.

He gazed blankly at the corner opposite Barnabas, where the pile of shriveled, lifeless ants had been before he ordered the cell cleaned daily. Crisp yellow straw now covered every inch of the floor, and it smelled like a harvest day.

"You have spoken to me of revolution, of dissent, and of preparation for a new order," Vitus said. "The prefect has all the information he needs to put you to death. Why should I not tell him these things?"

"My friend, why are you asking me? You are the one who has not spoken to him of these things. You must ask this question of yourself."

Vitus had hoped for an answer that would set his mind at ease and confirm the direction he was considering, but Barnabas was right, of course. He knew he could have been done with this whole affair a long time ago. He could have spent the time drinking wine, feasting, or getting a massage, but instead he kept visiting, kept thinking all day and night about Barnabas and his preposterous views of life.

"So tell Barnabas, why *do* you keep coming?"

Vitus sighed. "I don't know." He clamped his hands into fists, wanting to break something. "I don't understand many of the things you say. They're stupid, outrageous, but...."

"But what?"

"Sometimes you say something that's ridiculous, or even the complete opposite of what I believe, but the way you explain it, it seems so reasonable, logical, even. When I think about it after I leave here, I find I can no longer defend my position or believe what I used to believe."

"Yes! Yes!" replied Barnabas. "You got it!"

"Got what?"

"The truth makes sense! That is how you can know what is true and what is not. The truth is—just as you said—*reasonable*. It is coherent and simple and comforting. Untruth is the opposite!"

Vitus felt the explanation soak in like the lavender massage oil they used at the baths. The top of his head tingled, and he felt giddy for a few seconds.

Then he noticed the chain around Barnabas's leg, remembered where exactly they were, and began seething with indignation. "But the truth is *not* always reasonable," he said bitterly. "Look at yourself. You've been arrested because the high priest Caiaphas didn't like what you were saying. The truth is that your life is being squandered here in this prison cell, and there are greater odds of you being crucified than of you being set free." Wanting to be on the same level as Barnabas, Vitus stepped closer and squatted down on the straw so their faces were in line.

Barnabas gazed back with a maniacal grin. "Does it comfort you?"

With a scowl, Vitus stood back up and folded his thick forearms in front of himself. "Are you mocking me?" he asked. "In the beginning, I thought you were just another radical Jew! Another pigheaded extremist enslaved by your thousand and one laws. But I can't think straight anymore after having talked with you all these months!" Putting his hands to his head, he squeezed his skull. "It doesn't comfort me. It makes me angry! You don't belong in this prison cell. I'm not even sure you belong in this *world*."

He faced the wall and quietly banged his forehead against it. The light from the candle grew even dimmer, threatening to go out completely.

"Your anger is your hint that what you believe is not truth," said Barnabas.

Vitus groaned—a short, guttural plea like a dog about to bite. "Then explain it to me so that I can understand," he said wearily. "What is the truth of your being here?"

"Barnabas confesses he did not know the truth when he was arrested," he began, "but in hindsight it's very clear to him. The Creator had a special mission for this one that involved him being arrested and brought to this prison cell." He tilted his head down, staring at the floor in front of him as though he'd finished answering the question.

Vitus studied him for a moment, then asked, "And the Creator's mission for you?"

"To help open the heart of one who was imprisoned," Barnabas replied. "One who was ready to listen."

Vitus knew all the men currently in prison, and wondered which one Barnabas was referring to. "Is it the man in the cell next to you? The criminal we spoke of earlier, who tried to kill one of my men?"

"No," Barnabas said faintly. "It is a different prisoner. One who does not realize he is imprisoned, that his head holds him hostage, while his heart pleads to be heard."

Barnabas looked up at Vitus when he was done speaking, and when their eyes met, an unbearable, silent cry burst from Vitus's chest as he realized who Barnabas was referring to. This ridiculous young man with impossible ideals and unshakable convictions believed his duty was to go to prison solely to share the most precious teachings he'd ever encountered with an enemy of the Jewish people, a faithless Gentile, a Roman centurion whose name meant "lively."

After the shock wore off, Vitus considered Barnabas surely insane. But he couldn't shake the feeling that perhaps it was the reverse, that Barnabas was actually the sane one and everyone else, himself included, was lost in madness.

Just like the first time he'd visited Barnabas, Vitus found himself breathless and in need of air. He snatched his helmet from the straw and rushed to the door, hollering for Stone to open it.

Outside the cell, Vitus shoved the small basket into Stone's belly, ordering, "Divide this among all the prisoners."

Stone began to say something in response, but Vitus cut him off immediately. "Shut up and do as you're told!"

As he escaped down the hall, Vitus added, "And if I hear of anyone beating a prisoner without warrant, they will answer to me. Understood?"

"Yes, sir."

Vitus lurched up the stairs, ricocheting from one side to the other. Then he raced to the middle of the courtyard, where he fell to his knees, out of breath and out of time.

He had to make a choice.

* * *

Vitus squeezed his way through the market, heading to the praetorium, where he'd been told Pilate had gone.

When not in a city, a praetorium signified a general's tent within a Roman encampment. The praetorium in Jerusalem referred to a palace built by Herod Antipas's father. Pilate lived and governed there whenever he was in the city.

The market, surrounded by three columned porticoes, occupied a large public plaza outside the praetorium. Because it was a gathering point as well as a place for merchants, it was usually crowded, but today it was especially packed. As Vitus wove toward the praetorium's front entrance, he began to have to push and elbow his way through. The closer he got to the praetorium, the more dense and more agitated the crowd became, with angry shouts coming from all around.

Once past the sentries and safely inside the walls of the massive complex, Vitus stopped at a white marble fountain for a drink of water. The praetorium was filled with extravagant and opulent items like the fountain. There were two lavish buildings, each with their own banquet halls, baths, and accommodations for hundreds of guests. The immaculate grounds included gardens, groves, canals, and ponds with bronze fountains.

At the top of the stairs leading to a second-story room, Vitus spotted a fellow centurion with his back to him. Despite not seeing his face, Vitus recognized the muscular legs and V-shaped frame. It was Corvus—an ambitious pretty boy who'd recently been promoted to centurion.

Vitus, breathing heavily from hurrying up the stairs, started to ask him a question, but Corvus cut him off.

"Careful, old-timer," he said. "You don't want to have a heart attack." There was no hint of humor in his voice.

Ignoring the insult, Vitus asked, "Where's Pilate?"

Corvus removed his helmet and shook his head so that sweat from his thick brown hair sprayed in every direction.

Vitus growled under his breath as he wiped the spray from his face.

After a contemptuous laugh, Corvus replied that the prefect was inside. "Not that he wants anything to do with you," he added.

Vitus bulled past, using his shoulder to intentionally bump Corvus in the chest. Then he silently scolded himself for letting Corvus get to him so easily.

Inside the room, Vitus found the prefect peeking outdoors past one of the long orange curtains that separated the chamber from the small balcony adjoining it. Cradling his helmet at his side, Vitus approached.

"Centurion," said Pilate, noticing him immediately. "You're just in time."

"In time for what, sir?"

"Come, come. You shall see." Pilate pulled aside the curtain, motioning for Vitus to join him on the balcony. Like all the pilgrims below, he was wearing a white kerchief over his head. Vitus didn't know if it was simply a covering to protect his partly bald head from the sun, or to disguise himself as someone other than the prefect of Judea.

Out on the small balcony, Vitus could see the crowd was even bigger than he'd thought. Their furor was directed toward the larger, more formal balcony to his right, where prefects usually addressed the people.

"Sir," Vitus said cautiously, "you do know why they're upset, yes?"

"They're *always* upset about something, Centurion," Pilate said dryly. "Ever since I came here, I've heard nothing but complaints and criticism."

Vitus hoped he wasn't about to be subjected to a long tirade. Every new prefect seemed to lament the lack of respect shown them by the Jews.

The curtains fluttered in a gust of hot wind. Vitus squinted against the bright sun, watching the demonstrators yell and thrust their arms in the air. Near the back he saw a father carrying a toddler on his shoulders and wondered if they were there as protesters or as spectators.

"There is a rumor going around that you have intentions to raid the Temple's treasury to pay for the aqueduct," Vitus said.

"Is that so?" Pilate said with a shrug.

Vitus counted eight guards standing at attention on the main balcony off to their right. He assumed Pilate was going to speak to the crowd. "I'm quite sure they'll disperse if you announce there's no truth to the rumor."

Even though Pilate's head covering was the same color and material as the pilgrims wore, he'd wrapped it clumsily, and it had slipped down to his eyebrows. Vitus doubted Pilate knew how comical he looked.

"Sir," Vitus said, raising his voice over the protesters, "is there any truth to the rumor?"

Pilate tilted his head to the right. "Of course not," he answered. He wiped his mouth with the back of his hand, then repeated the same words. "Of course not."

Vitus noted three actions in Pilate's response that signified he might be lying. He tilted his head before answering, covered his mouth, and repeated the answer.

Pilate scanned the crowd below, smiling wryly when he found whatever he was searching for. "Centurion, understand this. These Jews will learn one way or the other who is in charge here."

A rotten apple suddenly whizzed between their heads and splattered against the column behind them.

"Who threw that?" Pilate asked. He scrutinized the protesters near the front.

"I didn't see, sir."

"I cannot tolerate this insolence! They'd tear me to pieces if they had the chance. And it's because of all these provocateurs—like the one you were to have reported to me about."

"Barnabas, sir."

"What?"

"The man you had arrested," Vitus explained. "His name is Barnabas."

"I don't give a damn what his name is," Pilate said. "What did you find? When can we crucify him?"

Vitus took a deep breath. Though he feared Pilate's ire at being disappointed, he was certain the alternative would be much worse, that his heart would rupture—probably violently—if he gave in. Barnabas wasn't deserving of crucifixion. He wasn't even deserving of being arrested.

From behind them, a guard pulled back the curtain and handed Pilate a bronze scepter. Vitus recognized the short, unadorned staff as the one the prefects used during formal occasions. He'd never seen it used when speaking before a crowd, though.

"Never mind," Pilate said as he hid the scepter inside his robes. "We'll discuss it later."

Vitus's relief was short-lived. It was replaced by trepidation about the already large crowd swelling even further as pilgrims, women, and children passed through, joined in, or stopped to investigate what all the commotion was about.

"Down with the pagan prefect!" someone shouted, not in Aramaic, but in Greek. Vitus heard it clearly and assumed Pilate had as well.

Curling up the corners of his lips in an ugly smile, Pilate said, "You know, I wasn't particularly fond of the Samarian unit at first, but they do have their advantages." He leaned forward, gripping the balcony wall with one hand and pointing down with the other. "Notice how well they blend in."

Vitus studied the crowd intently, spotting the Samaritans after a long search. They had no shields, helmets, or leg armor, and wore ordinary cloaks like all the Jews they were interspersed with. Their heads were covered with prayer shawls.

"It's time, Centurion," said Pilate. He put his hands on his hips, sticking his bony elbows out wide. "Time for these people to learn their place." He turned to Vitus, as if seeking confirmation, but instead just stuck his chin out and nodded his head.

Vitus gazed down again at the father carrying the toddler on his shoulders, then winced against a sudden pain in his chest. He didn't know what exactly Pilate had planned, but knew nothing good could come of it.

The energy of the boisterous, massive throng below reminded him of the bloodthirsty spectators at the Colosseum. He'd broken his leg there. Here, he held his aching heart, convinced it was next.

Chapter Twenty-Seven

"Keep your eyes closed," Jonah instructed Luke as he led him up the last few steps of a small, verdant hill. The morning sun floated over the eastern mountaintops while an angelic breeze wicked the sweat from their skin.

Jonah positioned Luke just right, turning his torso and raising his chin. "All right," he said, "open your eyes."

Before them lay an exquisite view of the towering walls and immense buildings of Jerusalem. Gently sloping mountains in the distance cradled the city. Massive sand-colored ramparts some forty feet high and eight feet thick protected the kingdom on all sides. White smoke from the Temple fires drifted gently into a sapphire-blue sky.

After watching Luke's face light up, Jonah breathed it all in himself. At last all the endless walking, sleeping on the ground, worrying about wild animals or being robbed in the middle of nowhere, was behind them. This was the only part of the journey he ever looked forward to.

"Does it look familiar?" he asked. Luke hadn't been to Jerusalem since he was five years old.

"A little bit, I guess," Luke answered. "It's unbelievable."

"You see those four towers farther inside the city?" Jonah said, pointing. "That's the Temple right next to them."

Luke blocked the sun with his hand and squinted, then yanked on Jonah's arm. "Come on!" he said and sprinted away. "Let's go there!"

Jonah laughed, then ran after him, delighting that his old body could still keep up with the youngster. Despite staying up all night watching over Luke, Jonah wasn't tired. He felt strangely invigorated since the bizarre events of the previous evening.

They caught up with Tiras and Ehud soon enough, though Jonah instantly regretted it. He assumed the sight of their destination would have softened Tiras a bit, but he could tell right away he was wrong. For whatever reason, Tiras seemed to be even more ill-tempered. He grumbled about the heat, the dust being kicked up, and the Roman soldiers—conspicuous in their crimson cloaks—intermingled with the crowd in the marketplace up ahead. In between his complaints, he lectured the boys about enemies of the Jewish people. He was especially vitriolic concerning the Herods, whom he blamed for a multitude of current problems.

When he paused his rant to take a breath, Luke asked innocently, "Has Herod Antipas or his father ever done anything nice?"

Tiras shot him a look of disdain. "Nothing at all," he asserted. "Why would they? They don't give a damn about us Jews."

Jonah certainly wasn't fond of Herod Antipas or his father either, but Tiras's statement irked him as being grossly distorted. "I know his father arranged for Egyptian grain to be imported during the great famine fifty years ago," he announced. "That saved the lives of countless numbers of people, including my own father and all his siblings."

Clearly affronted, Tiras opened his mouth to respond, but Jonah wasn't finished and cut him off.

"He also renovated the Temple into the splendor it is today. And he expanded the courtyard at least tenfold for us pilgrims," he continued. "As for Herod Antipas, things have been quite stable since he took power—very few famines or wars or invading armies."

Tiras gave a grunt and scowled at Jonah. Then he hurried ahead despite his limp.

Jonah caught Luke casting a sidelong glance at him, and the two of them couldn't help but snicker. It was the first time Jonah had gotten the best of Tiras on the entire trip.

The mass of people condensed as they approached the marketplace just outside the city walls. In Jonah's previous journeys to Jerusalem, he'd found that most pilgrims, no matter how arduous their journey, usually became joyful, giddy even, as they converged on the city, so he was perplexed that the crowd seemed more jittery than joyous. Hoping to understand why, he listened in on snippets of conversations.

"Indeed, what good thing ever happens in Galilee?" a sullen voice somewhere to his left grumbled.

Jonah knew there would be no answer, that it had been asked rhetorically. The Jews of Judea looked down on those from Galilee as crude and uncouth.

"Grandfather, did you hear the latest about Zebulun and his group of bandits?" a voice to Jonah's right said.

Jonah swallowed hard as he searched for the speaker. It had been over a decade since he'd spoken to Zebulun.

"That criminal? Who cares?" a raspy voice replied.

Though Jonah could hear their conversation, he couldn't locate them. The majestic view of the city he'd enjoyed a short while ago was gone, replaced by the tall butts of camels in front and a steady stream of pilgrims on either side.

"I heard he thinks he's the new King David," the grandson continued. "Says he's going to kick the Romans out, and the Herods too, then crown himself king."

Jonah wasn't surprised to hear it. In hindsight, he could see all too clearly who Zebulun was.

"Let me guess," the grandfather replied. "Zebulun has begun quoting from the book of Isaiah, yes?" He then proceeded to recite a verse in a sarcastic tone. "'The Spirit of the Lord God is upon me, because the Lord has anointed me to bring good news to the afflicted. He has sent me to bind up the brokenhearted; To proclaim liberty to captives and freedom to prisoners; To proclaim the favorable year of the Lord and the day of vengeance of our God.'"

"How did you know?" the grandson replied in an incredulous voice.

"Someone like that comes along every few years," the older man answered. "They think they're God's chosen one. Proclaim the righteousness of their cause. Cite examples of how they're fulfilling the prophecies." After a short pause, he added wearily, "Then they're either killed, imprisoned, or chased off. It's always the same...."

Jonah agreed. He'd seen it himself enough times too. It seemed like a messiah or new King David was forever on the horizon, never to arrive.

After a few more minutes of walking, they entered the bazaar outside the main gate. Jonah tilted his head up at the formidable front wall of the city, with its parapets and Roman soldiers leering down. From certain angles, Jerusalem seemed more intimidating fortress than sacred destination.

There were money changers and animal vendors inside the city, near the Temple, but they were more expensive, so Jonah and Tiras chose to do their business outside. Since it was required to pay the Temple tax in shekels, Tiras went to exchange money. Jonah and the boys stood in line to purchase an animal.

"What do you usually get?" Jonah asked Ehud as he surveyed all the animals for sale: goats, calves, lambs, doves, even a few deer.

"A lamb," Ehud responded. "A few times when we didn't have much money we had to get doves."

When going to the Temple, it was obligatory to bring a sacrifice. They were prescribed for the expiation of certain types of sins, although the more general purpose was expressing thanks to God.

A barefoot, dark-skinned slave in a knee-length tunic passed by, leading a bull on a rope. The huge, docile animal defecated with each step as it passed by.

"How much to buy a bull?" asked Luke.

"Probably two hundred dinars," Jonah answered. "More than all the rent we'd pay for our house for two years."

The odor of the cow manure wasn't even noticeable since the entire area was already saturated with the smells of animals and their excrement.

Jonah adjusted Luke's prayer shawl so it protected the back of his neck. "It's going to be a hot one," he remarked. "Make sure you keep your face and head covered." Amaryah had bought Luke a new prayer shawl for the occasion. Jonah knew both the material and the dye, and that it was destined to fade rather quickly, but for now it was as bright and orange as a setting sun.

As they shuffled ahead in line, Luke pointed at a plump goat gnawing on the rope that tied it to a stake in the ground. "Can we get that goat?"

Jonah shook his head. It bore too much resemblance to poor Graha from his childhood. "How about that old ram next to it?" he countered. "Looks like he's led a good long life."

Luke agreed. Then he and Ehud sneaked their way through the thick throng to join Tiras on the other line.

Everywhere Jonah turned, he heard not only different accents, but different languages. And though everyone in the marketplace wore similar looking garments, Jonah could detect differences among them. All the Jewish pilgrims had prayer shawls and wore ankle-length tunics, unlike slaves, soldiers, or Gentiles, whose tunics were usually knee-length. He could tell farmers from Galilee because they had a certain purposefulness to their stride that others did not. The poor were obvious because they could not afford dyed fabric, whereas those from abroad often wore fine, brightly colored robes.

There were also subtleties of skin color that Jonah could distinguish. Farmers and construction workers had the darkest and most wrinkled skin, whereas the more well-to-do and foreigners from more northern climates had lighter skin.

And the Pharisees, of course, always stood out, because they wanted to.

The Jerusalem festivals were held yearly, but most Jews made the journey to the Temple only once every few years or—depending on their distance from Jerusalem—once in a lifetime. Jonah had last come for Passover several years ago. Of the three pilgrimages commanded by the scriptures, Passover was the first of the year and celebrated the Exodus, as well as the beginning of the new planting season after the winter rains. Pentecost was the second festival, held during the late spring harvest, to give thanks and present the first of the crops to God. Sukkot was the final festival of the year and commemorated the wandering of the Jews in the desert for forty years. It also celebrated the last harvest before the onset of the winter rains.

After Jonah reached the front of the line, he only had to haggle a little before agreeing on a price for the ram. When he rejoined Tiras and the boys, they had just finished exchanging money. Ehud regarded the ram from head to toe, exclaiming, "That's a fine animal. Look at those horns, Father!"

Tiras dragged Ehud forward by the arm. "God doesn't care about the size of the horns," he grumbled. "Come on. Let's get *our* sacrifice."

Luke gathered a few sparse weeds from the ground and fed them to the ram. Jonah eyed the souvenir sellers from afar. They sold pottery in every shape with painted images of the Temple or with the word "Jerusalem" written in ornamental Hebrew letters. For the more affluent, there was jewelry and decorative perfume bottles. Over top of all the odors, Jonah detected the sublime scent of frankincense. Though he couldn't see the man selling it, he spotted his raised arm holding a lit stick, his deep voice announcing, "Incense! Best quality! Lowest price!"

Luke ran his fingers across the scratches on Jonah's forearms. "Do they hurt?"

"Not so much," answered Jonah, "but they itch." He'd thought long and hard about what to say to the boys when the inevitable questions came about the claw marks on his cloak and scratches on his arms. Ultimately, he'd decided to tell them the truth.

"Ehud's father says you made it up," said Luke.

"And you?"

"I believe you. So does Ehud. He says he saw it, but was too scared to move."

Wanting Luke to learn to trust his instincts, Jonah tried to reassure him. "You were right to want to start a fire."

"I know, but it *was* against the commandments."

"One of the hardest things to learn in this culture is balancing your best judgment and what the commandments demand. I'm forty-four and still struggling with that," he said with a laugh.

Tiras and Ehud returned with a stubborn brown calf on a rope. While Tiras pulled from the front, Ehud had to prod it from behind. Jonah heard Tiras explaining to his son, "...and the more valuable the sacrifice, the more pleased God is."

Luke went over and petted the animal on the solitary streak of white fur between its eyes; then the calf unexpectedly lay down. Luke thought it humorous, but Ehud was upset.

"Hey, what are you doing?" he exclaimed. "Get up!" Ehud pulled hard on the rope, but the calf barely budged.

Jonah was surprised Tiras could afford it. Tiras had already mentioned earlier in their journey he'd had to borrow money from his relatives just to be able to make the pilgrimage. While a lamb could be purchased for around four dinars, and a ram for eight, a calf cost *twenty*.

As the boys pushed and pulled every which way to get the calf to stand up, Jonah saw something he knew Tiras wouldn't be happy about. "I hate to bring this to your attention, Tiras, but you might want to reconsider your sacrifice."

"Jonah," Tiras began and paused, tilting his chin down. "God does not look kindly on envy."

Jonah caught him in another fake smile. "Neither does He look kindly on blemished sacrifices."

"I examined this animal myself. There's nothing wrong with it."

Though the calf weighed more than Luke and Ehud put together, they somehow managed to get it back to its feet.

"Leviticus twenty-four," Jonah said without elaborating.

Ehud wrinkled his nose and looked away in thought for a few seconds, then abruptly squatted down and inspected the calf's underside.

"Father!" he gasped. "He's right! Look!"

Tiras sat on his heels. "What? I don't see anything."

"The testicles have a scratch," said Ehud. "In Leviticus it says you must not offer to the Lord an animal whose testicles are bruised, crushed, torn, or cut."

Ehud, mouth agape, stared blankly up at Jonah.

Jonah stiffened his lips to suppress a grin. Catching Luke smiling at him, he winked in response. He might not know as much scripture as Tiras, or even Ehud, but Jonah had always remembered that verse from Leviticus because it seemed so peculiar.

Tiras yanked the calf harshly by its rope and turned back toward the vendor he'd bought it from.

Knowing that returning the calf would be no simple or short task, Jonah called out to him, "We'll go to the market inside and get breakfast for us, then meet you back here."

Though a few vendors were selling food outside the city, Jonah remembered from past visits there was a larger selection and better quality inside the city. He asked Ehud to hold their ram; then he and Luke headed for the main gate.

Once inside the city walls, Jonah and Luke encountered a bottleneck where the base of one of the praetorium's tall towers bulged into the narrow road. While they slowly inched forward, Jonah used the opportunity to scrutinize all possible escape routes—a habit leftover from his time with the bandits. He discovered a short, four-foot reinforcement wall adjoining the praetorium's ramparts and towers. It wasn't very wide—perhaps eight inches—and was slanted slightly downward, but he thought he could probably climb up and travel along it if he needed to. Other than that, the way in and out was alarmingly limited.

Luke asked something, but Jonah couldn't hear him over all the noise. There was a chorus of shouts ahead of them, sounds of vendors haggling in the marketplace behind, the braying of goats, mooing of cows, and swirling conversations all around.

"I said," Luke yelled in Jonah's ear, "is it true that Pilate is planning to seize funds from the Temple?"

Surprised by the question, Jonah assumed Luke must have overheard others talking about the prefect. Before he could respond, a heavily bearded Pharisee next to him answered.

"Yes, he wants it for the aqueduct."

"Things are going to get really ugly if he does that," Jonah commented.

"How much worse can it get?" said the Pharisee.

Jonah wasn't entirely sure what he meant. He knew that discontent ran high, but that was the way it had always been.

"This wouldn't be happening if Pilate's overseer was in his capital where he belongs, instead of Rome," added the Pharisee.

Jonah had no idea that the governor of Greater Syria was in Rome and not Antioch. He didn't know if this was common knowledge or not. Every visit to Jerusalem always brought an abundance of news.

Once past the tower, they continued down a short road that led to the market. Though Jonah remembered the area was usually crowded, it was especially dense now. There seemed to be some kind of protest going on. He and Luke had to squeeze their way through hundreds, perhaps thousands, of protesters. Angry cries filled the air. Fists pumped skyward above covered heads. Jonah had never seen so many openly defiant Jews gathered in one place. Now he understood what the Pharisee had meant.

As he listened to the protests, his attention was drawn to the large balcony everyone focused on.

"Down with Pilate!" a young man on the right yelled, his face red with outrage.

"Stop the thieves!" shouted a hoarse voice on his left.

Jonah scanned the balcony for the new prefect, but saw only eight Roman guards there. They stood at attention, four to a side, with an empty thronelike chair in the middle.

Luke tugged on Jonah's tunic. "Where's the market? I'm hungry," he said. The faint scent of freshly baked bread and roasted meat was wafting through the air.

"It's just up ahead," Jonah answered. He wiped a bead of sweat from his forehead, feeling apprehensive. The situation felt volatile, and there was no easy way out of the cramped conditions. If he'd known about the protest, he would have gotten their breakfast outside.

A tall centurion marched to the front of the balcony. He was young, with thick brown hair sticking out from his helmet. He raised his hand, signaling for the crowd to quiet so he could speak. When they did, he announced, "The prefect orders you to disband and cease your protest! Leave this area immediately!"

The crowd jeered in response and became even more boisterous. Someone hurled a piece of half-eaten bread that landed harmlessly behind the centurion as he exited. Jonah was surprised to see him leave without uttering another word. He expected a threat, an ultimatum, or at a minimum a repeating of the order.

As they continued squirming their way through the protesters, Jonah spied two men standing on a smaller balcony off to the side of the main one. One of the men was dressed strangely, with a prayer shawl drooping down his forehead all the way to his eyebrows. The other held a centurion's helmet under his right arm, and, despite the years, Jonah recognized him right away. His face was more wrinkled and his eyebrows were turning gray, but it was the same face with the same long scar on the cheek that had haunted Jonah's dreams for the past thirteen years.

Jonah gritted his teeth so hard that his jaw popped. How he wished he had a bow and arrow!

In his fury, he jerked Luke forward, shouting in his ear, "You see that centurion?" He was going to show him the man responsible for his father's death, the devil who'd arrested Thomas and had him scourged and crucified.

He pointed to the balcony, waiting for Luke's confirmation, then saw the man with the drooping prayer shawl turn toward the crowd and raise a short bronze scepter high over his head. Since scepters were the adornment of kings and rulers, Jonah wondered if the man might be the prefect trying to get the crowd's attention.

Luke pulled urgently on Jonah's arm, directing his attention to something nearby. "Look!"

The blood drained from Jonah's face and immediately raced to his extremities. There, a few yards away, was a man removing his prayer shawl and cloak, revealing leather armor and a sheathed short-sword. In his right hand, he held a long wooden club with a bulbous top. Without warning, he swung it at the closest person to him, striking a young man in the side of the head and sending him sprawling to the ground. Past him, Jonah could see other soldiers who'd removed their disguises and were also beating protesters, bystanders, anyone within reach....

Chaos erupted. Shouts turned from indignant to panicked. Everyone attempted to flee, but in different directions. Jonah found himself at the mercy of the terrified crowd. He was pushed one way and then the next, so that after only a matter of seconds he could no longer see Luke and had lost track of him completely.

Swept up by a mob stampeding toward the main gate, Jonah could not free himself no matter how much he struggled. It was the same as when he'd been caught in a storm on the Sea of Galilee. Fighting against the tide was futile. He'd have to wait, conserve his energy for when the conditions changed.

As the throng pushed him along the road, Jonah desperately looked for an opportunity to get back to Luke. When he again saw the short reinforcement wall adjoining the tall ramparts of the praetorium, he knew it was his only chance. Though he had no hope of going against the flow of the crowd, he could move sideways, so he pushed and squeezed his way over to the right. Then he used the tightly packed mass of people as a human ladder to help him climb up to the wall.

Once on top, everything slowed down. Seconds seemed like minutes as he slid his feet one at a time, shuffling back toward the place he'd been separated from Luke. He had to be careful to remain leaning against the wall behind him. If he were to bend even slightly forward, he would surely tumble off the narrow ledge.

He scoured the crowd, searching for Luke's bright orange prayer shawl, hoping it hadn't been lost in the madness. He called out Luke's name, but the noise was so deafening he didn't even hear his own voice.

Then, suddenly, he spotted him. A soldier had chased Luke into a corner and was closing in, club raised high over his head. Jonah leapt from the wall back into the hornet's nest, sprinting toward Luke who had managed to duck under the soldier's first swing at him. Before the second attempt, Jonah crashed into the soldier like a charging bull.

Clasping his arms around the man's throat, Jonah held him in a chokehold. Then he pried the club away and scrambled to his feet. As the soldier gasped to catch his breath, Jonah swung the club hard against the man's knee, making doubly sure he wouldn't be pursuing them.

Reaching out for Luke, Jonah yelled, "Come!"

He gripped Luke's hand tightly, leading the way out of the melee, dodging clubs and jumping over the fallen. They ran toward the main gate, making good progress until they arrived at the narrow passage where the base of the tower bulged into the road. There, everything came to a halt.

"Tell me what's going on," Jonah shouted to Luke. He then lifted him up by the waist so he could see over the others in front of them.

Luke was in tears when Jonah set him back on the ground. "It's a blockade!"

"What do you mean?" yelled Jonah. "Are they blocking the road so we can't get out?"

"No," Luke cried, "it's a wall of bodies. People are climbing over them!"

Jonah understood now. So many people must have been trampled at the bottleneck that their bodies had formed a barrier others now had to crawl over.

He pushed his way once again to the short reinforcement wall and helped Luke climb up onto it. Then he scaled it himself, and the two of them slowly made their way around the base of the tower.

"Keep looking up!" he commanded Luke. He was afraid that if Luke let his eyes drop, he might lean forward and fall off, especially if he glimpsed the pile of trampled bodies.

Once clear of the roadblock, they jumped down onto the stone road. Behind him, Jonah saw others on top of the wall, following his lead in using it as an escape route.

The two of them raced toward the main gate, Jonah clutching Luke's forearm so that they ran side by side. He refused to let go until they'd gotten safely outside the city. In the marketplace, Jonah spotted Tiras and Ehud. "Tell them to follow us," he hollered to Luke.

The four of them, plus the ram and calf, hurried away from Jerusalem. If there was one thing Jonah had learned in his life about encountering violence, it was to put as much distance as possible between it and yourself as swiftly as you could.

He tried to warn the hundreds of pilgrims still streaming toward the city, but they only looked at him as though he was mad.

After traveling about half a mile, Jonah told everyone to stop. He checked behind them to see if the carnage had spread beyond the city's walls. Content that it hadn't, he explained what had happened to Tiras and Ehud. As he did so, Luke began sobbing uncontrollably, mumbling, "Why? Why, God? Why?"

Jonah pulled him close, holding Luke's head to his chest and running his fingers through Luke's hair. "It's all right," he whispered. "We're safe now."

"I'll tell you why," Tiras declared, glaring at them both. "These are the end of days, and this is God's wrath!" He was nearly screaming. "He is angry with Jews for not following the commandments!"

Jonah let go of Luke, curled his fist into a tight ball, and swung it furiously. He struck Tiras squarely in the cheek, knocking him backwards to the ground.

Then he took Luke's hand in his and headed north toward the familiar roads of Galilee.

He never once looked back. He wasn't even tempted to.

Chapter Twenty-Eight

Azara waved goodbye to Hadassah's girls as they skipped away from her front door. In the four months since she opened her school, she could swear each of them had already grown an entire inch.

"You're doing wonderful work, Azara," Hadassah called out after taking each of them by the hand. "My son is greatly annoyed that his sisters can read just as well as he can and sometimes know things he doesn't!" She laughed gaily as the three of them disappeared around the corner of the stone wall.

Azara returned to her classroom, humming an old Persian lullaby her father used to sing to her. It had been a good day. All twelve seats of her desks had been filled, and despite her fears of the girls being unmotivated, she'd found the opposite. They were eager learners who had made tremendous progress in their studies for such a short amount of time.

"Esther," Azara called out to the next room, "Could you collect the wax tablets from the desks?"

Esther, one of five Jewish girls in Azara's school, had begun staying after class to help Azara clean and prepare for the next day. She was twelve—nearly thirteen, she liked to remind everyone—incredibly bright, and always unpredictable.

Esther trudged in with an exaggerated slouch. "As you desire, master," she said in a mock low and dreary voice.

Azara laughed at her. "What is that all about?"

Esther straightened up and spoke in her normal voice. "That's how Hadassah's slaves always act."

"You're right!" said Azara. "That was a good imitation. I didn't know you were an actor."

"I'm many things," Esther said. Stretching up on her toes, she did a quick spin, the dark hair that hung to the middle of her back flying parallel to the floor. "Actor. Scholar. Inventor."

Azara regarded the small, black mole on Esther's right cheek and how it made her seem slightly exotic. "And what have you invented?"

"I made a trap that caught the mouse who kept stealing our grain."

Azara smiled and shook her head in amazement.

"I named him Moses. He lives in a cage under my bed now."

Not only did Esther not mind being different from other girls, Azara noticed, she relished it. Each day she added something unique to her appearance. Today it was a small red flower tucked above her ear.

"Perhaps you can bring Moses to class," Azara suggested. "Show the rest of the girls."

"No," Esther said without hesitation. "They'd scream and then jump up on the desks."

Azara retrieved a well-worn straw broom from the corner. "Hmm, you're probably right," she agreed. "Better leave Moses at home."

She began sweeping the tile floor of the classroom, collecting dirt and a few dead flies into a small pile. "What do you think the girls would like better for the next storytime?" she asked. "I thought we'd do some more Jewish history: either the story of how the first Temple came to be destroyed, or how the kingdom split into Judea and Samaria."

Esther gave a dramatic sigh. "My grandfather used to tell me Jewish stories night and day. Every one of them was about a battle or an uprising or some sort of violence." She picked up another wax tablet, cradling it with the others in her left arm. "And *the Exodus!* Ugh! If I hear one more story about the river of blood and the escape from the land of pyramids and the forty years in the desert, I'll kill myself."

Azara couldn't help but grin at Esther's melodramatic display. She reminded her of herself when she was that age. "All right," Azara said with a twinkle in her eye. "No *Jewish* history then. How about I tell an old *Egyptian* story? It's about a great mouse pharaoh who was beloved by all the mice of the land and—"

"Mice?" Esther interrupted.

"Yes, it was a kingdom of mice," Azara said, maintaining a straight face.

Esther narrowed her eyes. "Is this a real story?"

"Of course," answered Azara. "Every young Egyptian boy and girl would know this story. It's been passed down for generations."

Esther looked skeptical. "What happens to this 'beloved mouse pharaoh'?"

"Well, I don't want to give the whole story away," she said, suppressing a smirk, "but the Pharaoh and all the mice of the land suffer through ten terrible plagues brought on by an immigrant mouse who betrayed the Pharaoh's hospitality and—"

"Oh! Let me guess," Esther interrupted again. "And the immigrant mouse who brought on the deadly plagues had been raised by the Pharaoh's own daughter and in the Pharaoh's own palace!"

Azara feigned surprise as she took a sip from her cup. "You know this story?" she said, then could hold it in no longer. She burst out laughing, spitting the water in all directions.

Esther erupted in giggles and snorts as well, and the two of them could scarcely catch their breath.

"I suppose," Esther said in between gasps for air, "I'd better set Moses free from his cage before he starts making it rain frogs in my bedroom!"

They both laughed even harder.

"But seriously," Esther said once she'd calmed down. "Do the Egyptians really tell the story of the Exodus, but from their point of view?"

"Why wouldn't they?"

Esther rested her chin on her right palm and studied the floor. "It makes sense they would, I suppose."

Bending slightly at the waist, Azara took a few more deep breaths to try to compose herself.

"How about for next week," Esther said, "you tell us something different? Maybe a love story?"

"A love story?" Azara touched her index finger to her lips. "A happy one or a sad one?"

"A sad one," Esther answered. "About a boy and girl who fall in love, but can't be together."

Azara knew what she was alluding to. Esther had confided to her she was in love with a boy and that the two of them sometimes met secretly at night. But her father had already betrothed her to someone else.

During betrothal, which could last several months to several years, the bride and groom continued to live apart while all the details of the agreement between the two families were worked out, including the sum the bridegroom's father would pay to the bride's father. It was not uncommon for the bride to never even see her husband until her wedding day.

"All right," said Azara. "I'll tell an old Greek story, about Orpheus and Eurydice. It's so sad that I cried for nearly an hour the first time I heard it."

Esther nodded firmly. "Perfect."

Then they looked at one another and burst out laughing once more.

Alternately holding her belly and wiping tears from her eyes, Azara wondered if it was possible to die of too much laughter. She hoped it was. She wanted to pass away being this happy, this connected to another person. She loved Esther like her own daughter.

A deep, rumbling thunder in the distance quieted them. Azara held her breath until it was over. She hated storms.

After collecting the last wax tablet, Esther asked, "Where do you want these?"

"On top of the dresser," Azara answered. Setting the broom aside, she went to the next room to refill her cup with water.

"You know, my mother was fascinated with the Buddhist teachings you told us about," Esther called out to her.

"Oh, really?"

"Well, not at first," Esther clarified, "but after I explained to her, like you said, that it's more of a philosophy than a religion, she listened to me. She was really interested in the idea of Samsara—that we're continually going around on a wheel of death and rebirth, seeking to satisfy our desires."

"Did she ask any questions?" Azara asked, returning with her cup.

"No, she never does when I tell her what I learned that day. She just likes to listen."

Azara saw Esther was absorbed by something on her dresser and went over to see what it was. At first she assumed it was the dresser itself. Imported from the Far East by her father, it usually caught everyone's eye with its beautiful curves and red paint. But it wasn't the dresser that had attracted Esther's attention. It was an intricate carving Azara had bought in Samarkand a long time ago.

"The craftsmanship is amazing," Esther remarked. "Who is it?"

"That's Shiva," said Azara. "Shiva is—"

"I know. Don't tell me," implored Esther. "Shiva is the name for God in Hinduism, right?"

Azara took a long drink of water and smiled. "Yes. Seems you remember everything I tell you. Where did you get such an amazing memory?"

"And the material?" Esther asked, examining its flawless white color. "I've never seen a mineral quite like it. Where is it found?"

"It's nothing they dug from the ground," Azara said. "It's ivory. It's from an elephant's tusk."

Esther ran her fingers along the edges of the small statue. "Have you ever seen one?" she asked. "An elephant?"

Azara was standing close. She could feel Esther's body heat and smell the faint fragrance of the red flower above her ear. "Yes," she answered softly, "when I was a girl traveling with my father in the East. I remember the first time I saw one, I pinched myself to make sure I wasn't dreaming it all. They're so big you can't even imagine."

Esther set the statue down and pushed it away. "I wish I had your life," she said. "I'll never see an elephant."

"You don't know that," Azara said, trying to comfort her. "Life is full of twists and turns you can't predict."

"I can predict my life easily enough," Esther answered. "It will be the same as my mother's, my grandmother's, and my grandmother's mother's.... I'll be stuck here in Galilee, shut up in my husband's house until I'm old and die."

Azara wrapped her arm around Esther's shoulder and squeezed her close. How she wished she could clap her hands and grant Esther's every wish. But she couldn't, and Esther curled into Azara's arms and quietly wept.

After only a minute, Esther pulled away and held her head high. "That's enough of that," she said, drying her eyes with her headscarf. "Forget what I said. God has plans for me." She nodded her head as if convincing herself. "I know He does. I just have to trust in Him." She picked up Azara's cup of water. "May I?"

"Of course," Azara replied. "I nearly drank it all, though. Let me go get you some more."

As she retrieved the jug of water, Azara heard the distant voices of men coming down the road in front of her house. "A customer told me he'd be stopping by today," she called to Esther. "That might be him coming now." When she finished refilling the cup for Esther, she scanned the area, her eyes falling on the bowl of dirty water near the door. It was for people to wash their feet before entering. "Here," she said, handing the bowl to Esther. "Dump this water in the back next to the cucumbers. Then refill it for me."

Esther took the bowl and went out the back entrance while Azara hastily tidied up her shop—dusting off bottles and straightening baskets.

To make space for her classroom, she'd moved her shop into the sole bedroom of the house. The small room was crammed with shelves of exotic spices, perfumes, ointments, and jugs of imported oils. The man who'd said he'd be stopping by was a physician, so Azara inspected her inventory of herbs and tinctures, noting with disappointment she was completely out of two of her more popular items—cumin, used for treating wounds, and asphalt from the Dead Sea, which was applied to boils.

Since she'd heard men's voices, not women's, she hid the bottles of perfumes under a scarf. Perfume sellers were looked down upon, especially by men, but Azara didn't mind. Perfumes constituted the bulk of her profits, and the wives of the rich were her most valued customers. Besides, she hardly noticed the additional scorn, having more than enough from being a woman, a Gentile, unmarried, and without children.

The men were closer now and Azara could make out what they were saying. One man in particular seemed to be greatly agitated.

"Are you not one of the leaders of this community?" he said, his voice rising. "Have you no authority over such matters?"

"We are not the Romans," came the exasperated response. "We do not imprison people or crucify them because they say something we don't agree with! She hasn't broken any laws."

"She most certainly has!" the man exclaimed. "She is teaching of false prophets and idolatry."

"That may be, but she is not a Jew. She is not subject to the laws of the Torah."

"Bah!" the man said. "If you won't do anything about it, then *we* will."

Azara rushed to her window and caught a glimpse of three men approaching her house. Behind them, the sky was growing dark—thick with rain clouds.

"Open up!" the angry man shouted as he stepped up to the door and pounded on it.

Azara kept the door closed and locked. "What do you want?"

She hadn't recognized him, though he did somehow seem familiar to her. She knew the other two. The stooped man with the ram's horn cane was a Jewish elder known to all throughout the community. He was head of a council whose responsibilities included arbitrating disputes and determining punishments. He'd already visited her three times to express concerns over her school.

"Please," the elder said gently. "We only wish to speak with you."

Azara opened the door a crack, but the angry man pushed it open further. He thrust his finger at her accusingly. "My wife told me you'd be teaching her mathematics and how to read and write," he said.

Now Azara knew who he was. It was Salome's husband—Esther's father—the only parent she'd never formally been introduced to, because he was always away working construction. Like his daughter, he had a black mole on the right cheek, only his made him appear sinister instead of exotic.

"That *is* what I teach them," Azara replied. She tried not to let her eyes fall on the neckless brute Esther's father had brought with him. She'd seen him many times before. He never said much, just glared at others with his unsmiling face and one good eye. Whenever there was cause for a stoning, Azara always saw him at the front of the crowd with a big basket of stones.

"Then where did she learn this nonsense about the four liberal truths and some prophet named Buddha?"

"It's the four *noble* truths," Azara explained calmly, "and Buddha was not a prophet. He was—"

"I don't care who he was," the man yelled. "I'll not have my daughter learning blasphemy!"

Azara put her hands on her hips. "I'm giving your daughter an *education*, and for *free* I might add. An education doesn't teach her *what* to believe. It gives her the knowledge and ability to think critically so she can decide for herself. If you—"

"My daughter will *believe* what *I* tell her to," he declared. A jagged, blue vein on his temple bulged toward his hairline. "Where is she anyway? Esther!"

Azara twisted to peer over her shoulder. Esther stood mutely behind her, holding the bowl of water at waist level. Her head was down. Face pale. Laughter long gone.

"Esther, get out here now!" her father commanded.

Azara opened the door wider for Esther to pass by. The elder squeezed to the front and began addressing Azara from just a few inches away.

"As you know," he said, "this is not the first complaint I've received." He had a high-pitched voice, and his breath reeked of onion. "While I appreciate, and respect, your desire to be of service to the community, I'm asking you once more, dear woman—for the sake of peace—to cease with this school of yours."

Azara had already agreed with him on a previous visit to keep her school's profile low and not have any classes outdoors under the shade of a tree, like the boys did when it was hot. Glumly watching Esther lace her sandals, Azara recalled the girl's courageous words from a few moments ago, wishing she, herself, trusted in God's plans.

There was a pause while the three men stared at Azara, awaiting her response. The thunder rumbled again, this time a little closer.

Though trembling with fear on the inside, Azara did her best not to show it. Violence was not uncommon in Capernaum, though justice was—especially if the victim was a woman and a Gentile. "I'll think about it," she replied, wanting more than anything for the three of them to go away.

She started to close the door, but Esther's father stuck his foot in, stopping it. "There's nothing to think about," he said menacingly. "Either you stop your heresy or we'll do it for you."

Azara refused to look at his hate-filled face or the brute's lazy eye. Instead, she pushed on the door with all her weight until it latched shut.

"Brothers, come," she heard the elder say. "We've said our piece. Let us leave."

Azara leaned against the door, locking it and listening for the sounds of their departing footsteps. She stayed that way—shoulder against the door, biting her bottom lip—long after she'd heard them leave. Then she began to pace back and forth, pondering what to do. It was already clear her favorite student was being taken from her.

The room grew darker, though sunset was still hours away. A sudden gust of wind whistled through the cracks in the front door. A basket of flowers from the students toppled from the windowsill and spilled on the floor.

Azara slumped onto her wool mattress and combed her hair. It was the only activity she'd found that consistently calmed her nerves. Doing her best not to give in to fear, she tried to think logically about the situation. As a shopkeeper, she could hardly afford to offend the Jews in a majority Jewish city. If they avoided her shop, she could expect a slow slide into poverty. But if she did as they wanted and closed her school, she could continue to live a reasonably safe and comfortable life, secure in her financial situation and social standing, however meek it was.

From a logical point of view, it didn't make sense to fight this battle, but she picked up the cup she had drunk out of earlier and flung it across the room anyway. It shattered into a thousand pieces when it hit the wall. Then she screamed and pulled her hair and told the world she hated it.

There was a ghastly flash of light, followed by a crack of thunder so loud Azara was convinced it came from her own courtyard.

Curling into a ball, she hugged her knees tightly.

She hated storms.

Chapter Twenty-Nine

The wooden wheel of the weather-beaten wagon was nearly as high as Vitus's shoulders. He rested his arms on top of it and calculated by the sun's position that they had about three more hours of daylight left. In the far north, rain clouds loomed once again, but he held out little hope for them heading in his direction and releasing their precious contents. He could only cling to the knowledge that the winter rains would eventually—imminently—come and relieve both land and its creatures of the endless hot, dry weather.

From behind him, he heard the familiar refrain of the civilian engineer berating the workers. They were near a ravine somewhere between Jerusalem and the Dead Sea. Exactly where, Vitus didn't know, nor did he care. He had been charged by Pilate with the ignoble task of overseeing construction of new latrines here. It was an act of retribution, Vitus knew, but he was powerless to do anything about it.

The official explanation was that the latrines were needed for a large construction project scheduled to begin soon, but Vitus felt fairly sure the latrines were mainly meant for Pilate. During his two-day journey by horse between Jerusalem and the Roman garrison at Masada, Pilate was known to complain there was nowhere to stop for a rest in the area. It was a long stretch of high desert with no nearby villages—or even trees.

The engineer stomped back to Vitus and the wagon, muttering all the while, "Those imbeciles. You've got to watch them every minute or they'll screw up."

Vitus didn't bother asking what had happened. He'd learned by now that every little thing upset the short, pot-bellied man. Like Vitus, he'd been born north of Rome, but had spent most of his adult life in Judea. The engineer oversaw various construction projects here and in nearby provinces.

"It's time for their last break before we head back for the day," Vitus said.

Though the engineer had all the necessary knowledge of latrine construction, Vitus had been made the one responsible for the project's completion, including ensuring it was done on time and on budget.

"They don't need a break," the engineer snapped. "What they need to do is fix their mistakes."

A tiny breeze picked up and Vitus pulled his sweat-soaked tunic from his back, hoping for some air to flow there. In order not to draw undue attention to himself, he wore civilian garb, dressing in an ordinary off-white tunic with a long piece of fabric wrapped in spirals around his bald head to protect it from the sun.

"In case you haven't noticed," the engineer continued. "We're behind schedule. And it's all because of these *idiots!*" He spat on the ground.

The workers were mainly dark-skinned Nabataeans, plus a few Galilean Gentiles. No Jews had been hired since they refused to work on the Sabbath.

Vitus knew the engineer would calm down in a little while. He always did. To give him time, Vitus walked up a small incline to get a view of the progress being made. Near a wilting, slumped-over cactus, he slowly shook his head at the absurd project. To him, it was all a waste of time and money. Latrines were for encampments and cities, not for uninhabited wastelands like this.

The groundwork was complete, including the gutter that connected to the nearby tiny creek. The walls were about half-finished, and the workers were currently framing rectangular slots on one side to allow light in.

The latrines weren't going to be impressive like the grand public ones in Caesarea, with their painted frescoes, mosaic floors, and fountains. This would be a small building made of crude materials with enough space for just five people to sit on one solitary row. Half of the building would be enclosed for the latrines, and half would have no walls and only a roof, to be used as a shaded area for resting and eating.

On his way back to the wagon, Vitus held his breath against a swirling cloud of dust. When it had passed, he prepared a jug of water for the workers. It seemed so obvious to him that giving them their allotted rest was the ethical thing to do. He couldn't grasp the engineer's perspective. Placing two fingers in his mouth, he let out a loud, high-pitched whistle—the signal for the workers to begin their break.

The engineer scowled at him, again spitting on the ground. "The prefect will surely be unhappy about the project taking longer than it was supposed to," he said.

"That's my concern," Vitus answered. "Not yours."

"It will reflect on me as well!"

"Why must you argue with me on this?" Vitus shouted irritably. "Why?" He couldn't understand why he had to fight so hard all the time to do the right thing. What was worse, he often seemed to be punished for it. It was as though the world despised virtue.

While the workers lined up at the wagon for water, Vitus stormed away. Now, he was the one who needed to calm down.

As he trudged up toward the edge of the ravine, his back pain flared, but it didn't take him by surprise. Vitus had begun to see a link between the aches in his body and what he was thinking about. The two things that most reliably triggered pain these days were Barnabas and the catastrophe in Jerusalem during Sukkot.

Though he longed to speak with Barnabas, Pilate had forbidden him from entering the prison. Pilate claimed it was nothing personal, that he was merely doing an organizational change—assigning prison guard responsibilities to the Samarian unit—but Vitus knew otherwise. Pilate didn't want him, or any other Roman soldiers, speaking to "that provocateur."

Vitus's only solace was that Barnabas was safe from crucifixion for the time being. After Pilate's disastrous blunder during the festival, he'd been harshly reprimanded by Rome. Another mistake like that and he could be recalled, his term as prefect cut ingloriously short.

The engineer's shrill voice rang out, carrying far and wide as it bounced off the walls of the ravine. "All right, that's enough lounging around," he chastised the workers. "Get back to it!"

Vitus searched the jagged bronze and amber walls of the ravine for a cave or an overhang, but there was no shade anywhere, no respite from the sun whatsoever in this barren place. Even with his sandals on, he could feel the scorching earth beneath him.

A gust of hot wind carried the faint sounds of voices and metal clanging from somewhere around the bend in the road. Vitus cupped his ear with one hand, and with the other tightly gripped the handle of his sword. He felt naked without his armor and shield. Though unlikely, bandits and rebel armies had been known to pass through the area.

Hearing quite clearly the snort of a horse, he relaxed. In Judea, generally only the prefect or a Roman centurion would have a horse.

A few seconds later a Roman contingent rounded the bend and approached. A centurion on a restless brown steed led the way. Marching between rows of Roman soldiers with glinting armor were four half-naked, sunburned men. They shuffled their feet, hands tied behind their backs, looking as though they might collapse with each step. One long rope bound them to each another. It looped around their necks, sometimes under and sometimes over their long beards.

Vitus groaned as he recognized the statuesque centurion halting his men right in front of the half-finished building.

"Are those latrines ready yet?" Corvus yelled to Vitus. "I gotta take a shit."

Corvus's men laughed heartily.

Vitus bit his tongue to prevent a taunt that was begging to be let loose. He didn't want to respond in his habitual way of hurling an insult in return, but neither did he know what else to do.

The engineer spoke up. "I'll make sure you're the first to know when they're done," he said. "You'll have to hold it for now."

Vitus avoided eye contact with Corvus. Though they were on the same side, he couldn't help but think of Corvus as a foe. He reminded him too much of his old archrival, Flavian.

The Roman soldiers squatted or sat as they drank from their waterskins. Some of them held their shields over their heads for shade, while others used them to sit on.

Corvus raised his sharp chin in the air. "Caught me some bandits while you're building a shit house," he said to Vitus.

Vitus chose his response carefully. "Congratulations," he said flatly.

Corvus stared at him a minute longer, then shrugged and dismounted.

Seeing that no water was being given to the prisoners, Vitus retrieved a jug from the wagon and gave it to them.

"What are you doing?" Corvus demanded. "They don't deserve any mercy. They're thieves and murderers."

"Just trying to help you out," Vitus replied. "You won't get much acclaim for having caught them if they all die of thirst on the way to Jerusalem."

Corvus grunted skeptically as he led his horse over to the stream to drink.

The prisoners gulped down the water recklessly, consuming all that was offered. When they finished the first jug, Vitus got them a second. He pitied them. They were all skin and bone, and the only thing awaiting them at the end of their long march was a torturous death.

By the time Corvus returned, the prisoners had gotten their fill and Vitus was carrying the jugs back to the wagon.

"I assume you'll ensure an adequate supply of spongia," Corvus joked as he mounted his horse.

Spongia were sticks with sponges on the end to wipe one's behind. They were a luxury in general, and out of the question for a remote location such as this.

Seeing the engineer shake his head, Corvus added, "What? No spongia? I'd have to use fig leaves?"

Vitus felt that old competitive spirit in him surge to the forefront. Words tumbled out of his mouth before he could stop them. "For you," he called out, "we'll make sure there's a good supply of nettles."

The Roman soldiers again laughed, especially when one of them held his butt with his hands and shuffled knock-kneed a few steps, a pretend grimace on his face. Corvus made a sarcastic guffaw, then pursed his lips into a pout.

Though Vitus saw his quip had the intended effect, he got no pleasure from it. Every time he resorted to that former way of being, he regretted it. Setting the jug in the wagon, he was surprised to see a tiny green shoot breaking through the ground near one of the wheels. It was a terribly inhospitable place to take root. Not only was the ground hard and dry here, it was in the middle of the road. The plant could easily be trampled by hoof, foot, or wagon wheel.

"The latrines look as though they're coming along nicely," Corvus announced over his men's laughter. He glanced at Vitus, then at the half-finished limestone walls. "I wouldn't be surprised if word got back to Rome on what a magnificent job you're doing. Perhaps the Emperor will put you in charge of all the latrines in the province, maybe even give you a new title." Corvus paused, pretending to be deep in thought, then proclaimed in a mock majestic tone, "Lavatorium Structor Maximus!"

His men laughed uproariously—slapping their thighs and howling.

Vitus caught Corvus's gaze rest on him for a few seconds, presumably waiting to see if he had a comeback. But Vitus didn't have one. He didn't even try.

A realization had come to him that the seed hadn't picked its spot. Where it had been planted was beyond its control. It had no choice but to make the best of things, to sprout in whatever conditions existed there. He wanted to be more like that seed. Specifically, to quit fighting the circumstances of his life, quit defending himself, quit attacking others in words and deeds. He saw with newfound clarity how these actions were just as Barnabas had advised, distractions keeping him both stuck and miserable.

Swallowing the insult, Vitus silently wished in return for the safe journey and well-being of Corvus.

"What are you laughing at?" Corvus said with a big grin at his men. "What would the Roman empire be without some nice facilities for people to shit in?"

Amidst more laughter, Corvus raised his arm and gave the command for his men to move out.

Vitus saw himself in the young centurion. He too had once been ambitious, had wanted to shape and mold the world because he knew how it was *supposed* to be. But not anymore.

Barnabas had drained every last ounce of vanity and arrogance from him, and he no longer knew what the world *should* be like. When Vitus had walked into that prison cell all those months ago, he thought he'd known something of the world and understood why things were the way they were. But it hadn't taken long before he realized his views were mistaken and unsupportable—built on a flawed foundation.

The only thing Vitus knew for sure anymore was his own ideas of how to make the world a better place had been horribly wrong. What was undeniable to him in the moment was that the world needed more humanity and less animosity.

As Corvus and his men marched away, they kicked up a miniature dust storm that slowly drifted toward Vitus. Closing his eyes in preparation, he heard the derisive laughter of Corvus's men and the engineer again berating the workers.

From the world's point of view, Vitus was on a losing streak. His counsel was no longer sought. He'd been relegated to supervising latrine construction. He'd been laughed at, put down, disrespected.

But despite all that—regardless of everything assaulting him from the outside, including the noise and dust and heat—he couldn't help but smile, for he felt an indestructible peace and strength on the inside. He had at long last found something he believed in with all his heart and soul.

It was an abiding, inclusive love that excluded none, not even his enemies.

Chapter Thirty

Jonah swatted a fly buzzing around his head, hoping the strike was enough to convince it to leave him alone. He and Luke were following the Jordan River north on the long journey back to Galilee. Along with dozens of others, they'd spent the day on the banks of the river, listening to the captivating orator, John the Baptizer.

Luke was the one who'd suggested they come. He seemed particularly enamored of the idea of being baptized in the river and having his past sins absolved. After the calamity in Jerusalem, Jonah was determined Luke have at least one fond remembrance of his birthday trip. He didn't want him trying to block out any memories of his thirteenth birthday the way he had.

During the Baptizer's passionate sermon, Jonah had been skeptical—identifying more with the two Pharisees and Sadducee in attendance. They'd stood at a distance with their arms crossed, their faces expressionless. Like Jonah, they had not gone for baptism in the water and had been content to stay back and listen. Unlike Jonah, they had likely gone there solely to find out which competing sect the influential rabbi was siding with.

"Do you remember Sarah from Cana?" Jonah called to Luke.

All the walking and climbing had exhausted Jonah's legs, and he nearly tripped over a fallen branch. It had taken them a day and half to reach the wilderness north of the Dead Sea, on the border of Judea and Perea.

"Probably not," Jonah answered his own question. "You were too young. Anyway, her father called on me last month for a problem with his eye, and we got to talking."

Ahead of him, Luke groaned and slouched his shoulders.

"He suggested a marriage between the two of you," Jonah continued, "and I agreed it was good idea. He comes from a good family and isn't short on money."

"Do I get a say in who I marry?" asked Luke, his voice cracking.

It was the first time Jonah had heard Luke's voice crack, and he noticed how Luke was more man than boy now. He had body odor, a neck nearly as big as Jonah's, even a few hairs growing in his armpits. He wondered if he had amorous feelings about girls yet.

"Of course," said Jonah. "But it's the father's responsibility, you understand."

Luke grumbled, then changed the subject. "Do you think the Baptizer really could be the messiah?"

"Where did you hear that?"

"From some pilgrims in Jerusalem."

Like many of his beliefs, Jonah usually kept his thoughts concerning expectations of a messiah to himself. While some hoped for a powerful leader, an ideal king who would unite the Jews and rid them of the Romans, others believed the messiah would be more of a divine figure with supernatural powers, particularly those of healing. Across the spectrum, most were united in the belief that the messiah would restore the dynasty of King David and usher in a time of peace and justice.

Except for Jonah. Though small in number, he and others like him did not expect a messiah at all.

"Why don't *you* decide," Jonah advised, concluding it best to keep his opinion to himself on the matter.

"Me?"

"Yes, *you*. Don't take anyone else's word for it," Jonah said. "Not even mine." He'd changed his mind on this trip about wanting Luke to be a dutiful, devout Jew. More than anything, he wanted him to think for himself.

"But how am I supposed to know?" Luke protested.

"How is *anyone* supposed to know?" asked Jonah. "Don't fall into the trap of accepting other people's beliefs as the truth. What you believe is entirely up to you. Giving that away is like giving away your right arm."

"Like my father?"

Jonah had no idea how Luke knew he was talking about Thomas. He hadn't even realized it himself, until now. "Yes," he said with a drawn-out sigh, "like your father."

After that, they traveled without a word between them until Luke broke the silence. "Why didn't you get baptized?"

"I didn't like what he was saying," Jonah replied.

"Really? I did."

Jonah felt a lump in his throat. That was not what he wanted to hear. "*What* exactly?" he asked.

"What he said about not committing violence, about being truthful and not taking anything that isn't yours, about being satisfied with what you have. And I really liked the part about beginning anew—discarding your past sins and resolving to live righteously. I want to honor the covenant by following all the commandments, just like the Baptizer."

Jonah was speechless. He wasn't sure they'd heard the same man speak.

"What didn't you like?" Luke asked.

When Jonah had heard the Baptizer speak, he'd mostly been reminded of Zebulun. His cousin had also taught some virtue, but ultimately it had all been self-serving. Jonah recalled the addictive sense of indignation that Zebulun had encouraged in the bandits. His cousin had taught Jonah and the others to cultivate it from the time they arose in the morning to the time they closed their eyes at night. From the rich to the Romans to Herod to the high priests, there was never a shortage of things to be incensed about. Every injustice, every perceived slight—not only to the bandits, but to the entire Jewish people—had to be rehashed day in and out.

Jonah pursed his lips and reflected on how brilliantly it had worked. The madder they'd grown, the more willing they'd been to carry out whatever Zebulun wanted them to.

"What I didn't like is that the Baptizer seemed to be scaring people," Jonah finally answered. "Telling people they'll be burned up if they don't do what he tells them to."

"But he was only telling them for their own good," said Luke. "He wants to save us."

Jonah choked on that last word—*us*. "Save us from what?"

"From God's punishment," Luke said. "From the lake of fire."

Luke's words were like tiny swords stabbing Jonah in the heart, threatening to break it in two. He held his hands, one on top of the other, over the middle of his chest against the pain. His fears were coming true before his very eyes. Luke believed in a petty god, a vindictive, spiteful god who threw tantrums when things didn't go his way. Convinced people like that were the ones causing all the needless pain and suffering, Jonah thought it better for Luke not to believe in god at all, like himself, rather than believe those lies.

As they trod down a well-worn path to a bend in the river to refill their waterskins, Jonah slowly formulated a plan. He wanted to let Luke make his own decisions, choose his own beliefs, even make his own mistakes, but he couldn't allow him to fall into the same trap that his father had. Jonah had failed to protect Thomas. He wouldn't fail to protect his son.

The first step to persuading Luke there was no god was to introduce uncertainty in the scriptures. If Jonah could demonstrate that fulfilling all the commandments was unattainable, then he could point him to the logical conclusion: that abiding by the covenant didn't make sense. How could it, if it was impossible to keep one's end of the bargain?

"It's great that you want to follow all the commandments," Jonah began, "but you need to know exactly what you're taking on. You already admitted you don't always say the Shema every night. And that's just *one* commandment."

Luke was now in the middle of the stream, straddling two half-submerged rocks and refilling his waterskin from a spout of water pouring over the small dam in front of him. Three men—Galileans, Jonah guessed from the looks of them—appeared on the trail. While one disappeared behind a large bush, presumably to relieve himself, the other two joined Jonah and Luke in refilling their waterskins.

Jonah acknowledged them with a nod, then continued his conversation. "Luke, do you know how many commandments there are total?"

Luke shook his head. Finished filling his waterskin, he moved to the riverbank to allow the two newcomers to use the spot. One of them was young, maybe five years older than Luke. After taking Luke's place, he announced, "Six hundred thirteen." Then he looked to the other man for confirmation. "Right, Rabbi?"

"Indeed," came the response. He'd said it pleasantly, and Jonah liked him immediately. He was middle-aged, at least thirty, Jonah guessed, and was standing knee-deep in the water.

Pleased with this new information, especially when he saw Luke's eyes grow wide, Jonah then had an idea to use the rabbi to help him make his point. "Rabbi," he said, "please explain to my son how he can follow all six hundred thirteen commandments in his life, especially when some of them contradict one another."

Jonah was sure what the man's answer would be. All the rabbis were quite predictable in their blind insistence on obeying the scriptures.

Instead of the rabbi, the young man spoke again. "What contradictions?"

Jonah had said that last piece without even thinking about it, but now he saw how it played into his plan perfectly. "I remember once a few years ago, I was reading the book of Proverbs," he explained. "It said, 'Do *not* rejoice when your enemy falls, and do not let your heart be glad when he stumbles.' And on the Sabbath a week or two later someone in our synagogue did a reading from Psalms and said, 'The righteous person will rejoice when he sees Your vengeance.' So which is it? Are we to rejoice or not rejoice when an enemy of the Jews is vanquished?"

Jonah did his best not to look smug for he knew he had cornered the rabbi with his argument. If the rabbi replied that one of the commandments was correct and the other wrong, he would be admitting to Luke there were flaws in the scriptures. If he answered instead that one should simply do one's best to follow all the commandments, he would be admitting that it wasn't possible to fulfill each and every one.

While the three of them awaited the response, the rabbi continued filling two waterskins as though it was the most important thing in the world to be doing at that moment. So completely absorbed was he that Jonah wondered if he'd even heard the question directed at him.

After pulling both waterskins over his shoulder, he finally turned to face Jonah. A curly strand of dark hair separated itself and dangled in front of his forehead. After brushing it aside, his friendly gaze settled on Luke. He moved close to him and laid his hand on Luke's shoulder. Then, with a tranquil smile, he said gently, though authoritatively, "In everything, treat others as you would want them to treat you, for this fulfills the law and the prophets."

To be polite, Jonah gave him a few seconds to elaborate. When he didn't, Jonah opened his mouth to wrap up his contention, but—to his dismay—found he could say nothing in response. His line of reasoning no longer made sense. In just a few words, the rabbi had destroyed his argument. He had explained to Luke how to satisfy his end of the covenant, and do so easily.

Jonah wanted to argue, to tell the rabbi that it couldn't be that simple, but he was too stunned to say anything. He just stood there, hands on his chest, convinced his argument's failure had sealed the fate of his breaking heart.

The rabbi departed the water, and the young man called out from the riverbank, "How much further to John the Baptizer?"

"Maybe a mile," answered Luke.

Elated, the young man bounded up the trail away from the river. "Wonderful!" he said.

The third man, finished urinating, emerged from behind the bush, calling out, "Jesus, did you fill my waterskin?"

"Yes, James," the rabbi replied in his same pleasant tone. The mischievous strand of curly hair again fell over his left eye, but it didn't seem to bother him and he left it there this time.

Jonah could do nothing more than watch the three of them disappear up the trail. The middle of his chest felt as if it was ablaze, as though it had been thrown in that dreaded lake of fire. But to his bewilderment, the flames weren't burning up his heart. They were just melting the thick crust of despair encasing it.

Part IV

Time Period: 28 CE (One year after Part III)

In 28 CE, Jesus began his ministry in Capernaum. He was around 33 years old. Tales of his miraculous powers of healing drew crowds to him. He used these opportunities to preach a very different message than Jews were accustomed to hearing. Word about him spread quickly throughout the village and the nearby regions, though not necessarily to Judea. He remained mostly unknown there until later, when he traveled to Jerusalem to teach outside the Temple.

Chapter Thirty-One

Azara wandered aimlessly through her house, from one dimly lit room to the next, shuffling her bare feet on the unswept tile floor. She was drawn time and again to a gloomy corner in her old classroom, where she liked to close her eyes and imagine herself dissolving into a darkness where time and space didn't exist.

She found the Sabbath the loneliest and most difficult day of the week. In a majority Jewish village like Capernaum, Gentiles observed the last day of the week and all its restrictions by default. Azara had no customers or visitors. The market was closed, and while all the Jews were enjoying fellowship at the synagogue, Azara was locked up at home.

Her only company was her diluted wine—a result of a word of caution that had spread throughout Capernaum about the water being unsafe. Such cautions occurred a few times a year. The remedy for sickly water was to add a little bit of wine to it. Azara never understood why that helped, but it always seemed to do the trick.

The only problem was that instead of mixing it nine parts water to one-part wine, she was mixing it five parts water to five parts wine, and was on her ninth cup of the day.

In the classroom, she ran her fingers across the dusty desks, hearing the ghostly voices of the girls who'd once sat at them. Even after a year she could still see them all—their curious eyes, fidgeting hands, endless questions pouring from their lips.

She raised the cup of watered-down wine to her mouth, tried to take just one sip, but failed miserably. Before she knew it, the cup was empty once more.

Her head spinning, she wobbled to the other room for a refill. At first she couldn't find the pitcher among all the unwashed plates and bowls. Then she followed the ants, whose line went from the half-rotted plums and celery, up to the windowsill, around the pitcher, and to a small crack in the wall. As she reached for the pitcher, she saw a solitary figure walking briskly down the road, a faded yellow headscarf hiding his head and face. It was early afternoon so she assumed he was headed to the synagogue, but instead he glanced around secretively then slipped past Azara's stone wall and approached her house.

After ensuring the door was locked, Azara hid out of view.

"Azara?" the man called quietly as he knocked.

His voice sounded friendly—and vaguely familiar—but Azara had learned to be wary. There were those in Capernaum who would hurt her if given the chance.

"Azara?" he called a little louder. "Are you home?"

"Who's there?" she demanded.

"It's Jonah."

"What do you want?" she asked, still unsure who he was.

"Sorry to bother you on the Sabbath. Is your shop open?"

At that, Azara opened the door. She couldn't afford to turn down business.

The man squeezed inside and quickly closed the door behind him. As he unraveled the headscarf from his face, she recognized him. He was one of her regular customers, a Jewish physician from the city of Magdala.

"Oh, it's you," she said, breathing easier. "Hello, Jonah. Haven't seen you in a while. I thought maybe you were avoiding me like the rest of them."

"Avoiding you?" he replied. "No. I've just been busy. Unfortunately, business is really good these days."

"I can imagine," she said. "There are so many sick people everywhere. Blind. Deaf. Paralyzed. Lepers. The whole world is full of death and suffering." She took a step back so he wouldn't smell the alcohol on her breath, then added, "My mother died giving birth to me."

Jonah paused from removing his headscarf and caught her eye. "I'm sorry," he said softly.

Azara blushed and looked away. She had no idea why she'd felt the need to tell him that.

Hastily uncovering the baskets and jars, Azara did her best to stand straight and speak slowly. She didn't want to slur her words. "What can I get for you?"

"Did my special order come in?"

Azara gaped absently for a moment, then remembered. "Oh, yes! I almost forgot about it. It came in a month ago."

"Sorry for the disguise," Jonah said as he shed his olive-colored, Romanesque cloak. "I got into town late yesterday and stayed with a friend, but didn't want to wait until the Sabbath was over to get this and head home. I hate traveling after sundown."

Azara shrugged. "If I had a copper coin for every time I've seen a Jew sneak around a commandment, I'd be richer than Herod." She was rummaging through her various bins and shelves for Jonah's order. "You already paid me for it anyway, so it's not as if you're buying anything on the Sabbath."

"Yes," Jonah affirmed with a sigh, "that's what I keep telling myself."

"Oh, I remember," Azara said. "I put it in the other room so no one would try to buy it. Would you be a dear and go get it? It's on top of the dresser." She didn't want to go herself for fear that he'd see her teetering.

"Sure," said Jonah as he strode into the dim classroom. "Is your hip bothering you again?"

"Yes," she replied, pleased she hadn't had to lie. "How come your son never accompanies you anymore?" she called out.

"I don't know," Jonah answered from the next room. "He always used to pester me about when I was going next, but he doesn't seem to care now."

"Maybe he was just coming to see the girls," Azara joked.

Jonah laughed. "Maybe. You know he did lose interest in coming with me right about the time you closed your school."

"Did you find it?" Azara asked. "Should be right on top."

"Not yet," he answered. "The older I get, the longer it seems to take my eyes to adjust."

"I understand. Same thing happens to me."

"I heard lots of stories about you wherever I went," Jonah said.

"About that 'wicked Gentile woman'?"

"Yes," Jonah said with a chuckle. "That's how I knew it was you they were talking about. I was impressed that you kept your school going as long as you did. I never did ask you, what was the proverbial 'straw that broke the camel's back' and made you close it?"

As she deliberated how best to explain it, the grief of losing her favorite student, Esther, ambushed her, and a whimper escaped her lips.

"Are you alright?" called Jonah.

"Yes," she lied. "I closed it because the men of this *fine* community couldn't tolerate their daughters and wives receiving an education—"

"Wives?" Jonah interrupted.

"Yes, the girls would always go home and tell their mothers what they learned. The men didn't like it. Most of the Jews stopped sending their daughters, so I had only Gentile girls. First they started harassing the girls, and then their families, so I called it quits. I didn't want anyone getting hurt."

The price Azara paid for not closing her school immediately had been steep. It was a rare Jew from Capernaum that visited her shop anymore, and she was forever looking over her shoulder when she left her house.

"Sorry to hear that," said Jonah. "The ignorance around here is suffocating."

Azara smiled at his words. She liked Jonah. "I appreciate your business," she said. "If it weren't for you and the Gentiles in this city, I'd probably be a beggar in the street."

"No need to thank me," replied Jonah as he returned from the classroom with a small leather pouch. "I come here because you're honest, and I can't get some of this stuff anywhere else."

Azara casually leaned against the wall to steady herself as she watched Jonah open the pouch and examine its contents.

"By the way," he said, "that's an exquisite dresser you have."

"Thanks. My father bought it in Samarkand about twenty years ago."

Taking a small pinch from the pouch, Jonah smelled it, then put it on the tip of his tongue.

"I had a heck of a time finding a supplier for—how do you pronounce the name of these herbs again?" asked Azara.

"Huang lian."

"I thought you told me you learned everything from your wife's uncle who lived in Egypt. That doesn't sound Egyptian to me."

"Definitely not. It's from the Far East. I learned about this one myself. A fellow physician gave me a sample when I was in Jerusalem. He said it worked wonders for stomach cramps, sore throat, and fever, so I tried it and found he was right."

Azara nonchalantly covered the dirty plates and rotting food with a large rag, hoping Jonah hadn't noticed them. "Fever?" she repeated. "My friend's mother has been suffering from fever for several months now. Headache. Nausea. Can't even get out of bed most days. I'm surprised they haven't called on you. Everyone knows you're the best physician around."

"Yes, my success rate is probably a staggering one out of ten—leaps and bounds ahead of the rest of my profession."

Azara laughed. She appreciated his modesty. He wasn't exaggerating by much. The reputation of physicians and their ability to cure was abysmal.

"Who's your friend?" asked Jonah. "Someone in Capernaum?"

"Yes. Her name is Miriam. She's the wife of Simon, the fisherman."

"Simon? Don't think I know him."

"Oh, you'd remember if you met him. Big guy with a big mouth. His wife tells me he's gone all the time lately—following some new rabbi. He goes by Peter now."

Jonah tied the pouch to his belt. "Guess I don't know him."

The prospect of spending the rest of the day in her house suddenly seemed unbearable to Azara. "Could you give me a pinch of those herbs, and tell me how to administer it?" she asked. "I want to take some to my friend's mother today. Maybe it'll help her."

She'd been meaning to visit for the past two weeks, but kept procrastinating because she abhorred being near people who had one foot in the grave.

Jonah placed a small amount of the herbs in Azara's palm. "Just mix with some hot water and have her drink it."

He pulled his cloak tight around his neck and wrapped the headscarf around his head and face. "I've got to get going," he said. "It's a two-hour walk back to Magdala."

Azara slid over to the window and scanned for anyone on the road. "It's clear," she announced.

"Thanks," Jonah replied. He winked at her with both eyes like a cat, then slipped out the door, hurrying away from her house.

* * *

Holding her breath against the bedroom's sickly, stagnant air, Azara crept quietly behind her friend, Miriam. Hazy sunlight from the bedroom's sole window shone on the straw mattress and dingy wool blanket that covered Miriam's mother. Unable to detect any sign of breathing from her motionless figure, Azara thought the woman surely dead.

Miriam squeezed her mother's pale, limp hand. "How are you feeling? Are you thirsty?"

Although the elderly woman opened her eyes a crack, Azara doubted she actually saw anything. Her gaze was blank and brief, and after murmuring something inaudible, she shook her head once slowly, then closed her eyes again.

Miriam ensured the gray stoneware cup sitting next to the bed still had water, then led Azara back out of the room.

"That's how she's been," said Miriam after they left. "Sometimes it seems she's improving, but then a week later she's worse than ever. When her fever gets so bad like this, she doesn't even know who I am. She just lies in bed moaning. Eventually she starts sweating—soaking her robes completely. After that she'll get a little better, then start the whole thing all over again."

Azara regretted the wine's intoxicating effects had worn off and were no longer numbing her feelings and anxiety. With a forced smile, she squeezed her friend's hand in sympathy.

Hearing men's voices approaching from outside, Azara turned to see Miriam's burly husband walk through the door. Biting her lip to hide her disappointment, she bowed her head and stepped behind Miriam.

With a disapproving leer at Azara, the big man rushed to his wife and hissed, "What is she doing here?"

"Hello, Simon," Azara said as dispassionately as she could.

"Please," Miriam whispered, "call him Peter."

"My apologies," Azara added quickly. "Peter."

"Get her out of here," Peter said crossly.

Azara was accustomed to Peter disliking her, but he usually just ignored her.

"Why?" asked Miriam. "She brought some herbs for my mother."

"I don't want him seeing her," Peter exclaimed in a whisper.

Hurrying back to the door, he announced, "Wait here, Master. I'll bring some fresh water to wash with."

Miriam grabbed Azara's sandals from near the front door, then escorted her out the back.

"I'm sorry," Miriam whispered while Azara laced her sandals around her feet. "You know how he is."

Azara nodded. Sadly, she was well acquainted with such treatment.

"I'll mix the herbs as you instructed and give them to her this evening," added Miriam. "I hope they help. Unless something changes, I fear she's not long for this world."

Azara gave Miriam a quick embrace before departing. As she walked through the rear courtyard to the road, she heard an inquiring voice from inside the house. "Who is that? Where is she rushing off to?"

Azara heard Peter's voice answer apologetically, "I'm sorry, Master. There was a vile woman here. I've sent her away."

"Why do you say she's vile?"

"She's a dog," he answered. "A Gentile."

Pulling her scarf snug around her ears to block out Peter's voice, Azara hastened for home. It was a twenty-minute walk, and the quicker she moved, the less chance she had of being accosted.

She watched a calico cat slink by with a lifeless bird in its mouth, and then three rambunctious boys tearing around the corner, wooden slingshots in hand. "There it is! The cat got it," one of them yelled.

Azara didn't recognize the boys, but knew they must be Gentiles. The Jews wouldn't allow activity like that on the Sabbath.

It had only been a minute or two since she'd left when she heard a voice calling to her from behind.

"Wait!"

As she turned to see who it was, the sun peeked out from the thick white clouds that had been veiling it. It was broad daylight, but she could scarcely believe what she was seeing. The voice was Peter's, and he was *running* toward her.

She nearly burst into laughter at the sight of his ungainly frame hurtling down the road. She'd never seen him run—hadn't even been able to picture him running—and yet here he was, bounding as fast as he could to catch up to her.

He arrived huffing and puffing, too out of breath to even speak. Holding up an index finger, he bent at the waist, taking deep, wheezing breaths.

"Won't ... you," he gasped after a few seconds, "come ... back ... for a bit?"

"Wh-What?" Azara stammered, positive she'd misheard him.

He held his right palm to the middle of his chest, which was usually a gesture of tenderness and sincerity toward someone, but Azara suspected it was merely because he was anxious about his racing heart. He took a few more breaths, then asked her, "Won't you come join us for dinner?"

Azara stared at him, awaiting the conclusion to his prank. Not only had he never asked her to stay for dinner, he'd never made the least effort to make her feel welcome in his home.

"Come," he repeated. "Stay for dinner."

"Why?" she asked, narrowing her eyes. She considered Peter to be the most arrogant man she knew, and the competition for that honor was fierce.

Peter pursed his lips until they lost all color. Then his bushy eyebrows drew closer to one another as he said, "Because Master desires it."

His answer made no sense to her. The rabbis and Pharisees were the ones insisting that every rule and commandment be followed at all times, under every circumstance. From the look on Peter's face, she was certain he knew his answer was insufficient.

"The rabbi desires an unmarried Gentile woman to join him for a Sabbath dinner?" she asked incredulously.

"Yes."

"Simon—I mean, Peter," she said. "I don't know what kind of trick you're trying to play, but I'm not interested in being the object of your little game."

"It's not that at all," Peter protested. He looked to the sky, then let out a half-growl, half-sigh. "Azara, listen," he said, softening his usual scowl. "I was reprimanded for my rude treatment of you. He told me to apologize and invite you back for dinner."

She was still skeptical, but it was the first time she ever recalled him calling her by her name, rather than "that woman." Deciding to put him to the test, she fixed her eyes on his. "So when are you going to apologize?"

Through his thick, red-tinged beard, she could see his jaw stiffen in response. He swallowed, then muttered through tight lips, "Please, accept my apologies for how I treated you earlier."

Azara didn't know whether to laugh or to cry. She had never seen Peter like this before.

"I accept your apology," she replied, "but I don't care to join you for dinner." She was greatly intrigued to meet this rabbi who had Peter so completely under his thumb, but thought it best not to press her luck any further.

"Azara, I beg you," Peter said. "I don't want to disappoint Master."

"What exactly did he reprimand you for?"

"I already told you."

"What were his exact words?"

"Why must you make this difficult?"

She put her hands on her hips. "I'm just trying to understand your sudden change of heart, that's all."

"He said, 'You shall not judge, lest you be judged.'"

Azara arched her eyebrows.

Peter hesitated, peering at her with the expression of a traveler who'd become hopelessly lost, then added, "'Else the same standards you use to judge others shall be applied to you.'"

Azara was sure he was making it up, but couldn't detect a hint of dishonesty in his voice. *What kind of Jewish rabbi would say something like that? Especially about a situation involving a woman and a non-Jew?*

"All right," she said, deciding she had little to lose. "I'll play along."

She waited for Peter to start down the road so she could follow behind, but to her surprise he insisted on walking next to her. For the duration of the walk, she contemplated what kind of a trap Peter might be luring her into. She'd long viewed him as more reptile than human, more cold-blooded than warm-hearted.

When they arrived at the house, she timidly followed Peter through the front door, then searched for the new rabbi who had insisted she be invited back. Scouring the small circle of men speaking in hushed tones, she recognized three of the seven. There was Peter's taller brother, Andrew, who had been a follower of John the Baptizer before the popular orator was executed earlier that year. She also knew Eli, a young man who delivered goat cheese to Azara's house. And Eleazar, who was a scribe—and also possibly a Pharisee. Though she'd seen him more times than she could count, Azara had never known for sure since he refused to speak to her.

"Where is Master?" Peter asked.

Miriam pointed to the room where her mother lay.

As Azara knelt to remove her sandals, Peter made a beeline for the bedroom. A few seconds later, Azara heard gasps as though something horrible or something wonderful had just happened. She looked up to see a stranger in white emerge from the bedroom. Following just behind him—to Azara's and everyone's shock—was Miriam's mother herself.

Peter stood behind his mother-in-law, his arms awaiting her imminent fall.

"What are you doing out of bed?" exclaimed Miriam.

"I am healed," her mother answered. "By the hand of this rabbi." She held her pale hand to his cheek, smiling at him as though he were her own son.

Azara set her eyes on the mysterious rabbi. He was middle-aged—in his thirties, she guessed—but he had a playful quality about him. He wore an unembellished, off-white tunic with sleeves that extended only midway down his forearms. Though his beard was closely cropped, his hair was tousled, whimsical, and a little on the curly side. Azara thought him ruggedly handsome, particularly his slightly mischievous smile and the dimples just above his beard-line.

Sneaking over to Miriam, Azara whispered, "Did you give her the herbs?"

Miriam shook her head.

"Then how?" Azara asked in disbelief.

Miriam made no reply, only kept slowly shaking her head.

Eleazar, the scribe, was the first to break the prolonged silence. "But it's the Sabbath," he objected.

Eli, standing next to Eleazar, spoke through hands still covering his mouth. "Rabbi, is what you've done right? Isn't healing on the Sabbath a sin?"

The rabbi grinned, looking as if he might laugh. "Is it right to do good on the Sabbath day, or to do harm?" he asked. "Is it right to save life or to kill?"

No one answered the rabbi's questions. Instead they gawked at Miriam's mother, who now moved about as though she'd merely risen from a short nap, rather than weeks in bed with a high fever.

"Come wash your hands," she called as she handed a heavy stone bowl to Peter. "We'll eat soon."

Miriam moved hesitantly from Azara's side, retrieving a large jug of water from another room and nearly tripping as she brought it. Emptying the jug into the bowl Peter held, she poured so quickly that some of it splashed onto the floor.

"It's all right," Peter said before she could apologize. "I think all of us are a bit shaken."

While the men washed their hands, Azara regarded Miriam's mother warily. Though she had heard stories of miraculous healings, this was the first time she'd ever witnessed one. She kept expecting Miriam's mother to faint or drop the bowls of food she was carrying to the small dinner table.

Even after Peter and the rabbi took their places at the table, Azara remained fixed to her spot near the doorway. She was gradually becoming convinced of the validity of the healing, but the idea of sharing a Sabbath meal with a scribe and a rabbi remained inconceivable to her. She had yearned all her life to be free of the stifling conventions of Galilean culture, yet she found it hard to now let them go. She felt unnerved being among people deliberately disregarding the deeply ingrained customs. Keeping one eye on the door, she half-expected soldiers to storm in and arrest them all for immoral conduct.

There were no chairs. Everyone sat on the floor. The knee-height, wooden table—crowded with brown clay bowls and a basket of flatbread—was not very long, and couldn't possibly accommodate everyone.

"Just squeeze in tight," advised Peter.

Eli went to the door and began putting his sandals on as the rest of the men, foregoing all tact, jostled for a seat as close to the rabbi as possible.

"Eli, where are you going?" inquired Peter.

"My apologies," he answered. "I have relatives visiting and I've already promised to join them for dinner." He furrowed his brow and kept his eyes on the floor. "I hope to see you again, rabbi. I have a few questions about what you taught in the synagogue today."

Miriam followed him out the front door, hollering for her twelve-year-old nephew to come to dinner.

Seeing that Miriam's mother had placed a few bowls of food on a nearby stool, Azara assumed this was where the three women would be eating. She felt relieved at not having to join the men at the table, but as she and Miriam began to sit, the rabbi called to them, "There is plenty of room here. Come. Join us."

An uneasy hesitation rippled among the men until Peter said, "You heard him. Make some space." He then caught his wife's eye and nodded to her.

Miriam took Azara by the hand, and the two of them squeezed in behind Peter so they were not at the table, which was impossible, but at least close to it.

A moment later Miriam's nephew darted in, coming to an abrupt halt at seeing all the people. Miriam rose from her seat and led him over to the table. "Barak, sit next to Azara," she instructed.

"Hello," Azara said warmly as the boy climbed over her legs and crammed in next to her. "Haven't seen you in a long time."

"Do you want a snakebite?" he asked her with a straight face.

"Sure."

He hissed and pinched her forearm.

"Ouch," Azara said with a laugh, then pinched him back.

Eleazar, sitting in front of them, turned and asked the boy with a feigned smile, "Did you wash your hands?"

Azara hadn't realized when she'd sat down how close she was to the scribe. She was astounded he'd consented to sit at the same table as her.

The boy examined the fronts and backs of his hands. They appeared clean to Azara, and apparently to the boy as well, because he stretched to the table and grabbed a piece of bread.

Eleazar frowned at the boy. "It's most important to follow the commandments on the Sabbath."

"Where is it written you have to wash your hands before eating?" the boy asked brashly.

Azara didn't think it unwise to wash hands before eating, but she understood the boy's dismay at having to follow yet another edict. "It's not," she said. She was no scribe or Pharisee, but she knew the written scriptures as well as any of them. In addition to having studied them with her old tutor, Farrukh, she'd also pored over the Torah again recently when she'd been teaching the girls.

Because of all the loud conversations around her, she'd made her pronouncement rather emphatically. By coincidence, their voices had all died down at the exact moment she'd spoken. Feeling her face flush as every head turned toward her, she regretted accepting Peter's invitation to return for dinner. He twisted around and glared at her now.

The rabbi, to her amazement, nodded and smiled. "She's correct," he said.

"But rabbi," said Eleazar, "eating with unwashed hands defiles a person."

Though the rabbi already held everyone's attention, he announced nonetheless, "Whoever has ears, let them hear." Then he locked eyes with Eleazar. "Don't you understand that whatever goes into the mouth passes into the belly, and then out of the body? But the things that come out of the mouth come from the heart, and these things defile a person. For out of the heart come evil ideas, murder, adultery, sexual immorality, theft, false testimony, slander. These are the things that defile a person; it is not eating with unwashed hands that defiles a person."

Eleazar peered skeptically at the rabbi.

"Alas for you, scribes and Pharisees, hypocrites," the rabbi continued. "For you wash clean the outside of the cup or dish, while within they are full of greed and self-indulgence." Though his words seemed harsh, he said them more as a plea than a rebuke. "You blind Pharisee," he said softly, "first clean the inside of the cup, that its outside may become clean also."

The scribe said nothing in response, but looked as though the rabbi had just explained that two plus two equaled five.

Azara understood his confusion. Scribes and Pharisees were rarely ever questioned. People deferred to their words—in gratitude or perhaps disgust—but never disputed their understanding of the scriptures.

She, for one, was impressed with the teaching. The rabbi had simultaneously attacked the oppressive rules that the scribes and Pharisees had piled onto the written commandments, and shown how it was one's words and actions— particularly those motivated by anger, greed and jealousy—that corrupted oneself, not disregarding some cryptic decree.

Miriam set a bowl of green olives on the table; then she and her mother squeezed in and sat down.

Turning to the rabbi, Peter said, "Would you do us the honor of the blessing?"

"As the head of the household, the duty and honor are yours," came the reply.

Peter bowed his head and said solemnly, "Blessed are Thou, O Lord our God, King of the Universe, who bringest forth bread from the earth."

Sabbath meals were the finest of the entire week, with the best and most rare foods. On the table were lentil stew, oil-cured olives, creamy white goat's milk cheese, a half-dozen foot-long smoked fishes, and a salad with lettuce, spinach, leeks, cilantro, roasted almonds, and wine vinegar.

Everyone ate with their hands, using bread to dip or scoop into the various dishes. Peter prepared a plate and passed it back for Miriam, her mother, Azara, and the boy, since they couldn't reach the table.

Though Azara was fond of all the food being served, she had little appetite. She mostly just scrutinized the back of the rabbi's head, wondering why he seemed so familiar to her. But even when she gleaned his name, it was no help. Jesus was one of the most common names around.

Neither Azara nor Miriam spoke a word during the meal. Azara thought the whole situation unreal—sharing a Sabbath meal while a rabbi answered questions and provided teaching. She was captivated by the presence and voice of this man who spoke with such conviction and authority, yet was so humble. Whenever a question was asked of him, his considerate reply always seemed like the obvious and logical answer.

Peter was laughing and smiling, and making sure everyone could reach the various dishes. Azara had never seen this side of him: thoughtful, pleasant, hospitable, jovial even. It was as if he'd been born again since meeting Jesus.

She had to admit that she, too, felt different in the presence of this unorthodox rabbi. Her persistent feelings of loneliness and sadness were strangely absent.

Toward the end of the meal, the myriad conversations faded away, and everyone listened to Peter's brother, Andrew, recount a recent experience. He'd been in a nearby city, outside its synagogue, and was advising some interested people on the lessons Jesus taught. Quite a large crowd had gathered to listen to him, until the temple authorities—the priests, scribes, and Pharisees—arrived with a small contingent of Herod's militia. After quickly disbanding the crowd, they warned Andrew not to come back. To reinforce their threat, a soldier struck Andrew on the side of the head with the blunt end of his sword.

As Andrew removed the prayer shawl from his head, revealing a nasty purple bump, Peter asked the rabbi, "Master, what are we to do in situations like this? My brother may have been killed."

Azara expected the rabbi to say something about the right to defend oneself, or perhaps an assurance of revenge in the near future. But instead, he exuded peace, saying earnestly to Peter, "Do not be afraid."

Then he addressed everyone at the table. "You have heard it said, 'Love your neighbor and hate your enemy.' But I tell you, love your enemies and pray for those who persecute you."

Azara would have thought him mad, except that he looked so tranquil and self-assured in his instruction.

Amidst uncomprehending stares, Jesus continued. "Blessed are those who are persecuted because of righteousness, for the kingdom of heaven is theirs." He was looking around the table as he spoke, pausing at each person and gazing deeply into their eyes. He even twisted and craned his neck behind him in order to see the women and the boy. When his eyes met Azara's, he said, "Blessed are you when people insult you, persecute you, and falsely say all kinds of evil against you."

While his words hung in the air, Azara held her hands to her heart and tried not to cry. It was if he somehow knew all the struggles she'd gone through in her life, not just being a woman, a widow, and a Gentile, but also her heartbreaking experience with her school. Despite her being one among many, she was convinced the rabbi was speaking to her alone.

In the ensuing silence, Peter slipped away from the table and began setting out small oil lamps made of clay in preparation for nightfall.

The rabbi picked up the empty breadbasket and held it upside down over one of the lamps. "No one lights a lamp and then puts it under a basket," he explained. "Instead, a lamp is placed on a stand, where it gives light to everyone in the house."

After removing the breadbasket, he raised the lamp an arms-length over the table. "In the same way, let your light shine out for all to see."

Everyone was still, and when it became clear he was finished, Azara excused herself from the group. She felt dizzy with the rabbi's words and wanted to get outside for some air. Her legs trembled beneath her as she walked, as though she was sailing across the Sea of Galilee. But of course she wasn't on the sea, and she realized it was the first time in her life she'd ever felt the ground beneath her so steady and firm. Her legs were trembling not because the earth was moving, but because she was completely unfamiliar with being on such solid ground. In the presence of this rabbi, the world finally made sense to her.

Azara leaned against the outside wall of the house, breathing in the scent of the sea and listening to a cacophony of birds flying overhead. The sky was a brilliant mix of fire orange and rich yellow, the vestiges of another faultless sunset. With the rabbi's penetrating words still echoing in her head, she couldn't help but wonder just who was this man. An authority on the scriptures who openly defied the commandments by healing on the Sabbath? Who advocated loving one's enemies? Who taught openly to both men and women, Jews and Gentiles alike?

She could only shake her head at the mystery of it all, even more so when the rabbi himself stepped out and stood by her side.

He smiled kindly at her as he ate a piece of bread. "Azara, do you really not know who I am?"

She searched his cheerful face and gentle brown eyes. She'd met thousands of people at the market or at her shop over the years, and rarely remembered their names or how they'd met. "I'm sorry, rabbi," she said. "You do seem familiar."

A stray black dog with matted fur ambled down the road in their direction. Azara recognized it. It was known for its surly demeanor and sometimes biting people. Head low, tail high, it headed straight toward them.

When the rabbi began to squat, Azara assumed he would pick up a rock to throw at it. It was a common practice to repel dogs—so common that one didn't actually need to pick up a rock, but only pretend to do so and the dog would run away. But instead the rabbi sat on his heels and held out his piece of bread.

"I wouldn't do that if I were you," she warned. "That dog bites."

To her astonishment, the skinny dog lowered its tail and trotted up to him without so much as a growl.

The rabbi patted it on the head. "He's not such a bad dog," he said as he fed it the bread. "What's his name?"

"I don't think he has one," answered Azara. "He's not very well liked."

"Not well liked? Maybe we should call him Motuk," the rabbi said with a wink.

Azara stared back blankly. That name was so familiar.

The rabbi leaned forward to pull a burr from the dog's tail. As he did so, a curly strand of his dark hair parted from the rest and dangled over his left eye.

Seeing that, it all came back to her. Eyes wide, she gasped.

"It's you!" she blurted. "Jesus! That adorable toddler I knew in Nazareth!"

He grinned in response. "It's been a long time, my friend."

"It's been over *thirty years*!" she exclaimed.

He stood up and faced her, then took her hands in his. "So it has," he confirmed. "I'm happy our paths have crossed again."

Overcome with emotion, she fell to her knees, grasping his bare feet and weeping. All her memories of him and that time in her childhood returned in a flash: her father, Old Man Omri's dog Motuk, Baruch and his gang of bullies, Jesus' parents Joseph and Mary....

He crouched so he was on the same level, then lifted her chin and met her eyes as though he knew her more fully than she knew herself. In his compassionate gaze, all her fears, worries, and questions receded, and her tears flowed unhindered.

Peter's booming voice interrupted their reverie. "Master," he called from inside the house. "We have melon! Come and get some."

Azara wiped her eyes as she made her way back up to her feet. In the luminous twilight that made everything feathery and dreamlike, she discovered a throng of people coming down the road. Some of them limped or hopped. Some of them used crutches or canes. Some of them had to be led because they couldn't see. And some of them had to be carried because they couldn't walk.

Azara didn't have to guess where they were going. She saw Eli at the front of the crowd, carrying a young girl with a deformed leg. His story of Jesus' miraculous healing powers must have spread through the village like wildfire.

The only reason they were coming now, instead of earlier, Azara knew, was so they wouldn't break the commandments. Since the sun had set, the Sabbath was over.

They crowded around Jesus—the ill, deformed, sickly, and infirm, sitting at his feet, looking up at him with desperate eyes.

He laid his hands on them one by one, healing them of whatever sickness they had.

As Azara watched the blind gain their sight and the lame walk once again, she thought that nothing seemed impossible anymore. It was as though the savior of the world had arrived to lift the veil of ignorance and illusion. She recalled one of her favorite passages from the Pali Canon, a collection of Buddhist scriptures: "When an illumined soul descends from heaven, there appears in this world an immeasurable, splendid light surpassing the glory of the most powerful glow. And whatever dark spaces lie beyond the world's end will be illuminated by this light."

Indeed, she thought. He was the brightest light she'd ever seen.

Chapter Thirty-Two

Transfixed by the goat tied up in front of his house, Jonah fumbled with the latch of his wooden gate and couldn't get in. He didn't own any livestock, so whose goat was it, and why was it in his yard? With a groan, he recognized the green foliage in its mouth as the leaves of his prized rose bush. He nudged the gate with his shoulder until it finally opened. The little brown beast continued chewing intently as it stared back at him. When Jonah got to within a few yards, though, it lowered its horns as if about to charge.

A glance at the rose bush confirmed the worst. The goat had already eaten every last leaf. Jonah cussed under his breath. There was no point now in moving the goat away.

"Bad goat!" Jonah chided as he changed course and went into the house. "Luke!" he called irritably, certain the teenager must have something to do with this. "Come here!"

While waiting for an answer, he rummaged through the familiar basket sitting on the table. Underneath a green palm leaf, he found pieces of flatbread and a large bowl. He smiled as his nose detected the scent of his favorite dish: a chunky stew Amaryah made with beets, kale, turnips, carrots, and parsley.

"Luke?" he called out again, a little louder.

Still no answer.

He knew Amaryah wasn't home. She'd told him before he left that she'd be spending the Sabbath with her sister, who lived in the tiny village of Hammat, three hours south of them.

The sun was already setting, and Jonah regretted his delay in arriving back to Magdala. He'd stopped for a brief rest along the way, but to his dismay had fallen asleep for nearly two hours. He hadn't realized the extent of his own exhaustion, and it made him wonder what other obvious things he was unaware of.

In the dim light of the hallway, he crept alongside the wall to Luke's room, then peered inside. He let out a weary sigh at the sight of the mess. Luke's bed was unmade; a dirty tunic and headscarf lay crumpled on the floor; and the top of the small dresser was covered with open scrolls of the scriptures and a half-eaten piece of bread.

Though Jonah hated it when Luke left food in his room since it attracted ants, he was more agitated by the state of the scrolls. They were expensive.

Just as he was about to move on, he caught something out of the corner of his eye. Moving close to the bed, he bent down and looked underneath. There, he saw a small viper coiled near one of the bedposts.

Far from hating snakes, Jonah actually appreciated them for keeping the mouse population in check. Mice were a scourge that ate the grain in the silos and devoured the crops in the field before harvest. Nevertheless, he grabbed Luke's walking stick from amidst the clutter and clamped the snake's neck to the floor.

While he waited for it to suffocate, he thought about the folklore that a viper in one's house heralded a forthcoming unwanted visitor. He hoped it was only a superstition. He had enough problems in his life as it was.

He wrapped the dead snake around the stick, then carried it out of Luke's room to the back door. With better light he saw the triangular head and black spots that signified it was poisonous. This made him feel slightly more justified in killing it, but still, if he'd caught the snake elsewhere in the house, he would have simply captured it to be released somewhere outside the city. The snake's unforgivable sin was that it had been in Luke's room.

Before taking the snake outside, Jonah first went out himself to check if the Sabbath was over yet. Not only was killing a snake in your house considered work, it also wasn't allowed to carry anything in or out of your house on the Sabbath. He was still a respected elder of Magdala, but wouldn't be for long if he was caught repeatedly neglecting the commandments.

Spying the setting sun between the rows of houses across the road, he determined that it was easily halfway below the horizon, meaning the Sabbath was officially over. He took a deep breath, dropped his shoulders, and exhaled sharply. Then he retrieved the stick with the snake and began trudging up the hill behind his house. His neighbors had small children, and he didn't want them to be frightened seeing a poisonous snake anywhere nearby. He was taking it to the bushes surrounding the ruins of the old grain silo, where a wolf, stray dog, or vulture would surely find the carcass.

Halfway up the hill he heard a man and a group of boys inside the ruin's dilapidated walls. A few steps later he recognized the voices of Luke and his friends. He also heard the voice of someone much older and stopped dead in his tracks when he realized who it was.

Zebulun.

Jonah flung the snake to the ground, cursing it and its legend that had come true.

"You can't be constrained by notions of a *fair* way to fight," Jonah heard his cousin say from the other side of the wall. "It's a battle of life and death, and the only thing that matters is that you remain alive. In this move, accuracy and timing are important. You have to make sure you strike the enemy squarely in the crotch. He'll be stunned for a second, and that's when you grab his weapon away from him."

Of all the days Jonah might expect his cousin to show up at his house, the Sabbath was dead last, but at least he understood now why there was a goat tied up in front of his house. When Jonah disregarded the commandments, he did so openly. He didn't try to manipulate them in any way. Zebulun, on the other hand, was one of those Jews who bent the rules to their breaking point so they could profess to always obeying them. On the Sabbath one was allowed to walk to the local synagogue from wherever one's home was in the village. Outside one's city the distance was set at five hundred yards, but the Pharisees decreed that distance could be doubled if one was following herd animals—like goats.

As Jonah searched for the easiest way to get inside the old silo, he heard Zebulun advising the boys: "It's absolutely paramount you know the reason you're fighting! If you have a righteous cause, you'll be victorious."

The silo's roof had collapsed decades, if not centuries before, and its crumbling walls, covered with moss and crisscrossed with vines, looked as though they were ready to fall as well.

Jonah winced at hearing one of the boys ask: "What about avenging the death of your father?"

It was Luke's voice. Jonah had lectured him on the painful subject several times and thought he'd gotten through to him. He didn't want Luke to sacrifice his future by trying to settle a score from the past. Since Luke was fervent about the scriptures, Jonah kept scouring them for verses that showed they didn't condone vengeance. Unfortunately, he couldn't find any.

"That's a righteous reason, indeed!" said Zebulun. "Luke, come here and try the move on me."

"How did you know his name?" one of the boys asked.

Before Zebulun could answer, Jonah climbed through a large hole in the wall and came into view. Luke hastened to hide his wooden sword behind his back, as did the other boys.

"I know many things," Zebulun replied after a glance at Jonah. "I even know that man's name."

Jonah, hands on hips, scrutinized his cousin's disguise. His dingy tunic was threadbare, and his faded "farmer's headscarf" was pulled loosely around his cheeks and chin so no one could easily see his eyes. Though Zebulun couldn't hide his broad shoulders and stout frame, Jonah thought his staff and goat compensated enough to render him more-or-less a common shepherd, rather than the notorious outlaw wanted dead or alive.

"Greetings, Jonah!" said Zebulun.

The four boys spoke in hushed tones among themselves, but much too loudly and carelessly to be secretive.

"How did he know that?" whispered one.

"He's Zebulun, I tell you," said another.

"Nah, Zebulun is nearly seven feet tall," the first replied.

Jonah knew almost all of the tall tales that had built up around his cousin. For those who had never met him, he was revered as a mythical warrior with supernatural strength and prowess.

Zebulun walked over to Jonah and lightly punched him in the arm. "Hey, Gladiator," he said with a grin.

Then he turned and approached the boys. "You've heard of Zebulun?"

"Who hasn't?" one of them answered. "He's famous. He's the only one who stands up to Herod and the Romans."

"Yes, I've heard of him too," said Zebulun, his chest swelling. "He's a virtuous, yet humble man."

"And invincible!" another boy said. "One time he fought off an entire Roman Legion."

Jonah bit his tongue to keep from laughing contemptuously at that one. Wanting to break up the conversation before there was any chance of Luke and his friends learning who the stranger before them really was, Jonah reproached the boys. "Your fathers are going to be very disappointed to find out you've been practicing with your swords. You know if the Romans or Herod's soldiers catch you, you'll be whipped."

They hung their heads and dropped their swords from behind their backs.

"Luke," Jonah said. "Go get dinner ready. We have a guest."

"Can't I stay with my friends?" Luke pleaded. "I already ate."

Before Jonah could respond, Zebulun did. "Is it not written in the book of Exodus," he began. "'Honor your father—'"

Zebulun didn't have to finish reciting the well-known verse. The boys, in unison, did it for him. "'...and your mother, so that your days may be long in the land which the Lord your God gives you.'"

They'd said it with more than a hint of sarcasm, and Zebulun couldn't hide his displeasure. "The prophets dedicated their lives to bringing the word of God to us, and you think it's some kind of game?" he snarled. "There is no higher purpose in life than to obey the commandments!"

Hoping to spare them—and himself—from one of Zebulun's extended tirades, Jonah raised his voice with a suggestion. "The Sabbath is over, and I'm sure all of you have chores to do," he said. "Yes?"

The boys stared at the ground, kicking at the dirt. None of them answered.

"An elder just asked you a question," Zebulun growled. "Look him in the eyes and answer."

They kept their heads down, but raised their eyes briefly to Jonah. "Yes," they said meekly.

"No. No. No," Zebulun said, his tone full of scorn. "You couldn't fight off a hungry fox with that halfhearted attitude, never mind the Romans." He reached out and lifted Luke's chin so it was parallel to the ground. "Sheath your swords," he commanded. "Then make a row and stand up straight."

The boys slid their handmade wooden swords inside the belts around their waists, then hurriedly lined up one next to the other.

"Much better," said Zebulun. "Now address him as *sir*, and answer him like men, not boys!"

With heads held high, they turned in Jonah's direction. "Yes, sir!"

"Not bad," relented Zebulun. "There's hope for you yet."

Pacing slowly along the line of boys, he stopped in front of each one and held his face inches from theirs as he spoke. "Remember who you are. You are the chosen ones, the descendants of Abraham and Moses and David. Never forget that the man standing next to you is your brother. Protect him, and protect this sacred ground, because you are *Jews* and this is *your* land! Do you understand?"

"Yes, sir!" they shouted.

Zebulun grunted his approval. "Now run home and do your chores."

As they sprinted away, he called after them, "Live your lives in fear of God, and follow the commandments!"

Luke led the charge back to the clustered stone houses of Magdala.

"He's fast," commented Zebulun.

Jonah nodded as the two of them headed in the same direction, albeit at a much slower pace.

The sun had dropped completely below the horizon, and twilight's rays caressed the evening sky in shades of amber and copper red. Jonah wanted to enjoy it, but couldn't. He was too anxious about what had brought his cousin for a visit.

"Where were you?" asked Zebulun as they walked. "I was surprised no one was home when I arrived."

Jonah contemplated his answer before speaking, that old sense of choosing his words carefully around Zebulun returning naturally. If Jonah explained that he'd been in Capernaum, then Zebulun would know he'd blatantly violated the commandments by walking home on the Sabbath. Since Zebulun had been traveling on the Sabbath too, Jonah briefly considered telling him the truth, but decided he didn't need to hand his cousin cause for confrontation. He was sure to get all he could handle as it was.

"Visiting a friend," Jonah replied, pleased with his sufficiently vague answer that wasn't dishonest. He had indeed stayed with a friend in Capernaum, and even though he didn't know Azara that well, he considered her a friend, too.

A screech from high overhead caught their attention, and Jonah and Zebulun watched as a hawk and an owl engaged in a mid-air fight, both of them plummeting perilously close to the ground before disengaging.

"A few more seconds and they both would've been dead," Jonah remarked.

"Sometimes that's what it takes," Zebulun said resolutely.

Though Jonah didn't understand what he meant, his gut told him not to pursue it. "I hear rumors you've got quite the army these days," he said.

"I'd like very much to have ten thousand men with weapons and armor better than the Romans," Zebulun said dryly. "And I'd like to be seven feet tall, too!" he added with a laugh.

Though Jonah wanted to know how many men Zebulun really did have, he didn't bother asking. He knew his cousin wouldn't tell him.

"What is the mood here these days?" asked Zebulun.

"Same as ever," replied Jonah. "People are still quite upset about what happened to John the Baptizer. It was one thing for Herod to throw him into prison, but quite another to have him beheaded. And at the request of his stepdaughter, no less."

"He got what he deserved," Zebulun muttered. "I could have protected him, but he was a damn fool who didn't know what was in his best interest."

Jonah said nothing in response. He could tell from Zebulun's comment that he had most certainly approached John the Baptizer to gauge his interest in being allies, and had instead been rebuked. Jonah had seen it happen before when he was part of the bandits.

Though the day had been humid and breezeless, a steady wind from the north now began to pick up. It rippled the tops of the tall green grass they walked through and carried the distant sounds of cows bellowing.

"I appreciate you not revealing your relationship to Luke," Jonah said.

"I wasn't sure what you'd told him, so thought it best not to say anything. Does he know about your past?"

Jonah shook his head. He and Amaryah had never told Luke about his bandit days, because if Luke ever divulged it, Jonah could be arrested.

"He knows about Thomas—that he was his real father, and that he was crucified by the Romans," Jonah said.

Zebulun walked stiffly and made a slight wheezing sound when he breathed. Jonah studied him out of the corner of his eye, noticing his crooked nose and bulging belly. He'd gained quite a bit of weight over the years.

"I saw him again," Jonah announced.

"The centurion?"

"Yes. We went to Jerusalem for Sukkot last year. He was part of that slaughter. I saw him with the prefect."

"He'll get what's coming to him one day," said Zebulun. "Who knows? Maybe at the hands of Luke. Did you know he's been practicing with his friends to avenge Thomas's death?"

Jonah grimaced at the reminder. "Yes," he said. "I caught him sneaking out at night once to do some sort of training with them."

"He is not without skill," remarked Zebulun.

"What do you mean?"

"I was only with them for a few minutes before you came," he said. "They were practicing with their wooden swords—the three others all ganging up on Luke as he was clearly the best one." Zebulun slapped Jonah on the back. "You should send him out my way for a week. Let me teach him a few things."

Jonah veered away from his cousin, putting some space between them. "Stay away from Luke," he warned. "I won't have you corrupting his mind the way you did his father's."

Zebulun gave a snort. "His father understood things that were well beyond your grasp."

Jonah pinched the back of his hand, a new habit he'd developed to restrain his temper when it began to flare. "I'm afraid we don't have anything special for dinner, but you're welcome to join us," he said as cordially as he could muster. Even though he reviled his cousin, Jonah's cultural beliefs about hospitality were deeply ingrained in him.

"Thank you. I haven't had dinner yet," replied Zebulun. "Where is Amaryah?"

"Visiting her sister."

"And how is her pregnancy going this time?"

Jonah stared at him in disbelief—flabbergasted that Zebulun knew Amaryah was pregnant. It made him wonder what his cousin *didn't* know.

"She's doing well so far," he answered. "But then the previous ones all went well too, until the very end."

"When is she due?"

"About four months."

When they arrived at the house, they washed their feet with a bowl of clean water Luke had set out. The night air was cool, and when the wind gusted, Jonah found himself on the verge of shivering.

"Luke," he called once inside. "Start a fire, please." He was glad the Sabbath and all its restrictions were over so they could warm up the food.

"I'm getting the table ready," Luke griped. "Can't you?"

"Just do it, please," Jonah implored.

Luke banged two cups down on the table, then went to the fireplace and began arranging the kindling.

Zebulun ambled slowly through the door, eyeing the interior of the house. He stared at the mosaic floor for a long time, and then the couch with its flamboyant red covering that Amaryah's uncle had brought from Egypt. "I see you live a nice comfortable life now," he commented.

Sensing the disapproval in Zebulun's voice, Jonah smirked upon seeing Luke had set out the "guest cups" they only used on special occasions. They were extravagant stoneware cups with handles on each side and multicolored Hebrew letters written above an artistic rendering of the Ark of the Covenant. They were sure to further provoke his cousin.

After filling the ornate cups with wine, Jonah invited his cousin to sit at the table with him. Zebulun held his cup at eye level, squinting at its intricate design. Amaryah had bought the cups on a trip to Jerusalem, and everyone who'd ever seen them had remarked on their elegance. Zebulun said nothing, merely frowning a little before lifting it to his lips. He drank all the wine at once, gradually tilting his head back as he neared the bottom of the cup. When he was finished, he let out a grunt and clutched the back of his neck.

Jonah surveyed him, not as his cousin, but as a physician. He noticed how Zebulun never turned his head or torso from side to side. And in addition to a crooked nose, a scar on his forehead, and several missing teeth, his whole body seemed extremely rigid.

"Your neck bothers you?" asked Jonah.

"I've got pains everywhere," replied Zebulun with a wave of his hand. "But what is one man's agony in the face of thousands who suffer at the hands of our enemies?"

Jonah swallowed the urge to guffaw. He hadn't heard that particular manipulation before, and wondered how long Zebulun had been using it. "So you're a martyr now?" he asked sarcastically.

Luke was behind Zebulun, squatting near the fireplace. Zebulun called to him without turning in his direction. "Luke, listen to me," he said. "Thomas— your father—understood that suffering was necessary. He took it on gladly so that others could bear the fruit of his adversity, so they would be able to live their lives free of Roman laws and taxes, free to raise their families according to Jewish law. He was a virtuous man who understood his sacrifice was for the greater good."

Luke had uncovered the embers they'd carefully buried in ash before the Sabbath began and was now blowing gently underneath the kindling. "How?" he asked. "What did he do?"

Jonah smiled at Luke's question. He leaned forward in his chair, pressing his elbows on the table and propping his head up.

Still making no effort to face Luke, Zebulun held out the cup in his hand, as if it was the answer. "Look around you," he said as he made a sweeping motion with his arm. He set the cup down on the edge of the table.

With a confused expression, Luke turned his head from one side to the other. "What am I supposed to—"

"Thomas lived a life that was the opposite of all this," continued Zebulun. "Everything you see is the result of abandoning the fight. You and your family live pleasant lives here under the yoke of Herod's rule. Do you know where the taxes you pay for this lifestyle go?"

"Answer Luke's question," Jonah interrupted.

"They fund the Roman army and Herod's militia," said Zebulun. He stared straight ahead, his small black pupils barely visible in the fading light. "Thomas and I made vows to put an end to such hypocrisy. We vowed to cleanse this land, to never stop fighting until freedom and justice were won, until we'd reclaimed this sacred land given us by Yahweh. It was—"

"You *still* didn't answer his question," Jonah said, raising his voice. "Why don't you tell him what his father did, what you did, what we all did? Tell him about the people who got hurt, the people who died." He could feel the heat of his temper rising up his spine. His face was already flushing.

"We fought our enemies!" Zebulun fumed. "That's what we did!"

Jonah squeezed the sides of his head with his hands. "Be careful, Luke," he warned, "or you might find *yourself* on that ominous list." He met his cousin's glare with one of his own. "How long is your list now?" he asked. "First, you said our foe was the Romans, then you added the Herods, then the Samaritans, then the Gentiles, then the rich Jews, then the Jews who don't agree with you. Where does it end?"

Zebulun finally turned in his chair toward Luke. "Some people always want to make it more complicated than it is," he said calmly. "You understand that, Luke. It's just like when Joshua approached Jericho and saw a man in front of him with his sword drawn. Joshua asked very plainly, 'Are you for us, or for our enemies?' It's that simple. There are only two sides."

"And one side is filled with hatred, violence, and delusions of grandeur," Jonah added.

Zebulun visibly stiffened, but kept his attention on Luke. "Do you know the book of Numbers?"

Luke nodded.

"Then you know that if we unite and fight against the enemies in our land, God promises to help us. The promise I've made—that I live my life by every day—is to do God's will. And God desires justice and a restoration of this land to its rightful owners."

"Ha!" Jonah yelled. "The only things you ever give are *promises*."

Fifteen years ago Jonah was sure he would have fallen for Zebulun's conniving words, but no longer. He saw right through the scheme. "Do what I say and I *promise* you justice and freedom and victory. But their fulfillment is always in the future. Very clever. Even in your wildest success, you never have to achieve any of them. Instead, you assure everyone they're '*just around the corner*,' forevermore coming down the road."

Zebulun stood and pivoted to face Jonah. "And what of you?" he accused. "You sit in this nice house with your gaudy cups and fancy furniture. What are you doing to lift the burden of oppression? What are you doing to help the poor? Or do you pretend that you don't see it? Luke, don't ever think independence and freedom come easily. They never come without tears, without heartache, without bloodshed!"

"Freedom?" Jonah repeated incredulously. "From what? Living under your rule was more burdensome than Herod's!" He slammed his cup down, wine splashing over the rim. "I see you so clearly now. You're just another pretentious zealot who promises a better future, who promises peace. But it *never* comes!"

"Peace is for fools and cowards!" Zebulun snarled. "It's the brave who do God's bidding, who fight the good fight. *You* have forgotten that struggle."

"You and your damn *struggle*!" Jonah jumped out of his chair, tipping it over so it fell backwards. "I'm so sick of—"

"It's not *my* struggle," Zebulun shouted. "It's *our* struggle! Yours, mine, Luke's, all of us! And you turned your back on it. You walked away!" He pounded his fist down, shaking the table so hard that his cup tumbled off the edge, shattering into a hundred pieces as it hit the floor.

In the ensuing silence, no one spoke, no one moved. There was just the sound of Zebulun's labored breathing and the wind whistling as it crept under the door.

Luke began gathering the broken shards into a pile, but abandoned it after only a few seconds. "What does he mean?" he asked Jonah. "What did you walk away from?"

Zebulun crossed his thick forearms over the top of his pot belly. "Send the boy away," he ordered, "lest he learn things you don't want him to know."

"No," Jonah replied defiantly. "He's not a boy anymore. Besides, he can handle the truth of his family's history."

Zebulun lowered his fat chin, fixing his gaze on Jonah. "Then tell him."

Jonah rested a hand on Luke's shoulder, then looked him in the eye. "Luke," he said somberly, "this is my cousin, Zebulun."

Luke wrinkled his nose at first, then his eyes grew wide.

"Yes, *the* Zebulun," Jonah said in response. "Thomas and I went to live with Zebulun and his family when our parents were killed."

Zebulun uncrossed his arms and dropped his shoulders. "After fifteen years in that house, we were evicted and penniless," he told Luke. "The great Sadoc found us wandering down the road and took us all in."

"Sadoc?" Luke repeated. "The outlaw?"

"He was no outlaw," said Zebulun. "He was a champion of the people, a fearless lion who undertook the impossible—trying to stir a nation of listless sheep to action."

Luke studied Jonah for a few seconds, then did the same with Zebulun. "So your fathers were brothers?"

Jonah nodded. Then they were all quiet again. Jonah used the last of the water to refill his cup. Handing the empty jug to Luke, he told him to go refill it.

After Luke left the house for the nearby well, Jonah and Zebulun continued standing in silence, both of them staring at the shattered remains of the cup on the floor.

"Why did you come here?" Jonah asked wearily as he slumped into his chair.

Zebulun sighed. "I brought something for you." Lifting his pack from the floor to the table, he began digging through it.

Jonah regarded a few strange items from the pack, things one wouldn't usually take on a journey away from home. In particular, there was an empty inkpot and a wooden cup with a long crack down its side. Jonah felt perplexed until he realized their significance. Some Jews would carry personal possessions with them solely so they could declare any spot they wanted to be their "home" on the Sabbath. Using this contrivance, they could travel as far as they wanted on the dedicated day of rest.

"I found these and thought you might like to give them to Luke," said Zebulun, rolling two stone dice toward Jonah.

Jonah recognized them immediately. They had been Thomas's favorite toy when they were kids. "You came all the way here just to give me these?" He plucked one of the dice from the table, examining its faded dots.

"And this," Zebulun said, sliding over a small dagger with a freshly wrapped leather handle.

Jonah left it on the table. "I already have a dagger," he said. "Several."

"It's for Luke. For his bar mitzvah."

"That was last year."

"Better late than never."

Jonah pushed the dagger away and put his elbows on the table once more. "Why did you *really* come here?"

"What? A man can't visit his cousin to say hello?" Zebulun objected.

"You haven't done that in the thirteen years since I left. Why now?"

Zebulun grunted and leaned back in his chair. "I need a favor of you."

"*You* need a favor of *me*?"

"I've heard of a new rabbi who seems to have some miraculous powers."

Jonah knew from his time with the bandits that Zebulun kept tabs on any and all potential rivals. New King Davids or messiahs were continually popping up. Personally, Jonah never took them seriously. Their popularity, even their lives, were usually short-lived.

"Who?" Jonah asked, wondering if he might have heard of the man.

"His name is Jesus. I heard about a wedding in Cana where he turned water into wine."

Jonah knew lots of men by the name of Jesus, but none of them qualified as rabbis. And certainly none of them could perform miracles.

"Never heard of him," said Jonah. "I'm sure he's just another charlatan. Why are you worried?"

"I'm not *worried* about anything," Zebulun said coldly. "I just want to know what he's about. Some of John the Baptizer's disciples have gone over to him."

Jonah massaged his temples against an imminent headache.

"And who knows," added Zebulun. "Maybe he could get a few things through that thick skull of yours about following the commandments. God knows I haven't been able to."

"Why don't you go and see him yourself?" asked Jonah, although he already knew the answer. With both Herod's militia and the Romans on the hunt for them, it wasn't wise for Zebulun or his men to be seen in public places.

"When you left all those years ago," Zebulun said with a frown, "I agreed to abide by our agreement that neither I nor any of my men would mention your involvement with us. The authorities, your neighbors—no one—has had the slightest clue about your past."

Jonah understood the implied threat if he didn't go to see this rabbi.

"You win, cousin," he conceded. "You always do."

Chapter Thirty-Three

Azara studied the sky overhead, particularly the ominous gray clouds moving toward them over the Sea of Galilee.

"Another storm's coming for sure," she said to her neighbor, Cyrus. "But not for an hour or two at least. You should have plenty of time."

Cyrus was winding a ratty, old rope over the top of Azara's red dresser, drawing it tightly to the floor of his wagon.

"Try not to scratch it," cautioned Azara. She'd just sold it last week—for about half of what she thought it was worth—and Cyrus had agreed to deliver it. In addition to fewer customers willing to buy from her, the last harvest had not been a good one. It had resulted in a spike in food prices, and in an effort to become more self-sufficient, Azara had traded the dresser for a milking cow.

Standing just out of reach of the twitching tail of Cyrus's donkey, Azara caught sight of a stranger trudging down the road toward them. He was carrying a small boy with shriveled, knobby legs, and he nearly tripped over a mangy, black mutt sprawled on the road.

Azara had a good guess what—or more precisely, who—the man was looking for. In the six weeks since Jesus started living in Capernaum, he'd healed a great number of its residents. Word of his healing powers had spread, attracting people from nearby villages. They arrived by the handful nearly every day. Most sought him to be cured of some illness, but many came simply to hear his captivating parables and unorthodox teachings.

Not everyone, though, agreed with Jesus' mandates of inclusion and loving one's enemies. A vocal conservative element, the old guard, opposed him. They were envious scribes, obstinate Pharisees, anxious elders, and others who abhorred what they viewed as a blatant disregard for the commandments and well-established Jewish customs. Jesus seemed to have little regard for the old ways. In addition to healing on the Sabbath and teaching non-Jews, he openly conversed with unmarried women, Samaritans, even Romans.

"Are you looking for the Rabbi Jesus?" Azara called to the man. She hated to be the bearer of bad news, but someone had to tell him.

"How did you know?" His grey eyes, weary and distant, searched Azara's face. The toddler he bore in his arms hiccupped and brushed his dusty bangs away from his eyes.

"Just a guess," answered Azara. "I'm afraid you've just missed him. He sailed away this morning to visit another city."

The man hung his head. "I'm sorry, Matthew," he whispered, kissing the boy on the forehead.

After Azara turned away, he asked her, "Do you know what city?"

"Bethsaida, I think," she replied. Jesus had often traveled by foot to villages within a day's walk. Today was the first time she'd heard of him using a boat.

The man made a long face, then turned and went back the way he came.

Frustrated she couldn't help, Azara pursed her lips as she watched his haggard form retreat down the road. Words from Jesus' talk the previous night echoed in her head: "For I assure you, if you have faith the size of a mustard seed, you will tell this mountain, 'Move from here to there,' and it will move. Nothing will be impossible for you."

Azara didn't know how to have faith like that, but she desperately yearned for it.

"Did you see the wedding procession last night?" asked Cyrus from atop the wagon.

The donkey swished its tail and jerked its hind legs against the flies harassing it. "Unfortunately," she answered, swatting at the bugs as well.

Usually she liked watching the festive ceremony of the bridegroom—adorned in his finest garments and a crown of flowers—arriving to fetch his bride. The procession, first to the bride's house and then to the bridegroom's, was always a lively affair with friends, relatives, and musicians singing, dancing, and casting flowers along the way. Sometimes they even carried the veil-covered bride on a chair.

But when the procession had come down the road the night before, Azara had viewed it gloomily from afar. She was unable to enjoy it, because she knew whose wedding it was: Esther's.

Cyrus spit out the long piece of yellow straw he'd been chewing on. "Knowing the groom's pompous father, it was probably quite the feast," he commented dryly.

Once a wedding procession made it to the bridegroom's house, the couple would disappear into a bedroom for the physical consummation of their marriage. Afterward they would hang the bloodstained sheet out the window for all to see that the bride had been a virgin. Then the seven-day celebration would commence in full force, beginning with a sumptuous feast.

Since Esther's father had pulled her out of Azara's school a year ago, Azara had only seen her a few times, most of them at the market with her father, but also, significantly, just a week prior, when Esther had knocked on her door late at night. She'd been distraught, sobbing over her upcoming wedding, and lamenting to Azara how she was still in love with some boy her own age.

It had been all Azara could do just to listen to the heartbreaking story. It reminded her, painfully, of her own forced and disastrous marriage when she'd been Esther's age.

Finished securing the dresser, Cyrus climbed into the front of the wagon and settled onto the bench. "Let's go, Aesop," he called, smacking the donkey's rump with a long, bare stick.

"I'll see you tonight," said Azara. She couldn't afford to pay him in coins and had instead agreed to compensate him by preparing a chicken dinner for him and his family. Though residents of Capernaum were fortunate to have fish once in a while, most meals usually lacked any animal protein. A chicken dinner was a special treat.

Azara's new cow bellowed from the other side of the stone wall.

"Sounds like she wants to be milked," Cyrus suggested as his donkey pulled the creaking wagon away.

Having had the cow for only two days, Azara was still getting used to its sounds and what they meant. "Yes, probably," she said thoughtfully, then headed back inside her house.

Before going to milk the cow, she added more water to the bowl of soaking chickpeas. Preparing the dinner would take her hours, and she'd barely started. Lost in thought of all she still had to do, she'd begun slicing an onion when she heard the cow bellow once more. Grabbing a bucket, she opened the door to go outside, but stopped at the sight of a large group of men marching down the road. At the front of the twenty or so locals, she distinguished the neckless brute with his large basket. Swallowing hard, she realized a stoning was about to take place.

Quickly, she closed the door, locked it, then pulled a chair over and wedged it in tightly. She had no reason to suspect they might be coming for her, but it was not unheard of for innocent people to be stoned.

Though stonings were relatively rare, Azara had witnessed several in her lifetime. They were the most severe punishment dispensed for disobeying the scriptures, resulting in a gruesome death lasting anywhere from twenty minutes to two hours. They usually took place outside the city walls, but not always. Like everything else, numerous rules dictated how to carry them out, including a requirement that two or more witnesses could verify the sin committed. If led by angry men bent on vengeance, however, rules generally did not apply.

Peeking out through a crack in the door, Azara spied the dog lying on the road as the mob approached. It turned its head toward the men, then rolled over, stretched to its feet, and trotted away. Capernaum was not a big village, and Azara recognized many of the men as they passed by, including the elder who'd advised her to close her school. A ragtag group of bare-chested boys followed at a distance, despite the regular warnings from the men to "Go home!"

Listening intently, Azara made out a few words among the men's myriad conversations—something about "sheet," "virgin," and "ran back to her parents' house."

Most of the nearly dozen sins the Jewish scriptures ordered stonings for were in the books of Leviticus or Deuteronomy. Azara iterated through them in her mind: idolatry, divination, blasphemy, adultery....

She gasped at the next one that come to mind: a woman claiming to be a virgin at marriage, but who was not.

Hastily tying a headscarf around her face so it covered everything but her eyes, she rushed out the door. She hoped it wasn't true, but nevertheless despaired it was. The crowd of outraged men were almost certainly headed for Esther's house.

Ignoring the pain in her hip, Azara chased after them—her conversation with Esther the week prior haunting her. After her wedding, Esther would be moving in with the groom's family, and she'd said she was going to meet the boy she loved in order to tell him goodbye. Azara had urged her not to go, because it was too dangerous. If she was caught out alone at night, or worse, with the boy, she would be in very serious trouble. Azara now feared that Esther hadn't heeded her advice, and that their goodbye had turned into something amorous, and now, tragic.

Glancing up at the sky, Azara saw the clouds from the east moving in more quickly than she'd predicted. Worse yet, they were growing darker, not so much gray-colored anymore as charred-wood black.

The mob came to a halt at Esther's house, blocking the narrow dirt road in front. It was midday, hot and humid, and the men reeked of body odor. As Azara pushed her way through the sweaty throng, she cynically considered how similar the Jews and Romans could be sometimes. While the Romans preferred to crucify people, Jews preferred to stone them. Both methods were a cruel and public form of punishment that resulted in a horrific death. Both methods had the same objective: to frighten people into obedience. The only difference was that the Romans wanted everyone to fear their power and obey their laws, and the Jews wanted everyone to fear their God and obey His commandments.

After squeezing past a lanky farmer she knew, Azara made it to the front. She saw Esther's father disappear into the house, only to reemerge forcefully pulling Esther out by her long, dark hair. Bending at the waist, her whole torso contorted to his vicious grip. Esther's mother, wringing her hands, peered out from the doorway behind them.

"Where is the evidence?" Esther's father yelled.

The diminutive, homely groom held up a large rumpled cloth. "Here," he answered in a nasal voice, throwing the bloodless sheet forward.

Esther's father regarded it with disgust, the jagged, blue vein on his temple throbbing as if it might burst. He threw his daughter forward violently so that she fell to her hands and knees on the dirt.

"Mother!" she wailed, trying to crawl back to the house.

But her mother only crumpled to the floor as her father slammed the door closed on her from the outside.

"Don't open it," he warned. Then he went up to the neckless brute and took two rocks from his basket.

Though she despised him, Azara still found it hard to believe he was turning on his own daughter.

"Not here!" the Capernaum elder called. "Take her outside the city." He raised his ram's horn cane, pointing down the road.

Like a sacrificial animal being led to the altar, Esther's terror-stricken eyes searched every direction for an escape. But there was nowhere to run. The crowd was in front; and stone walls to her right, left, and behind hemmed her in.

Azara wished Jesus was in town. He'd know what to do.

Overhead, dark clouds began to blot out the sun. The storm Azara had convinced herself was still far away—that she still had time to prepare for—was already here.

As the men argued about where to carry out the stoning, Azara again recalled Jesus' teaching about faith. She wanted to be inspired by his words, but instead felt ashamed. She didn't have faith the size of a mustard seed. She didn't even have faith the size of a speck of dust.

Though she had no clue what to do or say to stop this madness, she found her legs thrusting her forward, away from the crowd, toward Esther. She could only comprehend one thing at the moment: that her small, timid heart didn't want to beat anymore if Esther was stoned to death.

Over the men's boisterous debate and the hideous wailing of Esther's mother from inside the house, Azara called out in a shaky voice, "Have you no shame?"

The men stopped and stared.

"She's only a child," exclaimed Azara as she helped Esther to her feet.

Unable to see Azara's face because of her headscarf, the men murmured amongst themselves. "Who is that?"

As Azara surveyed all the enraged men, rocks in hand, she felt her time had come. She was making her last stand against the hatred of the world.

A large raindrop splashed on her nose. She pictured the half-cut onion still setting on her table, the chickpeas soaking in water.... Who would finish all the preparations for dinner?

Azara purposefully and unhurriedly removed her headscarf. She refused to hide anymore.

"It's the wicked Gentile whose school corrupted the minds of our women and daughters!" Esther's father announced.

Stretching her arms behind her waist, Azara pulled Esther in tightly to her back. She basked in the warmth of an intense fire burning within. Was this the holy place Jesus had spoken of the week before? His words resounded through her mind once more: "When you therefore shall see the desecrated sign of desolation, spoken of by Daniel the prophet, stand in the holy place."

She didn't know the answer, but standing there at the edge of the unknown, she felt more alive than she'd ever been. This solid, righteous place was her *true* home, and no one could take that from her. The spiteful mob could destroy her mortal body, but they could never destroy the light that blazed within, for it was eternal.

"These women are abominations in the eyes of God," shouted Esther's father. "Stone them both!"

He hurled a fist-sized rock through the air that ricocheted off the side of Azara's head.

As everything went black and she felt herself falling to the ground, Azara listened for the whisper of death calling her name.

But death was silent. There was only Esther's high-pitched scream piercing the darkness.

Chapter Thirty-Four

"So you think Roman rule over these provinces is coming to an end?" the one-eyed spy asked as they marched along the dirt road of the village. His colorless lips were curled into an ever-so-slight smirk.

Vitus leered at the round, leather patch over the man's left eye. "I didn't say that," he said testily.

He wasn't sure if the spy had been sent to catch him expressing dissent or perhaps insubordination to Pilate's rule, or if the situation had already passed that stage and the spy was part of some devious plot to make Vitus out to be a thief of tax monies.

After being condemned to degrading jobs for so long, Vitus was grateful for his new assignment safeguarding tax monies. He'd assumed the change of orders had been a reward for his diligence, competence, and refusal to complain about the menial tasks he'd been assigned. But he wasn't so sure of that anymore.

"I simply said that *everything* eventually comes to an end," added Vitus.

Officially, the spy was one of the new "tax inspectors" Pilate decreed were to now verify all tax monies as they were collected and moved throughout the provinces. But Vitus knew better. He may not be the insider he once was, but he knew full-well how increasingly paranoid his commanding officer had become. Pilate was convinced there were Romans within his own ranks who were determined to discredit him—traitors who wanted him out as prefect. The new "tax inspectors" and "administrative liaisons" everywhere were nothing more than spies who reported directly to Pilate.

"No man lives forever," Vitus continued. "Rivers stop flowing. Lakes dry up. Entire cities are razed to the ground. It's like the first Temple the Jews built. No doubt they thought it would last forever, and yet what is it now? Nothing more than dust."

"Dust?" the spy repeated. He was half Vitus's age, and though he wasn't a soldier, he dressed similarly to one, with a crimson cloak and a shortsword strapped to his waist.

A verse Vitus had recently read came to mind. "All came from the dust and all return to the dust." In his free time, he'd begun learning the written language of the Jews so he could read their scriptures firsthand.

"Says who?" the spy asked skeptically.

Vitus shrugged his shoulders, surprised that anyone would find the quote provocative. "That's from the book of Ecclesiastes."

"Ecclesiastes?" the spy said, his tone incredulous. "What is that? One of the Jewish scriptures?"

Vitus instantly regretted telling him the source. He'd been trying to interject some teachings into his day-to-day conversations, because Barnabas had long ago encouraged him to do so. But now Vitus felt as though he'd just given the spy evidence to be suspicious of his loyalties.

"Perhaps you've been here in the provinces too long," the spy said. "The Jews' ridiculous talk about the end of the world has skewed your thinking."

Vitus stiffened. "Or perhaps you haven't been in the provinces long enough to gain some respect for the culture here," he countered.

Behind them an arbitrary breeze brought the scent of the sea mixed with the stench of fresh dog feces. To the east, the sky was growing dark. Vitus had no doubt a storm was coming, but he was confident he and his eight-man contingent had plenty of time to make it to the small outpost on the outskirts of town. He'd been to Capernaum, one of several villages that dotted the coastline of the Sea of Galilee, several times before, and knew exactly how long the trip took.

"Hey, Commander," said one of the soldiers marching behind Vitus and the spy. He was helping to carry the heavy wooden chest with the tax monies. "Why *are* they always talking about the end of the world?"

It was a question Vitus would normally have enjoyed answering, but right now he was still too preoccupied with the spy's accusation. "I don't know," he said absently. "What do you think, boys?" At nearly fifty years old, he'd started referring to anyone younger than thirty as a boy.

"If you had to live by all their commandments, you'd be begging for the world to end too," a whimsical voice called out.

The soldiers laughed. Even Vitus couldn't help but grin. It hadn't taken him long to learn that the quick-witted young man was the jokester of the group. If Vitus needed a laugh, he had only to look his way. The jokester had a funny habit of grinning like an idiot and wobbling his head back and forth if you looked at him unexpectedly.

They were approaching the local synagogue—a meager, dilapidated building in the middle of the village. A scattering of doves pecking at the ground in front flew away toward the sweltering afternoon sun. Vitus wiped sweat from his brow and grudgingly inhaled the sultry air. Raising a fist over his head, he announced, "Let's rest here for a few minutes."

Despite there being a well in front of the synagogue, it was still a peculiar order, he knew. They had filled their waterskins and rested only a short time ago. But considering the heavy load they were lugging, he doubted any of them would complain.

The chest required six men to transport it, three to a side, bearing the weight on two seven-foot-long poles threaded through handles. Normally they'd have a donkey and cart for the hefty chest, but both were currently undergoing repairs: the donkey for a split hoof, and the cart for a fractured wheel.

"I've got a cramp in my foot again," Vitus remarked offhandedly, hoping the information would allay any misgivings about his order.

He wanted to stop at the synagogue to inquire about the miraculous healer he'd heard rumors about. Supposedly, the man had begun living in Capernaum a month and a half ago and had already healed a great number of its residents of their ailments. If the rumors were to be believed, he did so simply by touching them. When Vitus had learned the man's name—Jesus—he was beside himself at the possibility of having found Barnabas's teacher.

Sliding his laden pack from his shoulders, Vitus dropped it to the ground with a dull thump and a puff of dust. He'd gotten a servant six months prior, mostly to have someone else tote his stuff, thus safeguarding his recently improved, pain-free back. Unfortunately, the man was ill and couldn't accompany him on this trip.

The familiar swish-swish of someone sweeping reverberated from the entrance of the synagogue. Vitus ducked inside and spotted an adolescent boy on the other side of a crumbling stone column. After beckoning him over, Vitus leaned in close to one of the boy's deerlike ears and asked where to find the miracle-healer, Jesus.

The boy, wide-eyed and shuddering, wouldn't say. "I'll fetch the local rabbi," he replied instead, then dropped his broom and sprinted out the door.

Hoping it wouldn't take long, Vitus returned outside and began unlacing his sandal. Though he'd tried to make his inquiry as inconspicuous as possible, he noticed the spy watching him from under his brown leather cap. Vitus was sure his actions looked suspicious—entering a synagogue and whispering something to a Jewish local—but it was a risk he was willing to take. He couldn't pass up the opportunity of meeting the man Barnabas referred to simply as "Master."

Vitus's men, reclining against the trunks of palm trees or the walls of the synagogue, traded gossip and jokes in between sips from waterskins. Nearby, a pile of their scarlet-red rectangular shields were propped against one another, resembling a glowing bonfire. In its center, long, sharp javelins pointed skyward, glinting in the sun.

Vitus listened in on their conversations as he began massaging his foot. His cramp, minor to begin with, receded easily—which was perfect since it had already served its purpose of giving him an excuse to stop at the synagogue.

"No, that was Zebulun," Vitus heard the spy say.

"Then what *was* his name?" the jokester asked. "Commander, could you help us? Who was that windbag always yelling that the end times are here?"

Shrugging, Vitus waited for him to be more specific.

"Some well-known rabbi," the young man elaborated.

"Hmm," Vitus replied, scratching the side of his head in mock contemplation. "A popular rabbi who preached the end of the world was coming. That narrows it down to just a few hundred."

The men chuckled.

"The crazy guy," added the jokester, "who was always talking about the lake of fire, telling people to repent, lived in the wilderness—"

"You mean the agitator Herod put in prison?" someone called out.

"The Baptizer," the spy said resolutely.

"Yes, the Baptizer," the jokester confirmed. "He was adamant the world was going to end soon."

"It did," said the spy. "For *him*."

A few of the men sniggered, but Vitus didn't find the quip amusing. After arresting the rabbi, Herod had him beheaded, despite the fact the man hadn't broken any law. He hadn't killed anyone, robbed anyone, or incited people to take up arms. He'd merely said some things Herod didn't like.

"What do *you* think, Centurion?" the spy asked. "You seem to know a lot about this stuff." He made a broad, all-encompassing swing of his arm. "When will *all this* end?"

Choosing his words carefully and mimicking the spy's arm sweep, Vitus answered earnestly. "All this," he said, "will end when it no longer has a purpose to serve."

"Life has a purpose?" the jokester said dryly.

One of the men guffawed, spitting out his water in the process.

"You're born. You suffer. You die," offered another soldier.

"And if the gods smile on you," added another, "you win a few battles and have some fun with the enemies' women!"

The spy, sneering under his pointy nose, lashed out at them. "Shut up, you fools! I didn't ask you." He then gazed expectantly with his one good eye at Vitus. "Please, Centurion. Continue."

Vitus noted he had yet to see the spy laugh, or even genuinely smile for that matter. Scrutinizing the man's clean-shaven, acne-scarred face, he speculated at his intentions. If it was to gather enough evidence to convict Vitus of sedition, then precaution dictated Vitus keep his mouth shut. But then caution had never gotten him what he wanted in life. Quite the opposite.

"Understand there's a difference between the purpose of the world and the purpose of life," Vitus explained.

Peering at the dark-gray clouds moving toward them across the Sea of Galilee, he deliberated how best to get across his point. Like the Jews, Romans also believed in the immortality of the soul. While Jews learned that all souls—no matter the life they've lived—went to a place called Sheol upon death, Romans were taught that all souls went to Hades. Both Sheol and Hades were described as gloomy underground places where both the righteous and the unrighteous spent eternity.

"The purpose of your *life* is to choose your soul's path," said Vitus. "The purpose of *the world* is to give you countless opportunities to make that choice. We are—"

"What choice?" the spy interrupted.

Vitus recalled Barnabas's words from a year ago, the memory of that moment permanently etched in his mind: "Vitus, the choice is between inclusion and exclusion, between seeing others as oneself and seeing others as separate. That's what each of us has to decide—whether to serve others or serve oneself. Whether to listen to the heart or reject it."

He knew that simply reciting Barnabas's words would be ineffective. His listeners wouldn't understand it. In speaking with soldiers he had to focus on logical arguments, using imagery and concepts they could relate to.

"Imagine there are two armies going on a quest to find a hidden, vast treasure," he said. "And you have a choice of which one to join. One army is blue. The other is red."

Before continuing, he scooted away from the encroaching sunlight and further into the shade of the synagogue. "The blue army is about unity. They're like a band of brothers, ceaselessly striving to serve one another. Each soldier is honored as an important part of the whole. They stress inclusion and cooperation. In battle, the blue army fights honorably and as a united force. They take prisoners where possible and treat them well, and they never leave a fallen comrade behind. The ultimate sacrifice for a soldier in the blue army is to lay down one's life to save another."

The spy, sitting the furthest away from Vitus, cupped his hand to his ear and slid in closer.

"The red army is the opposite of the blue," explained Vitus. "Their focus is personal power—the individual reigns supreme. Each man is expected to look out for himself, and one's worth is determined by how well one performs on the field of battle. The strongest and most skilled are promoted, regardless of how they treat others. The weakest are viewed as a burden, usually cast off or left behind. In battle, the red army is fearless and brutal. They take no prisoners, and they're masters of trickery and deception."

Vitus scanned the men's faces, trying to discern if he was getting through to them. Some looked intrigued. Others had their eyes closed, whether in torpid slumber or deep reflection, he couldn't tell.

"If they prayed to the gods, the soldiers of the blue army would pray 'Make us whole.' The soldiers of the red army would pray, 'Let me prevail,'" he said in conclusion.

Lifting his waterskin over his head, he wondered what Barnabas would have thought about his armies analogy. In one of their last meetings, Barnabas had instructed him in no uncertain terms that Vitus had "an obligation" to share his understanding of the world.

After a long drink, Vitus tilted his head back at the sky. "That's it in a nutshell," he announced. "The world exists to help you decide which army you want to join."

"Which one did you enlist in, Commander?" asked the jokester. "I'll join that one."

The big-eared boy who'd left to fetch the local rabbi came into view down the road. A wraith of a man with a thin, white beard hastened behind him.

"And what happens after you choose?" asked the spy. "Do you then change your allegiance?"

"After you choose," Vitus replied, deciding to ignore the second question, "then the world tests you—repeatedly and intensely—to see how strong your convictions are." He made his way to his feet, patting dirt from his legs and buttocks as the rabbi and boy approached.

"You seek the Rabbi Jesus?" asked the pale, gaunt man. He had breadcrumbs in his beard, and his breath smelled of garlic.

Vitus nodded.

"Is he in trouble?"

"Not at all," Vitus reassured him. "I heard he's a gifted healer and teacher, and wanted to meet him. That's all."

"He left this morning to visit another city."

"Are you certain?"

"Absolutely," the man replied. "I saw him and his disciples get in the boat this morning."

"Maybe they just went fishing?" Vitus suggested hopefully.

"No. You don't squeeze that many men in a boat if you're going fishing."

Vitus was heartbroken, but did his best not to show it. "Come on, boys," he called with a glance skyward. "Let's get going. That storm's moving in fast."

He laced up his sandal, his thoughts turning to Barnabas. Though the young idealist was still imprisoned, Vitus felt reasonably assured of Barnabas's safekeeping from crucifixion. After the debacle during the Sukkot festival, Rome had made its displeasure known to Pilate. The prefect had to be very careful now. One more miscalculation and he could find his tenure cut short.

As Vitus led his men down the narrow village road, the sounds of chiseling rang out through the air. It was a common noise in cities along the coast, usually from carpenters building boats.

After only a few minutes, Vitus found their path impeded by a crowd of men. Usually people made way for Roman soldiers, but this group was intensely focused on something and didn't even notice Vitus and his contingent of eight heavily-armed men. Rather than yelling for the road to be cleared, Vitus stood on his tiptoes at the back of the crowd, trying to discover what held their attention so acutely.

He discovered two frightened women, one older and one younger, at the front of the mob. The older one had just finished removing her headscarf when Vitus heard a man proclaim the women were "abominations in the eyes of God." Then Vitus glimpsed an object fly through the air, striking the older woman in the head. As she fell to the ground, the other woman—a girl, really—gave a piercing shriek.

"What's going on here?" Vitus demanded in Aramaic. All heads turned toward him as he plowed his way through the crowd, the spy following in his wake. After a forceful push past a stocky man with a large basket, Vitus turned and faced them. Eyeing the rocks in their hands, he spat on the ground in disgust. He detested stonings.

Crucifixions were certainly no more humane, but in Vitus's experience, most of those sentenced to crucifixion at least deserved it. They were usually men convicted of robbery, murder, or treason. But the Jews stoned both men and women, and for ridiculous reasons like blasphemy, predicting the future, or worshiping nature, the sun, the moon, or a different god.

"Centurion," an elderly man called in a high-pitched voice. "This is a Jewish matter. It is none of your concern."

All Roman soldiers had been warned against taking actions that had the potential to further inflame tensions with the Jews. Though the prefect and others in the Roman command sometimes blundered badly, their policy was nevertheless to be as sensitive as possible to the Jews' laws and customs. Vitus, in particular, had been singled out by Pilate and advised rather bluntly that any meddling at all on his part would result in severe consequences.

After a brief, probing glare at the Jewish elder, Vitus turned his attention to the injured woman. She wasn't moving, and bright red blood trickled down the side of her head to the dry earth below. Kneeling next to her, the girl was sobbing and calling, "Azara! Azara!"

Vitus wasn't sure what to do next, or how any of this would end, but he knew he couldn't walk away just yet. He swallowed against the rising nausea in his throat as he contemplated how the old man was likely right. Nevertheless, Vitus replied matter-of-factly, "I'm *making* it my concern."

"This is *Galilee*, not Judea," a man at the front of the crowd argued. "Herod is in charge here."

Vitus gripped the handle of his shortsword, unsheathing it a few inches as he stepped toward him. Despite knowing nothing about the man, he felt an acute dislike of him and his ugly black mole and bulging vein on his temple. "At this particular moment," Vitus said with a cold stare, "*I* am in charge."

The one-eyed spy conversed in Greek with the Jewish elder. "What have they done?" he asked.

"Adultery," the old man stammered with a stomp of his ram's horn cane on the ground.

"The groom's father paid two hundred dinars!" someone yelled.

"Yes! And for a virgin, not a whore!" called another voice.

"Was this a marriage? Or the purchase of a slave?" Vitus asked mockingly before going to inspect the woman's injury.

Judging by the amount of blood, Vitus didn't think the wound particularly severe, but he'd learned that with head injuries, one never knew. Although the woman's eyes were closed and she was unresponsive, she appeared to be breathing normally.

The spy slinked over to him. "Centurion, this is indeed a Jewish affair," he whispered in Greek. "Let's be on our way."

Vitus considered his words, and how, finally—after more than a year—he'd gotten off Pilate's demeaning jobs list. He didn't want to go back to overseeing ditch digging and quarry work, or guarding horse stables, or supervising latrine construction. If he withdrew now, there was nothing incriminating the spy could report to Pilate.

The crowd murmured amongst themselves. Vitus overheard the elder tell someone to fetch Herod's soldiers from the market.

"The prefect has clearly stated we are not to interfere in internal Jewish affairs," the spy added. "Let us depart before the storm starts in full."

Galling as it was, Vitus had to admit the spy was correct. What the Jews chose to do to one another was beyond his authority, particularly in Galilee.

As he tilted the woman's head to get a better view of her wound, a lone raindrop splashed onto his hand. The sky grew darker by the minute, and a loud, rolling thunder echoed across the Sea of Galilee. Storms here, Vitus was learning, could be unpredictable, and hazardously quick.

He was about to stand and leave when two curious things caught his attention. The first was that the raindrop on his hand felt strangely warm, and he realized it hadn't been a raindrop, but a falling tear from the girl. The second was the injured woman's face. It wasn't just her physical beauty despite her age, it was the shade of her skin and the contours of her nose. In all his decades in these provinces, Vitus had learned the subtle physical differences separating Jews from Gentiles, and she appeared to be more Persian than Jewish.

"This woman doesn't look like a Jew," he declared. "Is she?"

Squinting at the sea of unsmiling, bearded faces glaring back at him, he waited for a response. "Is she?" he asked again louder.

"She is not," the girl whispered to him in between sobs.

The sky flickered from a sudden lightning strike to the east. It wouldn't be long before the thick clouds reached them.

"Take the Gentile," the elder proposed, "but not the girl. She is a Jew and has brought shame on the entire community. Leave us so we can do God's work swiftly before the storm."

Vitus slid his arms under the woman's limp body. "You lied to me about this being strictly a Jewish affair," he countered. "And now you expect me to believe anything else you say?"

As he lifted the woman from the ground, she opened her hazel-brown eyes, gazing vacantly up at him. With a gasp, the girl moved in close and caressed the woman's cheek.

Using both of her quivering hands, the woman clutched the girl's slender right wrist. "I'm not leaving without her," she said faintly in Greek.

The repulsive man with the black mole grabbed the girl's left arm, pulling the other way. "Leave her be, Roman! This is *my daughter*!"

Vitus's head swirled. "Your daughter?" he replied blankly.

A wave of indignation crashed over him as he comprehended it all. "You were going to stone your own daughter?"

"Leave them, Centurion. They're nothing to you!" a voice from the crowd called out.

The man's words, though, had the opposite of their intended effect. Vitus knew precisely what he had to do, no matter the consequences.

"Take us to this woman's home," Vitus ordered the girl. "You'll stay with her there." Then he raised his knee high and kicked the man holding her arm so that he stumbled backward to the ground, wheezing for air.

With her head bowed, the girl led the way into the throng. As the indignant villagers reluctantly parted, Vitus detected the faint scent of roses over the men's sweaty, odorous bodies. In the girl's long, dark hair, he spotted the source: entangled red petals left over from her wedding.

"I'll be coming to this village regularly from now on," Vitus announced to the mob. "If any of you so much as harm a hair on their heads, you'll have me to answer to."

He didn't honestly know if he'd be able to keep that promise. His actions would surely land him in hot water with the prefect. It was even possible he'd just written his own prison sentence.

But he felt strangely calm. Perhaps because he knew he had righteousness on his side. Or perhaps because he saw this was a test from the world.

And he wasn't about to fail.

Chapter Thirty-Five

As Jonah strode by himself along the familiar twisting road from Magdala to Capernaum, he barely noticed the majestic view of the Sea of Galilee or the clusters of yellow flowers dancing in the breeze near the shoreline. His thoughts were entirely focused on Luke's despondency and what could be causing it.

Jonah yearned for the days long past when the two of them had carefree conversations about what animals would say if they could talk or where the sun went after it set. Words between the two of them these days were vague and guarded. They could barely discuss ordinary things like the weather or chores without getting into an argument.

On his better days, Jonah convinced himself Luke was just being a normal moody adolescent. On his darker days, he tormented himself with thoughts that Luke secretly liked males, and not females. Jonah's best friend was unusually effeminate. And every time Jonah tried speaking with Luke about the marriage he'd arranged, Luke became sullen and refused to talk. If Luke preferred men, Jonah knew he had no hope of protecting him. The life of a homosexual, once caught, always ended abruptly and violently—usually amidst a hail of stones.

A bee buzzing past Jonah's ear startled him out of his reverie. The first thing he noticed was a lone white sheep on a far-off hillside. Though flocks of them were plentiful in Galilee, it was rare to ever see one on its own—unless it was lost.

The second thing he noticed was that the reeds near the shore had grown taller than him. Peeking through the long stems and verdant leaves, he spied several fishing boats on the sea. That was certainly nothing rare. Fishermen were out there day and night casting their nets, hoping to catch a few fish in the depleted waters.

Jonah leaned on his walking stick and sighed longingly at one boat in particular. Unlike the others, this one had its sail up and was whipping across the waves. For the past ten years, Jonah had been saving up and had finally accumulated enough money for two equally expensive items: the bride price for Luke's marriage, and a boat. He fantasized about sailing to someplace far away and unknown where he could drop all his worries and responsibilities.

When Jonah returned to the trail, he detected the scent of lavender, which meant he was approaching the large patch of it that marked the halfway point. In Capernaum, he hoped to finally meet the Rabbi Jesus. He'd heard from a friend who'd passed through the small village earlier that day that the famed rabbi was indeed in town.

It had been two months since Zebulun asked Jonah to go listen to the rabbi and report back, and Jonah knew he'd taken far too long. But it couldn't be helped. A few days after Zebulun's visit, Jonah had left for Tiberius to care for a wealthy man suffering from poor appetite and insomnia. The man had convinced him to stay for several days, and when Jonah returned to Magdala, he learned he'd missed Jesus, who had given a talk in the synagogue on the recent Sabbath.

Shortly after that, Jonah had fallen and hurt his knee. He hadn't been able to walk at all for nearly three weeks. Even now, eight weeks later, it still hurt.

His hopes that Zebulun might have forgotten about his request had been dashed by a surprise visit from a stranger that morning. Jonah understood from the man's cryptic message that not only had Zebulun not forgotten, his patience was at its end. Zebulun expected Jonah to report to him in three days, and since the trip to Zebulun's hideout in the mountains took two days, Jonah had no choice but to hope he could find and hear Jesus today.

To give his sore knee a break, he stopped at his usual spot along the route, sitting under a fig tree on a big basalt rock he'd nicknamed Patience. His conversations with the table-sized rock were rather one-sided, but he enjoyed them nonetheless.

In between sips from his waterskin, Jonah explained to Patience how he and Luke still vehemently disagreed about Luke's desire to avenge Thomas's death. As Jonah listened in vain for a potential resolution, he caught a glimpse of a woman in the distance. She was descending the same hill he'd recently gone down. He eyed her curiously, for it was unusual for a woman to leave the house without a male escort. Besides Azara, there was only one woman he knew of who dared travel wherever she wanted on her own, and he hoped to God it wasn't her.

She disappeared from view where the road curved and dipped into a cluster of bushes and trees. When she reappeared a minute later, Jonah cursed under his breath for he knew that graceful gait could only belong to one person: Mary.

Though she lived only a few houses away from him in Magdala, they hadn't spoken to one another in over two years. Not since the incident.

It had occurred while Mary's nephew had been visiting. He and Luke had gotten into a fight. Jonah hadn't known over what. He'd only known what he saw and heard in those few seconds: Luke screaming for help and someone on top of him raining down blows. Charging to the rescue, Jonah had kicked Luke's assailant off, then thrown him head first into a stone wall.

It was only after the fact that Jonah realized he'd overreacted. Luke had no cuts or bruises, and his assailant had merely been a skinny boy who happened to be as tall as an adult—a boy who was now crying and stumbling down the road toward Mary, who'd witnessed the entire scene from the roof of her house.

Besides a nasty bump and a three-day headache, the boy had suffered no long-term harm. The only lasting repercussion had been Jonah's guilt, Mary's scorn, and the dissolution of their friendship.

Pretending to be preoccupied with massaging his knee, Jonah pivoted on the rock to look the opposite way from his approaching neighbor. He didn't want to face her, and he was certain she wanted nothing to do with him.

But instead of passing by, her muffled footsteps came to a halt behind him, and after a short eternity, she cleared her throat and spoke.

"Jonah, my friend, I want you to know I've forgiven you," she announced in her silvery voice.

Jonah peeked over his shoulder at her. She was holding a small bouquet of the purple lavender flowers and standing impossibly straight. He'd always been envious of her ideal posture. Whereas many people perpetually bent forward or hunched over as though protecting some shameful secret in their belly, Mary always stood tall with her shoulders back, chest out, and chin level to the ground. In her elegant white headscarf and robes, she came as close as anyone he'd ever met to embodying what he thought an angel would look like.

"And I ask you, my brother," she continued, "to please forgive me my animosity toward you. I was wrong, and I'm sorry."

Jonah turned the rest of the way around. He studied her expectant eyes and the soft lines in the olive-brown skin of her face to try to determine if she was serious or not.

She was.

Pressing his hand into the rough, uneven rock, he steadied himself from a suddenly spinning world. Her unguarded, kindly gaze took him by surprise, and he had to look away.

"Will you?" she asked a few seconds later.

"Will I what?"

"Forgive me."

"Oh," Jonah said, laughing embarrassedly. "Of course. Yes, I forgive you." Not knowing what else to do, he offered her some water, but she waved it off. "But your anger was justified," he added. "I deserved it."

"No, you didn't," she said firmly. "We'd been friends for a long time before the incident. You made one mistake and I judged you for eternity. Nobody deserves that."

Jonah was speechless. To him, being the first to admit one was wrong was one of the most difficult things to do in life. Not only had she done that, she'd done it confidently. Jonah had always known her as being rather indecisive, but the tone of her voice left no doubt as to her conviction.

Mary sat down next to him. "Is this the rock you told me about once? You gave it a name, right? Perseverance?"

"Patience," Jonah corrected her.

"Oh yes, Patience. I'm glad I finally get to meet her." Mary patted the rock with her hand. "Actually, is it a *her* or a *him*?"

"I don't know," Jonah said with a chuckle. "How does one tell?"

Mary shrugged as a slight breeze unexpectedly picked up.

"Ugh, it's about time," grumbled Jonah. He pulled his sticky tunic away from his chest in the hope some air would flow inside.

Mary moaned and arched her back. "Thanks for the breeze, God."

Jonah was struck by the difference in their outlook. While he was bitter and held a grudge about the unbearably hot afternoon, she didn't seem to blame God at all, instead praising Him for a momentary gust.

"Where you heading?" asked Jonah. "Capernaum?"

"Yes. And you?"

Jonah nodded. "Hoping to catch that new rabbi in town."

"Jesus?"

"Indeed."

"Me too," said Mary. She explained that she'd heard Jesus' talk at the Magdala synagogue and had taken every opportunity since then to hear him speak. She'd been to five of his talks already.

Jonah wasn't surprised. Jesus' acclaim had spread dramatically in a very short time. In addition to healing the blind and lame, Jonah heard he'd also performed an exorcism. Supernatural acts were important because they provided the proof Jews needed of the rabbi's direct link to God, thus allowing them to trust completely in the rabbi's teachings.

"Do you know if he's giving a talk today?" Jonah asked.

She shook her head. "A lot of his talks are informal, spur of the moment," she answered. "When a crowd gathers, he teaches." She pushed herself up from the rock, then dabbed at her thin black eyebrows with a blue kerchief. "Shall we walk together?"

"Certainly," replied Jonah, rubbing his knee. "As long as you don't mind going slowly."

Normally he would be nervous about being seen with a woman who was not his wife, but fortunately everyone in the area knew Mary. By virtue of being of independent means and hailing from an affluent, well-respected family, she was able to do things other women only dreamed of.

"Not at all," she said. "I'm surprised you're out here. I saw you limping around the past few weeks. Didn't your doctor tell you to stay off your feet?"

Jonah laughed. "Yes, but I'm like all the rest of my patients. I never heed my orders." He pulled his waterskin over his shoulder. "Let's hope we're in luck today. I've been wanting to hear this rabbi for many weeks now."

Mary's almond-shaped eyes regarded him quizzically. "Didn't you tell me once you got more than your fill of sermons on the Sabbath?"

Jonah grimaced at her words. It was true he wasn't usually interested in hearing what rabbis had to say. He mostly blamed the Pharisees and rabbis for the wretched state of the world. He certainly couldn't tell Mary his real reason for seeking out Jesus.

"I'm intrigued to meet this particular rabbi," he answered. "I've heard so much about him: All the miracles, all the healings...." With the help of his walking stick, Jonah lifted himself from the rock and flexed his knee a few times.

"Aren't you worried about him taking business away from you?"

"Not in the least," he answered with a chuckle. He explained that far from hurting Jonah's business as a physician, Jesus was actually making his job easier. Jonah mostly catered to the wealthy and often treated the poor for free. It wasn't the well-to-do Jesus was healing, but primarily the indigent, thus alleviating Jonah's workload.

The two of them walked side by side, catching up on all that had transpired in their lives since they'd stopped talking to one another. During every lull in their conversation, Jonah's thoughts returned to Mary's first words to him in over two years: "Jonah, I want you to know that I've forgiven you...." Though he remembered her being sincere, he still felt suspicious. Of what benefit to her was forgiving him? There must be something he was missing. A righteous grievance—like he had against the centurion—was not something you just dropped without getting *something* in return.

When the next pause came, Jonah blurted, "I can't stop thinking about what you said to me back on the rock."

"I understand," replied Mary. "I was shocked when I heard it too."

"You were shocked to hear your own words?"

"No, when I heard Jesus speak about forgiveness. He's mentioned it several times already—how it's important to forgive others."

Although the scriptures often mentioned God forgiving men and women for their faithlessness, Jonah had never read any verse about God's *people* being asked to forgive.

"The first time I heard one of his talks," Mary continued, "a man asked him how many times he should forgive his brother who had wronged him. 'Up to seven times?' he asked. And Jesus responded, 'I tell you, not just seven times, but seventy times seven.'"

Jonah scoffed at the notion. "Preposterous. Why would anyone do that?"

"I'm not sure I can explain it," answered Mary. "What I think I understand from Jesus is that forgiveness is a way to return to a state of wholeness. It's something you do to free yourself of the past."

Jonah was unconvinced, though he had to admit *Mary* certainly seemed different. When they'd been friends before, she was often cynical and melancholy, but now she seemed the opposite.

The quiet, meager village of Capernaum at last came into view. It wasn't much to look at—just a collection of dingy, basalt stone houses huddled near the shore and a few modest docks with a small armada of weather-beaten fishing boats bobbing up and down on the waves. Like Jonah's hometown, it had a synagogue in the center. Unlike Magdala, though, Capernaum didn't usually stink. Magdala was known far and wide for the fish sauce it produced, but its residents paid for that renown whenever the winds changed direction and blew the stench of rotting fish guts toward the town rather than away.

Once they entered Capernaum, Mary led them straight to the home of Peter, where she knew Jesus to be staying. Peter's wife informed them that Jesus was having dinner at the home of Levi. Jonah was baffled by the news. He knew Levi, having treated him for boils once, and wondered why he would have invited Jesus for dinner, and more inexplicably, why a rabbi would have consented to eat at the home of a tax collector.

Mary suggested they go there, and, hoping to solve the mystery, Jonah agreed. They arrived at Levi's lavish two-story house a few minutes later. A sizable crowd had congregated outside the front gate. Jonah climbed atop a knee-height wall and spotted Levi. He was showing someone a grapevine that wove up a lattice attached to the outside of his house. When the two of them turned in Jonah's direction, Jonah recognized the man Levi was talking to. It was the same rabbi he'd met by the riverbank after going to see John the Baptizer a year ago.

"So that's the famous 'Miracle Healer from Capernaum,'" Jonah said to no one in particular. His initial mild curiosity to meet the man swelled to something much more than that. Not a week had gone by when he hadn't longed to happen upon that mysterious rabbi again.

Levi's servant was wiping dust off a long outdoor table. Many people preferred to eat dinner outside in the summer, especially when it was hot and the sun wouldn't set until late. Levi was no exception, and he had a beautiful, rather uncommon patio that was fully tiled.

After directing some men to bring out another table, Levi swung his arms over his head to get the attention of the crowd gathered on the road outside his house. "For all of you who were not invited," he hollered, "you're welcome to sit on the wall and listen, as long as you are quiet and don't disturb us."

A wave of relief washed over Jonah. He'd been concerned that Levi—not noted for his generosity—was going to turn them all away.

Jonah and Mary found a place on the partly finished wall that was only a few yards from the table. Once they sat down, Mary pointed at the queue of people at the far end. "You see the man kneeling, washing people's feet?" she asked Jonah. "That's Andrew, one of the rabbi's disciples."

Jonah recognized him as well. He'd been John the Baptizer's follower—the one who'd led him and Luke to the riverbank where the famous orator had preached and done his baptisms.

Mary then directed Jonah's attention to a stocky man with a red-tinged beard near the front gate. He stood awkwardly, nervously eyeing the crowd. "That's Peter," she said, "Andrew's brother. He's also a disciple."

Jonah sympathized with Peter's unease at being there. Tax collectors were thought of as traitors because they became wealthy by collaborating with Herod and the Romans at the expense of their own people.

"What kind of rabbi has dinner at a tax collector's house?" remarked Jonah.

"The kind who doesn't flinch at eating at the same table as outcasts and wretches," Mary replied matter-of-factly. She nodded toward the other end of the table, where some guests had already taken their seats.

Jonah saw she was right. The dinner guests included an abundance of sinners. Abram, the drunkard, was pounding on the table trying to make a point about something, though no one appeared to be listening. On his right an alluring, infamous prostitute was laughing gaily. And across from her sat the beardless Ezra, a money lender—generally held in the same esteem as prostitutes, since they violated the commandments by charging fellow Jews interest on loans.

While Jesus washed his hands, Levi disappeared into his house, then reemerged a moment later with a large brown sack like the ones that held lentils, wheat, or almonds at the market.

"These are some old tunics," Jonah heard Levi telling Jesus. "Take them for the poor. They're still in decent condition."

"Thank you. That's very generous," Jesus said as he took the sack in one hand and clasped Levi's shoulder with the other.

Levi then led Jesus to the other end of the table. As they passed by Jonah and Mary, Mary caught Jesus' eye and waved to him. Jesus acknowledged her with a brief smile.

Though several colorful pillows had been set on top of a rug for them, Jesus pushed his out of the way and sat cross-legged. The servant arrived, cradling a pitcher of wine in his arms, then carefully set it on the table in front of Levi.

A multitude of conversations were springing up, but Jonah was close enough that he was still able to hear Jesus and Levi over all the chatter.

"What a splendid pitcher," commented Jesus.

Jonah agreed. It had been artfully crafted and painted to resemble a cluster of grapes.

"Is it stone?" Jesus asked.

"Yes, I got that at the market here some years back," said Levi. "It's Persian." He poured its contents out into the mugs on the table until the pitcher was empty. "Please," he said, "accept it as my gift."

"But you've already given me a gift."

"No, the tunics were for the poor. This is for you."

Jonah smirked, thinking Levi rather ostentatious for giving away such an expensive item.

"How do you know I won't give this to the poor as well?" Jesus said with a glint in his eye.

"Do with it as you please, rabbi," Levi replied dryly as he lifted the heavy pitcher with both hands over the sack with the tunics. "It is yours."

Jesus pushed the tunics to the sack's sides so the pitcher fit in the middle.

Levi leaned in close to Jesus and asked him something. After Jesus nodded in response, Levi stood up from the table, raising his arms over his head and clearing his throat. "The rabbi has agreed to take a few questions while the food is being brought out, so—"

Abram, clearly inebriated, scrambled to his feet, but lost his balance in the process, nearly falling onto those next to him. "Rabbi, I beseech you," he cried out as he regained his footing. "Explain to us imbeciles about life. Well, not *life* exactly. What I mean is, more precisely, for example—" He wrinkled his nose and swayed as though a strong wind were blowing. "For example," he repeated, slurring his words, "my cousin is wealthy and happy, while I am poor and unhappy. How is this fair?"

"You have no money because you spend it all on wine," someone shouted, prompting laughter among the crowd.

"Yes, indeed," Abram said thoughtfully. "You may, of course, be right."

"Sit down, Abram," someone called.

"Rabbi, ignore him," said another.

Abram puffed up his chest and gathered himself. "But what of this?" he exclaimed. "My neighbor, who has nothing but the tunic on his back, is cheerful every day, while I am a miserable wretch. Tell us, rabbi, did God gift him with happiness? Or has he done something to earn God's favor?"

All eyes turned to Jesus, but instead of answering the question, he called out to Andrew, who had finished washing other people's feet and was now crouched over washing his own. "What say you to this question, Andrew?"

"But Master," Andrew protested, "he asked you. And my judgment is no comparison to yours."

"Fear not," replied Jesus. "I shall correct you if you're wrong."

Andrew rose to his feet, standing sheepishly facing Jesus. "My answer would be short, Master," he said with a bowed head. "And based entirely on what I've learned from you." He then turned to Abram. "I would say: A man reaps what he sows. Sow misery and you shall be miserable. Sow joy and you shall be joyful."

Jesus smiled warmly, nodding his approval.

Jonah respected Andrew's reply, though he was taken aback to realize how similar he, himself, was to the drunkard. While Abram cultivated misery, Jonah cultivated sorrow.

A Pharisee sitting on the other side of Mary spoke up. "My good sir, may *I* ask a question?"

Levi scowled at the man, presumably because he'd already asked non-guests not to intrude, but Jesus looked the man's way and said, "Please."

"Rabbi, we know how honest you are," the Pharisee began. "You teach the way of God truthfully. You are impartial and don't play favorites. Tell us then, what is your opinion? Is it lawful to pay taxes to Caesar or not?"

Jonah leaned forward to peek over at the man's face for he perceived immediately what a sly question it was. If Jesus said yes, then he could be accused of courting favor with the hated Romans. He could be called a traitor to his people. But if he said no, then he could be labeled an agitator and reported to Herod or the Romans, who then might arrest him.

Jesus looked displeased, muttering something under his breath before calling out, "Show me the coin used for the tax."

Someone tossed a Roman dinar to him. He caught it with one hand and held it up for all to see. "Whose image and inscription is this?"

"Caesar's," the crowd answered.

Jonah was intrigued with Jesus' response so far. Taxes were paid to the government that ruled a land, and without saying so himself, Jesus had made clear under whose rule the Jews lived.

The Pharisee held his hand to his pointy chin, squinting skeptically at Jesus.

"Render unto Caesar the things that are Caesar's," added Jesus. "And unto God the things that are God's."

It was a provocative answer, Jonah thought, for although it pointed out who was, in fact, the ruler of Palestine, it also suggested that it didn't matter as far as one's spiritual ambitions were concerned. One's heart could be given to God even while one's taxes were given to Rome.

Jonah fought back a grin as he pictured himself relaying this information to Zebulun. Those like his cousin, who believed freedom from their oppressors was both an ultimate and required first step toward any reconciliation with God, would positively choke with indignation at such a suggestion.

Jesus called to Andrew, who had just finished washing his hands and was now searching for a place to sit. "Come to this end," he said. "There's room down here."

Levi's servant continued setting dishes of food on the table: baskets of flatbread, platters of black olives, and leafy salads. Jonah couldn't see what every dish was, but he could make a good guess based on their smell. Steam rose from several large bowls that undoubtedly contained some kind of stew with fish.

"Some of you I've seen before," Jesus announced. "And you've heard my invitation to follow me. I say to those hearing me for the first time: Come to me, all who are weary and carry heavy burdens, and I will give you rest."

Jesus slowly scanned, one by one, the faces of those sitting at the table or on the half-finished wall. When his gaze came to Jonah, it was all Jonah could do not to look away, for he felt as though Jesus somehow knew everything about him: his troubled past, his difficulties with Luke, his deep shame and unending faithlessness. But strangely enough, Jonah sensed no condemnation or judgment from Jesus. It was as though the life Jonah was living was perfectly alright, and that Jesus knew—somehow really *knew*—that Jonah would overcome every obstacle in his path, that it was inevitable.

"Take my yoke upon you and learn from me," continued Jesus, "for I am gentle and humble in heart, and you will find rest for your souls. For my yoke is easy to bear, and the burden I give you is light."

While Andrew tiptoed past, Jonah considered the offer Jesus was making. He certainly longed for a path less burdensome than that of the Pharisees and scribes with their endless rules.

Jesus slid a few inches closer to Levi. "Move my sack and you can sit here next to me," he instructed Andrew.

A prominent lawyer familiar throughout Galilee slid his mug of wine out of the way and leaned over the table to get Jesus' attention. "Rabbi, how are we to know what you speak is the truth?"

Jesus, poised as ever, called on his disciple again. "What say you, Andrew? You've been my disciple for several months now. Have I spoken the truth?"

"Yes, Master," Andrew replied as he stepped gingerly past Levi. He stretched his arm toward the sack next to Jesus. "Indeed, your yoke is easy to bear and the burden you give is light." Unaware of the heavy pitcher that had been added to Jesus' sack, Andrew tried to lift it, but was instead pulled down toward it by the unexpected weight.

Jesus and the entire crowd burst into laughter. Even the stern lawyer couldn't help but snicker.

With a mock expression of determination on his face, Andrew took hold of the sack with both hands and pretended it was more than he could lift. The crowd howled with delight. Jesus laughed so hard he used the backs of his hands to wipe tears from his eyes.

When things finally calmed down, the servant signaled to Levi that all the food had been set out. Jesus then led them in a prayer of gratitude, after which the dinner guests began to eat. While they dined, Jonah whispered one of his observations in Mary's ear. "He's quite light-hearted. For some reason, I thought he'd be strict and austere."

"Yes, that surprised me too," she whispered back. "He's so good-natured, it's impossible not to like him. Even when he rebukes someone, it's never in a mean way. And if one does somehow get offended, it's quite hopeless trying to stay mad at him."

Jonah studied everything about Jesus, noting how he chewed slowly, appearing to savor each bite, even closing his eyes from time to time before he swallowed. Jonah could no longer hear any of Jesus' conversation as the noise level had increased substantially. In addition to the murmur of all the conversations, the table made a high-pitched squeal every time Abram pressed down too hard. He was sitting on the ground on his right hip, his legs beside him, leaning forward so that most of his weight rested on the table.

Unlike the fancy table Jonah knew Levi had inside, the outdoor table was made of thin, rough planks that were faded and worn from the sun and rain. Levi's exquisite painted serving bowls and mugs made up for the feeble table, though Jonah couldn't help but wonder if Levi had bought them, accepted them as a bribe, or perhaps seized them in lieu of taxes owed.

As twilight came to an end, the servant began setting out small oil lamps around the table. Levi positioned one in front of Jesus, and when the two of them had finished eating, Levi again consulted him, then announced, "The rabbi has consented to answer a few more questions."

The lawyer immediately spoke up. "Rabbi," he called almost frantically, then collected himself once he saw he had no competition. He brushed away crumbs from his beard, then asked "What should I do to inherit eternal life?"

"What is written in the scriptures?" Jesus replied curiously. "How do you understand them?"

"'You must love the Lord your God with all your heart, all your soul, all your strength, and all your mind.' And, 'Love your neighbor as yourself,'" the man answered, quoting popular verses.

"You have answered correctly," said Jesus. "Do this and you shall live."

Jonah could see by the man's glum expression that Jesus' answer did not satisfy him. The lawyer was noted for being a proud man, considered by many Galileans to be an authority on the scriptures.

"And who is my neighbor?" the lawyer asked.

Jonah understood the challenge implied by the question. Though it appeared simple on the surface, the query was really a test of Jesus' knowledge and understanding of the scriptures.

Jesus closed his eyes and was silent for a moment, then he began to tell a story. "A Jewish man was traveling from Jerusalem down to Jericho," he said, "when he was attacked by bandits."

Jonah knew well the road Jesus spoke of. Dubbed the "Way of Blood," myriad travelers had been assaulted or killed by robbers as they traveled it. He crossed his arms tightly in front of himself, thinking of Zebulun and his own wretched history being one of the bandits.

"They stripped him of his clothes, beat him up, and left him half dead beside the road," continued Jesus. "By chance a priest came along, but when he saw the man lying there, he crossed to the other side of the road and passed him by."

The priest's actions made sense to Jonah. He probably assumed the man was dead, and to make contact with a dead body was considered defiling— particularly so for priests, who were required to be ritually clean.

"So too," said Jesus, "a Temple assistant—a Levite—came to the place, saw the man, and passed by on the other side."

Jonah thought he knew where the story was going, that it was to be an admonishment of religious authorities for their hypocrisy, for choosing rules over people.

"But when a Samaritan on a journey came upon him," Jesus said, "he looked at him and felt compassion."

There were murmurs and groans at the mention of the Samaritan. The crackdown in Jerusalem during Sukkot was still fresh in Jonah's mind. The soldiers who had disguised themselves and infiltrated the crowd to attack the pilgrims had all been Samaritans.

"Going over to him, the Samaritan soothed his wounds with olive oil and wine and bandaged them. Then he put the man on his own donkey and brought him to an inn, where he took care of him."

As Jesus paused for a moment, Jonah glanced around at all the perplexed faces in the crowd, glad he wasn't the only one who didn't understand the point of the story so far. Surely Jesus wasn't suggesting to a Jewish audience that an ungodly, half-breed *Samaritan* was the honorable one.

"And the next day," added Jesus, "he took out two dinars and gave them to the innkeeper, saying, 'Take care of him, and whatever more you spend, I will repay you when I come back.'"

Jesus fixed his eyes on the lawyer. "Now which of these three would you say was a neighbor to the man who was attacked by bandits?"

The lawyer, like the rest of the crowd, was quiet and stunned. Jesus was not only suggesting the Samaritan was the righteous one, but that he was the only one of the three who'd followed the intent of the scriptures.

The lawyer, bowing his head, answered Jesus sincerely. "The one having shown compassion toward him."

Then Jesus said to him, "You go and do likewise."

In the silence that followed, a long-forgotten memory broke free of the dark recesses Jonah had condemned it to. It was of the ill man he and Thomas and Zebulun had found in the woods when they were kids. They had initially tried to help the man, Jonah now remembered, because they thought he was a Jew. When Zebulun had pointed out he was actually a Samaritan, they'd dropped the ailing man back to the ground and fled as fast as they could.

Jonah sat with the memory, so fresh and raw it seemed it had occurred only yesterday and not over thirty years ago. He'd thought Jesus' teaching had been directed at the lawyer, but wasn't sure anymore. Perhaps Jesus had been speaking directly to Jonah all along.

Filled with overwhelming remorse, Jonah pinched the back of his hand. Though it was a trick he used for controlling his temper, he hoped it might help him now refrain from sobbing ingloriously in front of everyone.

It did not.

Abandoning all hope of poise or dignity, Jonah wept bitterly and openly. Mary held a reassuring hand to the middle of his back in support, while Jesus thankfully continued to answer questions, keeping the crowd's attention.

Jonah's tears continued unabated long after the table had been cleared and half the guests had left. He finally regained his composure just as Jesus rose from his spot and made his way toward him and Mary.

"Good evening, Mary," he said cheerfully. He expanded his broad chest with a deep, obviously satisfying, inhale. "Ahh, the night air smells so good tonight."

"Hello, rabbi," replied Mary. "I'd like you to meet Jonah. He's a doctor from my village who's been wanting to hear you speak for some time."

"It's nice to see you again, brother," said Jesus. With an open palm, he patted Jonah heartily on the upper arm.

Amazed that Jesus remembered him, and still overcome with emotion, Jonah struggled for a response. "Yes. Definitely. It's—"

"Rabbi," the Pharisee next to Mary interrupted, "why do you eat and drink with such scoundrels—these tax collectors and sinners?"

With a smile and conspiratorial wink to Jonah, Jesus replied, "It is not the healthy who need a doctor, but the sick."

Jonah couldn't agree more. He felt as though his sick heart had just received a lifetime of healing in one evening.

Chapter Thirty-Six

Peeking through the crooked front window of the physician's house, Vitus looked for any indication that Ira's examination would soon be over. He'd risked coming to this remote place northeast of Jerusalem not for any centurion duties, but solely in the hope that the physician here could diagnose the cause of his servant's unknown malaise. Unable to see anyone or anything other than a tall antiquated dresser whose top was covered with wilted herbs, dried orange flowers, and a pair of antlers, Vitus cracked his knuckles and resumed watching the two men across the road working at a wine press.

One man, clad only in a white loincloth, was treading gingerly around a shallow basin that had been chiseled out of an enormous stone slab. Another man brought palm-woven baskets that were brimming with purple grapes. Each time he emptied them into the basin, he would shout enigmatically, "Camel's ass!"

Vitus regarded the two men jealously, longing for their carefree jobs— particularly now. He worried his relatively easy and dignified duties safeguarding tax monies wouldn't last much longer. The prefect was in the capital, Caesarea, preoccupied with other matters, so the repercussions of Vitus interfering in the Capernaum stoning had yet to be administered. Pilate had sent word for Vitus to remain in Jerusalem until he arrived, but Vitus had disregarded those orders, deciding his servant's rapidly declining health couldn't wait.

The two wine-press workers, though less than twenty yards from Vitus, paid him no attention. This reassured Vitus his disguise was reasonably convincing. To conceal his identity, he had not worn his helmet, armor, or anything else that might identify him as a Roman. Instead, he was attempting to pass himself off as an ordinary construction worker, a common sight in these parts. While most Jewish men and women wrapped themselves in ankle-length tunics, Vitus wore one that only came to the knees, as was standard for workers, servants, slaves, or anyone else who required mobility. His skin wasn't as dark as some of the locals', but it was a rich copper brown that didn't distinguish him too much from those native to this region. The only dead giveaway was his hairless head and face, bright blue eyes, and long scar on his cheek. To conceal all that, he wore a loosely fitted headscarf and did his best not to let anyone get too close.

Hearing the front door scrape open, Vitus turned, but neither the physician nor Ira emerged. Instead, out wafted plumes of sweet-scented, white smoke.

Several years earlier Vitus had come here seeking help for chronic headaches that no one and nothing could alleviate. After smudging him with the same white smoke, the doctor had advised him to stop eating almonds, and, much to Vitus's surprise, that solved the problem. He hoped for similar success now for Ira.

The doctor, shaking his head from side to side and muttering something inaudible, appeared through the smoke like an apparition. Pale and ghastly, he smelled like an oversmoked fish. He began chanting in an impossibly low and beastly voice as he faced different directions. Vitus, remembering the doctor had done the same thing with him, sat down on the rickety bench to observe.

Ira's volatile malady had begun two months before. On his worst days he would lie in bed from sunup to sundown, with a fever, no appetite, and a yellowish tint to his skin and eyes. On his average days he would complain of stomachaches, nausea, and a general lack of strength. On his good days he was able to perform the duties he was supposed to. He cleaned and polished Vitus's helmet and armor; prepared meals; fetched water; and carried Vitus's pack when he traveled. Ira was also adept at massage—something Vitus hadn't even considered when he'd accepted Ira's offer to become his slave for six years.

While the doctor finished his incantations, Vitus withdrew three coins from the leather pouch he had hidden inside his tunic. After Ira came out, Vitus placed the coins in the physician's outstretched dingy palm, then he and Ira set off on their ten-mile journey back to Jerusalem. Vitus was pleased to see the sun still high in the sky. As long as they didn't take too many rests, they should be back well before sunset.

Once outside the desolate mountain village, Ira began explaining the doctor's cryptic pronouncement.

"He said I should go to the Bethesda bath."

Vitus was familiar with that pool, one of several in and around Jerusalem. "Did you tell him you've already been to other pools?"

"Yes," replied Ira. "He said this one was special and that I should wait until the angel stirs up the water, then be the first one in and I'll be cured."

Vitus was skeptical, but admitted there was much he simply didn't know. He wouldn't have guessed in a thousand years that almonds were the culprit behind his headaches. "I guess it can't hurt," he said.

The foul odor of a dead animal began growing in intensity. Vitus traced the smell to a baited leopard trap set a short distance back from the road. Constructed with branches tied together with rope, and covered with leaves, it was made to look like a harmless tunnel. The leopard, seeing he could go either forward or backward, would enter the space oblivious to the danger. When he reached halfway and tugged on the piece of rotting meat hanging down, both the front and back gates would be released, dropping shut and sealing the leopard's fate.

Vitus knew a successful capture meant a boon for the poor people who lived here. Leopard fur fetched a steep price at the market. Still, he thought it an inglorious death for such a majestic creature.

"I'd like you to come with me to Capernaum next week if you're feeling well enough," Vitus announced. He'd been seeking any opportunity of late to go there. One reason was to check on the two women he'd saved from being stoned. The other was his hope of meeting the Rabbi Jesus.

In the two weeks since he'd rescued Azara and Esther, he'd returned once to look in on them by trading duties with another centurion who was heading there to retrieve a criminal captured by Herod's militia. Vitus had planned to stop by Azara's house just to make a show of it—to remind the men of the village that he was indeed making good on his pledge to protect the women. However, he'd ended up spending half the day there. He'd found Azara not only pleasing to look at, but pleasing to talk to as well. She was unusually well-educated. In the company of his Roman colleagues, rarely did anyone question Vitus's thoughts or beliefs. He simply knew more than anyone else. But with Azara he suspected he'd discovered his equal. They'd spent hours discussing Plato's teaching that the everyday world of the senses was not actually real, but a grand illusion, and that one's primary goal was to climb out of life's dark cave of ignorance.

"Sir," Ira said hesitantly. He stared at the ground, stooped forward even more than usual. "Thank you for taking me here. I don't quite know what to make of all the kindness you've shown me. It's not something I would have expected...." He left the sentence unfinished, his voice trailing off.

Vitus was fairly certain he knew the words left unsaid: "...from a Roman." No one expected generosity, or sometimes even decency, from a Roman. Vitus recognized he and his colleagues were often viewed as little more than amoral, godless heathens.

Ira stopped and pointed his knobby forefinger at something in the distance. At first Vitus felt nervous about what he'd detected, for these parts were known for robbers. But he took a breath and reminded himself that God was looking out for him. He had come to believe that whatever, or whoever, came his way was somehow for his benefit, even if he didn't understand how or why.

Spying a meager plot of green ahead of them, Vitus noted nothing special—just two hardy cedar trees and the patch of grass they sheltered. Then, out of the corner of his eye, he spotted two gazelles leaping gracefully across a vast yellow ridge.

There Ariseth Light in the Darkness 261

Ira spit out the herb he'd been chewing, then sighed heavily. "This affliction—it's my fault, sir," he professed. "My sins against God have been great. I haven't obeyed the scriptures well in life."

Vitus pulled his chin toward his chest and tugged his headscarf down to protect his nose from the blazing sun. Ahead of him, he could see three vultures circling below a tiny wisp of a cloud. "We each have our sins that stalk us in life," he remarked. Before he'd met Barnabas, Vitus had only a few regrets in his life. But once Barnabas helped him understand what exactly sin was, his remorse multiplied a thousandfold.

"Forgive me, sir," Ira said. "I am but an old man who doesn't understand much. How could you have sinned? You are a Gentile. You are not required to follow the commandments."

"Sinning is not confined to Jews," said Vitus. "To *sin* is to speak or act in a way that denies we are all brothers and sisters in the eyes of God. A sin is something done from a belief of separateness, that what you say or do to others has no consequences for your *own* happiness and well-being."

Ira slowly shook his head. "You are very wise, sir."

A sudden gust whistled through the multitude of ridges and crevices. The winding, rocky road they traveled was more like a trail than a road. Vitus doubted some of the passages were even wide enough for a wagon to fit through. When he noticed a pair of recent footprints in the dry soil leaving the main path and heading up into the harsh terrain above them, he wondered if they belonged to one of the Jewish holy men who lived in the caves here and spent every day in prayer and quiet contemplation.

Of course the footprints could also belong to a robber. Vitus was keeping an eye out for them, but wasn't overly concerned. He had no doubt he could fight off two or three of them if they chose to engage—maybe even four, depending on the circumstances.

Their conversation diminished over the next two miles as they gradually merged with their barren surroundings. There was very little life, plant or animal, here. No matter which way he looked, all Vitus could see was rugged, beige slopes and the occasional sun-bleached bones of a long dead animal.

Coming upon a narrow gorge, Vitus stopped to scrutinize the area. Traversing this type of passage would leave them exceedingly vulnerable between the towering walls of rock on either side. He listened for the slightest sound, but with neither a breeze nor any kind of running water nearby, it was dead silent.

"What is it?" asked Ira. He hadn't spoken loudly, but his voice nevertheless echoed far and wide.

Vitus put his finger to his lips, hushing him. "Let's get through here quickly," he whispered in Ira's ear. "Then we'll take a rest."

Halfway through the gorge, Ira pointed out a finely embroidered cloak stuffed behind a boulder. As he tugged on it, several small rocks that had been wedged in on top of the cloth came tumbling noisily to the ground.

Vitus's stomach clenched, and he quickly glanced behind them. "We need to get out of here," he hissed in Ira's ear. "Now."

As he backpedaled, Vitus squinted at the ridge twenty feet overhead, half of which was in bright sunlight. He scoured the cracks and dark shadows for signs of what he feared was about to take place.

Then he heard it. Alarming sounds echoing from every direction: men speaking in hushed tones, pebbles crunching underfoot, the muffled clanging of metal....

Vitus reached inside his sweaty robes and gripped the familiar handle of his shortsword as a skinny, wild-eyed youth stepped out from his hiding spot in front of them. He was clutching a rusty dagger and wore a ragged, fraying tunic that covered only one side of his bony ribs.

Others soon joined him: four more with swords and spears in front, five others blocking the path behind, two men with bows and arrows straddling rocks from above. They all had long, scraggly beards, worn-out sandals, and tunics not much better than rags.

Bandits. Twelve of them in all.

Vitus was surprised to see them this close to Jerusalem, where the Romans had significant troop concentrations.

"Travelers!" a voice boomed from on high.

Vitus tilted his head back, blocking the blinding sun with his free hand as he tried to locate the voice's owner. His eyes settled on a thirteenth bandit—a bull of a man with a bright red kerchief wrapped around his head.

"So we meet again," Vitus muttered to himself. Despite the years, he hadn't forgotten the infamous outlaw: Zebulun.

Instinctively, Vitus unsheathed his sword and held it in front of himself.

Zebulun's voice rang out again. "What, pray tell, is a mere peasant doing with a Roman sword?"

Vitus yanked off his headscarf. There was no point in hiding anymore, and it obscured his peripheral vision.

Zebulun howled in delight. "The Lord is a God who avenges! Praise be to the Lord!" he called triumphantly. "He has heard my prayers!"

Vitus wasn't concerned or even surprised he'd been recognized. He was busy searching high and low for a way out. Unfortunately, he saw no cave or dwelling to duck into, no secret tunnel, no rescue party on the way if he could hold them off for a while. The archers above were already loading their homemade arrows and taking aim down at him.

Zebulun held out a fat fist, and the men below lowered their long menacing spears and began closing in on Vitus and Ira. "You have oppressed my people. You have stolen our money and our land," he proclaimed. "You crucified my cousin—my flesh and blood! But today, Centurion, vengeance is mine!"

Vitus studied the emaciated, ill-equipped men approaching him. A few wore bronze helmets that were too big for them. Some had primitive shields that they weren't holding properly. A couple of them had pitiful leather armor. But as amateurish as they were, Vitus knew he could not defeat them all, so he called out to Zebulun. "It's me you want," he shouted. "Let this man go. He is a Jew in ill health."

"Sir," Ira protested, "I shall not leave you."

Zebulun hooted as though Vitus's request was a joke. "Do you really think you're in a position to be making demands?" he called from on high.

Though Vitus considered suicide a cowardly way to die, he turned his sword around, pointing it at his belly. "Then I shall deny you the satisfaction you seek!"

Zebulun laughed uproariously, but then consented. "Very well, Centurion. I will grant your wish."

Vitus pushed his servant forward with his free arm. "Start walking," he commanded.

Ira made a doglike whimper. "But sir—" he objected again.

"That's an order!" Vitus growled.

"Go, traitor!" yelled Zebulun. "And hurry, before I change my mind."

Ira slinked forward, dragging his feet across the dusty earth as the motley bandits in front squeezed against the sides of the narrow gorge. With a last mournful glance back at Vitus, Ira passed in between them and out of sight.

The vultures that Vitus had seen circling earlier now came lower. One of them landed on the jagged ridge high above.

"Fourteen years ago you slipped through my grasp, but there will be no escape this time, Centurion," Zebulun declared.

Vitus knew his foe was right. He'd always wondered how exactly his life would end. He used to think it would be in battle, but that was a different life. The time for fighting in his new life was over. He threw his sword to the ground. If he was going to die, he wanted to do it without anger in his heart, and with complete trust in God's plan for him.

As the embittered faces of his enemies closed in, Vitus looked up at the heavens—perhaps for the last time, he considered.

The sky was a peerless blue. Enchanting. Peaceful. Boundless.

It was a good day to die.

Chapter Thirty-Seven

Jonah slipped and slid, but persisted in climbing his way up the bone-dry hill of reddish dirt. At the top he spied the sentry he'd been expecting. The man had squeezed into the slim shade provided by a split in the rockface. Sitting atop a boulder, he had his elbows on his knees, propping his head up under folded hands. A handcrafted spear rested on his lap. When he heard Jonah's footsteps, he stood and lazily pointed his spear in Jonah's direction. "What is your business here?" he asked indifferently.

Jonah took a step back from the stone-tipped spear and recited the unimaginative pass phrase he'd been given: "The Lord is a God who avenges."

In response, the gaunt sentry lowered his spear and plopped back on the boulder. "Shine forth," he muttered under his breath.

Jonah had seen—more often than he cared to—the signs of someone who hadn't been getting enough to eat. In addition to the man's lethargy and emaciation, his cheeks were sunken and his skin was flaky. He was a lousy choice for a sentry, and Jonah wondered if Zebulun had assigned him the duty as some sort of punishment.

Through the overcast sky, Jonah detected Zebulun's camp, now no more than a mile away. It was nearly the exact opposite of a Roman encampment. There was no carefully laid-out outer defense, nor precise rows and columns of tents separated by passages and roads. Zebulun's camp was a jumbled maze filled with countless, minuscule dwellings that Jonah was dreadfully familiar with from his time in the bandits. Zebulun was forced to move his camp frequently as the authorities learned of each new location, so the "houses" they lived in were never much more than short mud-packed stone walls with branches and thatch thrown over top for a flimsy roof.

Despite descending the hill's sandy soil with careful, deliberate steps, Jonah still lost his footing and slid the last few feet on his rear end. After dusting himself off, he let out a weary sigh. It had been a long two days of travel, but at least it was over and he'd made it in one piece.

He'd followed the Jordan River south for most of the trip. Before he got to the area where John the Baptizer used to preach, he'd headed east, per his instructions, into a mountainous, barren area of Perea. The remote location of Zebulun's camp, Jonah recognized, was both a blessing and a curse: a curse because it was nearly impossible to grow crops there and water was scarce; a blessing because it was a long way from any Roman outpost; and Perea, like Galilee, was ruled by Herod Antipas, not Pontius Pilate.

For much of his journey, thoughts of Luke had occupied Jonah's mind. He was coming more and more to believe Luke's melancholy was a result of his misguided belief that he had to avenge Thomas's death. Having failed to convince Luke he had no such obligation, Jonah now wished he could just do the deed for him. At forty-five, Jonah was older than the vast majority of the populace and felt his life was mostly over. If fate was ever inclined to bless him with the opportunity to sacrifice his remaining days to safeguard Luke's, he vowed to himself not to hesitate.

When not thinking about Luke, Jonah had rehashed his conversation with his neighbor, Mary, on forgiveness. Though she'd claimed she was only relaying what she'd learned from Jesus, Jonah was having a difficult time with it. Her words had been preposterous. After all, nobody—rabbis, scribes, even Pharisees—spoke about forgiveness. Mercy, yes. Compassion, yes. But the idea of forgiving someone who had caused serious harm was nearly unheard of.

As they'd departed from the dinner at Levi's, Mary had explained that forgiving is like setting fire to the list of grievances between you and the other person, and that once burned up, you could go back to how things were before anything passed between the two of you. It was like beginning anew.

Jonah had to admit he liked the sound of that. For far too long he'd felt mostly incapable of enjoying life. If there was a way to draw nearer to that innocence, openness, and enthusiasm he had prior to his thirteenth birthday, then—no matter how crazy the idea—he was willing to try it.

At the outskirts of the camp, a strong gust of wind blew stinging sand against Jonah's legs. Another sentry, just as pallid and skinny as the first one, emerged from a makeshift guardpost and called out to him.

Jonah recited the pass phrase once again, but the sentry was unsatisfied and demanded to know what he wanted there. While Jonah explained, he studied the young man's curiously familiar face.

"Is your name Caleb?" asked Jonah after justifying his presence.

The sentry narrowed his eyes and leveled his spear. "How did you know?"

"Your father was Boaz?"

"Yes."

"My goodness, how you've grown," Jonah exclaimed. "I knew you when you were ten. I was friends with your father. The three of us used to fetch water from the river together."

Caleb stood his spear on its end beside him and scrutinized Jonah's face. "Were you the one who used to tell stories to us kids around the fire at night?"

Jonah nodded, feeling gratified that Caleb not only remembered him, but had a positive memory. "Is your father around?" he asked. "I'd love to say hello."

"He died five years ago."

Jonah lowered his head. "I'm sorry," he said. "I hope he went in peace."

"No, not really," replied Caleb matter-of-factly. "It was drawn-out and painful. Just like everyone else...."

Jonah grimaced, finding it hard to believe the food situation could have been so bleak for so long. But there was no denying Caleb's thin, colorless lips, nor that he was significantly shorter than his father had been.

As they wound their way through the camp, Jonah was dismayed to discover Caleb and the other sentry were actually in *better* condition than everyone else. Clearly, the rumors of Zebulun's "mighty Jewish army" were nothing more than wishful thinking. Listless adults with twiglike arms and legs stared at him with bulging eyes and blank faces. Even though it was hot, they wore cloaks over their tunics and had their headscarves wrapped tight, as though it was winter.

Caleb said nothing to any of the people they passed by, nor did they speak to him. Even when Caleb stepped over the outstretched legs of a young boy lying on the ground outside his house, no greetings or apologies were offered.

Jonah felt sickened by it all. Things had never been this dire when he was part of the bandits. He knew all these poverty-stricken people were from the countryside and had known nothing but hardship in their lives. Joining the bandits was always a last resort. Was this the best Zebulun could do for them?

A girl with a distended, bloated belly held out her hand as they went by. When Caleb ignored her, Jonah hollered for him to wait so he could give her the last of his almonds and dried figs. But Caleb didn't slow down in the least, and Jonah, worried that he'd get lost in the disorganized, sprawling camp, apologized to the girl and hurried after his guide.

Caleb navigated the labyrinth of makeshift houses with ease, often turning abruptly to cut through a tight alley just when it seemed they were at a dead end. Jonah shook his head at the pathetic one-room structures. They were not only tiny, some were so short, one could only crawl in. Roman tents would be more luxurious.

"Where is everyone?" Jonah asked. The number of people he saw was only a fraction of the number of dwellings.

"Resting," replied Caleb.

Jonah glanced up at the sky, surprised it was afternoon already. Thick, high clouds had been blocking the sun the whole day. That was a good thing. Otherwise, Jonah thought, it would be unbearably hot inside those miserable little huts during the midday nap.

They zigzagged their way to a strangely elongated house surrounded by a two-foot wall of loosely-stacked stones. Unlike the other dwellings, this one was an actual house, with a door and windows, and tall properly constructed walls. Caleb made a cryptic knock on the front door, then departed with a flat, ambiguous, "Good luck."

Jonah removed his sandals as the door creaked open. Zebulun called out to him in an unusually jovial tone.

"Jonah! What a pleasant surprise!"

Once his eyes adjusted to the dim light, Jonah saw his cousin and another man seated at a rough-cut, rectangular table. Plates, bowls, and mugs were arrayed in front of them. The faint smell of cheap wine floated on the air.

"You weren't expecting me?" asked Jonah.

Zebulun retrieved a battered old stool and set it near his chair. "Of course I was expecting you," he said, then waved Jonah over. "I just didn't know when you'd be here. Jonah, this is my second, Malachi."

Malachi was a diminutive man, half Jonah's age. He remained seated, tilting his head back and looking down his narrow nose at Jonah. Though his chair was an average size, his feet barely reached the floor. Jonah nodded politely, remembering how his brother, Thomas, used to be introduced as Zebulun's "second," meaning second-in-command.

"It's good to see you," said Zebulun. He patted the stool next to him, signaling for Jonah to sit. "Come. Eat."

Disconcerted by his normally sullen cousin's friendliness, Jonah approached the table warily. A male servant started across the room with a large bowl for Jonah to wash his hands, but Zebulun rose and met him halfway, taking the bowl himself and setting it in front of Jonah.

As Zebulun poured water from a jug over the bowl, Jonah washed his hands in the stream and surveyed the sparse interior of the house. It wasn't a big space, but a dark hallway in the far corner hinted at further rooms. A black and white goat hide had been hung in front of a nearby window. Jonah wasn't sure if it was meant to block the sun, prevent people from looking in, or both. On the table he noted a half-empty plate of finger-length dried fish, a pitcher of wine, and a cracked bowl that held some sort of cold lentil salad with olives.

"Your people are in very bad shape," Jonah remarked as the servant set a mug in front of him and filled it with wine.

"Yes, that's true," commented Zebulun in a more somber tone. "But not for long!" His fat face was red, and though it was hard to be sure, Jonah thought he was missing another tooth since they'd last seen each other six weeks ago.

"It's good to see you!" Zebulun said again as he slapped Jonah on the back.

"You already said that," Jonah replied suspiciously.

"Oh, did I?" Zebulun laughed and downed some wine. "Jonah's going to tell us about this Rabbi Jesus," he announced to Malachi.

"Why do you concern yourself with him?" Malachi retorted crossly. "He's just another charlatan."

"Perhaps," said Zebulun, unfazed. "But an extremely popular one. Tell us, Jonah, what's he like? Where did you meet him?"

Jonah sipped his wine, swishing it around in his mouth to rinse away the dusty film that had accumulated from the high desert air. "I attended a dinner with him at Levi's house in Capernaum," he began. "The rabbi gave some teachings while—"

"Wait a second," injected Malachi. "The rabbi had dinner at a *tax collector's* house?"

"Yes," replied Jonah. "He's a rather strange rabbi—has no qualms about fraternizing with sinners. He was sitting at the same table with a prostitute, a drunkard, and—"

"Not that loudmouth, Abram," said Zebulun.

"The same," confirmed Jonah, taking another drink from his mug. The wine had a bitter taste both during and after swallowing, but Jonah relished it nonetheless. "The rabbi knows the scriptures as well as any scribe," he continued, "though he has a unique interpretation of them."

"Is it true he's healed people on the Sabbath?" asked Zebulun.

"From what I've heard, yes," said Jonah.

"And how does he defend this transgression?"

"People tell me he says 'The Sabbath was made for man, not man for the Sabbath,'" Jonah answered. Wanting to know Zebulun's reaction, he fixed his eyes on his cousin's crooked nose until Zebulun felt compelled to respond.

"He's a strange rabbi, indeed," Zebulun finally remarked.

Jonah had expected indignation from his cousin, if not outrage. Anything, really, except indifference.

"Why aren't you eating?" Zebulun asked. "You're not hungry?"

"No, just thirsty," Jonah lied. He was actually famished, but his conscience wouldn't allow him to partake of the food knowing the people outside were close to starvation.

Zebulun motioned to the servant, who approached and refilled Jonah's half-empty mug.

"What else?" asked Zebulun.

"He didn't speak about this when I was there," said Jonah, "but I've heard from others he chastises the rich and urges giving to the poor."

"Good. Good," said Zebulun. He nodded approvingly to Malachi.

"He also preaches nonviolence," added Jonah. "One of—"

"You see what I mean?" Malachi interjected. He glared at Zebulun. "The Baptizer preached that weak-kneed drivel as well."

Zebulun turned from him back to Jonah. "And tell us what he says about the Romans."

Having gone the entire day without food, Jonah was starting to feel pleasantly inebriated by the wine. He couldn't help but grin as he began to tell the story of the Pharisee asking if it was lawful for Jews to pay taxes to Caesar or not. He knew it would not sit well with his cousin. After he relayed the part where Jesus answered "Render unto Caesar the things that are Caesar's," Jonah paused in anticipation of Zebulun's inevitable tirade against the hated *Roman oppressors*.

But it never came.

Zebulun just smirked, commenting dryly, "Interesting."

"I told you this would be a waste of our time," said Malachi. He stroked his patchy beard.

"Anything else?" Zebulun asked.

Bewildered by his cousin's aloof response, Jonah wondered if Zebulun might be drunk. Regardless, he next conveyed Jesus' story about the Good Samaritan. It wound up having a markedly different effect on Zebulun than it had on him. At the end, where Jonah had sobbed, Zebulun instead laughed raucously.

"So he's a jester?" Zebulun howled. "Going around telling absurd tales to make people laugh?"

The ridicule of a story that had touched Jonah so deeply was too much for him. He slammed his palm down on the table and leapt from his chair. "Why did you make me come here to tell you this?" he yelled. "It took me two days to get here, and it'll take another two to get back! And you just smirk and laugh at everything I tell you!" He gulped down the remainder of his wine and stormed toward the door. "I've fulfilled my end of the bargain," he shouted. "Now leave me alone!"

"Jonah, wait," called Zebulun in between snorts of laughter. "Don't leave yet. I've got a surprise for you." He got up from the table and started toward the hallway. "Come," he said over his shoulder. "I promise this will make your trip out here worth the while."

Jonah watched Zebulun's heavy frame disappear into the darkness of the hallway. Then he reluctantly followed. They proceeded past two closed doors before coming to the end, where two bleary-eyed guards sat, their spears leaning against the door behind them. One was falling asleep, and the other was sharpening a dagger with a flat stone. Seeing Zebulun approach, they scrambled to their feet and stood at attention.

"Open it," commanded Zebulun.

One of the guards leaned into the door as if it was going to take great effort, but the door opened easily and without a sound. In the center of the darkened room, Jonah gazed at a man slumped on the dirt floor. There was a bag over his head, and his wrists were tied with rope to a thick wooden support beam. He wasn't moving, and Jonah couldn't tell if he was dead or alive.

"What is this?" Jonah asked.

Zebulun led them behind the prisoner, kicking him in the thigh as he passed by. "Wake up," he said. "Time to pay for your sins."

The room was small—about six paces one way and five the other. Whatever its original intent, it seemed to serve now as a storeroom for shields. Dozens of them lined the walls.

With a sly grin at Jonah, Zebulun yanked the bag from the man's head. "A gift," he proclaimed.

Jonah lost his breath, and nearly his balance. It was the centurion.

Zebulun blindfolded and gagged the Roman with two long strips of leather while Jonah clutched the beam to keep from falling over. Jonah had fantasized about this meeting for years on end, but it had come so quickly and unexpectedly that he couldn't take it all in. The mere sight of the centurion's face brought back so many painful memories.

"I got you some toys to play with," Zebulun announced. He pointed to a couple of objects lying on the floor near the door, then went over to retrieve them. "Here's a nice little club." He struck it against the beam, making a loud crack. "It's very solid. You needn't worry about hurting your delicate doctor's hands," he said with a laugh.

Zebulun then held up a short whip with a wooden handle. "You'll like this. I had one of my men make it just for this occasion. It's a replica of the one the Romans use. Quite appropriate, don't you think?" He set it back down on the floor, then proffered the club.

Jonah took the ten-inch piece of hard wood hesitantly, holding it loosely in his hand. Mouth agape, he gazed at his cousin.

Zebulun shrugged. "That's it. No more toys," he said with a chuckle. "Can't risk you killing my most valuable possession. He's going to fetch a nice ransom." He stepped closer to the centurion and gripped the prisoner's tunic between the shoulders. With one swift movement, he ripped the fabric to bare the man's back.

As Zebulun ambled stiffly out of the room, he addressed the two guards. "Don't disturb them," he commanded. "Take a break for a few minutes, then stand watch at the front door of the house until I come and get you."

Before closing the door behind him, Zebulun called to Jonah, "Don't hurt him too bad. He's got to walk all the way back to Jerusalem after the prefect pays me."

For the first several minutes after the door latched shut, Jonah just stared at his enemy, twitching at the prospect of revenge. Then, without taking his eyes off the centurion, he set the club down and felt around for the flagrum. After finding it, he examined it closely, realizing it was probably nearly identical to the one used on his brother before they crucified him. Stretching his arm back, Jonah whipped the flagrum full force.

Thwack!

The centurion startled at the sound, his whole body tensing and drawing into itself. The small pieces of metal knotted into the whip's three thongs embedded themselves in the wood of the support beam. As Jonah pried each one out, he decided to dedicate the thrashing to Luke.

But as he stretched his arm back again, ready to begin, he was seized by a sickening thought: that what he was about to do would be in vain. There would be no satisfaction nor closure, because mere punishment wouldn't free Luke of the burden he believed was his.

In fury, Jonah hurled the flagrum to the ground with a dull thud and a puff of dust. Then he squatted with his head in his hands, ruminating about what to do.

The stench of body odor and urine was oppressive in the warmth of the dungeonlike room, and he wanted to tear the boards off the window to let in fresh air and light. But something even more pronounced bothered him. He had a bizarre sense that he and the centurion were not alone.

Slowly turning his head from one side to the other, he peered into the dimly lit recesses of the room. An assortment of shields faced him from each dingy stone wall. Most were crude, wooden, and homemade, though a few looked to be solid brass. Cobwebs connected them all, one to the other in an unbroken mesh.

Jonah held his breath and listened intently, but heard only the strained exhalations of the centurion through his gag. When he closed his eyes for a second, the presence enveloped him in a gentle warmth as it introduced itself.

It was fate. And it was smiling upon him.

Jonah's whole body shuddered as he comprehended the opportunity. Reaching inside his robes with a trembling hand, he unsheathed his dagger. With one flick of his wrist, he could free Luke from a past that didn't belong to him.

And if it resulted in Zebulun striking Jonah down in retaliation, then so be it. He'd gladly give his life to save Luke's.

Jonah inched forward on his knees until he was close enough to feel the centurion's body heat and smell his foul breath. He didn't need to deliberate how to carry out the deed. As a physician and former bandit, he knew the most unfailing way to ensure death was to slice a man's throat.

When a few determined rays of sunlight abruptly streamed into the room, Jonah surmised the afternoon sun must have finally broken free of the dense clouds concealing it. Now he could see everything clearly: the knobby Adam's apple of the centurion's throat, the thick stubble on his chin, the faded scar running down his cheek. And he could see, too, the deep creases and wrinkles in the Roman's skin that signified he had also lived a longer than usual life.

With a white-knuckled grip and a quavering hand, Jonah touched the dagger to the centurion's throat. Then, without thinking, he found himself reciting a prayer. It was the short, standard prayer of thanks always said before severing an animal's throat for a feast or special occasion.

Jonah gritted his teeth, cringing at his own words. This was not a gala or a celebration!

He broke off the prayer, but it was too late. Just as the sunlight squeezing through the cracks of the boarded-up window had erased most of the darkness of the room, so too had the tiniest bit of gratitude—even if in error—been enough to shift his prerogative. Jonah's resoluteness evaporated into the arid mountain air.

In frustration he plunged the dagger into the dirt floor as his mind began to reevaluate everything. He pulled at his hair, vexed by his own irritation and indecision. On top of it all, the stifling air of the cramped room was suffocating. He had to escape.

Lunging out the door, Jonah stumbled halfway down the hall before collapsing and hugging his knees to himself. Desperate for a reprieve from his madness, he latched onto the words echoing down the hallway. He couldn't see anyone, but he could hear their conversation.

"Forget the chariot, then," Zebulun was saying. "What about swords?"

"And bows," added Malachi's nasal voice.

"With three hundred dinars, I could certainly get you some good quality ones," a new voice responded. "But with all due respect, your people don't look as though they're in any condition to engage in battle. Perhaps you should use the ransom money to buy grain."

"I heard you the first time," Zebulun replied crossly. "That's my business, not yours. I know from experience there's no one more determined to win a battle than a hungry man with a hungry family. Do you—"

A knock on the front door interrupted their discussion: three sharp raps followed by a pause, then two more drawn-out knocks.

"It's the messenger," announced Malachi.

Jonah heard the door opening, then Zebulun immediately addressing the newcomer. "Well?"

"Sir," the messenger replied breathlessly, "your negotiator asked me to inform you they're refusing your offer. He also has it on good authority that the prefect is preparing a century of well-armed soldiers to begin a search for the missing centurion, and—"

"Damn them!" roared Zebulun. "Tell them I'll *crucify* him if we don't receive payment!"

"Your negotiator did not expect you to be pleased," the messenger said calmly. "However, he said this was to be expected in the first round. He gave me several suggestions and questions for you. May I proceed?"

Jonah heard a familiar grunt from Zebulun that meant go ahead.

"First, he said he doubts they'll change their decision unless the terms change," the messenger said. "He suggests you lower the ransom by a hundred."

"Two hundred dinars is still a lot of money," commented Malachi. "And it's better than nothing."

"Very well," Zebulun said grudgingly.

"Just a few more clarifications then, if you would," said the messenger. "Your terms are two hundred dinars to be received by sunset four days from now. In return, the centurion will be set free. Correct?"

"Yes," said Malachi.

"And if they agree to your demands, but need an extra day?"

"One extra day is fine," Jonah heard Zebulun say irritably. "But no longer than that."

"And must it be in dinars? What if they propose an equivalent or different form of payment?"

"Why would they choose anything else? That makes absolutely no sense!" Zebulun bellowed.

"I don't know, sir. These are questions your negotiator demanded I get answers to. He said he can't doubt the terms he offers, or the terms he agrees to. He needs to know every concession you're willing to make so he doesn't have to send me back here again."

"An equivalent is fine," Zebulun conceded. "Now get out of here!"

At the sound of the front door creaking open, Jonah thought to join the messenger on his exit from the camp. Then he heard Zebulun's last words of advice to the man. "Tell my negotiator," he snarled, "that his *doubts* are going to get him killed one day, and the sooner he gets over them, the better. Doubt is nothing more than weakness in disguise."

Zebulun's dire warning struck a chord of discontent with Jonah, because he realized it was doubt that had caused him to flee from the difficulty of killing the centurion.

That damn, ever-present doubt! Jonah had vowed not to hesitate, but here he was doing exactly that.

Hastening back to the room, he ripped his dagger from the ground, full of resolve to overcome any weakness within.

But at the same time, Zebulun's exhortation grated on him. Jonah had learned through years of grief and agony that Zebulun's suggestions, if followed, nearly always resulted in perpetuating misery rather than reducing it.

The light was still streaming through the cracks of the boarded-up window, and Jonah was struck by how different the centurion looked without his red-plumed helmet, metal armor, and crimson cloak. Stripped to the waist and hunched forward against the beam, he looked disturbingly frail and human. The sound of his labored breathing filled the room.

Jonah positioned the sharp blade of his dagger a few inches from the centurion's throat. Then he lowered it once again amid questions about whether doubt was really the enemy he believed it to be. Was it possible doubt and confusion opened the door to something new, something better?

Just as dawn arises out of the blackness of night, perhaps certainty was meant to emerge from the ashes of doubt. Maybe certainty that arises in the absence of confusion isn't certainty at all, but vanity and arrogance.

Swallowing his revulsion toward it, Jonah allowed the messiness of doubt to settle upon him. The feeling was like a thick fog in which he couldn't see far in any direction. He came to understand rather quickly why he so deplored doubt. It was because—if he was honest—he had to admit he didn't know every time which way was best. As a parent and a physician, he'd developed skill in *pretending* to know the answer. The skill had served him well. But in the absence of any such authoritative roles, doubt was simply another word for mystery.

And it was the mystery of life that had always enchanted him. This was what he'd left behind all those decades ago, he realized. It was the "not knowing" that he'd loved, and that had been replaced by the jaded, practiced certainty of adulthood.

He recalled his words from earlier that day, how if there were a way to return to the wonder of his youth, then—no matter how crazy the idea—he would try it. No sooner had these words passed through his mind than Mary's instructions on forgiveness returned to him.

"Forgiveness isn't complicated, Jonah," she'd said. "You forgive by remembering only the love you've given in the past, and the love that was given you. Anything not of love is to be forgotten. To forgive is to remember selectively. You give up your right to your own memories, and leave the choice to God."

To God?

Jonah recoiled at the thought. How could he trust God, when God was vengeful, spiteful, and sometimes downright vain?

He began pacing in a circle around the centurion. He felt as though he was standing on that cliff near his house, trying to decide whether or not to jump. He saw Jesus' serene face in his mind, and remembered how the rabbi was unconditionally friendly and warmhearted to all, even those who bickered with him.

"If only *You* were more like Jesus," Jonah accused God. "But no! *You* just want people to obey all Your ridiculous rules!"

Those words he'd shouted in rage so long ago thundered through his head again: *God! I'm through with you!*

That sentiment had most certainly been true fifteen years ago, but standing in that room, Jonah knew something else to be true as well. While he may have been through with God all these years, God had never been through with him.

With infinite patience, God had been watching and waiting for this exact moment to come—the moment when Jonah decided to step off that cliff, armed only with the promise of forgiveness and a sliver of faith in the ultimate goodness of his Creator.

His doubt draining away, Jonah fell, not into a never-ending abyss like he'd always feared, but into the passionate embrace of the Beloved. He wept with the realization that the warmth he'd felt wash over him earlier was not fate smiling on him. It was God welcoming a lost sheep back into the fold.

As he slid his dagger back into its sheath, he was filled with overwhelming gratitude for his life. His path had led him to the most valuable lesson there was, worth every ounce of pain and struggle he'd endured. Forgiveness, he now knew, was not about letting someone off the hook for their wrongs. It was about crying out to God, in the strongest terms possible, that you're ready to come Home.

Chapter Thirty-Eight

Turning her head to the side and holding her breath, Esther bent down and wrapped her arms around as much of the pale yellow straw as she could. Praying not to sneeze, she carried it quickly to the other side of the modest wooden shed. When she opened her arms to dump the load, the cow unexpectedly swung her neck to the side, the straw falling on her long forehead.

"Sorry, Saraswati," said Esther, patting the large bony cow on the side. She'd named it, at Azara's suggestion, after the Hindu goddess of knowledge, learning, and the arts.

The cow didn't seem to be bothered much, either by its exotic name or by the food dropped on it. After shaking the straw from its head, it grabbed a mouthful and began chewing.

The orange sun, low in the sky, cast a long shadow from the stone wall surrounding Azara's property. Azara was the one who usually did the evening milking, but she'd gone to pick wild figs for a dessert they were going to make using honey, milk, and cinnamon. That left Esther with the chore twice today.

But she didn't mind. She'd rather shovel manure from sunup to sundown than return to her old life with her father or her bridegroom—both of whom wanted her dead.

Two uneasy chickens sat on a shelf opposite Esther, eyeing her suspiciously as she came near and retrieved a knee-high stool. While sliding a bucket underneath the cow's udders, Esther heard a high-pitched scream in the distance.

Rushing to the front gate, she knocked over the stool with a loud bang, sending the startled chickens fluttering from their roost. Just as she'd unlocked the gate and was about to sprint out, she heard the hollering of boys and giggles of girls echoing through the air. It hadn't been Azara screaming, but just children having fun. Esther held a shaking hand to her heart and breathed a sigh of relief.

She always worried whenever Azara went out. Azara was the parent she'd never had, the one who believed in her and stood by her no matter what.

Since the attempted stoning, Esther and Azara had been free from harm thanks to the centurion and his promise to protect them. But he hadn't been to visit in nearly four weeks now, and they were both concerned, especially since hearing a disturbing rumor about bandits capturing a Roman soldier and holding him for ransom. Esther hoped to God it wasn't Vitus. She liked the centurion, but more than that, she thought he and Azara were made for each other. On his first visit the two of them had talked for hours on end, and he'd bought baskets full of herbs from Azara's shop, though Esther doubted he needed any of it.

After returning to the shed and perching on the edge of the stool, the cow swished her tail against some flies and struck Esther in the face instead.

"Saraswati," exclaimed Esther. "You be nice to me!"

But the ill-mannered cow did the same thing a moment later, so Esther bent the tail upside down over the cow's back, then secured it in place with a rope. The cow bellowed in protest as she struggled to free her tail.

"That's what you get," said Esther sharply. Resuming her place on the stool, she wrapped her thumb and forefinger in a circle around the base of one of the cow's two-inch-long teats, and squeezed. White milk gushed forth into the bucket. She did the same with her other hand, alternately gripping one, then the other.

When she was half finished with the milking, a black and white cat jumped on top of the weather-beaten gate of the shed and meowed.

"Are you back again, Orpheus?" Esther called out. She peered at him, noticing a fresh scar near his right ear. "Where have you been? In Hades looking for your beloved Eurydice?"

The cat bounded gracefully to the ground and approached, then stood on his hind legs, pawing at the air.

"Ready?" asked Esther. She pointed one of the cow's teats toward the cat's head and squeezed. A stream of milk arced through the air, and the cat contorted to catch it directly in his mouth.

Two flat clangs of the "gate bell" abruptly announced Azara's return.

Using some rope, a pulley, and an old bell, Esther had created the contraption so that it tolled whenever someone opened the gate. They had a secret signal that let Esther know it was Azara coming home: Azara would open the gate, then let it close a little, then push it open again to make the bell ring twice.

"Esther?" Azara's voice called out.

"Here," answered Esther from the shed.

"Why was the gate unlocked?"

"Sorry. Thought I heard you earlier and was going to go out, but it wasn't you."

"Well, be more careful next time...."

"I will."

Azara's smiling face appeared over the shed's shoulder-height wall. "Did you collect the eggs yet?"

"Wanna see a trick?" replied Esther.

"Sure."

Esther squirted another stream of milk through the air, and the cat again caught it in his mouth.

Azara laughed. "That's marvelous! Did you teach him how to do that?"

Esther nodded.

"You never cease to amaze me." Azara opened the shed's gate and strode toward the chickens, who had resumed their place on the shelf. Stopping halfway there, she exclaimed, "What did you do to Saraswati's tail?"

"She kept swatting me," Esther protested.

"All right," conceded Azara, "but maybe you could do it in a way that's a little more pleasant for her." She placed her basket full of puny wild figs on the ground, then untied the rope holding the cow's tail. With the tail hanging normally, she retied it to the cow's right hind leg.

Esther was impressed. Azara's solution had accomplished the same aim, but in a kinder way.

"There you go, Saraswati," said Azara with a pat to the cow's rump.

Esther shook her head, annoyed at how much she still had to learn. She was constantly comparing herself to Azara—a game she played to see how she measured up to her teacher. Physically, she was already as tall as Azara, though not nearly as shapely. She didn't have Azara's splendid, thick eyelashes, but neither was she missing any of her teeth.

Where Esther believed she fell dramatically short was in her words and actions. While the world often frustrated her to no end, Azara seemed to possess some godlike power that allowed her to disregard the awful parts of the world and only see the good. Azara had a phrase she lived by and repeated often: "What you send out to the world comes back to you. Hate begets hate. Love begets love."

Esther wondered if the saying was from the Rabbi Jesus. He'd had quite an effect on Azara. Since meeting him, Azara no longer complained about her hip or financial situation. In fact, she no longer complained about anything.

As Esther resumed milking, she breathed in the familiar, not entirely unpleasant, mix of musty manure and recently harvested straw. Azara hummed a song as she sprinkled some grain on the ground and shooed the two chickens from their roost. After a few clucks of protest, they leapt off the shelf, flapping their wings furiously to make a soft landing on the ground.

"I saw Saraswati's calf yesterday," Azara commented as she gathered the brown eggs they'd been sitting on. "He's getting quite big now."

"Does he have horns yet?"

"No," said Azara as she squatted to retrieve an egg from the bottom shelf.

When Azara stood back up, Esther saw her out of the corner of her eye swaying and clutching for the wall. "Are you alright?"

"I'm fine," Azara answered after a brief pause. "Just stood up too fast."

For the first two weeks after Esther's father's rock struck Azara in the head, Azara hadn't been able to do much. She'd had nauseating headaches and was dizzy all the time.

Esther thought constantly about that day—her wedding, the painful consummation of her betrothal, the horror of the bloodless sheets, and the attempted stoning.

She took a break from milking to poke at a pimple on her chin. "Saraswati's a girl," she announced.

"Yes..." confirmed Azara, arching her eyebrows.

"Did she bleed?" Esther asked as she forced herself to leave the pimple alone. "I mean her first time," she explained. "Did she bleed?"

"You're asking the wrong person," Azara said with a laugh. "My tutor never lectured on the details of bovine mating."

Esther crossed her arms, sulking. She didn't find it funny. The fact she hadn't bled her first time having intercourse had nearly cost her her life.

"Listen," said Azara. "I've never heard of a girl not bleeding her first time, but I want you to know I believe you."

Azara's words nearly brought tears to Esther's eyes. Esther's father certainly hadn't believed her, and her mother had been too weak-willed to ever disagree with him.

Azara leaned against the cow's side, gazing down at Esther with her big, hazel-brown eyes. "You said you didn't have sex with that boy you loved, and I trust you told me the truth."

Esther frowned and slouched on the stool. "Love."

"What?"

"You said *loved*," Esther clarified.

"Oh," replied Azara, wrinkling her nose. She set the eggs in the basket on top of the reddish figs. "You're still in love with him, huh?"

"Unfortunately," said Esther with a sigh. "I think of him every day."

It was mostly quiet except for the contented chewing of the cow and the distant sounds of children playing. Then came a loud knock at the front gate.

Azara jolted like a cat caught off guard. "Who could that be?" she asked with a frown.

Esther had learned that Azara always got nervous whenever someone came late in the day, since it was rare for anyone to visit her shop near sunset. It was actually rare for anyone to visit her shop at all these days. Most of the men of the village had forbidden their wives to buy from her, and certainly no Jews in Capernaum would do business with her anymore.

The boycott had resulted in two unexpected twists, though. The first was that several Gentile families who'd never frequented Azara's shop before, now came regularly. They purchased common herbs and oils they formerly bought elsewhere. The second twist was that Azara secretly met Hadassah and other wealthy Jewish women in back alleys of the market to sell them perfume and cosmetics. With food prices so high, Azara needed all the help she could get.

Esther couldn't see over the wall, but a timely gust of wind told her who it was. Riding on the breeze was the unmistakably strong scent of lavender, and whenever Mary stopped by, she always brought a small bouquet of the purple flowers with her.

"It's all right," said Esther as she resumed milking. "It's Mary."

Mary was from the nearby village of Magdala. She and Azara had met at one of the Rabbi Jesus' talks and had quickly become best friends.

"Hello? Azara?" Mary's voice called out from the road.

"How did you know it was her?" asked Azara as she walked to the gate.

"It's one of my many talents," Esther said mischievously.

A single, dull clang of the bell proclaimed the gate had been opened.

"I have wonderful news," Mary's voice sang.

Esther stood up from the stool to peer over the shed's wall. Upon seeing Mary, she deliberately pulled her shoulders back and straightened her spine. On those unbearably long days when she was cooped up because Azara was out and about running errands, Esther often practiced walking and moving like Mary.

"The rabbi," Mary said, after giving Azara a quick embrace, "has agreed to come give a talk at our club!"

Azara hopped up and down like a little girl.

It was one of the traits Esther admired most about her. Despite being nearly forty years old, she could still muster the excitement and playfulness of a child.

Esther rushed out to join them, and found herself pulled into an exuberant hug by Azara.

"Oh, that's wonderful news indeed," exclaimed Azara.

"He said he'd come next week," Mary added.

After initially resuming Esther's studies, Azara had decided, at the urging of Mary, to invite other girls—as well as their mothers. Mary argued that not only were girls starved for education, but their mothers were too. Most of them had never been taught to read or write, nor did they generally know anything of the world beyond Galilee.

Though Azara had worried about further exasperating the tensions, not only between Jews and Gentiles in the village, but also between women and men, Mary had convinced her to proceed with three simple suggestions. One was for Azara to not call it a school, but instead "The Daughters of Abraham Torah Study Club." This would set off less resistance in the men, she'd contended, and also make it more difficult to garner support if they again wanted to close her down.

Mary's second suggestion was to let it be known that Mary—a Jew—would be the teacher. Her third argument was the clincher. She'd said, "Azara, my dear, meaningful change is impossible without stirring things up a little."

They'd had their first "club meeting" two days ago. Though only one brave family from Capernaum had brought their two daughters, Mary had personally brought nine girls and their mothers from Magdala. While Azara had instructed the girls in reading, writing, and history, Mary had focused on their mothers' spiritual education. Then, after a lunch break, they'd switched classes and taught another two hours.

Esther was just as excited as Azara that the rabbi had agreed to give a talk. He was held in high esteem by the majority of Capernaum's residents, and his visit would certainly legitimize the club.

Azara and Mary were dancing now, one arm draped around the other's shoulder, alternately kicking their legs in the air. Esther wasn't sure whether to laugh or cry, so she did a little of both. In her family, she'd never seen women play and express themselves, even when they were out of sight of their husbands, fathers, and sons.

"Jesus is coming! Jesus is coming!" the two women sang, then giggled.

Esther loved to hear Azara's silly laugh. It made her feel there actually was justice in the world. If anyone deserved to be happy, it was her.

As Azara and Mary gripped each other's wrists, leaned backward, and began spinning around, Esther chastised them. "Azara, be careful!" she cried.

The two of them did stop spinning, but only because Esther's admonishment threw them into a fit of uncontrollable laughter.

"Yes, *mother*," Azara jested. She plopped down on the ground, still chuckling, trying to catch her breath.

Appreciating the irony of it, Esther laughed along with them. She recognized, in that moment, that she was completely happy. It was a gladness she'd never known before, as if she'd been let into some secret chamber where life's mysteries were revealed. And the mystery being unveiled to her now was of such a magnitude that she trembled.

It was a revelation that the highest order of love was fiercer than the mightiest warrior, and love at this level would enter into *any* battle—no matter how hopeless the odds.

It was this kind of love, Esther understood, that had saved her from being stoned; that had taken her in, provided her a roof over her head, and food to eat every day. It was this kind of fierce love that was teaching her how to read and write, and to question the ways of the world.

It was love of this order that was sitting next to her on the ground, laughing so hard that she snorted.

The last, rich rays of dusk blanketed everything in a cozy amber hue, and Esther inhaled the magic of the moment. For the first time in her life, she let it all in—every ounce of good fortune and kindness. It filled her to the brim, and she wanted, more than anything, to pay it back. She didn't know how, when, or where, but she vowed in that moment to repay to the world every drop of love given her.

And then some.

Chapter Thirty-Nine

Vitus scratched underneath his armor at the flaky, tender skin of his shoulders and glanced up at the two doves cooing from the branch above. In addition to recovering from one of the worst sunburns of his life, Vitus's nose intermittently throbbed with pain, and the soles of his feet were healing painstakingly slowly from countless blisters.

But none of it bothered him much. He was happy just to be alive. Only a week and a half before, he'd been released from being held hostage by Zebulun's bandits. And here he was in Capernaum, breathing the fresh sea-scented air, relaxing under the shade of a tree, and preparing to host a feast.

The woman he'd rescued from being stoned last month exited the courtyard of the nearby farmer's house and waved to him.

"He said yes," she called.

A contented grin slowly spread across Vitus's face, not so much because Azara's neighbor had agreed to sell five chickens for the feast, but because the alluring woman was coming to walk by his side.

"I was sinking—" Azara said as they started toward the market.

"You were *what*?" interrupted Vitus. He pictured her on a leaky boat on the Sea of Galilee.

"*Thinking*," she replied. "I know. I know. It's a bad habit that's gotten me in a lot of trouble," she added with a laugh. "Just can't seem to help myself."

Vitus chortled along with her, admiring her capacity to poke fun at herself.

"Perhaps you have a secret ally among the prefect's deputies," said Azara.

She was referring to their earlier conversation, when Vitus had told her he'd thanked the prefect for paying his ransom, and Pilate responded that he'd done no such thing.

"Yes, I suspect that too," commented Vitus. "Can't figure out which one it would've been, though."

In addition to *someone* in Pilate's inner circle paying the ransom, Vitus had also gotten away with a relative slap on the wrist for interfering in the Capernaum stoning. He'd only had to pull guard duty over the weekend. Either someone from on high was looking out for him, or he was in the midst of the best run of luck in his life.

"How do you know they even paid the ransom?" Azara asked. "Maybe Zebulun gave up and decided it was for the best to let you go."

"They didn't have my blindfold on very well," Vitus explained. "As they led me out of their camp, I saw men unloading a wagon filled with wheat. I counted the containers and figured it was at least two hundred dinars worth."

"Maybe they'd just bought it, and it was sheer coincidence it arrived as you were leaving," Azara suggested.

"I don't think so. First of all, I overheard the wagon's driver arguing that he was to take me back with him. Zebulun wouldn't allow it though. He had me dropped off several miles away, saying I had to walk back. Secondly, everyone there was so thin and sickly. If they could have afforded to buy that much grain before, then they would have done it already."

Vitus inhaled the aroma of fresh bread as the distant sounds and smells of the market up ahead began to reach them.

"I've always wondered about that," remarked Azara. "The rumors here are that Zebulun has a mighty army of thousands of Jewish warriors, and that it's only a matter of time until they liberate the people."

Vitus scoffed aloud at the notion. "It is *they* who need to be liberated. They live like animals there on that desolate mountaintop."

Over the clamor of carts creaking on the road, kids playing, dogs barking, and people haggling, there was a vendor's sonorous, baritone voice half-hollering, half-singing, "Fresh pomegranates! Last of the season!"

Vitus delicately picked at the peeling skin on his nose as he caught a glimpse of a carpenter meticulously chiseling the hull of a new fishing boat. "What do we need at the market?" he asked Azara.

Azara and Esther had enthusiastically agreed to help with the feast. While Vitus was in charge of the arduous tasks of butchering and roasting the chickens, they'd do all the rest.

"Do you already have bread?" asked Azara. "Or should we get more?"

"Better get some more," said Vitus.

The feast was for the ten soldiers who'd traveled with Vitus safeguarding the tax monies chest. He wanted to host a celebration of his good fortune, and to show his comrades his appreciation.

"I also need some artichokes for the salad," Azara said, "and some dried pears to make compote."

Vitus reached into his leather pouch and gave her four coins. "That should cover the bread," he said.

"I don't know how much bread costs in Jerusalem," replied Azara as she tried to return two of the coins, "but that'll buy enough for at least twenty people here."

"Never underestimate how much a Roman soldier can eat," Vitus joked. "Besides, there's no shortage of people these days we could give leftovers to." He handed her two more coins. "Is that enough for the rest?"

"More than plenty," she answered, staring at his nose again.

"Does it really look that bad?"

"Not at all," she said. "I was just remembering a salve I sell that will help it heal faster."

Vitus's broken nose had been a parting gift from Zebulun. He'd struck him with a hard little club while Vitus was still blindfolded. Before they released him, they'd taken Vitus's sandals and robes, forcing him to trudge naked through the high-desert and wilderness back to Jerusalem.

"And remind me to give you some fresh aloe for the sunburn and blisters," added Azara.

Vitus unsuccessfully suppressed a grin. He actually liked being taken care of, but didn't like others knowing it. He felt elated to be with Azara again. In the five long weeks since they'd last seen one another, he'd forgotten how much he enjoyed her company.

"Are you sure we shouldn't go check on your servant?" asked Azara. "What was his name again?"

"Ira," he replied. "No. There's not much one can do when he gets this way."

When Vitus and Ira had set out from Jerusalem, Ira had been feeling rather vigorous, but he'd suffered another attack of his symptoms as they'd neared Capernaum. Vitus had left him with the rest of his men at the military outpost on the outskirts of town.

"I've ordered my men to look in on him from time to time," Vitus added, "but he'll just be lying in bed the rest of the day."

They reached the edge of the market where two rival vendors were selling barley. They stood in front of bulging bags of grain spread out on opposite sides of the road, bartering with a bevy of customers. Barley was a poor man's wheat for making bread. Demand for it always increased whenever food prices shot up.

People going to and from the market made an exaggerated detour around Vitus. With the bright red plumes atop his helmet and the sun glinting off his armor, he stood out like a king among peasants.

"How long do you need?" he asked Azara.

She scanned the dozens of people at the market. "It looks rather busy today," she said. "Half an hour at least. Why?"

"You told me the Rabbi Jesus is often at the synagogue studying the scriptures with his disciples, so I thought I'd wander down that way."

"All right. Good luck," said Azara. She turned toward the market and disappeared into the crowd.

Vitus walked leisurely in the opposite direction. The synagogue wasn't far away. Nothing was very far away in the small village.

He'd only walked for a minute when a house's fresh yellow paint caught his eye. As he stopped to admire it, a gangly boy wandered out its front door, yawning as he stretched his arms.

"Go on! Get going!" yelled an angry voice from inside the house. "That's your punishment!"

The boy shrugged, then picked up a yoke and two buckets. He didn't seem to be too upset about it, and Vitus smiled to himself, recalling his own recent *punishment* that had been anything but. He'd been sentenced to weekend guard duty, and his first assignment had been to move three prisoners to another prison. To his delight and astonishment, one of the prisoners had been Barnabas.

Vitus guffawed aloud as he thought about it now. Who said God didn't have a sense of humor?

The move had been due to overcrowding, since the prefect liked to arrest people, but not release them. And after Pilate's reprimand from Rome, he was reticent to execute anyone without an irreproachable reason.

As the boy with the yoke strolled down the road in front of Vitus, the empty wooden buckets hanging from either side swung back and forth, making a rhythmic screeching sound. As a handful of doves flew past, Vitus reflected on how Barnabas was now in a much better place. Not only would he be getting a greater quality and quantity of food in the different prison, he would have a larger cell that was above ground and had a window.

When Vitus had escorted him through the streets of Jerusalem, Barnabas had been in surprisingly good health and spirits. He hadn't gone blind from being in a dark cell, as Vitus had seen happen to other prisoners. And his words were his most profound yet. Vitus was still trying to take in the enormity of Barnabas's teaching about the concept of free will. He replayed the conversation once again, every word of it having been indelibly ingrained in his memory.

"God will not violate the free will of any man," Barnabas had said. "That would defeat the purpose for which He made him. God created man in His image to better know Himself, and He granted His creation free will in all things. Man is free to believe what he wants. To ensure he is not forced, God abides by a rule of his own making: that there is forever a balance between the two primary energies, between love and inclusion on one side, and fear and separation on the other."

"But that's chaos," Vitus had objected. "Why all the confusion if God desires men's hearts to return to Him? Why doesn't He simply show Himself by standing on the earth as tall as a mountain for all to see?"

"You misunderstand the beneficial role of chaos," Barnabas responded. "It is the confusion—the tangle of truth and illusion—that set the stage for free will. Man is not only free to believe whatever he wants; he is even free to believe in God Himself. If God were to make Himself known by standing on earth, He would violate the free will of those choosing not to believe. He does not want anyone coming to Him out of fear or obligation, but because they truly desire to be with Him. It must be their *choice*. That is why Master has come, to give a gentle push to those on the verge of making this choice."

"Why is it so important to make this choice?"

"Why is it important to heal when one is ill?"

"You're saying the undecided are sick?"

"Not always physically, but yes. They are blind to their own goodness."

"But isn't your revered Master violating people's free will? Is he not tilting the scales with his teachings?"

"He speaks in parables to avoid violating anyone's free will. Those who are ready for the lesson will hear the truth. Those who are not will draw different conclusions. But you are accurate that he is 'tilting the scales,' as you put it. He once told me he can see the impact his life will have, and the ensuing rebalancing that will result."

"Rebalancing?"

"Yes. If new teachings come into this world that dramatically increase the understanding and likelihood of love, then balance dictates the opposite energy must also be allowed to increase. Master says the dark forces will corrupt much of his message. They will pervert his teachings to become tools for manipulation and control, rather than their original intent of compassion and inclusion."

"So he knows his teachings will become corrupted?"

"Indeed. He told me numerous wars will be fought in his name. Millions of people will suffer and die. But still it is worth it, he says, bringing this *good* into the world. For though they can cloud and deform his message to a certain extent, they will not be able to wholly undo all the light his words contain."

As Vitus stepped to the side of the road to let a smelly donkey pulling a rickety cart pass, he wondered how many more times he'd have to contemplate that discourse before finally understanding it all.

The donkey came to a stop just past Vitus and refused to go any further. The young man riding atop the cart whipped the obstinate beast on its hind end several times, but still it wouldn't budge.

Vitus could squeeze past them, but he was in no hurry. The rundown synagogue was already in sight, only fifteen yards ahead. He drank from his waterskin, noting that the meager synagogue was in even worse shape than he remembered. Large cracks in the walls zigzagged from top to bottom, the exterior was in need of both fresh mortar and paint, and the roof was sagging badly.

The young man climbed down from the cart and tried to pull the old donkey forward, but the only thing that gave way was its head—the rest of its body leaning stubbornly in the opposite direction.

Surmising the donkey knew about the well in front of the synagogue, Vitus called out, "Perhaps it's thirsty."

The youth momentarily turned his head toward Vitus, but then continued his futile effort to get the donkey to move.

Voices echoed out from the synagogue's slightly crooked entrance, and Vitus spied two men coming out. They wore faded brown tunics and had identical long sharp noses and bushy eyebrows. The taller one strode toward the well as the stocky one with a red-tinged beard tripped on the uneven stairs and stumbled after him for a few steps.

A third man emerged behind them, wearing an off-white tunic with sleeves that were too short. Though his robes suggested he was of ordinary means, he had a regal quality about him. He was as handsome a Jew as Vitus had ever seen, and the lock of hair dangling over his eyes softened his bold masculinity.

"Peter, will you never tire of this question?" Vitus overheard him say. His tone was lighthearted, and he had an easygoing smile on his lips as he rested a hand on the back of the man who'd tripped.

The taller one turned his head over his shoulder. "Knowing my brother, doubtful," he jested.

"Don't make it more complicated than it is, Peter," said the man in white. "Try this time to just get a *feeling* of what it's like." Turning to the taller man at the well, he asked, "Andrew, will you fetch us some water?"

The youth with the donkey apparently decided to take Vitus's advice. He gave up on trying to yank the beast forward and instead retrieved a beat-up bucket from the cart. He took it over to the well, where Andrew offered to fill it for him.

As he lowered the bucket, Andrew's two companions sat on the ground, leaning against the waist-high stone wall around the well.

"The kingdom of heaven," the man in white explained, "is like treasure hidden in a field. A man found it, and he concealed it. Then in his joy he goes and sells all that he has and buys that field." As he turned his head to the side to look at Peter, a breeze rustled the lock of hair hanging in front of his left eye. "Do you understand?"

Peter nodded, but slowly, unconvincingly.

"The kingdom of heaven," the man began again, "is like a grain of mustard seed that a man took and sowed in his field. It is the smallest of all seeds, but it grows larger than all the garden plants and becomes a tree. The birds of the air can come and make nests in its branches."

The donkey slurped noisily from its bucket, and the crank on the well squealed as Andrew turned it once again to retrieve more water.

"I see," Peter replied thoughtfully, though his furrowed eyebrows betrayed his words. "One more?"

"All right," the man said, still smiling. "Last one. Close your eyes. Relax."

Andrew pulled the bucket up the last few inches and set it on the ground next to his companions. After dipping a cup in the bucket, he offered it to the man answering the questions, but the cup was waved off. Instead, he made a motion to Andrew to fetch the bucket.

"The kingdom of heaven is like nothing you've experienced before," he said with a grin. "It is like an unexpected splash of cold water that awakens you from a bad dream." He then nodded to Andrew, who promptly dumped the bucket of water over Peter's head.

Peter gasped at the shock, then vaulted to his feet with surprising agility and started chasing his brother. "I'll get you for this!"

As the two of them darted to and fro around the well, the third man laughed uproariously. Vitus couldn't stop from laughing along with him. He admired that a grown man could still be fun-loving.

The donkey, having drank its fill, reluctantly moved on, and Vitus began following behind the cart.

"It was Jesus' idea," Andrew yelled as he dodged Peter's attempts to catch him.

Vitus stopped in his tracks. *Jesus?*

It hadn't even occurred to him, but it made perfect sense. Here was a man as playful as a child and as wise as a sage. Vitus beamed with delight. At last, he was going to meet Barnabas's beloved Master!

Peter, having given up on ever catching his more nimble brother, returned short-winded and sank to the ground next to Jesus. "Tell me, rabbi," he said as he scowled at Andrew, "will *all* who follow you enter the kingdom of heaven? Even certain tall and misguided *jesters*?"

Jesus laughed again as he gave Peter a cloth to dry off with. "Not everyone who says to me, 'Lord, Lord!' will enter the kingdom of heaven," he answered. "Only those who actually do the will of my Father in the heavens will enter. For even the Son of Man came not to be served, but to serve, and to give his life to redeem many people."

In clear sight now that the donkey and cart had passed, Vitus found himself the focus of attention of the three men. Under the withering glare of Peter and Andrew, he stopped mid-stride, suddenly feeling ashamed of his armor, sword, and gaudy crimson cloak. Who was he to intrude upon the rabbi?

"Hello," said Jesus. In contrast to Peter and Andrew, the rabbi's expression was soft and welcoming.

Vitus opened his mouth to reply, but nothing came out. In deference, he removed his helmet and held it at his side. Then he cleared his throat and responded with a raspy, "Good morning."

"Would you like some water?" Jesus offered.

Vitus shook his head. Though there were many things he wanted to ask, for now he had only one concern. "Rabbi," he called, "my servant is sick in bed, unable to move and suffering terribly."

Jesus didn't hesitate. "I will come and heal him," he said, rising to his feet.

"Oh no," replied Vitus, still feeling embarrassed. He motioned for Jesus to sit back down. "I do not deserve to have you come under my roof. Just say the word from where you are, and my servant shall be healed. For I myself am a man under authority, with soldiers under me. I tell one to go, and he goes; and another to come, and he comes. I tell my servant to do something, and he does it."

Jesus peered at his two disciples. "Truly, I tell you," he commented to them, "I have not found anyone in all of Palestine with such great faith."

Vitus shifted uneasily from one leg to the other, anxiously awaiting Jesus' next words to him.

"Go," Jesus said. "As you have believed, so shall it be done for you."

Relieved at the words, and knowing Ira was surely cured, Vitus bowed his head in appreciation. He felt indebted, not just for his servant's healing, but for all the remarkable changes in his life—all brought about by this unassuming rabbi and his teachings.

Though their exchange was brief, Vitus was content. Barnabas's "Master" had more than lived up to his expectations. The rabbi could have said no to his request, that he wouldn't help a Roman. He could have told Vitus to stop being a soldier, that he couldn't expect to be let into the kingdom of heaven with that career. But he didn't. He let Vitus know through his words, and his very presence, that everything was alright exactly as it was, that the only change ever needed by anybody was to have a little more faith.

Before turning to leave, Vitus glanced past Jesus and his disciples at the dilapidated synagogue, deciding then and there to finance its reconstruction. It was the least he could do for the new life he'd been given: one redeemed from pride, conceitedness, and vanity.

Chapter Forty

"What did *I* think about the talk?" Luke repeated as he searched his mind for an answer that might make his father proud.

"Yes," confirmed Jonah. He squinted against the sun's late afternoon slant. "Did you find anything appealing or provocative?"

"From *either* of the speakers," added Amaryah.

Luke avoided his parents' expectant gazes by looking past them at the boatloads of people still arriving down at the shore. The rainy season was over, and it was a near perfect day here in the countryside on the northern tip of the Sea of Galilee. Overhead, feathery clouds drifted leisurely in the blue sky, much like the boats with their ash-white sails skimming across the wide expanse of the sea below. The immense leaves of the squat date palms near the shore swayed in the breeze from the north. Luke loved this season and this location. He had so many fond memories of the times he and his family used to come picnicking here.

"I liked what the first speaker had to say about how dying with a closed heart is a great tragedy," he finally answered.

"Me too," his mother agreed.

As Luke searched his father's clean-shaven face for his reaction, he ran his fingers across the stubble that had started to grow on his own chin. He had to decide, fairly soon, if he wanted to grow a beard, like most Jewish men, or be a nonconformist, like his father.

Jonah nodded in response to Luke's answer as a gradual smile spread across his face. "Yes, that was my favorite part too. Especially when he said that the greatest achievement one can make is to die with an open heart, with malice toward none."

Luke recalled that part of the talk, when the man had spoken about a successful life being one in which no matter where you started or where you journeyed, you returned to love. But Luke didn't know what to think about it. Like most others, the idea of judging his life by the measure of love he gave was an entirely new concept for him.

"And the second speaker?" Jonah asked. "How about Jesus' talk?"

Luke appreciated that his father was asking his questions as if he genuinely wanted to know, as if Luke was an adult, not a child. Unfortunately, Luke didn't know what to say to his question, so he just shrugged.

"Nothing?" Jonah said curiously.

Though Jesus was, by far, the most famous rabbi in all of Galilee, Luke had never heard any of his talks prior to their sojourn here. Luke had enjoyed it when Jesus told his storylike parables, even if he wasn't sure he understood their point. But what he liked most was not anything Jesus actually said, but simply his presence. Luke felt so peaceful and content just to be near him and hear his voice. Everything seemed so clear, uncomplicated, just like it had during their first brief meeting at the Jordan River a year before.

"What about when he said it's better to give than to receive?" asked Jonah.

Luke nodded as Amaryah scooted forward to sit between him and Jonah. She smelled like roses. Jonah had given her rose oil for her recent birthday, and she'd been wearing it every day since.

"What did you think of his new commandment?" she asked Luke.

The new commandment had been the last words of Jesus' sermon. He'd told them "to love one another."

"I like that it's simple," Luke replied. "Probably not easy, but definitely simple." The instruction reminded Luke of the first time he'd met the rabbi, when Jesus had greatly simplified for him how to follow all six hundred thirteen commandments. Jesus had boiled down all the teachings of the Torah into one rule: "In everything, treat others as you would want them to treat you."

Luke's five-month-old sister, Aliyah, awoke with a tiny yawn and a stretch. Amaryah wrapped her hands around the baby and took her up from the small, yellow basket where she'd been napping.

"Well, if you follow just one commandment, I pray it's that one," Jonah said sincerely. "You're still young. Don't make the same mistake I did. Don't live your life full of bitterness, with anger at others and at God."

His father had consistently tried to hide his grudge toward God for the bad things that had happened in his life, but Luke had always known about it. For reasons he didn't completely understand yet, his father's resentment had abruptly disappeared after his return from a visit to his cousin Zebulun's camp six months back.

"You're not mad at God anymore?" Luke asked.

Jonah seemed taken aback by the question, but then answered earnestly. "No. I realized all the negative qualities I ascribed to God were my own doing. While it's true other people introduced me to the evil ideas, *I* was the one who took them up and made them my own." After Amaryah cradled Luke's sister into Jonah's arms, he set the baby on his knee. "It wasn't God's fault," he added as he began bouncing his knee up and down.

The baby giggled and cooed, and Luke couldn't tell who was happier: Aliyah or her father. She'd been such a blessing for their family—the first of the last five pregnancies that hadn't been a miscarriage.

His father was as cheerful and content as Luke had ever seen him, and as he tossed the baby in the air and caught her, Luke couldn't help but grin. He was happy for his father's newfound joy in life. He'd earned it.

"Are there any almonds left?" Amaryah asked.

Luke rummaged through the food basket next to him, but found only one stray almond on the bottom. "This is the last one," he said, holding it out for her. "I'm hungry too."

"Yes, we all are," replied Amaryah. "Jonah, let's head back already."

It was their third day here, and like most everyone else, they'd long since eaten the last of the food they'd brought.

"We'll go soon," Jonah said. "Just a little longer."

"He's *not* going to declare himself king," Amaryah said with a tone of exasperation. "That would defeat everything he stands for. Let's *go*."

A rumor had spread through the crowd that Jesus was going to crown himself king, and he'd specifically chosen this beautiful location east of the Jordan River and miles from the nearest village precisely because it was under the jurisdiction, not of the Romans or Herod Antipas, but of the Galilean ruler's more tolerant brother, Philip.

"I hope you're right," said Jonah.

Unlike his father, Luke hoped the rumor was true. Nothing would make the people gathered here happier. "You don't think he'd make a good king?"

"No, it's not that," replied Jonah. "If he declared himself king, it would mean the end of his ministry. The Herods or the Romans would crucify him."

The baby started to cry, and Jonah held her to his shoulder, patting her back. "It would also mean I misunderstood his teachings," he added as an afterthought.

"About forgiveness?" asked Luke. Ever since his father's return from visiting Zebulun's camp, he spoke about forgiveness as if it was some magical cure for everything. He'd told Luke numerous times about how he was able to forgive the centurion he blamed for killing his brother, but Luke couldn't fathom it. How could forgiving someone possibly make things even?

"No," his father answered. "I understand the kingdom of God he speaks of to be a spiritual state—not a physical location on Earth." Despite his persistent pats to her back, the baby cried even more.

"She's probably hungry too," said Amaryah. "Let me feed her. Why don't you and Luke see if you can find someone with extra bread to sell."

While Jonah stood and dusted himself off, Luke climbed atop a nearby boulder to survey the massive throng. He hadn't seen so many people in one place since his visit to Jerusalem. When they'd first arrived here three days ago, there had only been a few hundred people, but every half-day the number seemed to double, and the total of men, women, and children was now in the thousands.

The story of Jesus healing the well-known lunatic, Amos, a week earlier had spread both rapidly and distantly. It attracted those from villages many miles away, as well as pilgrims making their way to Jerusalem. They all wanted to meet this remarkable healer and listen to what he had to say. And even though everyone was hungry, no one would leave. There was too much anticipation of what might happen next.

"Why don't we try this way," Jonah suggested after craning his neck in every direction.

Luke hopped off the boulder, and the two of them set off into the crowd.

"I saw Joab down by the shore earlier," Luke hollered over the din. "He said he's decided to sell that boat you like, so I told him you'd buy it. He wants you to stop by sometime next week."

"No, I can't afford that," replied Jonah.

Luke shook his head in confusion. "What do you mean? You told me a year ago you nearly had enough saved up to finally buy a boat."

"Yes," Jonah said, then paused. "But I had some unexpected expenses six months back."

"Like what?"

His father hesitated again, pursing his lips and glancing up at the sky before answering. "Well...I bought a new tunic," he said. "And food prices were really high for a while."

"Food?" Luke said incredulously. "You could buy enough food to feed a village for an entire month with the money it takes to buy a boat."

"True," Jonah said thoughtfully. "But hopefully longer than a month."

"Jonah!" a woman's voice called out. "Hello!"

Luke turned to see Azara, the Gentile teacher who'd had the girls' school in Capernaum. She was winding her way through the crowd toward them. As she exchanged greetings with Jonah, Luke scanned eagerly for Esther, whom he'd heard was living with Azara now.

"My goodness, Luke," exclaimed Azara, "you've grown *a lot* since I last saw you. You look so much like your father. Another four inches and fifty pounds and you and Jonah could be twins."

Luke grinned at that. Though his relationship with his father had been strained of late, he still possessed his boyhood yearning to be like him. He felt proud to tell people his father was Jonah of Magdala, the best physician in all of Galilee.

As if straight out of one of his dreams, the crowd suddenly parted and Esther emerged right in front of him.

"Hello," she said, her gorgeous amber-gold eyes locked on him.

Unable to tolerate her penetrating stare for long, Luke searched instead for the unique touch she'd surely added to her appearance. It didn't take him long to find it. Her dark hair, which usually hung straight down to the middle of her back, was instead interwoven into braids that extended from behind her ears. Luke had never seen hair styled like that before. He thought the braids resembled pigs' tails.

"I like your hair," he said shyly.

"Thanks," she replied, swinging her head back and forth so the braids whipped from side to side.

"Esther didn't like Jesus' talk," blurted Azara.

Jonah pivoted toward the teenager. "Why? Was it too hopeful and inclusive?" he asked with a wink.

Azara laughed at his sarcasm. "I think that's what I like best about him," she commented. "It's so easy to despair of the world these days, believe that the future is bleak, but he's not pessimistic at all."

"No," replied Esther. "I didn't like when he said 'Everyone who asks will receive, and anyone who seeks will find, and the door will be opened to those who knock.'"

"Why not?" asked Jonah.

She glanced at Luke, before turning to Jonah. "Because it's not true," she said. "I've asked. I've sought. And I've knocked, but the door still hasn't opened."

"Me too," said Luke faintly. He peered longingly at the bewitching black mole on Esther's cheek.

Jonah waited while two bronze, bare-chested men passed in front of him. "What have you been asking for, Esther?"

She pulled her lips in tight in response.

"I've already tried. She won't tell," said Azara. Then, glancing suspiciously at Esther's doe-eyed gaze at Luke, she added, "But I might have an idea. Jonah, your order came in a few days ago. When you come get it, I think the two of us need to talk."

The crowd was particularly dense where they were standing, as it was a throughway for people either arriving or leaving. Working-class Gentiles from Decapolis, Phoenicia, and Galilee mixed together with Jewish travelers on their way to Jerusalem for Passover. From barefoot children in rags to well-dressed pilgrims with immaculate prayer shawls, people old and young, rich and poor, flowed by in a never-ending stream.

"When do you think you'll stop by?" asked Azara.

Jonah didn't respond. Luke wasn't even sure he'd heard her. His father was gaping fixedly into the distance at someone or something. Luke looked in the same direction, but noticed nothing out of the ordinary.

Azara raised her voice to be heard over the arguing couple passing by. "What is it?" she asked.

"That man," said Jonah, pointing. "I know him. He's the son of a high priest in the Jerusalem Sanhedrin."

"You think he's here to take in Jesus' message?" Azara asked.

"Or maybe to *spy* on him," Esther said mischievously.

"That's exactly what I was wondering," said Jonah, his voice trailing off.

Luke didn't know and certainly didn't care at the moment. He only knew he couldn't bear to be in Esther's presence like this. He wanted to talk to her, but didn't feel comfortable with the adults around. Esther's slender body had developed even more since the last time he'd seen her. Her breasts were bigger and her curves were curvier. But all he really wanted was just to hold her hand.

"We were just on our way to catch a boat back to Capernaum," Azara announced. "We'd better get going. See you next week?"

"Certainly," replied Jonah.

Esther again locked her eyes on Luke. "See you next week?" she whispered.

He mouthed the same words his father had said, then watched glumly as the two women walked down the hill toward the shore.

"Maybe we'll have better luck if we split up," Jonah proposed as he handed Luke two coins. "Let's meet back with your mom and the baby in a half hour."

Luke tucked the coins into a little pocket on the inside of his tunic, then departed in the opposite direction his father went. He decided to head to a small alcove where he'd seen the rabbi and a group of men disappear into. Luke would look for food to buy on the way, but his primary goal was to find the Rabbi Jesus and ask him Esther's question, because it was the same as his. He wanted to know why his longstanding, one-and-only prayer to God had gone unanswered.

As he climbed the hillside, he could see Galilean farmers working their fields and orchards across the river. From this distance they looked like slow-moving ants toiling in tall grass.

Luke called out every few seconds to the endless families and groups he passed, asking if they had any bread or food to sell. No one ever answered, and if he happened to catch anyone's eyes, they just shook their head. He scoured for anyone eating, but everyone seemed to be waiting around, like his father, to see if Jesus was going to proclaim himself king of Palestine.

Stepping gingerly through a patch of ankle-high, orange flowers, Luke was careful not to disturb any of the dozens of bees diligently collecting pollen and nectar. On his approach to the trees and bushes that formed the alcove, he recalled his days of playing and exploring in this magnificent, uninhabited place. The alcove had always been one of his favorites.

Its narrow entrance was now blocked by Mouse Man, as he was known to all the children in the area. It wasn't that he was small or timid like a mouse, he was actually heavyset and loud. The children referred to him as Mouse Man because he had a pet mouse that accompanied him wherever he went. Luke could see the miniature, gray rodent sitting atop the man's shoulder—its tiny black eyes fixed on the block of wood the man was whittling into the likeness of a camel.

Certain that Mouse Man was the gatekeeper and wouldn't let him through, Luke walked past him to a hidden deer trail he knew about. It was a short, winding path that led to the far end inside the alcove.

After ducking under the protruding branch hiding the trailhead, Luke glimpsed through the foliage a group of men lounging on the ground, drinking from waterskins, and listening to Jesus. He recognized a few of them, including his father's friend, the physician whose name was also Luke.

These men, Luke guessed, were not mere disciples, but the rabbi's shaliachs. Whereas disciples were like distant cousins, shaliachs were like immediate family. They formed the rabbi's inner circle, often leaving their own families behind to travel with and serve their teacher. Their duties included managing crowds, finding lodgings, collecting donations, and, most recently, giving talks on behalf of Jesus. Though the rabbi currently had many, many disciples, Luke guessed his shaliachs numbered only about a dozen.

During his public talk, Jesus had spoken of an upcoming preaching tour that would soon begin. He and his shaliachs were going to spread Jesus' message of a loving, compassionate God, and forgiveness and goodwill toward one's fellow man, far and wide beyond Galilee.

Luke made his way cautiously along the trail, trying to avoid stepping on any twigs or brittle brown leaves that might make a noise. He listened intently to the rabbi's words in the hope his question might be answered before he even asked.

"I am with you for only a short time," Jesus was telling the others, "and then I will return to the one who sent me. Do not lay down any rule beyond what I determined for you, nor declare law like a lawmaker, or else you might be dominated by it."

Through a gap in the vegetation, Luke caught a clear glimpse of the man who'd had such an impact on his father's life. Jesus was seated cross-legged under the shade of a tree, his face friendly and untroubled as he spoke to those gathered. That he always seemed so calm was one of the qualities that intrigued Luke the most. It was as if there wasn't a problem in the world that was worth the price of losing his peace of mind.

"Do not be afraid when you hear of wars and revolutions," Jesus counseled. "Such things must happen first, but they do not mean that the end is near."

Luke was taken aback to see his neighbor Mary among the men. She was sitting impossibly straight, a white prayer shawl draped over her head. Luke had heard she'd become one of his more devoted followers, and judging by how close she sat to him, the rumor was most certainly true. Luke had never heard of a rabbi accepting a woman as a disciple, but then Jesus was no ordinary rabbi. He seemed to relish breaking rules he deemed harmful or unjust.

Mary noticed Luke approaching the end of the trail and waved him over. Jesus paused in his teaching as Luke emerged into the clearing and sat down next to Mary. She playfully tousled Luke's curly, brown hair, commenting on how long it was getting.

Luke was afraid he'd be admonished for sneaking into their circle, but Jesus seemed to have stopped his discourse only to acknowledge and welcome him.

"Good to see you again," he said. He reached over and softly rested a hand on Luke's shoulder, just as he'd done at the Jordan River the previous year. "Luke? Right?"

Luke nodded—surprised, and also pleased, the rabbi remembered him.

"How is your father? Is he here?"

"Yes," answered Luke. "He's doing well. Thank you."

"And how are you? You look troubled."

Recognizing his chance, Luke hastened a query. "May I ask a question?"

"Of course," replied Jesus. "Questions are free." He then held out his hand, grinning slyly, and said, "An answer will cost you one dinar, though."

Luke reached in his pocket to see how much money he had before everyone's laughter revealed to him that Jesus was joking. Blushing, he forced a grin.

"Go ahead," Mary encouraged him. "Ask."

Luke stole another glance at Jesus. He'd heard he was a carpenter, and the rabbi certainly had the keen eyes and rugged hands of one. "I want to know," Luke said in a slightly quavering voice, "if an unanswered prayer is God's way of saying no."

Mary extended a hand in support, gently massaging the back of his neck for a few seconds.

"Or if maybe it's something He can't do," added Luke. Though he hadn't noticed before, Luke now saw that Jesus had a yellow and black caterpillar crawling on the back of one of his hands.

"With God, all things are possible," Jesus replied resolutely. "Whatever you pray and ask for, believe that you have received it, and it will be yours."

The answer, Luke thought, seemed custom-tailored for him. What he'd prayed for, he only half believed was possible.

As the caterpillar inched its way to the edge, Jesus flipped his outstretched hand over so it could keep crawling. "And whenever you stand praying," he added, "if you have anything against anyone, forgive him, so that your Father in the heavens will also forgive you your wrongdoing."

Luke didn't know if it was his proximity to Jesus or the way he had worded it, but forgiveness all of a sudden made sense to him. It was absolutely a way to make things even, but it made them even between you and God. Forgiving another opened the door to forgiveness of oneself.

Mouse Man hollered to the group from the alcove entrance. "Your chore boy is on the way, rabbi. I see him."

Not knowing if he'd ever get another opportunity like this, Luke tried to get answers to his father's questions about the kingdom, and whether Jesus would make himself king. "Are you going to lead our people like Abraham and Moses before you?" he asked. "Create God's kingdom on Earth?"

Jesus smiled warmly. Using his free hand, he brushed away the curly strand of hair that was dangling over his forehead. "My son, God's kingdom isn't something you can see," he replied with gleaming eyes. "You won't be able to say, 'Here it is!' or 'It's over there!' for the kingdom of God is *within* you." He placed great emphasis on the word "within," holding a fist to his chest as he'd said it.

Mouse Man shouted again. "He's here! Shall I send him in?"

"Yes, please," called Jesus as he rose gracefully from his cross-legged position. He gazed at Luke, then at everyone in the circle, and repeated his last point. "Be on your guard so that no one deceives you by saying, 'Look over here!' or 'Look over there!' for the child of true Humanity exists within you. Follow it! Those who search for it will find it."

As the caterpillar again reached the edge of Jesus' hand, he bent down and held his palm next to Luke's. After the caterpillar inched onto Luke's hand, Jesus departed for the other end of the alcove. The man sitting in front of Luke turned around, eyeing Luke and the caterpillar with a curious smile.

"Luke, this is John," said Mary.

"Hello," Luke said politely.

"Thank you for your questions," said John. "You found a way to put into words exactly what many of us have wondered about."

With his dark, weathered skin, thick forearms, and calloused hands, John looked like the typical rough fisherman so common in these parts—only his demeanor and words weren't coarse. He exuded kindness, his eyes soft and peaceful. Luke liked him instantly.

"Our time for rest will soon be over, and we'll have work to do," John announced. "Did you have any more questions, my child?"

Normally Luke wouldn't like being called a child, and it felt a little strange coming from John, who Luke guessed was the youngest of the men there. But the way John had said it so fondly made Luke wish he *was* still a child.

"About what?" asked Luke.

"About anything," John said with a shrug.

Jesus called out for Andrew, Peter, and James. As Luke watched the trio stand and go to him, he worried he didn't have long before all the men were called away.

"I have a friend," Luke answered, although the *friend* was actually himself, "who says when we die we don't go to Sheol. We just return to the earth, and the worms eat our flesh until there's nothing left. He says when you die, there's nothing. You simply cease to exist."

"And?" John asked with raised eyebrows.

"And," Luke said, "I want to know the truth." He released the caterpillar onto a green leaf of a nearby bush.

John ran his fingers through his beard, lost in thought for a few seconds. "If we are to speak of truth," he began, "then we must speak of love, for there is no higher truth than love. Before you were, there was love, nothing else. You are, quite literally, made out of love."

With an affectionateness Luke hadn't experienced since he was a babe at his mother's breast, John reached out and held Luke's hand in his.

"And into this all-encompassing love you shall return one day," he said tenderly. "There is nothing you can do, nothing you can say, nothing you can even think that will prevent it."

His words were like a balm to Luke's ears.

"The only thing you have control over is the manner in which you return to love," added John. "The journey is entirely yours."

Jesus called out to John and two others to come to him.

Luke, wondering what the fuss was about, watched John depart for the far end of the alcove. When the chore boy tilted his basket forward for Jesus and the others, Luke spied two meager dried fish and five small loaves of bread.

"Master, this is all we have," one of the men said. "It's not even enough for our own dinner, let alone this crowd."

"It will do," Jesus replied. "By the grace of God, they'll all be fed."

"Impossible," a dissenting voice declared. "There must be five thousand people here."

At first Luke agreed; but then he wasn't so sure. Nothing seemed impossible for Jesus.

He was like a gift from God.

Afterword

Jesus never charged anyone for the healings he performed, the enlightening parables he told, or the wisdom he instilled. In that spirit, the eBook version of this novel is offered at no cost*.

But it is not free. You are asked to make a donation to one of the following charities** that would doubtless be near and dear to Jesus' heart:

- Giving Sight to the Blind: www.Seva.org
- Helping the Lame to Walk: www.LimbsInternational.org
- Healing the Sick and Wounded: www.DoctorsWithoutBorders.org
- Lifting the Poor Out of Poverty: www.TechnoServe.org
- Ending Persecution: www.Amnesty.org

Alternatively—or even better, *mutually*—you could buy the print version of the novel and gift that to someone who doesn't have access to the eBook version (e.g., family, library, friend, ... or even foe). 20 percent of the profits from the print version will be donated to the charities listed above, while the remaining 80 percent will go toward funding goodwill projects by the author.

Please post a review and be sure to include your donation information, as it will inspire others to also give. When donating, leave a note or comment mentioning the book for the organization's tracking purposes.

* Depending on the distribution/outlet, the electronic version may not be entirely without cost to the reader, but certainly at the minimal price allowed.
** The charities listed were selected because their outreach is global (i.e., not restricted to any one country).

Final Thoughts

What if—instead of money, fame, or power—we based each decision on whether it brought more peace, goodwill, and understanding into the world? What if increasing love was the ends, and also the means?

We, too, can be a light unto the darkness. And collectively we can shine a light bright enough to lift this world out of chaos and confusion.

To contact the author, visit: www.Facebook.com/ThereArisethLight

Discussion Questions Focused on Your Own Life and Journey

Part I

- Was your religious upbringing more like Jonah's or Zebulun's? How were you taught to view God and the scriptures? Have these views evolved over the years?

- What are your beliefs about God being the source of both good *and* evil as Isaiah 45:7 says?

- Vitus's split-second decision to lead the charge to save General Gaius changes the course of his life. What abrupt decision have you made that ended up strongly shaping your future?

- When Jonah returns to his village and sees it has been ransacked, he's furious with God. Have you ever held a grudge against God? Blamed God for some misfortune in your life? Explain.

- Has there ever been a point in your life when you were no longer in love with God, but afraid of God?

- At the end of Part I, life becomes too much to bear for Thomas and he gives in to hate. Have you or anyone you've known gone down that path?

- Like Jonah and Thomas, nearly everyone has had some dramatic childhood experiences that strongly shaped them. What are some things you went through that influenced your beliefs about the world and yourself? Do you still hold to these beliefs? Why or why not?

Part II

- The covenant is a central theme in Part II. Do you have your own covenant? Explain.

- The family dynamics between Jonah and Thomas and Zebulun play out strongly in Part II. Assuming for a moment that you chose your parents and siblings (or even extended family like aunts, uncles, cousins, etc.), why might you have chosen the ones you did?

- When encountering the Roman soldiers, Thomas is blinded by his thirst for vengeance. Have you ever been blinded by a desire to get even? How did it turn out—for you, and for the other person?

- Jonah "doubles down" on his belief that God will see to it that things turn out alright. He then finds himself lost, angry, and confused when it doesn't happen. Have you experienced anything similar?

- When Vitus is trapped inside the carpenter's workshop, all seems lost. Have there been times in your life when things seemed hopeless, but you persevered nonetheless?

- When Jonah blames the turmoil and unfortunate events of his life on his failure to follow the commandments, did you agree with him? Do you believe there is causation between adhering to a religion's tenets and what happens in your life? Why or why not?

- While Farrukh is pragmatic and accepting of the world as it is, Azara is idealistic and excited at the prospect of being someone who changes the world for the better. Where do you fall on this spectrum?

- When Thomas is near death, he receives great clarity on the life he has lived. Under what circumstances have you received the most clarity on your life?

- Have you ever experienced failure on the magnitude of Jonah (at not being able to safeguard his little brother)? How did this affect you in your life?

Part III

- Both Jonah and Vitus experience in Part III what we would call today a "midlife crisis." No matter your age, have you gone through a prolonged period of doubt, confusion, and lack of desire to live? Looking back on it, does it make sense to you now?

- Have you ever, like Jonah, considered taking your own life? What, or who, pulled you through it?

- Put yourself in Luke's place. How might you have reacted at his age at being told you have to avenge your father's death?

- What "leopards" have you wrestled with that threatened to steal everything you hold dear? How did the fight change you?

- With Barnabas's help, Vitus realizes his name fits him well. If you know the meaning of your name, does it fit you? Have you grown into it?

- Vitus finds something he believes in with all his heart and soul. Have you found something like that? Does your life reflect it?

- Azara opens her school at great cost and risk to herself, because she feels it's the right thing to do. Have you ever done anything similar? Would you want to?

Part IV

- Put yourself in the place of Azara or Vitus at the stoning. What might you have done in similar circumstances?

- Have you ever, like Jonah, "turned your back on God"? If so, what were the circumstances and how long did it last?

- Barnabas states in Part III that "Confusion always precedes clarity." And in Part IV, we see Jonah coming to the same conclusion. Do you agree? Has this always been the case in your life?

- Do you have examples of when you've chosen forgiveness over vengeance?

- Have you ever felt like Esther when she wants to repay all the love and kindness shown to her? What were the circumstances?

- What was your reaction when it was revealed Jonah was the one who paid the ransom for Vitus? Does the thought of doing something like that appeal to you?

- Of the three protagonists (Azara, Jonah, and Vitus), whose struggles did you most relate to?

Discussion Questions Focused on the Book

Religious/Philosophical:

- At the end of Part II, Jonah accuses God of breaking the covenant with him. Do you agree? Why or why not?

- What is your opinion of how Thomas was willing to sacrifice everything—his own life, and that of others—for the cause he believed in?

- Did you agree with Jonah's initial decision not to treat the woman with the toothache? What would you have done?

- Barnabas claims in Part III that he would be no different than any other prisoner if he had lived their life. Did you agree? Why or why not?

- Discuss whether you agree with Barnabas when he says in Part III: "(T)he choice is between inclusion and exclusion, between seeing others as oneself and seeing others as separate. That's what each of us has to decide—whether to serve others or serve one's self."

- In Part III Azara opens her school and faces dire consequences as a result. Do you see any parallels to anything like this occurring in this day and age?

- Discuss the points of the conversation Vitus recalls between himself and Barnabas concerning free will, chaos, and rebalancing.

- In Part IV Jesus said, "Be on your guard so that no one deceives you by saying, 'Look over here!' or 'Look over there!' for the child of true Humanity exists within you. Follow it! Those who search for it will find it." What do you think he meant by this?

General:

- How original and unique was this book?
- What did you like best about this book?
- What did you like least about this book?
- What other books did this remind you of?
- What did you think of the book's length? If it's too long, what would you cut? If too short, what would you add?
- What will be your lasting impression of this book?

Characters:

- Did the characters seem believable to you? Did they remind you of anyone?
- Which character could you relate to the most?
- Which characters did you like best? Admire the most?
- Which characters did you like least?
- Which secondary characters stood out for you?
- Which character in the book would you most like to meet?

History:

- Did you learn anything new about the Bible or life in the first century?
- If you were familiar with the stories of the centurion in the Bible, does the character of Vitus fit who you'd envisioned? If so, how? If not, why?
- What was your impression of Pontius Pilate before reading this book? Did the rendering of Pilate change that impression? Or reinforce it?
- Is the portrayal of Jesus in this book similar or different from what you've learned? If different, which portrayal do you like better? Why?
- Would you want to live in first-century Galilee or Judea? Why or why not?

Impressions:

- Which events or scenes stood out for you as memorable?
- Which passages or chapters of Part I (or II, III, or IV), if any, drew you in the most emotionally? Have each member read their favorite passages out loud.
- What were some of the major themes? Are they relevant in your life?
- Share a favorite quote from the book. Why did this quote stand out?
- What feelings did this book evoke for you?

Theatrics:

- If you were making a movie of this book, who would you cast?
- Which artist would you choose to illustrate this book? What kinds of illustrations would you include?
- What songs or albums does this book make you think of?
- Which places in the book would you most like to visit?

Author:

- If you got the chance to ask the author one question, what would it be?
- What do you think the author's purpose was in writing this book? What ideas was he trying to get across?
- What else struck you about the book? Were you glad you read it? Would you recommend it to a friend? Did this book make you want to read more work by this author?

Acknowledgments

For their editing, assistance, or just plain old encouragement, I would like to thank Jenellen Fischer, Carol Gaskin, Krista Hiser, and Inessa Love.

Also by JV Love

The End of Sorrow: A Novel of the Siege of Leningrad in WWII

A love that would not die...
A city that would not surrender...
A war that knew no bounds...

The date is June 21st, 1941, and Adolf Hitler is about to lead Germany into what would become one of the bloodiest, most barbaric wars the world would ever know. His invasion plan, Operation: Barbarossa, calls for taking the northern Russian city of Leningrad in a matter of weeks, but as the troops reach the outside border of the city, the Soviet resistance stiffens and a stalemate ensues. Hitler calls for continual bombardment of the city and cutting off all outside supplies. He boasts that the city will starve to death and the German forces will march into a ghost town.

Follow a cast of lovers, heroes, and fiends as they struggle through one of the most horrific human dramas ever created. For 900 days, the citizens and soldiers of Leningrad, Russia endured one of the worst sieges in the history of mankind. Some would find the inner strength to light the way. Others would descend into madness.

"The Classical Russian form lives on: This novel is no pale imitation. ... The End of Sorrow is a triumph of craft. A rock-solid, gratifying choice for discerning fans of serious literature." – ForeWord Clarion Five Star Review

Excerpts from reviews on Amazon
"This is one of the best books I have ever read! ... I have read thousands of books in my life, but this is one I will certainly never forget!" – Tim

"This book is one that I hated for it to end. ... I highly recommend this book. In fact, I wish I could read it again, without knowing how it ends." – Anonymous

"I was swept away - surely the best compliment to any writer. Highly recommend." – Miss Melly

Historical Notes

It is nearly impossible to specify exact dates, or even years, for events that took place in the time of Jesus. Instead, scholars often give a range of time in which an incident likely occurred. For narrative consistency, this book uses the following timeline:

- Jesus is born sometime around 6 BCE.
- Herod the Great dies in 4 BCE.
- Pilate becomes prefect of Judea in 26 CE.
- Roman Emperor Tiberius retires from Rome to island of Capri in 26 CE.
- Jesus visits John the Baptist around 27 CE.
- John the Baptist is executed sometime in 28 CE.
- Jesus begins his public ministry and healings in 28 CE, shortly after John the Baptist's death.

It should be recognized that Jesus invariably repeated his teachings in slightly different contexts and for slightly different audiences. It is safe to assume that whatever record exists of his teachings in the Bible, we can be assured he used much the same words on many different occasions. The Bible, in fact, records several such instances. This novel uses Jesus' actual words as recorded in the scriptures with minor additions or deletions in order to fit the context of the conversation or scene in which it takes place.

It should also be noted that scripture from the Old Testament is quoted mostly verbatim since it had already been written; however, one needs to bear in mind that the New Testament—for the timeframe of this novel—does not yet exist. It would not be written for another two to four decades.

Biblical quotes and references have been taken from multiple versions and translations of the Bible. The book title is from Psalm 112:4 (King James version): "Unto the upright there ariseth light in the darkness: he is gracious, and full of compassion, and righteous."

PART I
Chapter 1
- People: Jonah, Thomas, and Zebulun are fictional characters based on Jewish culture, attitudes, and beliefs of the time.
- Fact/Note: King Herod (Herod the Great) died in 4 BCE after ruling for over three decades.
- Fact/Note: The Nabataeans invaded Galilee and Judea in 4 BCE. Hearing of the violence and unrest there, Varus, the governor of Greater Syria, called upon the Nabataean kingdom to provide assistance in restoring order. King Aretas of

Nabatea was all too willing to oblige, giving his troops free reign to loot and plunder the lands of his former adversary, King Herod, as they made their way to their objective of Sepphoris.

- Fact/Note: The large, elaborate ceremonies of bar mitzvahs is a modern-day phenomena. In the first century, they were usually commemorated by a visit to the local synagogue and a celebratory dinner at home.
- Scripture Reference: "Let man have dominion over fish" – Genesis 1:26
- Fact/Note: Certain varieties of fig trees produce fruit several times a year.

Chapter 2
- People: Marcus Trebellius Vitus is a fictional character based on what is known of Roman legionnaires of the first century.
- People: Flavian and Romanus are fictional characters.
- Fact/Note: Publius Quinctilius Varus was the Roman governor of Greater Syria from 7–4 BC. Prior to that he governed the province of Africa from 8–7 BC.
- Fact/Note: Though the record is not clear, it is believed that the Roman strength in Syria at this time included the III Galencia, X Fretensis, and either VI Ferrata or the XII Fulminata. Responsible for protecting the Roman Empire from the powerful Parthians, Varus was restrained in the immediacy and the number of troops he could send to Galilee and Judea.
- Fact/Note: It is believed that the minimum height to become a Roman soldier was 5'10" to 6', which was considered tall for the time.
- Fact/Note: A Jewish man named Judas, son of Hezekiah, led a revolt during this time and captured a large store of weapons from an arsenal in Sepphoris, the capital of Galilee.
- Fact/Note: Two thousand of Herod's former troops formed an armed band and terrorized the Judean countryside during this time.
- Fact/Note: A slave named Simon, who used to belong to Herod, crowned himself king and burned down Herod's palace in Jericho during this time.
- Fact/Note: Athronges, a shepherd, and his four brothers conducted raids of terror and led a rebellion against the Romans during this time.

Chapter 3
- Scripture Reference: "I form the light, and create darkness" – Isaiah 45:7
- Scripture Reference: Regarding Samson's strength—Judges 16:3; Samson slaying 1,000 Philistines – Judges 15:14-16
- Scripture Reference: "Everyone who is arrogant in heart is an abomination to the Lord" – Proverbs 16:5
- Scripture Reference: God causing the ground to open up and swallow Korah and his family – Numbers 16:31-32
- Scripture Reference: God punishing descendants of evil-doers – Exodus 20:5
- Fact/Note: After Israel's fall to the Assyrians, those of Samaria began to intermarry with the Assyrians, contrary to Deuteronomy 7:3-5. This is why the Jews considered the Samaritans "dogs," or "half-breeds."

Chapter 4
- Fact/Note: It was approximately 300 miles from Cyrrhus to Galilee. Roman armies generally averaged twenty miles a day, so it would have taken them about fifteen days to march there.
- People: General Gaius is a historical figure. He commanded the Roman legions sent to Judea and Galilee.
- Fact/Note: The Romans based their gods on the Greek gods. For example, Zeus became Jupiter, Ares became Mars, Poseidon became Neptune, and Hades became Pluto.
- People: Silas is a fictional character.
- Fact/Note: The Cantabrian Wars (29–19 BCE) were the final stage of the two-century long Roman conquest of Hispania.

Chapter 5
- Scripture Reference: Moses destroying sixty cities, plundering livestock, and slaughtering people in Argob – Deuteronomy 3:3-7
- Scripture Reference: Fear God – Deuteronomy 6:13 & 10:20
- Scripture Reference: Not owning property that belongs to another – Leviticus 6:2-3 and Deuteronomy 22:11
- Scripture Reference: Against stealing – Exodus 20:15 and Leviticus 19:11
- Scripture Reference: Not touching a dead person – Leviticus 21:11
- Fact/Note: In the Old Testament, dogs are generally held in low regard. To compare a person to a dog was considered an insult. See the following passages for references to dogs: 1 Samuel 17:43, Proverbs 26:17, 2 Kings 8:13, Exodus 22:31, Deuteronomy 23:18, 2 Samuel 3:8, Proverbs 26:11, Ecclesiastes 9:4, 2 Samuel 9:8, 1 Samuel 24:14.

Chapter 6
- Fact/Note: Like many wounded of his time, Flavian contracted tetanus. Author Richard Gabriel estimates in his book, "The Ancient World," that 80% of those with tetanus would die within three to six days.

Chapter 7
- Scripture Reference: "Heathen are sunk in the pit they made" – Psalm 9:15-16

PART II
Chapter 8
- People: Azara and her father, Aziz, are fictional characters based on what is known of Gentile (non-Jewish) people of the time.
- People: Jesus of Nazareth, and his parents, Joseph and Mary, are historical figures. The New Testament of the Bible tells the story of Jesus' life and teachings.

- Fact/Note: Herat, in modern-day Afghanistan near the border with Iran, is an ancient city with a long history. It is still a substantial and lively city today. Samarkand, in modern-day Uzbekistan, dates back to 1500 BCE. It was a pivotal city along several converging routes and was renowned for its craft production.
- Fact/Note: The series of networks and roads of ancient times that connected the Far East all the way to Egypt and Europe are referred to today as the Silk Road, but it should be understood that that term is a modern-day invention.
- Fact/Note: Alexander the Great's conquests (334-323 BCE) extended as far as the western edge of modern-day India.
- Fact/Note: Marriages in first century Palestine were generally prearranged by the father. A father was more concerned about the marriage of his sons than about the marriage of his daughters. No expense was involved in marrying off a daughter. The father received a dowry for his daughter, whereas he had to give a dowry to the prospective father-in-law of his son when marrying him off.
- People: Farrukh is a fictional character.
- Fact/Note: The Mahabharata is the older of the two major epics of ancient India (the Ramayana is the other). Texts of the story date to around 400 BCE, though its origins are thought to be as old as the 8th and 9th centuries BCE. Full of philosophical and devotional passages, the Mahabharata includes works such as the Bhagavad Gita.

Chapter 9
- Fact/Note: Sadoc, his brother, Judas, and their father, Hezekiah were genuine figures in Jewish history.
- Fact/Note: There were several various units of currency in circulation in first-century Palestine. Besides the Roman dinar, there was the pruta, or mite, and the Jewish shekel.
- Scripture Reference: "The Lord is a God who avenges" – Psalm 94:1

Chapter 10
- People: Ephraim, Servanus, and Damian are fictional characters.
- Fact/Note: Judea was in the Roman province of Syria, and, in addition to other taxes, every man was to pay 1% of his annual income for income tax. The crop taxes included 1/10 of grain crop, and 1/5 of wine, fruit, and olive oil.
- Fact/Note: Yom Kippur is one of the holiest days of the year for Jews. Known as the Day of Atonement, Jews traditionally observe the holiday in synagogue services, along with fasting and intensive prayer.
- Fact/Note: The incident of a Roman soldier breaking wind during the procession of pilgrims, and the resulting Jewish protest was an actual event, though history records it as happening later than it does here. See "Bandits, Prophets, and Messiahs" by Horsley and Hanson.

Chapter 11
- N/A

Chapter 12
- N/A

Chapter 13
- Scripture Reference: "The Lord is a God who avenges" – Psalm 94:1

Chapter 14
- N/A

Chapter 15
- People: Aaron is a fictional character.

Chapter 16
- People: Hezron is a fictional character.
- Fact/Note: The incident involving a Jewish protest against a Roman soldier setting fire to several scrolls from the Torah was an actual event. See "Bandits, Prophets, and Messiahs" by Horsley and Hanson.

Chapter 17
- N/A

Chapter 18
- Fact/Note: Renowned for their skill at trading, the Sogdians were an ancient people of Iranian origin. Their language was in widespread use along the Silk Road.
- Fact/Note: By means of the ancient Silk Road, Eastern and Northern Europe imported rice, cotton, wool, and silk from Central Asia. It exported skins, furs, fur animals, bark for skin processing, honey, cattle, and slaves.

Chapter 19
- Fact/Note: Evidence suggests that Romans carried out crucifixions by use of a pole, or a pole with a crossbeam (i.e., a cross). Both worked equally effectively at bringing about a long, tortuous death.

Chapter 20
- Fact/Note: Though crucifixion is thought of as an ancient and obsolete form of torture, it is still carried out in parts of the world today. If you're interested to know more, Amnesty International does a good job of reporting on it.

PART III
Chapter 21
- People: Shem and Moshe are fictional characters.
- Fact/Note: A Galilean accent was viewed by those from Judea similarly to how a deep Southern drawl is viewed by some Northerners in the United States. This was one reason why Jesus was viewed with contempt by some of the learned priests and rabbis from Jerusalem.
- People: Hadassah is a fictional character.

Chapter 22
- People: Pontius Pilate is a historical figure. Pilate was in fact a prefect, not a procurator. It was not until the rule of the emperor Claudius that the title of Roman governors changed from prefect to procurator.
- Fact/Note: Joseph Caiaphas was a high priest appointed in 18 CE by the Prefect Valerius Gratus. In the New Testament, he is said to have been the one who organized the plot to kill Jesus. He was also involved in Jesus' Sanhedrin trial.

Chapter 23
- N/A

Chapter 24
- Fact/Note: Though movies like to depict the hallways of dungeons and crypts lit with torches every few yards, it is highly unlikely this was ever done. Torches do not burn very long and so would have needed to be replaced quite often, perhaps two times an hour or more depending on what they were made of. Another reason is that ancient torches produced an incredible amount of smoke, so that having an entire hallway or room lit with torches would have made the air unbreathable rather quickly. The far more likely alternative was for a person who had to go to the dungeon to carry a torch with them down the dark hallway. For an extended period of time in a room, a candle likely would have been used since it would have lasted much longer and not put out so much smoke.
- People: Barnabas is a historical figure. It is known only that he donated the proceeds of some land to the early Christian community, and that he and Paul the Apostle undertook missionary journeys together. Though there is no evidence that Barnabas was ever arrested by Pilate, nothing at all is known of Barnabas's life prior to his mention in the Bible of meeting the apostles after Jesus' death.
- Scripture Reference: "Eye for eye, tooth for tooth" – Exodus 21:23

Chapter 25
- People: Luke, Tiras, and Ehud are fictional characters.
- Fact/Note: The cubit was an ancient form of measurement. It was the distance from the tip of the middle finger to the bottom of the elbow.

- Scripture Reference: "The Lord is gracious and compassionate, slow to anger and rich in love" – Psalm 145:8
- Scripture Reference: God destroying Sodom and Gomorrah – Genesis 19:24
- Scripture Reference: God and Jericho – Joshua 6:20
- Scripture Reference: God and the Amorites – Joshua 10:10-11
- Scripture Reference: God and the plague under King David – 2 Samuel 24:25
- Scripture Reference: "Fear the Lord and judge with integrity" – 2 Chron. 19:7
- Scripture Reference: "Eye for eye, tooth for tooth" – Exodus 21:23
- Scripture Reference: Killing of all the firstborn in Egypt – Exodus 12:29
- Scripture Reference: Moses sentencing a man to death for gathering sticks on the Sabbath – Numbers 32
- Scripture Reference: Read Numbers 14 for more info on Moses after the Exodus. If not for Moses' intercession, God would have struck down all the people with plague for their initial refusal to capture Canaan. Instead, they were forced to wander in the wilderness for forty years, all of them twenty years of age or older dying before seeing the Promised Land. In addition, the ten spies who gave a fearful report of the difficulties of capturing Canaan were struck down and died of a plague (Numbers 14:37).
- Fact/Note: In addition to the ibex and deer, other Israeli mammals include the hyrax, gazelle, jackal, wolf, boar, fox, hare, hyena, caracal, and badger.
- Fact/Note: Though many people, even those who live in Israel, are unfamiliar with the history of leopards in the region, the big cats have lived there for thousands of years. Archaeologists working in the Negev desert in 2013 uncovered a 5,000-year-old leopard trap alongside one that is estimated to be 1,600 years old. In 1965 the last leopard in Galilee was killed by an old Bedouin goat herder, and in the same year Bedouins killed a leopard in the Judean desert. There are efforts currently underway to preserve the few remaining leopards in the region.

Chapter 26

- People: Stone and Corvus are fictional characters.
- Fact/Note: Pilate did indeed make plans to get money from the Temple treasury to pay for the incomplete aqueduct.
- Fact/Note: Jesus informed most all of his disciples that they would be killed for spreading his teachings. Though unverifiable, Christian tradition holds that Barnabas was martyred at Salamis, Cyprus, in 61 CE.

Chapter 27

- Fact/Note: Pilate's premeditated assault on the Jewish protesters was documented by Josephus and other sources. There is disagreement among scholars over when this event occurred, with some claiming it was a year or two prior to Jesus' journey to see John the Baptist, and others stating it happened later in Pilate's career as prefect. Though many protesters were beaten, the number of actual casualties ranges wildly, with some estimates as high as several thousand.

Chapter 28
- People: Esther is a fictional character.
- Scripture Reference: Read the Book of Exodus for more info on how the Israelites escaped from slavery in Egypt.
- People: Esther's father, the brute, and the Jewish elder are fictional characters.

Chapter 29
- Fact/Note: The distance between Jerusalem and Masada was about thirty-two miles, but it was difficult terrain that would have taken two days to travel.

Chapter 30
- People: John the Baptist is a historical figure mentioned in the Bible.
- Scripture Reference: "Do not rejoice when your enemy falls" – Proverbs 24:17
- Scripture Reference: "The righteous rejoice when he sees Your vengeance" – Psalms 58:10
- Scripture Reference: "Treat others as you would want them to treat you" – Matthew 7:12
- Fact/Note: Though Jesus did indeed pay a visit to John the Baptist and get baptized, it isn't clear if this was a one-time, short event, or if he stayed with John the Baptist and his disciples for an extended amount of time. It is only known that this meeting between the two occurred prior to Jesus beginning his ministry.

PART IV
Chapter 31
- Fact/Note: Adding wine to the water, whether they understood it or not, did a decent job of killing bacteria in the water and was a common practice in the first century.
- Fact/Note: The smallest unit of currency was a copper coin called the pruta, or mite. It was the equivalent of today's penny.
- Fact/Note: Genesis 1:5 states of the creation of the universe: "And it was evening and it was morning, one day." Since evening is mentioned first, Jews observe a new day as beginning at sunset, thus the first meal of the Sabbath is taken at sunset of Friday. The last meal of the Sabbath is taken in the late afternoon on Saturday.
- People: Simon/Peter, and his brother Andrew, are historical figures found in the Bible. Originally disciples of John the Baptist, they later became disciples of Jesus (John 1:40-42).
- People: Peter's mother in law is a historical figure mentioned in Matthew 8:14–15, Mark 1:29–31, and Luke 4:38–41. One theory of her ailment is that she had chronic malaria—a common disease of the times.
- Fact/Note: Though some of the following foods are cultivated in modern-day Israel, they were unknown in the first century. All of these foods came from the Americas (which would remain unknown for over a thousand more years): corn,

potatoes, avocados, chocolate, tomatoes, bell peppers. In first-century Galilee and Judea, there is evidence to support that they ate beans, lettuce, spinach, beets, kale, radishes, turnips, carrots, artichokes, black cala, leek, onion, garlic, cucumber, and squash. They also likely used a lot of herbs, dried and fresh: mint, cilantro, parsley, marjoram, and oregano. They ate fruits that included apples, pears, figs, grapes, dates, melon, and also various nuts like walnuts, almonds, carob, and pistachios.

Chapter 32

- Fact/Note: Most houses in Galilee in the first century were either multi-family, multi-generational, or both. It was rare for just one family to be living in a house.
- Scripture Reference: "Are you for us, or for our enemies?" – Joshua 5:13
- Scripture Reference: "God promises to help us" – Numbers 10:9

Chapter 33

- Scripture Reference: "Faith the size of a mustard seed" – Matthew 17:20
- Scripture Reference: The following verses prescribe stonings: Ex 19:12-13; Heb 12:20-21; Num 15:32-36; Lev 20:2; Lev 20:27; Lev 24:10-16,23; Deut 17:2-5; Deut 13:6-11; Deut 21:18-21; Deut 22:13-21; Deut 22:23-24; Lev 20:10; Jn 8:3-5; Ex 21:28,32
- Scripture Reference: "Stand in the holy place" – Matthew 24:15

Chapter 34

- Fact/Note: The written language of the Jews at the time was mostly Hebrew, but sometimes Aramaic.
- Scripture Reference: "All came from the dust" – Ecclesiastes 3:20

Chapter 35

- Scripture Reference: Stonings prescribed for homosexuals – Leviticus 20:13
- Fact/Note: Archaeological evidence suggests that the Sea of Galilee was depleted of its fish stocks in the time of Jesus. One theory holds that the indigent and dispossessed farmers converged on the sea and contributed to overfishing.
- People: Mary of Magdala, more commonly known today as Mary Magdalene, became a well-known follower of Jesus. Though some early Church doctrine cast her in a negative light as being one in the same as a Mary mentioned in the Gospels who was a prostitute, there is no evidence anywhere in the Gospels to support the claim. In fact, Pope John Paul VI publicly acknowledged this in 1969.
- Scripture Reference: Forgive "seventy times seven" – Matthew 18:21-22
- People: Levi, also known as Matthew, is a historical figure and one of the twelve apostles mentioned in the Bible.
- People: Abram is a fictional character.
- Scripture Reference: Against charging interest – Exodus 22:25–27, Leviticus 25:36–37, and Deuteronomy 23:20–21
- Scripture Reference: "A man reaps what he sows" – Galatians 6:7

- Scripture Reference: "Lawful to pay taxes to Caesar?" – Matthew 22:16-17
- Scripture Reference: "Render unto Caesar" – Matthew 22:21
- Scripture Reference: "Come to me, all who are weary" – Matthew 11:28
- Scripture Reference: "Take my yoke and learn from me" – Matthew 11:29
- Scripture Reference: "For my yoke is easy to bear" – Matthew 11:30
- Scripture Reference: "What should I do to inherit eternal life?" – Lk. 10:25-37
- Scripture Reference: "Why do you eat ... with such scoundrels?" – Lk. 5:30-31

Chapter 36
- People: Ira is based on a centurion's ill servant mentioned in the Bible.
- Fact/Note: Though the Jewish and Gentile methods for producing wine were identical, Jews were only allowed to drink wine made by other Jews. A small wine press would have a treading floor: a rectangular basin about five feet long and three feet wide. The grapes would be crushed there, then left sitting until the residue settled to the bottom and the fermentation process began. Then a filter hole would be opened, allowing the juice to flow to a small reservoir two feet farther down. There, the juice would be collected in big narrow-necked jugs and sealed with mud corks.
- Fact/Note: Jews who sold themselves into slavery often did so on an agreed upon timeframe, not necessarily for the rest of their lives. One reason to sell oneself into slavery was to pay off debt.
- Scripture Reference: Regarding waiting until angel stirs the water – John 5:4
- Scripture Reference: "The Lord is a God who avenges" – Psalm 54:1

Chapter 37
- People: Caleb and Malachi are fictional characters.
- Scripture Reference: "The Sabbath was made for man" – Mark 2:27

Chapter 38
- Fact/Note: The earliest known mention of the Hindu goddess Saraswati is in the Rigveda (circa 1700-1100 BCE).
- Fact/Note: In this day and age, it is known that not all women bleed following their first intercourse. This occurrence undoubtedly led to false accusations in ancient times.

Chapter 39
- Fact/Note: Some of the oldest known paints were milk-based, with pigment from egg yolks.
- Scripture Reference: "The kingdom of heaven is like" – Matt. 13:31-32, 13:44
- Scripture Reference: "Not everyone who says to me, 'Lord, Lord!'" – Matt. 7:21
- Scripture Reference: "For even The Son of Man came not to be served, but to serve" – Mark 10:45
- Scripture Reference: "My servant is sick in bed" – Matthew 8:5-13

- Scripture Reference: Centurion financing synagogue's reconstruction – Lk. 7:5

Chapter 40
- People: John is a historical figure and one of the twelve apostles mentioned in the Bible.
- Scripture Reference: "Better to give than to receive" – Acts 20:35
- Scripture Reference: "Love one another" – John 13:34
- Scripture Reference: "In everything, treat others as you would want them to treat you" – Matthew 7:12
- Scripture Reference: "The door will be opened to those who knock" – Matt. 7:7
- Scripture Reference: "I am with you for only a short time" – John 7:33
- Scripture Reference: "Do not lay down any rule beyond what I determined for you" – Gospel of Mary 4:9-10
- Scripture Reference: "Do not be afraid when you hear of wars" – Luke 21:9
- Scripture Reference: "With God, all things are possible" – Matthew 19:26
- Scripture Reference: "Whatever you pray and ask for, believe that you have received it" – Mark 11:24
- Scripture Reference: "Whenever you stand praying, if you have anything against anyone, forgive him" – Mark 11:25
- Scripture Reference: "The kingdom of God is within you" – Luke 17:20-21
- Scripture Reference: "The child of true Humanity exists within you" – Gospel of Mary 4:3-7
- Scripture Reference: Feeding of the 5,000 – Matthew 14:13-21

Made in the USA
Monee, IL
30 May 2024

59148135R00189